GERONTIUS

GERONTIUS

James Hamilton-Paterson

All rights reserved. Published in the United States by
Soho Press, Inc.
853 Broadway
New York, NY 10003

First published in 1989 by Macmillan London Limited,
and reprinted 1989

First U.S. edition, April 1991.

Library of Congress Cataloging-in-Publication Data
Hamilton-Paterson, James.
Gerontius : a novel / James Hamilton-Paterson. —
1st U.S. ed.
p.   cm.
ISBN 0-939149-48-6
1. Elgar, Edward, 1857-1934—Fiction.   I. Title.
PR6058.A5543G47   1991
823'.914—dc20   91-6441
CIP

AUTHOR'S NOTE

This novel starts from an event: a six-week journey to the Amazon which the sixty-six-year-old Sir Edward Elgar made late in 1923. Almost nothing is known about this trip. It is not certain why he decided to make it although impulsiveness and restlessness were characteristic of him. What he said and thought and did in those weeks are a matter for fancy. Such is a point of departure for a work of fiction, as it was for Eduard Mörike nearly 140 years ago when he began *Mozart's Journey to Prague*.

The issue of truth in a novel whose central character is a man who did once live is not easily settled. Elgar was an artist whose life and music have been documented by modern biographers and scholars such as Percy M. Young, Michael Kennedy, Jerrold Northrop Moore and Diana McVeagh. Theirs have been my reference works.

My greatest debt, though, is to the music. It is much – and boringly – debated whether it is permissible to infer biographical facts from a composer's music. Yet that morbidly sensitive Englishman who experienced every note he wrote and could describe one of his own works as 'the passionate pilgrimage of a soul' is somebody this listener feels he occasionally inhabits more or less without presumption. Those affinities for people we could never have met are the more pungent for their element of invention. On this basis, then, the novelist proceeds with all due recklessness. I have deliberately taken a liberty by turning the shadowy Helen Weaver, to whom Elgar was briefly engaged in his twenties, into a more substantial character capable of bearing narrative weight. In so doing I have given her a new nationality and a background quite different from that of a Worcester shoe merchant's daughter. For the rest, I tried to be as factually correct as was interesting.

When I investigated the Booth Line records for this particular journey a couple of very minor discrepancies with received Elgarian scholarship did come to light. These concern the cruise ship herself, RMS *Hildebrand*. Firstly, the various ship's logs and documents which are still preserved show her captain's name was J. Maddrell, whereas Elgar biographers who mention the trip at all invariably call him 'Mandrell'. Secondly, a story is sometimes quoted to the effect that the weather was so bad on the first part of the outward leg that the *Hildebrand*'s pilot could not be put off at Holyhead and had to be taken on to Madeira. This is odd because Madeira was the third port of call. The first was Oporto, the second Lisbon, both of which were major ports with a constant traffic of vessels belonging to the Booth Line and various other British companies. Madeira was seven hundred miles further on; for a Liverpool-based pilot needing immediate passage home it makes no sense. The implication is that on this particular trip the ship missed out the first two ports and went straight to Madeira. It didn't, however. The *Hildebrand*'s log (which lists the dates and times of arrival and departure at every port) shows that not only did she call at Oporto and Lisbon but took exactly as long getting there as she always did – not what one might expect were the weather as bad as is always stated.

So one wonders about the source of this curious, but quite unimportant, incompatibility of accounts. It looks as though the information might originally have come from Elgar himself. He could well have mis-remembered the captain's name, while far younger men proud of their fortitude have been known to exaggerate the storms at sea they have survived. Nobody bothers to check a returning traveller's tales for veracity at the time, certainly not over such trivial details. Thus may a novelist sixty-four years later speculate on them affectionately.

To my acknowledged indebtedness to the authors named above I should like to add my sincerest thanks to David Peate of the Booth Steamship Company Ltd and Janet Smith of Liverpool City Libraries for their great courtesy and help.

for Ronald Blythe

A train was travelling northwards from London through the grey squalls of a winter's afternoon. From a corner seat in one of its carriages a man watched his country with the scurried perspective of a railway traveller: crossing fields at a bias, chipping off the corner of a hill, barked at by sudden brick walls and engulfed in tunnels. Desolate suburbias came and went and the tarred telegraph poles kept pace. As daylight diminished rain streaked the glass at flat angles, blurred and wobbled the scene, pooling at the corners of the pane in trembling pockets. It occurred to this man (who had dog hairs on his otherwise immaculate trouser cuffs) that he had spent much of his life in a compartment, alone and quite still, while outside it an activity called travel went on whose images beyond the window – ever different, always the same – represented not distance but time flashing by. Days, months and years had reeled past until here he was towards the end of a lifetime not going anywhere at sixty miles an hour.

After a while he fell asleep and sleeping dreamed a vivid dream. Later, when events brought back the inessentials of this dream, the fragments had about them a satisfactory, vatic air as if they were true parts of the man he believed himself to be.

He is to climb at last.

Although from his father's house it appears amid the rockfield no bigger than a candle, this column has surely cast an immense shadow across his life.

He begins the climb. Even at this early hour of morning the sun is bald and white. Above him the cedarwood rungs recede into blue glare against which the coarse stone column tapers upward.

'Get on, boy,' shouts Rahut from near his heels. 'D'you think you're the only one?'

The words of this corrupt acolyte ought to bully away the last of the dreamer's confidence. He has been declared a day-tripper, no longer someone who has tirelessly observed this limestone candle for years and in all weathers, far enough away to imagine the spiritual flame blowing from its tip night and day in invisible rags like a beacon summoning worshippers, sceptics, the curious, the petitioners, the humdrum devout from all corners of the world. This unseeable smoke from a man's blazing soul has wafted like incense across the skies of Syria and Cilicia. At festivals such as Sniffing the Breezes entire parties of picnickers walk from Antioch to sit on the ground at a respectful distance, singing impious songs about spring, eating dates and idly spitting the stones in tiny trajectories towards their saint. For Simyun is indeed their saint; and while it is permissible for them to treat him with a certain familiarity and spit date-stones at him from a mile away it is a big mistake for outsiders to be heard scoffing. Tourists do well to leave their witty remarks at home in Athens or wherever it is they come from with their noisy manners and bundles of biscuits stuck all over with sesame.

Climbing this ladder to this man today, now, is a terrifying honour. Yet shouts from below the dreamer remind him that so far as Rahut is concerned this ascent is not the end of many years' living in Simyun's illustrious shadow. Rahut sees only another petitioner he has vetted for his master's monthly ration, one more in a succession of climbers whose coins he has pocketed. For this Rahut is comptroller of Simyun's portals. He admits the world to his master's presence, exercising at times a quirky capriciousness. If now and again he allows a beardless village nobody up the ladder it is because he has already turned away some rotting archimandrite or fabulous sage who has crossed seas in a leaky boat just to ask the saint's advice. The locals often wonder if Simyun knows about the money Rahut is making. Not only is there the matter of audiences. He also permits the concessions of traders and hucksters whose stalls ring the column's base from far enough away that their cries cannot disturb Simyun's meditation. It is

Rahut who chips pieces off the column for them to sell and it is Rahut who gathers those rarest and most prized relics of all, the scented blackish coprolites which every month or so the saint lets fall to the sand beneath. Men have crossed deserts for weeks just to acquire a single fragment of these potent, fragrant truffles. They are embodied in lockets, rings, reliquaries, medicines; it is said there is enough healing in a single one of Simyun's bowel movements to cure the ailments of the entire world.

Why, then, amid this waft of chicanery does the dreamer still bother to climb? After so many years of living in this shadow he has to ask a question of the man who is variously considered a saint, shaman, madman, freak. The stories are famous, of course: how he joined a monastery when he was sixteen and dismayed his fellow-monks by his excessive austerities. They say he had himself buried upright in a hole in the ground, the sand filled back in and packed up to his chin, thus passing the livelong Syrian summer in a forgotten corner of the monastery garden. It is claimed he spent more and more time thinking up increasingly inventive privations. One Lent he had himself walled up in his cell for the entire forty days with nothing but a single loaf and a pitcher of water and when at the end they broke down the wall they found both loaf and water untouched and Simyun unmoved from the precise posture of prayer in which the masons had last seen him. It is commonly believed that he was finally dismissed from the monastery not only because he made his brothers feel they were positive sybarites by comparison but because his superior believed Simyun was taking a perverse pleasure in such performances. Whatever the reason he went off into the desert and sat on a tall stone without shade or food, relying on his disciples (for he was already famous) to give him bread and water. They say it was to escape his own disciples that he began to raise his platform ever higher above them until he lived as he does today at the top of a column fifty-eight feet tall. Already he has spent seventeen years standing on a circle of stone which measures three feet across and is ringed by a wooden parapet fitted with a crude lectern against which he may lean to doze, for up there he might literally fall asleep and keep on falling.

It is hard to believe a mere showman would have endured a fraction of such privations. After all, it is not Simyun who makes any money from his feat but Rahut. What accrues to Simyun is world-wide fame (for which he cares nothing) and the respectful pilgrimage of the wisest men of the age (for whom he temporarily forgoes his visionary agony to deal with their requests for advice). Sometimes he writes letters at his lectern by way of reply, handing them over in silence to ecclesiastical hierarchs who are hanging there on the uppermost rungs of the ladder fifty-eight feet above the stony ground, their eyes on a level with his ankles, the tendons of their hands gleaming in the unshaded blaze in which he lives. These letters are then carried to all parts of the world, to Asia Minor, to Constantinople, Athens, Alexandria, to be read to the churches there.

Why is the dreamer climbing? Why is he allowing the ground to fall away, the distant booths to come into view with their motley of relics, their brilliant bolts of Chinese silks brought by the traders' caravans from the other end of earth? What might this man know which could conceivably profit him, raised as the saint has been for so much of his life above the plane of ordinary mortals? Hands and feet dumbly answer rung by rung. The climber cannot say how he knows, but he nonetheless does know that this man is not like those bogus anchorites of Alexandria who live on fallen obelisks and are supposed to be carnal in the grossest ways with all manner of passers-by including, it is said, sheep and goats. The Emperor Julian himself referred to them as 'filthy and superstitious'. Simyun, to whose life people are drawn as moth to flame, has not the least thing in common with such layabouts. He thrives on denial; his pains have made him pure.

The dreamer is nearing the top. From overhead comes no sound, no cleared throat, no scuff of shifted position, no murmuring of prayer. Only, this blue emptiness and dazzle which surrounds him is pervaded with a faint and uniform hiss as of the sun's rays racing through air. The universe is filled with his heart-beat: not a sound from below, not a sound from above. Off to his right, maybe a foot away or maybe a million miles, a vertical black line runs. It is the rope of knotted leather strips which the saint uses to haul up his water-skins and frugal meals, for except on days of Audience an uncured thong is Simyun's only tangible link with the world beneath. On days of Audience such as today Rahut puts up this ladder for the upward pilgrimage. This itself is something of a test of a supplicant's sincerity for it bounces and flexes at each footfall and the narrow curved stonework against which its top rests seems designed to shed rather than support ladders, to send them skidding off into space on either side. There have indeed been accidents. The mayor of Sisan, Simyun's birthplace, was killed a year or two ago when the top of the ladder slipped. He had gone to ask Simyun's blessing on a plan to turn the saint's home town into an official shrine but whether a commercial interest lay beneath this apparently pious scheme is not known. Clinging like a beetle to the toppling ladder he made a descending arc across the blue Syrian heavens and smashed against the desert. Amen. Some said he was drunk. Simyun never spoke of the matter.

In fact it is believed the saint is protected by God from all that is trivial or defiled, that only the worthy ever get to address him. This seems unlikely, for how else would he remain in touch with the dark doings of this world such that his advice is treasured for its wise and practical nature? Yet perhaps God does protect Simyun from all agencies of physical harm, maybe in recompense for the terrible pains he inflicts on himself in sacrifice. His mere existence has been politically contentious and an attempt was once made to poison his food. But as he was hauling it up it is said a great hawk came swooping out of an empty sky, cut the thong with its beak and carried the food off in its claws, letting it fall to the ground a safe distance away. And even today on the very spot there grows a twisted black tree of a kind no-one has ever seen before whose wood is so hard that even a scimitar cannot nick it. The dreamer has himself seen this tree but would not presume to judge the truth of the tale. On the other hand he does know that boys from his village used to go out by night and shoot at the saint for target practice as he stood there outlined against the constellations. And yet never once was he hit, which is almost incredible given that even at fifteen Badur was reckoned the finest bowman of the Three Cities. Indeed, on one of these excursions Hadath was himself injured by an arrow of Badur's and this can only be reckoned the saint's kindly retribution, for the wound hurt abominably the rest of that night yet was cured without trace by morning. Thus it is ordained that none may harm Simyun but Simyun himself.

And so the dreamer has arrived. His left hand is now holding the topmost rung. On a level with his eyes are two naked feet and ankles, hugely swollen. Both his hands could not encompass one of the saint's ankles, so puffed up and black are they. The air is filled with an extraordinary smell – extraordinary, that is, because there are no flowers here. How did he expect a saint to smell? Surely no worse than a sick animal, having had no washing but winter rains for seventeen years. What one eats also determines how one smells, and Simyun eats no meat but only the simplest bread and pulses. Nevertheless there is a faint scent of flowers, although no flowers the dreamer recognises. Maybe now and then Rahut sends up some supplicant's precious gift, a vial of rare attar, priceless essence of blooms which open in Tartary or China at the other end of those great caravan trails.

The feet before his face are so huge their pain fills the entire circle of stonework. Between them, embedded in the stone itself, is an iron ring from which a black chain leads up against stained rags. He raises his eyes to the dazzle of the sky. Simyun is tethered by the neck around which is an iron collar set with inward-facing nails. It pierces to the heart, the sight of this transfigured animal whose neck is bloated and cicatrised by the ever-unhealing wounds of seventeen years. Otherwise the man is black with the sun where he is not grey with ragged hair and beard.

'At last you are here, then.' His voice comes down to the dreamer who is startled at how gentle and young it sounds. A creature like this, all iron and sinew and suffering, should have a voice to match – the voice of a raven, the cracked cry of a prophet. Is this perhaps the greeting with which he addresses all his visitors? 'Why do you hesitate? Step up. Don't be alarmed, boy.'

He may be all-knowing but how is it he doesn't see the evident impossibility of fitting another person onto that tiny island of stone? A scarred hand reaches down at the end of an arm like the branch of a tree which has been blasted by lightning. The arm seems so long as to be endless, as if stretching to another world. Then the hand grasps the dreamer's wrist and pulls him to his feet and he is astonished to find the area is larger than he imagined – so much so, indeed, that there is even room to pace about. He is filled with wonder, with awe. The proximity of sainthood is overpowering. What manner of man is this? For, looking about him, the dreamer now sees he is in a land of its own. They are standing in a small courtyard bounded on three sides by a stone parapet; on the fourth side is a cool white pavilion with slender spires and windows from which puff out damask curtains. Through an open doorway is a view of a cool green garden, red and white flowers, the fraying spatter of a fountain. The sound of birdsong and water pours through to them in the courtyard.

'I don't understand,' he says, suddenly frightened to look at the saint. 'Are we in paradise?'

'Ah, maybe we are,' says Simyun. A butterfly floats through the doorway and alights on his wrist where it opens and shuts its brilliant wings as if breathing sunlight. 'Whatever paradise may be.'

'You don't know?'

'It's all paradise.'

The dreamer thinks of Simyun's awesome sufferings. He suspects he is after all one of those desert mystics, no matter what his powers. The man appears to read this thought.

'For me suffering is my particular path, my gateway. It is not so for most of the world. I was once as saddened as anyone by the pain of the world. I used to argue that a merciful God hardly needed offerings of involuntary pain from his often guiltless creatures. That notion made me sadder still until I realised there is no God who needs or wants anything. There is pain just as there is wind or cold. I further discovered that I *am* the nonexistent God, just as you are. So my pain is a wilful gift to myself which has enabled me to see in different ways.'

The dreamer ought to be utterly confused by these blasphemies and obscurities. At any rate the question which stands for him and which he has carried like a pearl up the ladder to present to Simyun vanishes from his mind. The saint takes his arm and leads him to the parapet. On all horizons the view stretches: the distant white buildings of Antioch, the pinkish nearby hills, Mount Admirable. He can just see his house with the vineyard nearby, Rastul's herd grazing.

'Before I learned how to do away with time,' says Simyun in his young man's voice, 'I would stand here and watch the changes as they occurred. The city, for example, has practically doubled in size since I first came here. There is less cultivation in the hills but more traders with their caravans. I used often to be overwhelmed by the beauty of the world. At other times when my legs were on fire from standing, my head was on fire with noon, my neck was ablaze with the drag of iron and nails, I could not rise above my pain and the very landscape became listless and hateful. Often I cursed the nonexistent God for my self-inflicted exile. I imagine that strikes you as perverse?'

He cannot reply. If this is sainthood then the real and actual world of its speech and living leave him without words. Yet there is something about it which can be understood.

'But it eased. It always does if you keep on. Then I saw the same landscape but differently. You thought my life up here was either one long beatific vision or a boring wasteland of suffering? Well, it is neither. A lot happens here, you know. One notices everything: ants crossing the stones, lizards in the cracks, birds in the sky, the seasons' changing. Can you imagine how exciting it is when winter storms leave one roaring in space, the ground invisible below a fog of sand? Or when in spring the lightnings strike all round? At such moments I find it easy to remember I am wearing chain and yet so far no lightning has come close enough to singe me.'

As he speaks the dreamer notices it is rapidly becoming dark. There are feeble yellow lights in the far city, closer orange glows marking the traders' dung fires. There is a brilliant sliver of new moon in the sky among the limitless starfields.

'Now and then a strange beast used to prowl below,' remarks Simyun. 'It looked like half-lion, half-gazelle. It had a choking tawny smell like musk and burning carpets. It came very rarely but when it did it lay on the ground at the foot of this tower and looked up and I saw its eyes were glowing. Then the eyes would leave its body and float up towards me, revolving slowly like gems – rubies, garnets, I can't tell the stone. When they reached me I plucked them from the air and immediately I could be through my fists everything the beast had ever been. I could see far countries and feel sharp climates; I tasted carrion and fresh kid; I was the music a shepherd makes alone in the desert; I knew strange tongues. Once I was filled with longing by these things, by a ravenous yearning to pad about inviolate through all the marches of the world for myself, hearing and tasting and doing and seeing like my beast.'

'When did he last come?'

'Three years ago. He will never come back because I now know who he is.'

'And who is he?'

'Myself. I can see with his eyes and hear with his ears any time I want. I never realised it, that's all. I thought I had to wait for him. I think I have killed my significant beast.'

The dreamer doesn't understand why the saint speaks half sadly as if he had murdered a real thing. He turns from the parapet and, glancing towards the dark pavilion, is surprised to see a single lighted window with behind the curtain the filmiest suggestion of movement within the chamber beyond. At once he thinks of a waiting bride but as soon as this impious and foolish notion defines itself he dismisses it. Anchorites have no brides, saints no desire for mistresses, visionaries who can walk amid beasts and angels in the sky surely have no need of company. The night breeze through the passage from the courtyard beyond brings with it something so sweet he cannot tell if it falls on his ears or his nose or whether he tastes it in the air. He is so laved by it his entire skin absorbs it from every direction, a ravishment such as he has never known.

'What is it?' he asks.

'What it is. Call it what you like. Music, why not?'

And at once it gathers in his ears and he perceives that it is, after all, music. But it is quite unlike anything he has ever heard before, so beautiful and strange and new. It arouses a longing in him that is akin to pain and nothing seems worthwhile but just to hear that sound and go on listening to it for ever.

'Can you hear it?'

'I *am* it,' Simyun says. 'You too, of course.'

In the luminous night he glimmers beside him, no longer a tortured saint on swollen black feet and chained by the neck like a dog. He is powerful, lithe. His hands rest on the parapet like a captain's conning his ship as it forges outward across serene seas. He is confidence.

'Can you remember your question?' he asks. 'No, you've forgotten it. Never mind. Don't bother with being mortified. I'll tell you how it was with me instead, and that will answer it. I was sixteen when I left home with my brother to become a monk. He was a year or two older, more mature, more sensible. He went to an order at Tunis in Cilicia; I entered the Brotherhood of Mysteries over on the far side of Mount Admirable.' A pale sleeve raises to point to the east. 'But from the first I was not like the other novices. It was not that I was any holier or more pious and nor was my faith any greater than theirs. Much of the time it was rather less, actually. Throughout my novitiate I hated doing anything with the others, whether it was attending services or prayers or just gardening and working in the kitchens. I always yearned for my cell or the desert. I didn't mind my fellow-men, you understand, but I knew their mere presence blurred me in some way. I couldn't concentrate. I believed I had a mission but I was unsure what it was. My superiors despaired of me, condemning me as guilty of the sin of abominable pride thus to set myself apart from the rest of the community. "Maybe I am called to be a hermit," I told them. "Maybe I should leave the Order and go alone into the desert among the snakes and the little foxes to shiver at night beneath a quilt of stars." "You are not fit to be a hermit," they told me. "You may have the fortitude but you lack the humility. You do not wish to efface yourself; you have no desire to become lost."

'They gave me punishments, indulgences. But even as they did so they were playing my game. I became notorious throughout the Order as the most-punished novice. I added to that notoriety by devising mortifications of my own which outdid the worst they wished to inflict on me. At last they wearied of me as incorrigible, divisive, mad. I was expelled, not so much with curses as with absolutions as if I had been a crazed dog they feared might seek revenge if too harshly turned away. Hardly a model monk, you're thinking, and you're perfectly right. What, then, was this ridiculous mission of mine? If I tell you perhaps you'll find it hard to believe, it's so simple and unmomentous. It was this: to be myself. By *creating* myself, by uncovering my divinity I could reveal the divine to the world. It was not in me to be a monk among others but it was in me to be what a poet will one day call me, "the watcher on the column", which of course also implies that I am watched. Thus I am an example, a revelation. Pain is a gateway, not an end in itself. There are many gateways, this is mine. I recommend it to no-one but I commend to everyone the garden which lies beyond.

'Most of the people who come to see me are fools. No, that's uncharitable . . . not fools perhaps but not ready to understand which questions to ask. They want to know what they should do to lead a good life. You weren't going to ask that? No; you're already too thoughtful. Good and bad are human value judgements without the slightest meaning. There, that's the language of saints. I see you once imagined yourself going on an immense journey to a land across the desert so distant that our whole world winked out on the horizon at your back. You fancied you eventually came across a group of creatures or people roasting and eating one of their own kind. And you thought you had at last identified the common enemy, the anathema, until one of them said, "We have heard there are monsters elsewhere in the world who commit the ultimate blasphemy with their dead and lay them in the earth for worms and foxes instead of taking them back into the common body with honour and love." And you didn't know what to say.'

'It's true,' the dreamer admits. 'I did once imagine such a thing.'

'Well, now you must go,' says Simyun. 'You already know what to do to be yourself.'

'Do I?' He is lost. Already the night is over, or at least the sky is becoming light. He cannot bear to leave this man, this music which still streams from the shadowed garden beyond the pavilion.

'It isn't music,' comes the voice. 'You merely *hear* it as music. Somebody else might perceive it as colour, another as a scent, still another as a vision of extraordinary cities. It never ends and nor will it ever leave you. It is the garden itself. You need only discover the gateway but no-one can help you do that. We are unique. None can do it for us although sometimes things can happen of their own accord, out of a clear sky. Be alert. Use well the interval and don't be dismayed. Anyone who searches is forced into exile, even if it is only sixty feet up a pole. Perhaps going on long journeys is helpful after all because I can tell you that one day, in many more than a thousand years' time, a certain Jew will travel a great distance from a cold country and visit this place. He is a rabbi, one of the Hasidim, maybe more thoughtful even than most. He will stand on what he is told are the ruins of this very column and look across at Mount Admirable as the sun is rising, just as we are now. So overwhelmed is he that he instinctively covers his face. Then he goes home to his distant country and in time he writes down his discovery. What he writes is this: "As the hand held before the eye conceals the greatest mountain, so the little earthly life hides from the glance the enormous lights and mysteries of which the world is full; and he who can draw it away from before his eyes, as one who draws away a hand, beholds the great shining of the inner worlds." '

From somewhere beyond the parapet there sounds a strange note very like that of the ram's horn Shofar the Jews blow in their synagogues.

'It appears that I can see into the future but I'm often less certain about the past,' Simyun admits. 'For example, *Who built this tower?* I'm quite sure I didn't: I'm no mason. I'm equally certain nobody else would have done it for me. And if they did, who paid for their labour? Sometimes I even wonder if I may not have *invented* it. Maybe I dreamed it into existence one night as I lay on my rock below. Another mystery to ponder on,' and he gives a slight laugh.

As the dreamer turns to him his arm bangs against the wooden lectern and a clawed brown hand steadies him. His head sinks to the level of a pair of monstrous feet from whose rotting toes curl yellow nails. He looks up in awe and against the sky's sudden glare glimpses the silhouette of unkempt hair and beard, the iron collar clamped around the running sore of neck, the fall of black chain. As he begins his descent the Shofar sounds again. In no time he feels Rahut's hand on his ankle.

'That was damned quick,' says the acolyte, chewing a fresh quid. 'Straight up and straight down, eh, boy? Don't suppose he had much to say to *you*. Never mind,' he adds half to himself, 'we can fit an extra one in before noon.'

Once more the Shofar sounds and the world jerks to a halt.

The jerk woke the sleeper in the train. The lights in his compartment, whose sole occupant he was, had not been switched on, possibly out of deference to his slumber. Consequently the window had not turned into a black mirror obliging him to stare at his own reflection and that of the plump, buttoned upholstery which the LNWR considered suitable for their First Class travellers. Instead he could make out scattered lights, signs of a city, hints of dockland. At once from the darkness beyond the rain-speckled pane came the sad blare of a ship's siren.

'It ought to be dawn,' thought the man sleepily to himself, for by chance it was the very note which, twenty years before, he had written for the Shofar in his oratorio *The Apostles*: a clear C to herald the rising of the sun, the beginning of a new day. This thought stirred another, far more recent, memory as of a fading dream which slipped obliquely away beneath the full realisation of who and where he was: Sir Edward Elgar OM arriving at Liverpool on a late afternoon in November 1923 to embark on a voyage up the Amazon. Above him the netting of the overhead luggage racks bulged with the two light leather cases his valet had brought to Euston from the club in St James's. Beside him on the seat lay a cane, an overcoat and a hat. In the guard's van was a metal cabin trunk full of the sorts of things a gentleman might need for a six-week cruise into the primaeval heart of the world's largest unexplored tropical jungle (the phrasing was that of the cruise company's handout). The cabin trunk was stout and japanned. The valet, who had bought it a week previously in the Army & Navy Stores, thought it looked quite the thing: serious and intrepid. Unlike all his master's other tin and steamer trunks this one was double-sealed against termites, the locks were acclaimed proof against even the most nimble-fingered lascar or coolie, the hinges and corners were reinforced with brass. Empty, it weighed a ton. Edward had himself classified it as appropriate in the sense that Alice would have approved the air it gave off. Privately he thought it faintly absurd to go cluttered up with so many suits of clothes for so short a time. The memory of the trunk in the guard's van now brought him a whiff of vexation, reminding him that for all his best intentions it had in the end turned out impossible to make this trip as he would have liked, light and unencumbered. Instead he was dragging baggage behind him which dated back far beyond last week and the Army & Navy. But then he supposed one did not shed sixty-six years merely by abandoning habit like a heap of clothes smelling of mothballs. Nor was he sure he really wished to.

Imperceptibly the train started again, this time achieving no speed beyond that of a noiseless gliding past unlit deserted platforms without name which had the air of wharves. He did not quite recognise anything but the mere fact of knowing this to be Liverpool made it familiar from the old days, those penniless days of a quarter century ago when he had so often come to conduct his own works in the hopes of making a name (a name! the futility!), staying with Rodewald in Huskisson Street. It was, he suddenly realised, exactly twenty years to the day that Rodey had died, having nearly single-handedly turned the largely amateur Liverpool Orchestral Society into an ensemble capable of playing the best of the moderns: Wagner and Strauss as well as Elgar himself. Poor Rodey. How typical it was that so powerful a champion of music in England should have been a textile magnate – precisely the sort that ignorant London snobs had made their jokes about – the trade of music and the music of tradesmen, and so forth. Twerps, the lot of them; so pig-headed and cloth-eared they couldn't hear that for decades the heart of English music had beat in the provinces, hundreds of miles from the capital with its society dunces and fashionable virtuosi playing pot-pourris of Sullivan.

Well, damn them, men like Rodey had helped change that although the poor man had scarcely lived to see it: dead at forty-three but not before *Pomp and Circumstance* no. 1 was dedicated to him and not before his orchestra got first sniff at both it and no. 2. How the twerps had gnashed their teeth in London! More to the point, the awful suddenness of his death had inspired the Largo of the second symphony which was far more his memorial than the King's. Well. It all seemed so long ago now. How could he, Edward Elgar, already be sixty-six? It was as if Rodey appeared in the shadows on the other side of the compartment, unaged, to confront the old buffer opposite him.

'Still visiting Liverpool, Edward?'

'Hardly at all for years. I'm just passing through. Off to South America. The Amazon, in fact.'

'The Amazon? My dear Cocky, what on earth for? Don't tell me Gerontius has conquered the cannibals?'

'Good Lord no. At least, not so far as I've heard. No, it's more of an adventure. A bit of a jape. Just to get away from it all.'

'It all, Cocky? H'm. What does Alice have to say about *it all*?'

'I don't live my life just to . . .' he began huffily, but then, 'Alice is dead.' *Could* he have forgotten for that instant?

'Oh Cocky. My dear man; I'm so sorry. For you, I mean, not for her. After all, I'm dead too.'

Silly, such conversations. Yet nowadays after the great evisceration of the war conversations with the dead went on all the time and all around, so much realer were the departed than the ghosts who remembered them, the words heard than the words spoken. Thus, long after the dim figure opposite had been reabsorbed into the London & North Western Railway's plush upholstery and become pure shadow the warm and questioning voice lingered: 'Oh Cocky, what are you writing now? What great work is brewing for that ungrateful world?'

And there was no answer he could give. There was no way he, the living, could say, 'Oh Rodey . . . Dear old man, I'm finished.' And just then the train stopped, doors began to open, people to shout for porters.

'Sir Edward,' from the doorway. Hell, they'd tracked him down already. But it was only Tom Shannon the choirman's son come to see him onto the boat. Stepping out of the glossy carriage to the platform Sir Edward Elgar might have been caught in a series of sepia pictures for the *Pall Mall Gazette*: an obviously distinguished man of a somewhat military bearing, grey haired and grey moustached, buttoning his coat and adjusting his hat against the squalls of November rain which blew inwards between the train's glistening roof and the fretted overhang which sheltered the platform. This was Sir Edward Elgar the public figure – not so easily recognised as in the heyday of the prewar years, maybe, but still with the same appearance of purposefulness. A close observer might have noticed that Edward Elgar, on the other hand, was vaguely trying to fit the wrong hand into the wrong glove and had about those deeply hooded eyes a remoteness like one lost in a strange land.

It was only when they reached the quay that the cruise passengers could appreciate quite how bad the weather was and how it was shortly going to affect them very much indeed. Railway travellers were, after all, used to sliding effortlessly through the worst storms, no more attention needing to be paid to the sluicing blusters beyond the carriage panes than that someone might get up and lean his weight on the leather strap to force it and the window a final notch tighter. But here, huddled in the open-fronted sheds, the boarding travellers were reminded they had come to the end of solid land. In the brilliance of overhead derrick and bunkering lights they caught glimpses of rigging bowed into arcs by the wind, of rain-slicked paintwork, buffeting tarpaulin and – beyond the ship's hull – an impression of the wild surface of the Mersey. Certain of the passengers must from the moment of dressing that morning already have supposed themselves magically a thousand miles up the Amazon beneath tropic skies brilliant with parakeets; their clothes were absurdly light for an English winter evening. They almost ran aboard, one hand pressed to their hats, up the gangway with its slapping canvas sides, to be handed down over the calm, warm threshold smelling faintly of oil and brass polish by immaculately-uniformed officers.

Edward stood a little apart from the rest in the sheds, seeming not to mind the gusts of rain in the open doorway. He had clearly been recognised by several of his fellow-travellers but gave no sign of having noticed their glances in his direction, their whispers. The squalls beat the flaps of his overcoat against his legs but he disdained to turn up his collar. He might almost have been relishing the elements as proof of his presence here, on this dock, on a dark winter's evening in the north of the world. Head tilted back and face wet with rain he examined the *Hildebrand* from stem to stern as his home for the next month and a half. He saw an elegant small liner, graceful almost to the point of daintiness, with a grey hull below the white strake, white upperworks and the all-black funnel of the Booth Steamship Company. He was a well-travelled man and his eye was practised enough to judge the vessel's tonnage at about seven thousand and its length at some four hundred feet. He was surprised that so large a craft would be able to go a thousand miles up any river, even the Amazon, and wondered how many feet of water she drew.

He shook hands briefly with his escort and walked in a soldierly manner up the gangway. When he was halfway up a clout of wind caught the side of his head, lifting a spurt of grey hair and twirling his hat away into the sky. For an instant a dockside light caught a pale reflection from the maker's lozenge in its crown before it vanished over the Mersey towards New Brighton. The *Hildebrand*'s officers were most perturbed as they welcomed him aboard.

'It's only a hat,' he told them gruffly and then a steward led him along a neatly-caulked deck with a strip of green carpet running down its centre. On the left were cabin portholes, curtained and with lights burning inside. On the right was a line of larger, seaward portholes through which could be glimpsed the edge of the quay and wooden pilings. This passageway, after the blustrous weather outside, was warm and quiet and trembled slightly underfoot. Polished mahogany handrails ran along both walls. Eventually, after certain turnings, the steward's gleaming heels stopped outside a door with a brass figure 2 on it.

'Your cabin, Sir Edward.' He unlocked the door and helped his passenger over the few inches of coaming. 'Steward Pyce, sir. I shall do my utmost to ensure your trip will be happy and comfortable. I'm entirely at your disposal, sir. Should you need anything you have only to ring the bell. Meanwhile I shall have your luggage sent along as quickly as possible.'

As he spoke he was helping Edward out of his wet coat, tut-tutting as he felt the sodden velour facings. 'With your permission I shall take this away with me and have it thoroughly dried. Dinner is not for another two hours, sir. Captain Maddrell does still hope to be able to sail with the tide, that's in about forty minutes, but they say there's quite a sea running out there tonight and perhaps in the circumstances he'll prefer to delay a little.'

'I hope not,' said Edward. 'Personally I came to travel, not to sit tied up to a Liverpool quay.'

'Ah, you're a good sailor then, sir. Not like some others aboard, I should fancy, judging by . . .'

'The rougher it is the better I like it. Oh, and you might be so good as to ask them to be careful with my trunk. I have some instruments in it.'

'Certainly, sir. They'll treat it like it was eggs.' Steward Pyce made a pecking gesture with his upper body, all that was left in this democratic postwar wasteland of a servant's bow, Edward reflected as the man withdrew.

Outside, Pyce walked noiselessly off up the carpet mimicking his passenger's gruff bravado under his breath. ' "The rougher it is the better I like it." Ho. Says you. They all do, don't they? They all think they're the best sailors who ever set foot to deck until it blows a bit and then watch 'em not turn out for breakfast. Restaurant empty and the cooks all sitting on their thumbs in the galley looking at half a hundredweight of toast getting cold. Evening sir, madam,' he raised his voice and adjusted his vowels as other passengers passed in the wake of their own steward. Eventually he tracked down Hempson and ran his finger along the list his colleague was holding. 'Elgar. Number 2. Says he's got a trunk with trombones in it and to be careful with it.'

'Not another bloody musician? We've already got a band aboard, ain't that enough? Trombones, indeed.'

'Ought to be thankful it's not a joanna, mate.'

'It'll weigh,' said the man sagely, 'it'll weigh. Not one of 'em but don't bring a ton of junk for six weeks. "Kindly be dashed careful with that, my man. That one's got my medals in it." ' Hempson had lost three fingers near Arras six years ago and had pronounced views about the officer class.

Meanwhile Edward was sitting on the edge of his bunk, staring through the open doorway at his small sitting room with its shaded lights and writing desk. In one hand he still held a booking slip which read 'Sir Edward Elgar OM. Cabin Deluxe no. 2'.

' "Happy and comfortable . . .",' he said to himself. 'What on earth am I doing here?'

He got to his feet, throwing the ticket on the bunk. In the sitting room he stood beside the writing table and riffled the tops of the headed stationery in the rack so that the Booth Line crest shimmered with a faint husking sound. It was the vacant gesture of a man newly arrived in a hotel bedroom unable to think of what to do next.

It was when, in response to the bugle, he took his seat in the restaurant that Edward finally appreciated how at variance were the actuality of the cruise on which he had embarked and his advance fantasies of it. He had vaguely supposed a small, intimate group of civilised persons, none of whom had the faintest connection with music, being carried for a breathing space to an exotic land and back. He had imagined diverting, worldly conversations, tales such as those found in Conrad and Maugham told over dinner by rubber planters returning to their jungle fastnesses. He had even speculated about – well, why not admit it? – some flutter of interest at the taffrail, a moonlit equatorial night bringing him and an indefinite feminine presence into contact like amber and silk to rub a brief crackle into his old life. In short he had imagined shedding himself for a few weeks and entering a little world so absorbing and self-sufficient it would be almost an imposition having to write dutiful shipboard letters home to the ever-dwindling tally of friends and family.

It was in the restaurant he discovered the *Hildebrand* was carrying nearly sixty First Class passengers, thirty-eight of whom were making the round trip. There were another three hundred-odd Steerage passengers to be picked up in Oporto and Lisbon – mainly Portuguese migrant workers, he gathered, bound for Brazil and their fortunes. There would be no need ever to clap eyes on them; but even so, merely knowing about fresh hundreds of people tucked away on another part of the ship destroyed the last remnants of his fancy of quiet intimacy. He did, however, discover he had been placed at the Captain's table and as time went by he was to find this mere fact created some kind of invisible bulkhead between those select few who shared this table and the rest of the First Class. Tonight the Captain was not at table. He had sent his apologies via the Chief Steward and was sure his guests would appreciate that he was preoccupied with getting under way in one of the severest storms for some years. The Booth Line prided itself on the punctuality of its steamers on the Madeira–Para run but was no less proud of its safety record. Shipping companies always operated in the shadow of the most recent maritime disaster, such disasters being regular enough to remind them that modern engineering was not invincible. Not three months ago the French steamer *Député Emile Driant* had foundered off Dungeness with the loss of seventeen lives. While Captain Maddrell was wrestling with such problems on the bridge his passengers ate their first meal aboard still tied up to the dock in Liverpool.

Edward was introduced to a dozen people whose names more or less passed through his mind leaving few traces. Some of them seemed to fall so readily into 'types' that he felt excused the laborious gallantry of trying to remember what they were actually called. There was one of those mysterious knights of commerce whose very nationality was vague – Sir Somebody Pereira – port wine, most likely, or rubber. Or even slaves, who could tell? Two spinsters going back to some benighted mission in the depths of nowhere, all shiny knuckles and good works. A young man, practically a boy – Peter? Patrick? – going to take up his first post as a clerk in Alfred Booth & Co.'s offices in Manaos. A young woman in her twenties, rather modern, a Miss Air, self-described ominously as 'an artist'. There was even an explorer or botanist named – incredibly – Fortescue, with a red face and vague moustache: the sort of features which become visible only when surmounted by a pith helmet.

They all chattered as they ate, more, it struck him, out of excitement at the impending voyage than from a real desire to make acquaintance. Towards him they maintained that exaggerated respect which he had long since come to recognise and often to connive at. The food was good; he ate it largely in silence and listened to their conversation. But towards the end of the meal his reserve was overcome – maybe by the wine or even by the others' high spirits – enough to remark:

'I'd take a small bet that this company will be a good deal quieter by the same time tomorrow. Rather less numerous, too.'

'I imagine, Sir Edward, that you speak figuratively?' said one of the spinsters. 'I hardly think *betting* on the way Providence sees fit to dispose the weather . . . ?'

'Will anyone here offer me odds?'

'Well really, Sir Edward . . .'

'You think it'll be rough then, sir?' asked the Booth's boy. His evident apprehensiveness seemed to be shared by a majority of those at the table.

'My steward certainly thinks so.'

'Ah, one of those old sea-dogs, is he?' asked the explorer sceptically.

'More of a puppy, I should say, in every sense. But he claims friendship with the Marconi man in whom nowadays all wisdom is vested. Even old sea-dogs have given up lifting their muzzles to the sky. They shove up aerials instead.'

'It's quite miraculous and mysterious,' said the other spinster, giving him a sharp look he could not interpret.

From somewhere overhead came a melancholy C, loud enough to thrill the panelling and the table and the deck beneath their feet.

'Maybe we're off at last?'

But the glimpses of lamplit quay beyond the portholes remained unchanging. However, several guests took this as the moment to leave the table. As Edward himself stood up the first spinster made a nervous leaning gesture with her chest which implied that the eight or so feet of air between them was a momentarily intimate space.

'Despite our little contretemps I really must tell you, Sir Edward, how immensely honoured we are to have you with us.'

He muttered something. 'Muh, ah, very kind.'

'But I should explain that it's a particular honour for me. You see, I sang in the chorus at the first performance of your wonderful *Apostles* in Birmingham.'

'I am sorry, madam, that you should have thus wasted the precious hours of your youth.'

'Wasted? Sir Edward! It was the greatest possible privilege. It was probably the single most memorable event of my life. For all that it was so long ago I remember it vividly. The year was nineteen hundred and three.'

'I shouldn't wonder. But I believe the only thing worth remembering about that year was Rock Sand winning the Derby and the Two Thousand Guineas *and* the St Leger. Two to five on. Not much chance for a killing with a horse like that. Now if you will excuse me?'

'*Pig*,' he said to himself as he strode off down the passage to his cabin. 'Pig-pig-pig.' But then, as if to convince himself that his rebuff had been justified, 'She's ghastly. Is there no end to these dried-up creatures who hover around choral societies like vultures? I expect her friend sings drawing-room ballads in K sharp. Cursed pair of sirens.'

'Pig.'

He let himself into his cabin. His trunk had arrived and seemed to take up most of the bedroom floor. Its new lacquer glittered malevolently. Coffin, strongbox . . .; certainly it had the air of buried things about it, either of things decayed or of things concealed. Because he had not wanted valeting by a stranger he had not given Pyce the key. He now laid out his own night things, uncovering in the depths of the trunk several polished mahogany boxes with rounded edges, brass carrying handles and keyholes. The lid of each was inlaid with a rectangular ivory wafer where a name could be imprinted; they were all blank.

He read for a while in his dressing-gown, wishing to take refuge from that part of his brain which was vibrating with events, his day's travelling, the new surroundings. Beneath these lay the deeper upset of a life made suddenly rootless and aimless. His present existence seemed encompassed by the dingy walls of clubs and flats despite his recent move from Hampstead back to Worcestershire. Now that Alice was gone the London place had outlived its purpose. In relief he had returned to the county of his birth where he could finally turn his back on that endless metropolitan coming-and-going which had made Severn House so difficult to work in. Visitors, dinners, receptions, theatre-parties; telephone, telephone, telephone. Lady Elgar had revelled in it. Only he had known that each time the footman opened the front door another bar remained unwritten and another few pence unearned to pay that footman's wages. *Footmen.* Dear God, he was a composer. Why did he have to live like a character in *Earnest* where young moneyed swells could mess about at the piano while the butler brought in cucumber sandwiches? Damn them all, he thought, without trying to identify 'them' or, for that matter, having to decide whether he himself were included. A little hummock of bitterness heaped itself momentarily, lurched him and rolled on even as the other, the reading part of his brain resisted its interfering with the kind of serene melancholy he hoped might permit sleep.

Why had he brought Tennyson to read, of all people? Griefs,

longings, loves, ships, boxes, death. The rumble of wheels above the dreamless head. He closed the volume and went into the bedroom. As he did so the carpet transmitted another C to his slipper-soles which was then taken up muffledly by the air within the panelled box of his cabin. This time although the sound died away the carpet remained trembling. When finally he laid his head on his pillow he could hear distant machinery and marvelled at the smooth tumblings of steel, the tons of hot castings and whirling axles on which his life would depend for the next month or two. For a moment he was conscious of savage pressures in boilers studded with bolts.

'Calm sea. Prosperous voyage. Codswallop.' On the brink of sleep more jumbled phrases came to him: 'The watcher on the column' and 'autumnal man'. It was what came of leafing through Tennyson before going to bed.

He awoke once during the night, his eyes opening onto a dim circle of light. His first thought was of a hospital or nursing room, one of those places of disquiet and transience whose doors have round observation panes let into them through which white-caped heads were visible from time to time like a muster of ghosts waiting to be joined. Another operation? The pitching of the room still further bemused him. Just before a doleful calm panic set in he remembered where he was and consciously stopped his pyjama'ed arm before it could reach the switch on the bedside lamp. He was on his way to Brazil. *Brazil?* He must be mad. Therefore the circle of light was the curtained porthole giving onto the shelter deck. The *Hildebrand*'s plates quivered to waves and machinery. For a moment the motion was disagreeably like his recurrent attacks of Ménière's disease which had so debilitated him during the war; but once he knew the movement was real and not a trick of the inner ear he began to enjoy it. It was surely rougher now than it had been on any of those crossings he had made to the Continent – rougher, come to that, than on his transatlantic trips to New York in the *Mauretania*. After a particularly violent lurch which made the toothglass in the bathroom rattle in its retaining ring he thought it might even be rougher than it had been for the Mediterranean cruise with the Royal Navy in 1905.

For a while he debated getting up but gradually an inertia stole over him which was more like abandonment. Why worry? Things had run their course. If by some wilful alchemy his emptied life now consisted of being in a plunging steel box heading towards a dark continent he had never wished to see, why not? As soon do that as continue desolately shifting between the unsettled poles of Kempsey – still all packing cases which he now feared to unpack – and the London clubs where he lived out of suitcases. What drearier rut for an artist than that which led between servile slipperdom in the shires and the billiard rooms, smoke rooms and theatre crush-bars of the city? The shunting back and forth, the search for a quiet place where the departing Muse might once again be persuaded to settle: such very restlessness guaranteed it never would. Perhaps, then, in Brazil. Perhaps what had deserted him in fading England was now waiting among the energetic canopies of vast forests, its jewelled wings folded. It seemed unlikely; but then everything did.

It is the moment between dusk and dark when the forest stops breathing in and prepares for its night-long exhalation. With the vanishing of sunset's colour the water slides around the river bend like liquid slate, its surface scrawled faintly with poolings and involutions. The first fireflies blink over the mud among the rot and tangle at the jungle's edge. At the last moment of visibility a shadow comes and goes on the water although the air above seems to hold nothing more substantial than moths and midges – certainly nothing which could draw beneath it the outline of jagged wings. This slow flap as of membranes supporting a most ancient thing crabs its way upstream at an angle and is lost almost as soon as the eye thinks to have seen its shadow. A strange cry comes from invisible mid-river and at once a thousand frogs burst into steady unison.

Anybody who has felt nightfall's breeze off the river expire beneath damp heat rolling out of the jungle may also sense behind the rising whoops and screams and chitterings the combined tension of ciliary muscles as unnumbered pairs of eyes adjust their lenses to the dark on all sides. Only man becomes more blind. Yet there is a man here at this moment, watching this scene. It would be better to say he surveys it, for he is not standing on the shore but high above it. There is a small clearing from which the branchless trunk of a dead tree soars straight up. Its base is swathed in moss;

above this the shaft rises, glimmering where bark has peeled in scrolls. At the top is a makeshift platform of branches lashed roughly together in a roc's nest and on this he stands.

There is about this figure a great attentiveness. The very fact of its watching changes the scene in some way. In every direction for a thousand miles night hides the unrecorded, the inchoate. But this tiny patch of Brazil is different: it is being observed and experienced. It is even being loved. For the smells and sounds of the forest, as they rise from below and reach across from the adjacent jungle canopy, are fond to him. Even the stinging insects which cluster about exposed skin are familiar, a necessary part of the mysterious cycle in motion about his axle-tree. Years of this rigorous pursuit have sharpened his night vision and he easily identifies various animals which pass the foot of his tree. In fact there is a lamp in this eyrie but so content with the darkness is he that tonight, as often, he has delayed lighting it. Once he does so his night vision will be destroyed for the rest of his vigil and it is a faculty he is loth to lose. Meanwhile the sky flickers soundlessly to distant lightning. Sometimes he smiles when it crosses his mind to wonder what people would think if they could see him standing up here in the dark being eaten by insects. Those who didn't know might suppose him mad – the victim, maybe, of some self-imposed penance. And those who did – well, they too might find something extreme in a mode of behaviour which so courted discomfort and even danger.

There is a sudden breath of air across one cheek. He is tremblingly alert but does not move his head. His ears strain for the sound of something he can sense approaching, for whose arrival he yearns. A heavy body moves through the undergrowth below, but it is not that. A night bird crossing the river cries *chakk-chakk, chakk-chakk*, in a crescendo as it passes overhead. Following the sound with his eyes the watcher glimpses a blunt head crossing a starfield. It is not that, either; its diminishing cry is swallowed up. But in this limp tropic air there is a new tautness. Out there is some creature for which he has affinity. His sensibility has honed itself and is seldom wrong. Again the breath of air although the night is still. He imagines a light furry weight settle on the back of one hand or on his neck. Despite himself his skin crawls. He feels for the lamp and strikes a match.

The flare of light alarms certain creatures. There is the sound of wingbeats as a dazzled bird rushes for darkness. From the foot of the tree comes a startled snapping of twigs. But other things home in on the light and circle it in ecstasy. Beetles batter the platform with a crack of shards, carom off the lamp glass. The watcher is being spun into a whirling cocoon of insects. He catches the sparks of eyes, flashes of plumage. They are a wonder to him, the extravagant colours, the tigerish markings. It is this prodigality he chiefly loves: this profusion of colour and design intended for neither the light of day nor the eyes of man. The revelation of this concealed world has made the days less pre-eminent, less shallow.

And then he feels again the close breeze at one cheek and this time makes out a darting at the light's edge. Finally it comes completely out of the darkness to him: a moth the size of a pipistrelle clad in soft gold down. It settles on his shirt-front and he gazes down at it expectantly and with wonder. He notes the rapid tremble of its forewings, a stiff blur as it crawls an inch or two closer to his throat. Presently it stops and relaxes and he can see its hindwings are patterned like watered silk. Delicately its anus deposits an amber drop of liquid on his shirt. He stares into its eyes and thinks of his own hundred faces in those tiny gold seeds. The antennae are thick as beige feathers; the moth holds them high like the horns of an oryx making it look both quizzical and fierce. Slowly its abdomen pulses.

Seen from out on the river the light at the top of the tree is bright but scarcely illumines anything. It is there, high up in the air, for itself, on its stalk like a single dandelion opening short yellow petals. If a boat were to pass in midstream it would appear a lone bloom indeed, maybe the only light in an entire dark continent. Because it is unique it is a focus, a centre of activity, a contemplative node. To be carried past it out there on the dark current would be to have one's attention monopolised, for as long as it remained visible, by nothing more complex than a light up a tree. But as the boat rounded the bend and a swathe of forest extinguished it the mind would be unable to let go the image it retained. From now on the journey would be different, the night itself changed by the fact of having seen this: a lone figure standing on its high wooden tower in the middle of Brazil, motionless and waiting in the mothy air.

The next morning Steward Pyce almost concealed his disappointment on finding Cabin no. 2's occupant positively chipper.

Looking for all the world like a displaced squire Edward was striding about the shelter deck saying happily fatuous things under his breath as the ship lurched and fell. Through the tightly-dogged portholes were visible steep wastes of green–grey water marbled with the scud of broken foam. The *Hildebrand* bounced and slammed, its twin screws vibrating as their tips gashed the surface and then quietening as they were thrust back beneath a deep tonnage of water.

'By golly, that was a corker! 'Morning, Pyce. Any chance of breakfast yet?'

'Every chance, I should say, sir. There'll be quite a lot of it to spare this morning.'

'Coughing in their stables, are they? So much for the Jolly Jack Tar supposed to be lurking within every Englishman. I think I win my bet.'

'I'm afraid they are not all blessed with sea-legs like yours, Sir Edward. And the Marconi man says it will probably get worse. There's been a transmission from an American vessel out in the Atlantic to the west of us and they're taking it green quite badly. We've not even been able to put the pilot off at Holyhead like we usually do. He's still aboard and looks like being so for some time yet. The Captain says he's not keen on dropping him at Le Havre: wants to keep well clear of Biscay and I'm glad to hear it.'

Edward made an agreeably rolling progress to the restaurant where his spirits were still further lifted by the vista of empty tables. Only a few of them had been laid, their cloths dampened with water. At these a handful of breakfasters was sitting. As he passed they greeted each other with convivial nods in mutual recognition of their superiority to the landlubbers still groaning weakly in their bunks below. At his own table he found Captain Maddrell himself and Miss Air the 'artist'. His estimate of her went up.

'I was beginning to despair, sir,' the Captain said after he had introduced himself. 'I could hardly believe we had only one decent sailor at this table. It seems we have two. Now you will think it rude of me, sir, but I really must be excused. This weather has us all aback — or it would have if we had sails.'

'Of course,' said Edward. 'Besides, I'm sure Miss Air and I will feel all the safer knowing you're going back to the bridge to steer this tub.'

'In that case you'll be distressed to learn that I'm going to do no such thing. As a matter of fact I'm going to bed. I've been steering this tub, as you put it, all night and it's time to turn in. But don't worry; you'll be in good hands. Why don't you pay us a visit later on if you're interested? See how the old *Hildebrand* runs?'

'Oh, I'd like that. How do I get to the bridge?'

'Just ask any of the stewards or an officer. You'd be most welcome. If you're feeling really intrepid we might even be able to say that the Master of the King's Musick actually took the helm.'

'I say,' said Edward when the Captain had left, 'there's a forthright sort of cove. Nary a word minced. That's quite jolly. I love bridges, especially when there's a bit of a swell . . . I'm sorry we didn't talk last night. I'm not much at meeting people, you see. All I know about you is that you're Miss Air the artist.'

'Please do call me Molly, Sir Edward. I imagine it'll prove quite difficult to keep up an indiscriminate formality all the way to Brazil and anyway, one needs to reserve the right to be formal for those special cases one wants to keep at arm's length.'

'Well, thank God for an honest person. That's two in as many minutes. If this keeps up I'm going to enjoy this trip. Do you suppose it's the proximity of a watery grave which knocks the bunkum out of people?'

'Not in my case, Sir Edward, though I can't speak for the Captain. I'm afraid I'm seldom less frank than I am at this moment. It has never done me the least good.' She could hardly interpret the look she caught coming from, it seemed, his very skull so deep-set were his eyes.

'Oh, I . . .' he began. Then, 'I really can't resist your name. Might I pass you the *marmalade imaginaire*?' With a courtly gesture he set the earthenware marmalade pot on the dampened cloth in front of her.

'I thought I'd already heard them all. I think it's very dashing of you to be original while breakfasting on a sinking ship.'

'Oh, are we really? Mightn't the Captain have told us?'

'Captains don't like panic. It scares them more than drowning. But it's true I don't know that we're actually *sinking*. We keep going up and down but on balance I'd say we go down further than we come up. These things are cumulative.'

Later he took from his trunk a blank leather-bound book

portentously labelled 'Journal' in gold lettering on its spine. He had decided to keep a diary of the voyage, although 'decided' was perhaps too intentional a word to describe having bought it impulsively on seeing it in a stationer's. It had been the day he booked his passage – equally on impulse, since here he was on the high seas barely a fortnight later. Despair had a way of making one do things which then took on an air of spurious purpose. A ticket to a far place, a new leaf ... It seemed implausible. And yet ...

I

Boarded in terrible weather. Lost my hat. What idiotic phantasy was it of a little steel island detaching itself from these depressing shores & sailing away into sunshine with a select complement of souls aboard? The ship's a monster – well over a hundred yards long – albeit an elegant one & seems full of cocky stewards, shifty men & made-up women <u>smoking</u>. Unsure about my immediate fellows since most are too busy down below trying to turn themselves inside out. Molly Air has style & a fine name (?ch. in <u>opera</u>?). Capt. Maddrell's breezy & I think mayn't be above poking fun at us. Difficult to mind much. His job isn't to be sociable but an expert ship-driver. Ancient landlubbers like me must be as trying as those people who used once (once!) to come up after concerts & start off, 'I'm afraid I'm thoroughly ignorant about music, Sir Edward, but I want to tell you ...' Still, Maddrell has invited me up to the bridge later – his organ-loft – so I ought to be flattered & am.

Hempson and Pyce were enjoying a cigarette and a bottle of sherry filched from the bar. They were comfortably asprawl on First Class sheets and tablecloths in no. 1 Linen Store, a warm and rocking nest with a good many steampipes crossing its walls and ceiling. Each lay on racks on either side of the narrow gangway dividing the room, Pyce with his boots on a pile of face towels, Hempson with his on a heap of pillow cases. Now and then they would stick out a hand and the bottle or a cigarette would be passed across. This was only one of several bunk-holes scattered throughout the ship where members of the crew could go into illicit retreat, chiefly to smoke and drink and philosophise. On this particular morning the two men had company: a pregnant cat asleep on a deep litter of freshly-laundered table napkins.

'They're here again,' Pyce was saying. 'Dickins and Jones.' This was their nickname for an unlikely pair of confidence tricksters who from time to time joined the cruises under a variety of names.

'I saw 'em. Same cabin as last time, if I remember right. Gave 'em a wink, too, as an old pal.'

'What did they do?'

'Nah, po-faced. Professionals, aren't they? They've got their job, we've got ours. Live and let live, say I.'

'Right, and good luck to 'em. Except I hope it's not *my* passengers they fleece. I don't need the bother, I really don't. It's always the rich ones who cut up worst.'

'Like that Yank you picked on?'

'How in hell was I supposed to know he was a ruddy magician, Hemp? Bit of a misunderstanding, that's all.'

'You said. Still, probably best to keep your nose clean this time around. Otherwise Chiefie'll dump you. You watch him, Ernie. That one's got a streak of meanness in him.'

'Not the only streak he's got. Seen that new waiter with the hair he's put aboard? Blimey.' The two men smoked in silence for a bit, staring up at the wood slats supporting the linen on the shelf above. When Pyce next spoke the suddenness of the sound made the cat stretch all four legs stiffly out without opening an eye and then twist its head still deeper into the linen so its throat lay uppermost with a somnolent pulse ticking. 'And what about this new MO, eh? A rum 'un all right. Shouldn't fancy his sick parades.'

'Douggie says he's knife-happy. Likes a drink now and again, too, so I've heard. And they say there was something funny about him resigning the Army. He's dark.'

'What was that, then?'

'Nobody seems to know. Could be a streak there, too.'

'Ah, the old *Hildebrand* gets worse and worse . . . Do you ever wonder what we're all doing? I mean, tooling backwards and forwards across the Atlantic. Of course, I *know* what we're doing, making a living, but . . .' Pyce blew an inarticulate cloud of smoke over the sleeping cat. 'Sometimes I get thinking about it and it all suddenly seems funny. But when I try to explain, like now, it all goes back to being obvious. We're making a living. But the Old Man's only a bus driver, isn't he? This is just the number 11, except it goes to Brazil instead of the Town Hall or the Red Lion. So what's all this stuff for?' He gestured largely with the nearly empty bottle. An amber ejaculation of sherry flopped across the bedsheets. 'All this classy stuff, all that champagne and oysters and caviar and dance bands. You don't get caviar and dance bands on the number 11. Know what I mean?'

'I know what you *are*,' his friend told him kindly. 'Bit squiffy.'

'You do know, Hemp. You know exactly what it's like when we get to the other side. The sun beating down and the shithawks up in the sky and trees as far as the eye can see and the blokes there just living their lives when up comes the *Hildebrand*, the old number 11, regular as the timetable promises. I mean, what do *they* think about it all? About us? Where do they think we're going? We just sail past chucking stuff over the side and laughing and giggling. You've seen 'em, Hemp. You can't throw a dried pea over the rail without some little brown scrawny bugger paddling up in a tree trunk to nick it. There's nothing we chuck over they don't go for: empty tins, old crates, ends of rope. They can use it all. I dunno. What is it we're doing, driving round the ruddy globe dancing and giggling and throwing stuff away?'

'Do give over,' Hempson said. 'And pass me that bottle before you spill it all . . . You rotten blighter, you've scoffed the lot.'

'It spilt a bit.'

'Know what you are, Ernie?' Hempson's tone was half cross, half affectionate and something like envy gave an edge to his accusation. 'You're a trouble-maker. You've got the mind of a trouble-maker, you have. Me, I've had enough trouble.' And he stared at his own gappy hand. But Pyce wasn't looking. He was following the contours of the lumps in the cat's belly very gently with a fingertip.

'Am-az-on,' he murmured in time with his caresses. '*Am-az-on.*'

Edward, exploring, found the ship's library empty but for a man in a white mess-jacket busy with a rag and a pot of beeswax. For all its overtones of clubland – reinforced by the ghosts of half a million cigars and pipes wafting in from the carpet and furnishings of the smoke room next door – the place had the air of being used rather than consulted. A brisk marine smell hung about the pages of the books he took down at random. Also quite different from the volumes in London clubs (which seemed to acquire a uniform walnut hue as if they had become pickled in gloom) these were unusually pale about the cover and spine, presumably from having been taken up on deck.

And a weird selection they were, too, shelved without much attempt at classification. Between a Baroness Orczy and Conan Doyle's *The Lost World* he found the same edition of Longfellow he remembered his mother having. There was a shelf labelled 'Geography and Exploration' on which were a handful of novels as well as books dealing largely with South America: *Bouncing Gold: the Story of Rubber, In the Jungles of Venezuela, Where Stood Stout Cortez, An Economic and Regional Geography of South America* (in excellent condition), *Secret Rites of the Amazon Tribes* (all the photographs torn out).

Browsing with amusement and pleasure he selected a couple of good yarns for bedtime reading. Looking up he caught sight of a handsome brass ship's chronometer on the bulkhead above the shelves. Ten-thirty surely counted as mid-morning, a reasonable time for visiting bridges? He was just turning away when something made him look more closely at the books in the top shelf. There, outwardly no different from any of the dozens like it on either side, was volume I of Caroline Alice Roberts' *Marchcroft Manor*. On tiptoe he reached it down. Inside the cover he found a cancelled Ex Libris sticker for someone in Gloucester he had never heard of, then a rubber-stamped rubric in violet ink: NOT FOR TROOPS, itself cancelled and 'The Booth SS Co. Ltd' printed opposite. Opening it haphazardly he found Julian De Tressanay's sentiments on discovering that he had just inherited the Marchcroft estate:

> '*I, who have never thought of landed property, except to expatiate on the criminality of its tenure in general, and now I, of all people, I suddenly find myself the possessor of a large domain and old Baronial mansion, every stone of which could probably bear testimony to the dread of violence and oppression committed by its rapacious feudal owners . . .*'

Poor Alice. How painful to recall her second-hand radicalism from that distant era of Ruskin and Octavia Hill. Even more painful to wonder whether he might not have caused its demise as well as that of her writing itself. One more damned sacrifice . . . He searched, not over-zealously, for the second volume but failed to find it. He had never known what to say about her own stuff. She had given up novels on their marriage and from then on he had avoided having to pass judgement on her poetry by setting it from time to time. As he left the library he pondered the Arch-Jester's nasty little jab. Why that particular book of all books on board this particular ship of all ships?

A short time later as Pyce conducted him to the bridge there were other things which welcomely claimed his attention. Having passed from panelled and carpeted reaches through iron doors into more workaday regions thickly covered in sticky white paint he vaguely expected the bridge to be windswept and was surprised to find it calm and warm. Nobody staggered in and out with running oilskins. Mugs of tea tilted their circular brown puddles securely in metal holders. Neatly-pressed trouser-legs braced themselves easily apart; peaked faces stared ahead through streaming rectangular panes. They might all have been watching a motion picture of a tumultuous seascape but for the movement of the tea and the yielding at their hips. He clutched at a brass something and tried to foresee the *Hildebrand*'s various tilts and plunges.

Captain Maddrell, evidently a short sleeper, was standing slightly to one side of the helmsman on his grating, glancing into the binnacle as the man held the bows as nearly head-on to the south-westerly advance of waves as possible.

'I think we can ease off a point or two southwards, Skinner,' he said.

'Aye-aye, sir.' The spokes twirled.

The Captain went into the chart-room whose louvred door was dogged ajar and could be seen bending over a lit table on which lay maps, dividers, protractor, ruler. Looking round, Edward could see into another, similar room full of ebonite panels, knobs, switches and ranks of glowing valves. The Marconi man sat at his wireless, his back to the bridge, earphones on his head, away in some aetherial world of his own where electric blips and scratches announced human presences also abroad on these tossing wastes of ocean. Now and again his hand flexed on the Morse key as he added his own instrumental voice to some arcane dialogue.

Abruptly the Captain reappeared, uncapped a speaking-tube, blew into it and spoke. The inscribed plate above the speaking-tube – one of a bank arrayed like little organ-pipes – read 'Engine Room no. 2'. Then he turned.

'Mr Mushet, Mr Mushet. You're a lucky fellow and no mistake. A free holiday in Madeira. Next time we'll arrange to bring the wife and nippers.'

But the man he was addressing, standing to one side in a white jersey and stained cap, was maybe soured by the news. Eloquent as to his dismal thin beard he only stared out of a side window back to where the tip of Cornwall might have been many hours ago.

'It's not to be helped, Mr Maddrell,' he said at last. 'Not if a man will sail in the first place, that is.'

'You're an old woman, Mushet.' The Captain was clearly not put out. Cap pushed well back on his head so that the stubby black visor winked over his fringe in the light he was mischievously at ease – at home, Edward thought, in a way he had not been down below in the restaurant at breakfast. In the air these men shared was an equable passion. Their least movement – hand on brass, twirl of wooden spokes, raising mug to lips – had something in it of loyalty to each other and to their living island. Sir Sidney Colvin, as much Conrad's friend as Edward's, had recently read him a passage in which one of that writer's sentences had stuck in his mind as a true perception of a world from which he felt himself excluded. 'The ship, this ship, our ship, the ship we serve, is the moral symbol of our life.' *Moral*. Where was its equivalent in the lonely business on which he had expended his own years? Where the morality in such untrammelled selfishness? His mind gave something like a mutter of envy for whatever crucial experiences of muscle and eye and instinct that writer must have had with whom he shared a birth-year. One could so easily tire of the inner voice, always unassuaged like a bully yapping and baiting. Wistful bully, wishing now to have lived more brightly, to have had time off in the unequivocations of action.

'Sir Edward,' the Captain interrupted his self-disgust from across the bridge. 'Come and meet a miserable man.'

It was *that*, it occurred to him as he went over: not for many years had he remained in a room ungreeted for so long, nor had he been summoned so amiably by a stranger. There was something in the Captain which reminded him of the old gardener at Birchwood who had taught him hedging, coopering, a dozen other basic crafts, now scornful, now taciturn, very occasionally shedding a word of praise like a dead scale. But how Edward – hands scratched and blistered, sweating in his thorn-proof trousers – had glowed at the word! Such men were in charge of their lives, responsible for what befell them. They might really say anything to anyone with impunity. Absurdly, he yearned for their acceptance as he had never longed for applause, never had wished to throw himself upon those vegetable rows of fur and feather receding into an auditorium's shadows, gloved hands whirring against glittering bosoms like things dead and dry fretted in a hedgerow.

'Mr Mushet, I'd like to introduce the *Hildebrand*'s most illustrious passenger: Sir Edward Elgar, Master of the King's Musick – Mr Mushet. The unfortunate Mushet is our pilot – or rather he was when he was needed. Normally a cutter takes him off at Holyhead but in these conditions it couldn't be done. We might have carried him on to Le Havre, but the French coast is as bad as ours at present. The tales the wireless man is telling nearly make us inclined to skip Oporto and Lisbon and plough straight on to Madeira. His best chance of a short holiday is in Madeira.'

'But couldn't you have put him off on the South Coast safely to the east of the Isle of Wight, say?'

'Good heavens, Sir Edward, ours is a commercial shipping line. We don't make wide detours, burn up valuable coal and delay our passengers for the convenience of the world's Mushets. He's a vagabond, is Mushet. Never boards a ship without a toothbrush, a spare pair of socks and his papers. For all he knows an hour's trip down the Mersey can turn into a passage to the Ivory Coast. That's the life, eh?'

'Not when a man's fifty-two and feels the sun.' The pilot spoke still gazing out of the window as if expecting the skyline of Liverpool to heave into sight.

'Mr Mushet,' the Captain explained, 'sailed on this ship for nearly five years within recent memory, Sir Edward, and not once in that time did we ever hear him complain of feeling the sun.'

'And nor *would* a man who treks to and fro between Iceland and Norway.'

'You had another route in those days?'

'The Captain here's referring to the war.'

Edward looked around the bridge as if some vestige of that

awesome conflict were still visible as splashes of dried blood or the odd shell casing overlooked in a corner. 'This ship served?'

'It did indeed, Sir Edward, and most gallantly too. Three of us on this bridge today were bluejackets in her throughout the duration: that's First Lieutenant Simon Givens yonder. Have a warmer and I'll tell you. Tea or cocoa? We don't touch coffee on the bridge although if you wish it we can have a steward descend to more Bohemian zones to fetch some. But our galley understands cocoa. It talks cocoa in its sleep.'

'Cocoa would be splendid. Incidentally, I must correct you rather belatedly as to something you said at breakfast and just now when you introduced me. I'm not the Master of the King's Musick, you know. In England they reserve that kind of thing for the right sort of man. Cambridge academics mostly, I believe; *real* composers.'

Judging from a sharp glance the heat with which this was said was not lost on the Captain but he only said mildly, 'Then I stand corrected, sir.' As if to cover the moment's awkwardness he moved purposefully to place himself once more by the coxswain, watching waves and compass. His posture was that of a doctor attentive and silent next to a patient, deliberately not feeling the pulse but listening to all the sounds of a living body.

'She loves it,' he said happily. 'Feel her. Tight. She thrums. Not a groan anywhere. When I first caught sight of her my thought was, "H'm; pretty ship. Soft, maybe." But I was wrong. Wrong about the soft, I mean, for that was in late '13 when she was in civil trim and the old world was still going strong. She was young then, not three years from her maiden voyage. Black hull, white strake and upperworks, black funnel. Neat, graceful. No clutter anywhere. Something after all of a steam yacht about her, what with that sheer, light stern. The masts –' and through the blurred glass the fore-truck jabbed at the shattered sky '– were both white up to the halfway point and the topmasts plain varnished wood. They should have kept that, in my opinion. Maybe they'll change it yet.

'Ah, it was happy running in those days. Only ten years ago but it's not the same world we sail across today and they're no longer the same ports we reach, either. Not merely that they've changed physically because Pará, for example, Manaos, they've hardly altered at all. A few motor cars apiece, maybe, but not much different. It's the feel, I can't put it more exactly than that. There are no edges to anything now?' He glanced for confirmation at his distinguished passenger as if he had suddenly remembered, half-apologetic, that there stood a man who had already been over forty at the turn of the century and who no doubt felt even more acutely the falling-away of what had once seemed permanent.

'Well, as I say, she was a pretty ship. But then the war came and the Admiralty bagged her for their own.'

'Did you have guns?'

'Eight. When they converted her to HMS *Hildebrand* they changed her quite a bit. All her upperworks were grey and later on they painted the hull grey as well. So elegant she was.' The Captain might have been remembering a woman glimpsed in his youth who had on the instant set up a model for the elusive thing, the object which wounds fervently before it vanishes. 'I can see her now, sitting on the water in Scapa Flow, light as a dove. But she had claws. They gave her six quick-firers and two 11-inch howitzers before assigning us to the Northern Patrol: either Iceland to St Kilda or 20 degrees west to the Norwegian coast. We were supposed to maintain the blockade of Germany, which meant boarding any ship we intercepted. If we found a German raider we were to engage it.'

'And did you?'

'Oh, several times. The worst was in 1917. We were on convoy escort work by then, a "Q" ship. We were taking a convoy into the Clyde when torpedoes began scurrying about. Wherever you looked you could see their white tracks. The place was crawling with German submarines. The *Drake* took a fish amidships right next to us while we were pounding away at one of the subs on the surface. To this day I think we killed it for it disappeared in a cloud of smoke and steam.'

'Surely we got it,' said Mr Mushet. 'If we didn't we're not the heroes we've been telling everyone we are.'

There was nothing of reproof in his tone. The Captain said mildly, 'Oh, heroes. H'm. They were good days, weren't they?'

'The *Drake* went down,' objected the pilot.

'Capsized at anchor. She made it after all to Rathlin Sound. Notice served. Minimal losses.'

'But was this ship ever hit?'

'Never once, Sir Edward. Oh, plenty of times by shrapnel, odd rounds of this and that, slight damage to upperworks. But never anything serious. Never anything serious at all. You couldn't believe it, a dainty tropical cruise ship with borrowed teeth prowling the sea with submarines for company without getting a hole in her. For that matter, coming through arctic weather with her heart uncooled. None of our sister ships on this Brazil run was as lucky. All three of them went down in 1917, you know. *Hilary* was torpedoed in the North Sea, so was the *Antony*; and the *Lanfranc* was sunk too, for all that she'd been converted into a hospital ship. By the time she was de-commissioned the old *Hildebrand* was the only one left. Still is, come to that, although they keep talking about building another *Hilary*. But I'm not sure the trade's there as it used to be before the war. Those were our great days. You're aboard a real survivor, Sir Edward. The *Hildebrand*'s the last of the old world, *our* old . . .' he let the sentence wander off. 'You'll forgive me I hope, sir,' he resumed. 'I have a weakness. I like to talk about my ship. Damned selfish of me. I'm afraid I'm sadly ignorant of music.'

'Thank God for that. I am too.'

Several of those on the bridge looked round with surprise before fixing their faces back where they had been, attentive to the ocean ahead as if it could hardly be distinguished from their Captain's narrative.

'Ignorant, Sir Edward? Surely you're joking. Or perhaps . . . If it comes to that I suppose I'm aware of my own ignorance of the sea. No man can ever really know the sea. No doubt the same might be said of music. They're things of a lifetime.'

'That's a grim thought. Personally, I was just making a living – and not very much of one, either, for a good many years. It was a trade, that's all. It served me for a while. I'm thoroughly bored by it now. If you ask me there's a lot more to living than sitting at a table breaking one's head over a tune. This, for example.'

Staring at him now Captain Maddrell saw something boyish in the distinguished and slightly portly man, excited by being at the front of the ship as it bounded along over precipices of water, dropping and slamming and rising again.

'I can see why you despise us,' said this man.

'I despise you, sir? Where could you get that idea?'

'I mean us passengers. We're cargo, that's all. A fretful, moaning cargo which has to be appeased. Too many changes of clothing to be serious.'

'No, sir. We none of us feel that at all. Though since you're so frank I will admit that in general I'm always apprehensive when I wear my social cap. I'm no hand at table talk, as you'll have realised at breakfast this morning. I . . . well, the Purser's an excellent man for that. He's never so happy as when he's helping to plan games or getting the band to play a special tune for the couples.'

'The band? You don't mean there's a blasted band aboard?'

'Yes, sir. For the dancing. Tommy Hawtree and the Melodeers, I believe they call themselves.'

'Great God. This is awful.'

II

Really, discovering there's a band aboard has chilled me rather. First Alice's book . . . Next they'll start 'Salut d'Amour' or 'Rosemary' in the middle of an otherwise blameless sole meunière. It's hardly a new idea, bands on board passenger ships – look at the wretched 'Titanic' & remember those trips to Sanford in America – but I suppose it was yet another part of my silly phantasy – that at least one could get several thousand miles away from music. The time can't be far away when it'll be virtually impossible to hear silence. Motor cars and aeroplanes everywhere, bands everywhere, maybe even the wireless will find a way of setting a nigger minstrel to dog the heels of every last sane man on earth. Oh! I feel querulous but don't want to be. It isn't <u>me</u>, but it has come to serve as me just as it serves everyone else old enough to be too lacerated & weary to put anything back in its right place.

The <u>bridge</u> – exhilarating! I felt <u>dis</u>-honoured before such plain men as Maddrell. All those dratted honours of mine – those meaningless bits of gold and ribbon I pretended to covet for Alice's sake – they fell into dust as he spoke about the war aboard the 'Hildebrand'. I only ever felt honoured by the OM although it was such a new Order nobody in Worcester thought it worth a fig in 1911. That was the year after Florence Nightingale received it on her death-bed. 'Too kind, too kind . . .' she murmured but those present swore she had <u>no idea</u> what it was; as far as she was concerned they were giving her the Last Rites. But when I first heard the King was intending me to have it in the Coronation Honours List – that first dreadful thought like a telegraph message whizzing through the brain – <u>Oh, they don't want me to write anything more</u> – & then at last the pleasure &c. Ten or fifteen years earlier my honours could have come as encouragement; as it was they fell into my life with the dead weight of full stops. I know it's stupid to think of my life as ending with that List in 1911 but that's the thought which came & betrayed me. Probably the very moment of this ship's launching, judging from what the Captain said. Such interlocking trivia . . . So when he talked about the war I felt I'd been neutered – hadn't even any son to have hung maggoty and inglorious on that barbed wire like so many thousands, had been too old for this body to have been worthy even of a common grave with them – I had just to make <u>tunes</u>. (In any case the best tune of the war was 'Keep the Home Fires Burning' by Ivor Novello I think although immodestly I can't get out of my head that he might never have written such a good one had I not done P&C first – the falling fourths altho' his are concealed as falling thirds which are really appoggiaturas). What a mockery that I should have had a <u>sword</u>. What better sign of official impotence than the awarding of an outmoded weapon? Maybe one day the King will dole out diamond-studded Mills bombs or gold-plated Webleys to pink-cheeked dodderers. The sword, of course, went into the ground with Alice three years ago, stupid damned thing, I couldn't bear to see it. It's in the best place, in all senses. It was what she wanted for me & that part she can keep as far as I'm concerned.

Well, finally it seems I've wasted my life. It's a hard age at which to drink spider-juice but I submit. Suddenly on the bridge this morning I felt the flimsiness of all my substance, but not so much because I'd missed something. Quite the contrary – it was because of something of which I've had all too much: myself. I doubt it ever occurs to people who are not cursed with this 'urge to create' (whatever that is) how, far from living in sublime communion with one's Muse, one grows thoroughly to hate her. Oh I do hate that familiar voice – her voice, my voice which has ever since I can remember provided a commentary on everything I looked at, everything I did, every moment of my life. When one is a child one is spellbound by a voice which speaks with such immediacy to ear & eye & nose. 'Translate me,' it used to say & the sun made a tune on the skin of my forearms as I sat in classrooms with high windows. 'Take me down,' it said, speaking as aspen leaves trembling uneasily, their white always seeming to blow against late afternoon banks of dark cloud – water meadows with a few lonely cows and me. The voice was always at once of exhilaration & sadness. It's the sadness one remembers best with increasing years: the exhilaration has come to feel like empty gesturing. Those Shed books I take down and look at still, those various boyhood scribblings which still remain unused (few indeed) – no longer bring back those days as immediately as they once did, despite what I tell myself & friends. They merely bring back all the other occasions I've tried to re-live them. No more the real moment, the whizzing imperative, the yell by which things served notice that they were ripe to give dictation. Yet still that fossil voice demands my fossil attention. Not even Wordsworth had the power to stop once he'd reduced it to a trade. We'll never understand it. People tell me about my 'imperishable gifts to Humanity' – kindly, as they think. Well enough for Humanity, say I. But those of us who are haunted by that cracked old voice & plagued by that sniveller who demands more & more attention – we're the ones left with ashes.

The egregious Pyce has just been in to ask whether I would wish him to unpack my trombones and have them polished. I can't understand the fellow's impertinence – I give him far less trouble than any of the other passengers who are still supine in their bunks endlessly ringing for soda or beef tea yet he singles me out for such silly pranks. I shall think of a way of putting him in his place. Trombones indeed. Knavish he is.

In any case plenty of people become distinguished literary gentlemen. Why should I not have been at ease enough with my own Muse to have turned myself into a distinguished musical gent? I may <u>look</u> like one, I may <u>sound</u> like one but underneath it all I know I'm not. Nothing to do with class or anything like that – Parry's not a musical gent because he went to Eton but because he writes music like one. I started out by being wayward and have ended by being at war. Why? <u>I've not written enough</u>. Stanford writes more in a year than I ever did in ten. So did Mackenzie, even if the results were narcotic. (How kind of that newspaper critic reviewing 'The Troubadour' when he said the audience were reluctant to leave the theatre afterwards, forbearing to explain that snow was falling outside, the theatre was delightfully warm and the entire audience comfortably asleep.) My own efforts seem largely to have gone into warfare with myself. But why?

The gale blew throughout the second and third days of the voyage and the Captain, apprised by wireless of conditions off the coast of Spain and Portugal, kept toying with the idea of proceeding directly to Madeira. This was no light decision since eleven of his passengers were bound for Oporto, including the knight of commerce at Sir Edward Elgar's table. A further eighteen were headed for Lisbon. The remaining passengers were also expecting to go on short excursions at both stops, to wine lodges at Leixões for the ritual tasting of ten-year-old port and in cars from Lisbon to the Moorish town of Cintra. There they would wander on wobbly legs to the castle of Pena on the summit and through the grottoed Gardens of Monserrate dug into the hillside.

In the event the *Hildebrand* kept to her scheduled course, reaching the mouth of the Douro at midday on November 18th. Such had been the effects of the weather on her passengers, however, that practically no-one disembarked at Leixões clutching their Booth Line tramway coupons for the seven-mile ride into Oporto. Even Edward himself felt out of sorts, as much from the contagion of finding himself aboard a ship of invalids as from any real sickness. They sailed again at 11 pm, arriving at Lisbon the following noon. Still Edward kept listlessly to his cabin except to take tea in the Café aft of the smoke room. There he met Molly Air. Through the portholes were glimpses of white subtropical buildings against a grey sky, looking bleak and uninviting.

'We can console ourselves that we shan't be missing it at its best,' she told him as they shared a table. 'Cintra and all that, I mean. I made the excursion myself in early June a little while ago and it was ravishing then, just as Byron described. You cool yourself up there in the courts and halls of the castle, it's all glittery arabesques and fountains and arcades. Then you're whirled down straight to the Estorils, baking riviera beaches with gardens behind them full of oranges, pepper trees, mimosas and eucalyptus. Everywhere there are geraniums and bougainvillaea: nothing but savage colour and bright heat to remind you of all those marvellous long miles between you and England. But it wouldn't be the same in November, especially not in weather like this. Cintra would just seem cold, the castle gloomy, the beaches deserted. I'm afraid of that out-of-season feeling, aren't you? It suggests time rushing by and emptiness. It also always seems to imply that everyone else knows something you don't and is elsewhere.'

He hardly knew how to respond, taken aback by the vividness of her description and her tone. That little rhetorical turn 'aren't you?' was somehow informal enough to suggest intimacy but without the least presumption. It casually implied a friendship stretching back several years, precisely the sort of thing which normally made him bristle.

'I didn't know you'd made this trip before?'

'Eighteen months ago. I went to Manaos on this very ship but I came back on another. An adventure, I suppose. Having got to

Manaos I thought well, it's silly to come all this way for just five days and then go straight back home again. So I simply caught a river steamer and went on to Iquitos in Peru. That's another thirteen hundred miles upstream. It's a strange feeling getting further away from the Atlantic and ever closer to the Pacific. It really is like breaking through into the other half of the globe, the one which doesn't have all the familiar place-names. Except for Darien, of course.'

'You don't mean to tell me that you made the trip on your own? Surely your . . . er, husband . . . ?'

'If by that you mean unaccompanied, yes. But it was all right, you know. The Iquitos steamers also belong tc Booth's.'

'But what made you embark on such a trip in the first place?'

'Sir Edward, are you good at answering direct questions about yourself?'

'Not a bit, no. I had no business asking. Pray accept my apologies.'

'Oh, I don't need them. All I meant was it would take time for me to tell you enough for it to seem less like an act of wilful truancy. One explanation would be simple: I'm an artist and a botanist. I like painting exotica. The further into Brazil we steamed the more I realised how much I loved tropical land-scapes. All that grand gloom, sudden colour, huge skies full of clouds straight from the lungs of the jungle. I thought if Marianne North could have done botanical paintings in Sarawak and places then so might I in the Amazon. It's still far less explored even than Borneo and hundreds of times bigger. I want to be the first to paint peculiar orchids, huge gorges with unnamed falls whose spray drifts like smoke for miles. I want to see things no-one else in England or Europe has ever seen before. No doubt it sounds silly to you, but those are my reasons.'

'All of them?'

'Well no, of course not. I've grown apart from my family. Different views, you know. Also I was a nurse in France for a year before the Armistice. You can imagine it was all but impossible to go back to being demure, dependent, innocent if you like. Since when I've never been able to settle – along with thousands of others like me, I'd think. But I need hardly tell you about war, Sir Edward.'

He wondered what this Modern Woman meant. Surely not the

Boer War? Perhaps a son, two sons slain at Ypres, the Somme? Maybe it was just that she was still young enough for someone of his age to have no particular past; beyond a certain point any personal history would strike her as equally likely. As far as she knew he might once not have been a composer, might at forty have held a commission in the Dragoons, have served – for heaven's sake – in the *Crimea* even though he had not actually been born.

'I think you're very brave,' he said.

'But I'm not.' The creases from her nose to the corners of her lips were accentuated by her seriousness, a natural mask her face assumed along lines of old horror or resolve. 'I'm finally doing what I want. I should think that took abominable selfishness rather than courage.'

The Café was practically deserted. The continued absence of most passengers was emphasised by the occasional wan couple or jovial stranger who moved about the ship looking for diversion. Sometimes it seemed as though Molly Air and he were the only people aboard a vessel carrying them off to some unspecified place and for some unguessable purpose – to found a new race, maybe, or collaborate on a new ballet safe from the interruptions and curiosity of the metropolitan world.

'And what *is* Manaos like once we get there? If we ever do?'

'Wonderful. On the way down. You presumably know it was the centre of the rubber boom twenty years ago? I'm afraid a cad of an Englishman, a Mr Wickham, put paid to it by smuggling rubber seedlings to Malaya or somewhere out East with a similar climate. Or maybe his name was Wickstead and it was Ceylon? I heard so many people grouse about it I've quite forgotten the details. In any case Manaos's glory is fading. It already has that marvellous feeling of decadence and nostalgia even though the economy's only just beginning to suffer. People wander around moaning about going broke but they don't do anything much about it. Just mope in cafés and spit in the river and mop their foreheads and laugh. Most of the real brigands have moved out or are mellowing. The foreign business community is ageing visibly. Nothing much now between the older generation of entrepreneurs – especially Germans: you wait till you see them, concerts at the Schiller Institute – and boys like the one at our table – Peter? – who are all homesick. Fever-meat, I'm afraid. They're invalided home within six months. All day they sit on clerks' stools perspiring, and they live

on quinine. Poor things?' She finished this fervent sketch inter-
rogatively as if to discover where Edward's heart lay.

Promptly at eleven that night the *Hildebrand* sailed for Madeira.
The next morning found Edward restored to health although the
sea was still far from calm. As he breakfasted the ship plunged,
wood creaked, somewhere in a distant pantry several glasses
broke. In a short while Molly joined him at the Captain's
otherwise empty table and her presence further invigorated him.
How old was she? He could not be certain. Her war service was a
clue to a minimum age but when the previous afternoon she had
referred to feverish clerical boys it was as if whole generations lay
between them and herself. So unused had he become in his self-
imposed stuffiness to lively and voluntary talk by strangers that
after the reassuring stagnations of clubland and the shires he was
adrift. If this sort of thing typified modern shipboard life then he
had yet to find his sea-legs.
    Meanwhile a good proportion of the other passengers were still
keeping to their cabins, ministered to by stewards, stewardesses, a
harassed nurse, an ex-RAMC medical orderly with a red
moustache and finally the ship's doctor himself, Dr Ashe. From
previous experience Edward expected the doctor to be friendly,
perhaps jovial, even booming. Dr Ashe on the contrary had a
derisive, acidulous face and prowled the shelter deck corridors
with his red-moustached orderly trotting behind him bearing a
white enamel kidney bowl, empty. He looked as though he were
quite prepared to watch a passenger's canvas-shrouded body
weighted with old belaying pins slide from a tilted plank to raise its
own momentary headstone on hitting the ocean. Edward, not in
any case drawn to doctors as a race, made a mental note to remain
aggressively well for the rest of the voyage.
    Some time after breakfast a message reached him from Captain
Maddrell saying the bridge needed some new conversation and
would he care to step up? So he spent his fifth morning at sea once
more surveying through thick glass the tousled Atlantic, cocoa
mug in hand. The Captain was quite unrepentant about not
having skipped the first two ports of call.
    'I know if we'd gone directly to Madeira we would have been

through this weather several days sooner,' he said. 'But we're in business. It would have meant not taking on two hundred and fifty Portuguese migrant workers, a considerable loss to the company. Mind you, I bet the poor devils are regretting having sailed with us, packed in down there below decks. On some lines they travel no better than cattle, and pleased to be able to do even that. You can hang over the rail and watch 'em come aboard: black soft hats, long shapeless jackets, cheap fibre suitcases and those young–old faces – real Mediterranean types. Now and then I think it's really only modern slaving we're engaged in here. I know they're not physically forced to go but even so . . . There are things which drive a man as effectively as whips and shackles, it seems to me. The difference being that people like me are supposed to be able to carry them into exile with a clear conscience. But I know that Brazilian coast, Sir Edward. It can change a fit man into a tottering skeleton inside half a year, and these fellows often don't even start fit. Well, there it is.'

'Our Captain's a humanitarian, wouldn't you agree, Sir Edward?' Mushet the pilot turned away from his customary place in one corner, which for all his unsettled way of life he appeared to fit much as a ship's cat will be found habitually curled up on a discarded towel in its allotted retreat.

Edward did not answer directly but when he did speak it was to say: 'I suppose desperate men must take gambles. Brazil has to be developed and our own history shows that the sort of people who found colonies and spread civilisations are seldom meek and mild. Look at Australia, conquered by a rabble of convicts and deport-ees. But I must say I do applaud the Captain's views. When we're onlookers we cover things up by the phrases we use. We say "a new life" as easily as we say "a spot of bother" even when both might entail death. I was once myself carried away by an event where people were actually being killed.'

'War, Sir Edward?' The Captain looked knowingly round at him as though he too had once watched shells explode with an eye to their colour.

'Of a kind. Not one of ours, though. We were wintering in Italy, my family and I, in early Nineteen – I suppose in '08, it must have been. I was trying to write a symphony or some such rot. We were actually in Rome when riots broke out. I think there was a general strike – I seem to remember all the shops being closed and the trains stopped and I couldn't get manuscript paper for love or money. We heard a lot of shooting one morning and my daughter Carice insisted on going with me to see what all the fuss was about. It turned out that the troops had opened fire on crowds of demonstrators. It's a terrible thing for an army to have to shoot its own countrymen. The rioters were Socialists, but even so. When we reached the Piazza di Gesù it was all over – I was too late, as usual. But you know how even the aftermath of dramatic incidents is as exciting sometimes as the events themselves? The streets were full of soldiers and bright sunshine: glittering fixed bayonets and shining badges and buttons. The square itself was empty except for the cavalry picketed along one side. The brilliant uniforms, the gleaming steel all under that intense Italian sky made one heady. The air, I remember, was quite still. Some of the poor horses were nervous and the echoes of their hooves clopped round the piazza and from the side-streets leading to it from all directions you could hear the restless crowds, backed up and murmuring. The smell of gunpowder was everywhere. There was something *historic*, barbaric even, which I confess I found intensely thrilling. I mean it wasn't at all hard to imagine the Colosseum two thousand years ago, the flashings of steel, the roars and groans of the crowd, and then tiny individual human screams lost in the middle of all that implacable baying. Then we suddenly noticed bloodstains on the cobbles: in one place a whole puddle of blood with dust settling on it and all sorts of red scrapings and daubings as if bleeding people had been hurriedly dragged away. And everywhere around the walls there were white pocks in the old stonework. But only afterwards did I really feel shame that for quite some time – until I saw the human evidence – I had enjoyed it.'

For a while Edward stared ahead in a kind of horror, quite unsure how what had begun as reminiscence should have been turned by some malicious inner voice into confession. But the Captain said helpfully: 'The human animal, sir. It's in all of us, like as not.' Then, 'Would you be at all interested in the engine room? Our Chief down there is always happy to show off his infernal den.'

Edward gave a start. 'I say, I should. But there's just one thing since I'm here . . .'

And for fifteen minutes Sir Edward Elgar took the helm of the *Hildebrand*. The cox stood with his back to the bulkhead, at ease, looking nowhere in particular as Edward initially gave the spokes several nervous twitches and finally, beginning to sense the ship's weight and desire to turn her head, spinning the wheel. Captain Maddrell took up his customary position behind the helmsman, enough aside to read the compass over his shoulder, giving advice.

'Feel her through, Sir Edward. See that series of rollers ahead? She'll slice the first two but the next one will begin to turn her. You need to lay off to starboard a few points . . . bit more . . . hold her there. Oh, feel how she takes them? There's a real heart to this ship. But the weather's slackening. I believe we're through the worst.'

'It looks no different to me. But I say, this is a lark.' For, whatever anguishes and peppery despondencies had contrived to mould this grey-haired man into the simulacrum of a courtier, the deep eyes were full of a far younger happiness. As he watched a path sort itself out of the malleable wastes ahead he might have been conning a skiff past a notorious weir on the Severn fifty years earlier, so avid and childish was his expression, such pleasure was there in the feeling of lively wood beneath the hand, so beguiling the illusion of captaincy over his immediate or ultimate fate.

That night the wind dropped, the sea lessened and the *Hildebrand* ran out from beneath the westernmost edge of a slab of cloud which pressed down over Europe like funerary marble. The first stirrings of night life were felt as the more resilient passengers threw off malaise and donned formal dress. The carpeted corridors and stairwells which had previously lain empty but for the lugubrious tread of the doctor and a few diehards now trickled with highly polished shoes as circulation began returning to the ship's arteries. At the heels of certain of these shoes – not all of them women's – trailed whiffs of Guerlain.

'Odd how quickly one recovers . . . I say, Bernard, it's odd how quickly one recovers.'

'I heard you.'

'My dear, you *do* look ever so slightly fragile. But terribly brave, too. Like a meringue on the Western Front. Rather becoming, I should say. Goodness, when I think how badly I wanted to die this afternoon and now I'm ready for *anything*.'

'I can well imagine. But as far as this girl's concerned *anything*'s off the menu at present.' Just then a tall waiter emerged from a door and hurried by, leaving an impression of oiled hair and long lashes. '*On* the other hand . . .'

'On the other hand if that's on the menu you might just force yourself to a little nibble.'

'I rather think one might stretch to a mouthful . . . For the first time I'm beginning to be glad I came. *What a sheik.*'

'Well you can't have it, you're still too tottery. In your present condition you might keel over entirely. There's nothing at all chic about being buried at sea. Not when you were planning to lie in state at St Michael's, Chester Square, surrounded by loyal subjects in wildest mourning. Anyway, did you see the look he gave me?'

'I did. Pure dismay. I shall reassure and comfort him at the earliest opportunity.'

'I really think, Bernard, you'd much better leave that one to me. For the sake of your health.'

'You're so *caddish*, Desmond.'

'Howling.'

And the giggles and Guerlain died away.

Elsewhere quite, in a middle-aged saloon, two middle-aged ladies had been persuaded to try their luck in a friendly game.

'I suppose just this once,' one of them was saying dubiously.

'A little flutter never hurt anyone,' insisted her new partner whose silly-ass monocle nearly disguised a certain canniness of expression. 'We shan't be playing for money. Just matchsticks or something. Well, *pennies* then.'

'I'm an awful dunce at cards,' said the other middle-aged lady. The two men swapped glances.

'You'll soon get the hang of it,' urged the man with the monocle. 'Look, why don't we have a dry run to clear away the cobwebs?'

An hour later it could be observed that his beady expression had changed to one of glumness.

'It's coming back to me now,' his partner was saying.

Still later unspoken recriminations hung in little black clouds over the table.

'One never really forgets a card game, does one? It's like bicycling. One may get a little rusty but the knack never disappears completely, I find.'

'I wish I could say the same for the money we've been losing,' said the man with the monocle bitterly.

'Oh dear oh dear, I'm awfully sorry to be such a dunce.' And had the two men been less distracted they would surely have noticed the look the ladies briefly exchanged, for it was one of pure mischief. 'I tell you what, why don't we do something quite unladylike and play poker instead? Then it's everyone for himself.'

But there was no doubt luck was running against the monocled man that night. The ineptness his erstwhile partner had shown in her bidding seemed at last to have settled down into the occasional moment of recklessness. The rest of the time she made respectable little wins and by the end of the evening's play had done rather well.

'Goodness,' she said, 'you *did* have some awful hands, Mr Barstow, you poor man. I can't think what got into the cards tonight. Normally I'm the one forever trying to make a pair of fours sound like a straight flush or whatever it's called. Why don't we all try again tomorrow? Your luck will have changed by then. Do let's.'

That same evening also marked the beginnings of several shipboard romances. The shared oppression and enforced reclusiveness of the first days of the voyage made for flurries of alliance as eye caught speculative eye. Gentlemen in full fig came upon each other preening themselves anxiously before washroom mirrors and remarks were heard about 'the corker in the blue dress with the little dog'. The younger element soon found their way into each other's cabins (where all sorts of shrieks and evidence of high jinks were wafted into the corridors by opening and closing doors) while the youngest element of all, two morose boys of ten, met at dinner and loathed one another on sight.

But things were as yet exploratory, uncertain. What everyone asked themselves was, 'Am I going to get any fun? And if so, when might it start?', a question hardly confined to newly-assembled cruise passengers.

'What do you think?' asked one of the card-playing ladies of the other as they prepared for bed in their shared cabin. 'I quite fancy my Mr Monocle. *Barstow* – such a reliable, straightforward name and, unless I'm much mistaken, a straightforward gentleman. Straightforwardly greedy, I mean. Did you notice his tiepin?'

'Oh yes, and his cuff-links. Whereas mine . . .'

'I'm afraid there *was* something ever so slightly déclassé about yours, wasn't there? All that talk about nipping over to Brazil to settle some contracts. You saw his hands? That one's accustomed to lugging something far heavier than a briefcase.'

'Golly, how Sherlockian we're becoming in our old age.'

'My dear, a commercial traveller's a commercial traveller, dress him up how you may and send him to the other side of the world if you will. No, I don't think you can look upon that one as a man of substance. Bad luck.'

'Never mind. It was a start, wasn't it?'

'I'm going to turn the light out now. *Ow*. How very hot these glass shades become.' The two ladies lay and listened to the engines and the sea catching at the rivet-heads only an inch or two of steel plating away from their blanketed feet. From somewhere – maybe the deck above or the deck below them – came an occasional muffled strain of dance music, a sedate waltz as befitted the lateness of the hour. 'Yes, it's a start. I like the look of things. You know that feeling? It's going to be an interesting trip.'

'Mm. What price Sir Edward Elgar, though?'

'Under no circumstances.' The voice came from the darkness in a firm tone as if its owner had come up on one elbow to make the point.

'Dearest, just think . . . Position, wealth, and I'm sure I remember hearing his wife died recently.'

'*Absolutely not.*'

'Well it seems a pity. Rather a waste, I mean. He has the eye, did you notice? And don't come all over virtuous, it's such a bore. A touch hypocritical, too.'

'I suppose he has, yes. Yes, of course I noticed if you insist.'

'Oh I do insist. I also reserve the right to imagine you becoming more *predatory* as the voyage wears on. Anyway, I thought we'd long since agreed that anyone with the eye was fair game.'

From either bed there came the sounds of two old friends from whom little was hidden quietly enjoying a joke.

'I forbid you to have designs on the Master of the King's Musick.'

More laughter. All around them in the starlight the wave-tops wrung their hands unseen and fled continuously astern.

Oblivious of how his presence was already beginning to affect the plans of at least two people aboard, Edward was at that moment returning to his cabin after a bluff evening with new acquaintances. Still restless with smoke and chatter he postponed sleep for a while and instead settled down at the desk with his Journal.

III

Maddrell was complimentary on my helmsmanship in a gruff sort of way. Told him it wasn't unlike conducting & nor is it. As a beginner one had the same feeling of being run away with and then of immense power & one's least act will cause everything to skid off or sing. Maybe I should have been Captain Maddrell although it's by no means certain what sort of a composer he might have made. Probably rather good: well-made light music which everybody likes to hum and which earns.

Well I could do that too, and did it, except that I never wanted to have to. If only I could have made a halfway decent living out of 'serious' stuff I would probably have dabbled quite pleasurably in the odd 'popular' piece – & why not? it's perfectly respectable to be a tunesmith. That time hearing someone whistle the viola tune from Alassio in the street – who it was or where they heard it lawd nose but oh! the pleasure. It's the greatest compliment a composer can be paid (but compliments don't buy groceries) and I thought yes, I took the tune down so that other people could hear it too. I would certainly much rather have done salon pieces which people could whistle than all those glees and part-songs for beastly little choral clubs to massacre earnestly. One of those odious commissions (for a pittance, naturally) actually paralysed me with hatred. My hand would not move across the page. It took five days to write a line, such bosh, nobody would have wanted to whistle it & we ate bread that week but precious little else.

I did once tell somebody (pompous ass that I am) that I was folksong, mainly a retort called forth by their endlessly trying to get me to say what I thought about the 'new music' (esp. V. Williams) and all that Cecil Sharpery. Perhaps it wasn't so far off the truth. If ancient folksongs were the distillates of a culture & its language then it wd. be surprising if I who knew the sound of the wind on the Malvern Hills quite as well as Piers Plowman had not occasionally captured something of the essential melody which lies beyond mere tune. And anyway if folksongs are songs the folk sing then 'Land of Hope & Glory' – curse every one of its bars – surely qualifies. Not something I ever want to hear again, not even whistled in the street. How I've come to detest the thing! You can't joke with the public: they know nothing but what they do know is always enough to hang you. All my music has now shrunk to that single tune, quite undeserved what's more since it wasn't my idea to put words to it but the King's. They don't fit – of course poor Jaeger was right about that drop to

E – whatever words had been shoehorned into it wd. have sounded vulgar. But dear old Nim didn't have the full weight of the House of Saxe-Coburg-Gotha bearing down on him, only consumption, and that makes a man unafraid of kings. Mind you I don't regret the original tune as it was in P&C – it knocked 'em for six as I knew it would – but I never intended a thing which came to me one morning while I was probably sawing wood or something (the rhythm?) should become a perennial excuse for a national bellow.

Well, it was the box office & I played to it & God knows I needed to. One surely can hardly blame penurious artists for trying to make a bit of chink, even a living when they can tho' in the long run it never pays because you get labelled by the public's taste, fickle & ignorant as it is. Nobody now gives much of a damn for any of my music, only a remaining handful of dear ones who remember the great times; now we're fellow-dinosaurs who haven't yet crept decently down into our coal-seam and joined the fossils of a forgotten age. But I do live and breathe, I lash my tail & still can bite & take pleasure in doing so. The single exception to the fate of everything I've written seems to be 'Land of Hope', belted out with bombast & that has anyway become national property – it's no longer by me, just another of those purple tunes like 'Rool, Britanyah' and 'Gawd Save' which make the public climb onto its hind legs and yell with a tear in its eye (two tears if there's a pint in its stomach). Oh, foolish! spending a lifetime despising the British public's musical taste & I realise now my scorn was misdirected. It was really self-loathing for bothering with such things anyway. One is an artist & there's an end to it. No use trying to suck up to posterity – posterity's inscrutable & doesn't pay last month's gas bill. When dreamers of dreams get turned into national figures you can be damned sure their dreams are misunderstood. Poor old Kipling, now – a case in point. He complains he's so well known by a famous line here and there but never by the next line which undoes it & still less by all those hundreds of poems which lie unread in the Collected Works. Alas it's the same for me & probably for all of us. The people who are known by whole pages at a time are either a hundred years dead or Arthur Sullivan which amounts to the same thing. I know some of my things are alive and will last but it won't be me who reaps the least benefit from them – nor ever did – just a lot of conceited asses not yet even born, conductors & fiddlers & bawlers who are more thought of than the composers without whose music they would be nobodies. Or coxswains.

Later

We've all lost our faith, those of our generation – Hardy, Kipling, Conrad – we all went through the motions of producing stuff as if everything were all right, or at least still possible – as if that eye in the sky were still looking down with compassion. But it isn't; & since that filthy war we all know it never was – such scenes of carnage it wd. have to have witnessed unblinking – & now we've all woken up to the fact that it's dead. It's all as dead as the machinery roaring everywhere (soon no more horses, no more hooves clopping through the streets, no more friendly smells of fresh sweat & honest dung). I'm like a man who as a child once heard a marvellous bird sing in a miraculous tree & has spent a lifetime trying to take down its song – only to discover too late that it was only a cuckoo clock, springs & pulleys & cogs.

What a fool!

Later that night the *Hildebrand*, relieved of the sensation of butting into banks of solid felt, flew easily with its complement of sleeping lives high above an unseen terrain of mountains, crevasses and plains of silt. Among these suspended sleepers none at that moment knew where he was nor where he was bound, and there was at least one who even on waking might not have wished to settle on any particular landscape the reposeless slow whirling of his unease.

When dawn broke on the port side a grey track of smoothly undulant water led from the ship to a cream-and-gold focal point on the horizon. By the time the sun had risen in a sky which had in it only a few remaining tatters of cloud the water was gentle. It had also taken on shades of transparent indigo and blue which mark warmer latitudes and on which suds sit blindingly white for as long as it takes a ship's hull to pass. Gradually passengers began emerging on deck, pale and rubbery and uncertain in their dress, to blink at the ocean. Taking heart at the sight they all disappeared again and up from below, like the scent of fresh toast, there drifted the subdued clatter of crockery and silverware as the first solid nourishment for nearly six days displaced the nightmare memories of beef tea and water biscuits. It was a breakfasting ship whose decks Edward strolled with Molly.

'I know it's customary to observe that we all become different people when we travel,' she said, 'but I really do feel reborn. No doubt I shouldn't say so to a celebrated patriot but now we've left that storm behind I really think we're at last out of the clutches of England. I'm afraid for me the country has a malign aura of gloom which extends far beyond its coastline, like territorial waters or something. Now you're shocked, I bet.'

'Only by the news that I'm a celebrated patriot. I didn't know that.'

'Surely you're joking, Sir Edward? Knighted for services, friend of Royalty, composer of national songs?'

'I suppose I love my country – the few remaining bits which haven't yet been ruined by concrete and asphalt and other industrial eyesores, that is. And maybe I love my countrymen – some of 'em. But as an artist yourself you should know that artists don't have countries in the way other people do. If they're as unlucky as I've been then bits of their work – invariably not the best bits, either – get taken up and people go around saying how exactly they fit the national mood. All of a sudden an ordinary Worcestershire countryman, which is what I am, finds himself touted as the embodiment of John Bull. It's not a role I relish.'

'Oh . . . But I thought, well, Master of the King's . . .'

The ferocity with which he cut her off made her stare straight out over the rail like a ticked-off child who dare not look at its accuser.

'For the last time, I am *not* the Master of the King's Musick. That post is currently held by Sir Walter Parratt and has been since the eighteen-nineties. I am no longer the master even of my own music, let alone the King's.'

The sheer pain of this last sentence, spoken as he turned abruptly away to stare at the black funnel uttering its racing black coils, silenced her instinctive protest that this was positively the first she'd ever heard of it.

'I'm extremely sorry if I offended you.' She did not say this especially meekly but more with the dispassion which comes from being accustomed to ordinary bad behaviour. That was what one had to say; it was thus one sued for peace.

'Offended? I'm not offended. I'm just bored beyond bearing that wherever I go people feel they've got to talk about music, music, music. Damn all music! Why ruin a perfectly beautiful morning with this incessant gabble about *music?*'

The injustice of this fresh outburst, instead of silencing her as it had silenced so many, actually stung Molly to say an unthinkable thing. Not knowing nor even caring whether this man beside her embodied the State or an Art or was merely some kind of distinguished-looking puppet she said:

'That is probably the most childish thing I ever heard a grown man say. We were talking about patriotism; it was *you* who suddenly began a tirade about music. Five years ago I was watching horribly wounded men die – boys, most of them, children even – and not one of them behaved in such a nursery fashion. You've evidently lived a very indulged life, Sir Edward.'

She walked away up the deck and vanished down a companionway. He was left staring at the impassive slide of water, the speed of whose hissing lacework of foam reminded him of how fast he was being carried ever further from the known, or at least the familiar. *What on earth was he doing here?* He'd never wanted to come on this stupid trip. Who had taken this mad decision for him? Who had recommended this very shipping line? Sybil, damn her. And the thought came and went too fast to be put into words, like a sick chord, 'How dare Alice leave me like this?' while that same fleeting sound also encompassed her chiding 'South America? Oh Edu, I hardly *think* . . .' He had a sudden glimpse of the frightening and empty waywardness to which a life was subject once ordinary domestic restraints had dissolved. What was to prevent . . . ? And the answer always came, Nothing. Nothing might prevent anything. And the dazzling wound in the water was forced open beneath his eyes to close raggedly somewhere under the Red Ensign at the stern, the scar of the ship's wake stretching back and back to the vacant line of sky and water.

Whatever crossness or self-pity might have swallowed him for the rest of the day was staved off by the appearance at his elbow of Steward Pyce in a white mess-jacket.

'I have a message for you, Sir Edward. Chief Engineer Stanford presents his compliments and would be happy to see you at your convenience in the engine room.'

Edward continued to stare downwards. 'Stanford? Is that really his name?'

'Chief Engineer Stanford, sir. Yes sir.'

'Dear God. I suppose there isn't a cabin boy named Delibes, is there? Or a grease-monkey called Dvořák aboard? No Saint-Saëns in the stokehold?'

'No sir.' Pyce was perplexed. 'No foreigners aboard. Not as crewmen, leastways. And certainly no Germans. I can't see any of the lads wanting to share a berth with a Hun.' Then, evidently wondering whether he might not have been a little outspoken

(Elgar, now, that didn't sound particularly English, did it?) he added a conciliatory 'Bygones be bygones, sir, of course. Water under the bridge. Live and let . . .'

'Show me.'

As Pyce led the way below Edward said 'I wonder if you would be so good as to get me a couple of things?'

'Of course, sir. All part of the . . .'

'I need a small bucket – well, perhaps a large tin with a stout handle and some light cord. Say about thirty feet. Can you do that?'

'Stout cord, sir. Light bucket. Can do, sir. Any particular . . . ?'

'Just those, thank you Pyce. When I say bucket maybe that would be a bit large. More of a can with a handle. Hold about a quart, shall we say?' And as they both stooped to enter the first of a series of round-cornered metal doors set rather high in the wall Pyce caught the words 'my instruments'. It's his bloody trombones, the Steward thought. What on earth can he be up to? He tried to imagine any activity – regardless of plausibility – which could possibly involve such equipment. He gave up as he ushered his passenger through a last hatchway, grasping the lintel with an extended hand so the distinguished grey head might bang itself on nothing harder than his knuckles.

Edward passed into a racketing cavern where sound and smell merged into one another and became the single effluvium of power. The noise itself was a sustained low howl and monstrous panting as though the *Hildebrand*'s metal flanks heaved with her efforts to drive through the ocean. An hour later he returned to the upper air deafer and with the uncertain tread of an invalid. Once in the bright breeze he was again conscious of the onward rushing of the ship, a feeling now informed by images of the implacable force of great engines. Never mind, he thought, only for a few weeks. But as the memory of that appalling breakfast-time conversation with Molly Air re-surfaced a familiar swell of despair rose up from beneath and then receded, leaving him beached on the exposed deck like a castaway. 'We could none of us have foreseen how stranded we should become,' he thought, and, 'We do not belong here.'

Yet once again his desolation was broken into by the sudden appearance of Steward Pyce. This time the man carried a coil of light cord and a small metal drum which had been roughly pierced at the rim and fitted with a wire handle.

'Were these what you had in mind, sir?' After some thought and a speculative conversation with Hempson he had decided that this was part of the equipment for a new game his passenger had devised, something like deck-quoits but involving throwing things into a tin rather than over a peg. The string was probably to enable a player to twitch the tin at a distance to spoil his opponent's aim. He had not yet decided on what these people would be throwing into the tin – coins, probably, even bloody sovereigns, seeing the money some of them could afford to leave lying around on their dressing-tables. Well, you had to be idle rich to come on a jaunt like this in the first place, didn't you? Upwards of forty-eight quid was what the round trip cost a First Class passenger. Forty-eight quid.

'Just the thing,' his own passenger was saying, looking pleased for the first time. Gloomy sort of cove, Pyce reflected. You'd hardly have thought an old jam tin from the galley would cheer him up like that. 'Is this thing clean?'

'Clean, sir?' What was this? 'Oh yes sir. Cook gave it a good washing out.'

'Well, very good then. That'll be all.'

From the way in which he put tin and cord at his feet the man was not going to be more forthcoming. A little disappointed Pyce withdrew but only to the ample cover of an engine room duct whose mouth perpetually gulped the cool wind of their passage. He fiddled idly with the latch mechanism controlling the angle to which the duct could be swivelled so that any passenger on deck might suppose him properly occupied, while every now and then covertly watching the distant figure at the rail. Suddenly it stooped in the stiff manner of the portly and tied one end of the cord to the handle of the tin. Then Sir Edward gave a swift glance about him and, evidently reassured that he was not watched, began to lower the tin over the ship's side. There was a pause during which his grey hair was twitched by the breeze then a sharp 'God damn it!' reached the Steward's ear. Sir Edward could be seen hauling in the cord hand over hand very fast. On the end was nothing but a piece of bent wire.

Pyce, who from the moment his passenger had begun lowering the tin had known what would happen, smiled to himself. 'Silly beggar,' he thought. 'What did he imagine at fourteen knots?' He moved off to another part of the deck but not so far away that Sir

Edward would not be able to spot him almost immediately. He was not at all surprised by the man's appearance at his side within minutes.

'I'm afraid you'll think me a complete idiot, Pyce,' Edward began, offering the bent wire. 'I was fiddling with that can when it somehow unhitched itself and fell overboard. I wonder if I could trouble you for something a little stouter? A bucket perhaps?'

As he went to fetch one the Steward pondered this inept little falsehood and pondered still more the outcome of an attempt to lower a heavy galvanised iron bucket into the whizzing sea. 'Probably pull his stupid arms off,' Pyce told the stores man with satisfaction.

'Lose a perfectly good bucket in any case. Give him this one, look, it's patched. Hanged if I'm turning over a new one.'

'Don't you worry, I'll do it for him. Better have some proper rope while you're at it.'

Up in the sunlight he approached Edward blithely, swinging the bucket.

'Now then, sir, you want some sea-water.'

'Oh, Pyce. Er, well, while you're here with a bucket I wouldn't mind some of that *as well*.' And his distinguished passenger shot him a hot unreadable glance from his deep-set eyes. 'But not here.'

'No sir, it'll be easier if we do it from the stern.'

'Afraid not. No, I want it from up front.'

'You want water from the bows rather than from the stern?' This isn't eccentric, he thought, it's stark staring. 'I think you'll find it's pretty much the same water, sir. Sea up front and sea behind.'

'That's maybe what it looks like to you, Pyce, but I can assure you it isn't at all the same to my instruments.'

'No sir?' The man was going to give his trombones a drink, that was the only possible thing. Pyce wondered whether he should see the MO − informally, of course, just to find out if there was any chance of this man going right off his chump. There had been that American last year who had tried to walk on the water. You just couldn't tell. It usually wasn't the noisy ones at all; it was the quiet, well-mannered, purposeful sort you had to watch.

'Well, sir, if it's from the bows you'd perhaps better let me get it for you. It's a tidy drop to the water up there and that bucket's going to weigh a bit when it's full.'

Together they made their way forrard past the bridge to the very

bows where the deck narrowed to a cramped clutter of ironwork –
windlasses, chain lockers, a small derrick – and the stem plunged
vertically to cleave the water far below like a sharp grey headland.

'You shouldn't really be here, sir,' said Pyce as he let the bucket
fall to the water trailing an impeccably-judged length of slack, then
extricating it with an expert flick the moment it had begun to fill. It
had taken a fraction of a second. Soon the bucketful of Atlantic
came up over the rail, the water still revolving as the last
effervescence cleared. 'There you are.'

From an inside pocket Edward produced a silver hip-flask which
he unstoppered and plunged into the bucket. When it was full he
corked it.

'Very much obliged, Pyce. You can throw the rest away now; I
have what I need.'

From his vantage point on the bridge Captain Maddrell had
been watching with puzzlement.

'That steward, Pyce, what the hell does he think he's up to?' he
said, presumably to Mr Mushet who was slouched in his customary corner nearby.

'Is that the musician fellow he's got with him?'

'You know damn well it is. Pyce should never have taken a
passenger up there. I don't care if it's the Prince of Wales, he's not
being given the unrestricted freedom of *my* ship. Company regs are
quite definite on the point. If some passenger takes a header into
the briny from the bows we won't have a leg to stand on in court.
Look good in the *Echo*, wouldn't it? "Booths Murder Nation's
Composer".'

Allowing a discretionary ten minutes to elapse before sending
for him the Captain had Pyce uneasily climbing the bridge stairs.
This was emphatically not the steward's territory; he normally had
nothing to do with the ship's officers, being answerable to the Chief
Steward. Once on the bridge he stood to attention, conscious of
how out of place his white mess-jacket looked amid the blue serge
and knitted pullovers of professional mariners.

'At ease, Pyce. You again, eh? I want an explanation.'

'Sir, Sir Edward insisted, sir.'

'Did he, by Jove. And if he'd insisted on taking all his clothes off
and climbing the ruddy mast you'd have given him a leg-up, is that
it?'

'Sir, of course not, sir. But he's my passenger sir . . .'

'Blast your passengers. What in God's name gets into you? That American fellow. Scandalous. Right, you know Ship's Regs.'

'Sir.'

'Clear breach. I'll get Chief to dock your wages. Now get off my bridge. If it happens again I may bring back the old naval tradition of keel-hauling. D'ye know what keel-hauling is?'

'No sir.'

'Not very nice is what it is, Steward. Not very nice at all. Go.'

But much to his own surprise Pyce stood his ground.

'It's about my passenger, sir.'

Captain Maddrell, who had already turned away, inflated his face in a fine imitation of disciplinary rage.

'Are you deaf, Pyce?'

'No sir. But Mr Elgar, that is Sir Edward . . .'

'Good God man, who's Master of this vessel?'

'You are sir.'

'Then d'ye think a captain wishes to hear a steward's impertinent complaints about a passenger? Don't you think he might have better things to do, like getting us all to Madeira in one piece?'

'Sir. But I think he's mad.'

'Probably the only thing you two have in common, then.' Over by the window the pilot gave an acidic snort. 'Whatever it is I don't wish to hear it. For the last time, get out.'

All right Kaiser Maddrell, thought Pyce as he gave an unnautical salute and left the bridge, I've done my bit. If the old idiot starts prowling your ship gibbering and waving knives at people I'll be the first to go and put my feet up with Hempson in the galley.

The *Hildebrand* ploughed on another mile or two before Captain Maddrell spoke aloud. 'What d'ye think that damnfool steward meant, "mad"? Did Sir Edward strike anyone else on this bridge as mad?'

Long familiarity with their captain enabled the others to recognise this as rhetoric and nobody spoke. But their unexpressed replies hung on the air: 'No madder than most civilians.' 'Aren't all passengers?' 'What does it matter?' The Captain alone answered his own question with the sophisticated thought that to a man like Steward Pyce anyone of a higher social order and an artistic bent probably did strike him as an alien being.

Inside Cabin no. 2 Edward was happily opening the polished

mahogany boxes he had brought. He would have unpacked them the first night but fearful for their safety in the ship's violent movement had left them among the shirts and suits and under-wear which largely filled the massive cabin trunk. Now at last he had them ranged on the writing table. From the porthole above it a brilliant stream of light, bounced first off the sea and then reflected from the white-painted shelter deck outside, fell onto the wooden surfaces. The grain shone, the ivory nameplates gleamed, the brass sparkled. Some quality of the light in these reflections, some persistent afterglow from a lifetime's forgotten summers filled him with quiet exuberance. Unlocking the tallest case he drew off the cover of a microscope, a handsome brass instrument with a choice of three objective lenses. Peering down it to assure himself that it was none the worse for its rough passage he flexed and swivelled the concave mirror underneath to gather the light into a single disc of glare. Satisfied he opened a second case, a nest of glass slides each fitting into its grooves. He lifted out one or two and held them up. None was cracked. Light winked off their polished edges, made momentary jewels of the stains, the rubies and topazes and amethysts set at their centres. The last of the cases yielded a compact field kit: small bottles of dyes and reagents, various tweezers, spare slides and cover-slides, tiny gummed paper labels, mapping pen and a thimble-bottle of indian ink.

About all this equipment there hung a subtle air of professional-ism, for although it was beautifully maintained clearly none of it was new. Various blots and spillages inside the compartments hinted at long use while inside the lid of each box was an old paper label inscribed 'Ruthven Jevons MD, Bombay'. Edward had not liked to remove these labels: it had seemed presumptuous for a mere hobbyist. Besides, he always had in the back of his mind to track down this doctor, discover when – and if – he had died, and how such personal things should have found their way into the anonymous mart of the saleroom.

It did not cross his mind that the unknown doctor might, like himself, finally have tired of his life's work and have willingly swapped the tools of his trade for some congenial new pursuit. It was thus, shortly after moving into Severn House, he had impul-sively but without regret sold his Gagliano violin and bought a billiard table with the proceeds. Golly how cross Alice had been . . . And now over the last eighteen months an obsession with microscopy had grown so it almost displaced – or perhaps was complementing – a lifetime's varied hobbies. Woe to artists with a scientific bent! he might once have said, thinking of fatal distraction and of Saint-Saëns, among other things a competent enough astronomer to have had a telescope built to his own specifications. Woe to artists whose talent is seen as subtracting from their genius! For Edward there never had been a time when bouts of intense creative work had not alternated with a lassitude full of loathing for music. At such periods the hedging-and-ditching, the chemistry experiments, the bicycling, the barrel-making, the kite-flying, the motoring had seemed like remissions from a long and nagging illness, stretches of normality when an ordinary life became possible once more. Yet always it had returned like a malign influence, the half-hated half-loved imperative, as if with its monstrous egoism it was making the claim that beneath the guise of seriousness the little crazes merely concealed the one part of him which was truly serious and which consumed him.

With nothing but pleasure he now tipped the contents of his hip-flask into a carefully-rinsed toothglass and with an eye dropper took a sample of the sea-water. For half an hour he bent over his microscope, bathed in sunlight, occasionally grunting. 'Oh look!' he would murmur. 'Oh how perfect!' Far beneath him the engines prowled peacefully in their confines, the ship hummed along so steadily it might have been on wheels. Shadows fleeted past the porthole as the last passengers hatched out and fluttered to the upper regions trailing fragments of conversation.

' ". . . well, not at any rate with *that* dress," I told her . . .'

'Betty's *taste* . . . !'

'. . . buy some more in Funchal . . .'

Sometimes the grey-haired man at the table prepared a slide, light flashing off silver tweezers as he delicately settled a tiny wafer of glass to cover the bead of moisture containing the specimen. Finally he sat back and rubbed his eyes before going to the cabin trunk and rootling in it like a schoolboy with a fine disregard for crushed shirt-fronts. He came up with two books, one of them obviously new: Minchin's *Introduction to the Study of the Protozoa*. The other was Murray and Hjort's *The Depths of the Ocean*. Back at the table he spent the next hour leafing through their pages, often peering down the microscope to verify his identifications.

When the bugle went for luncheon Edward was much restored and went with every expectation that he would see Molly Air and be able to apologise to her. But she was not there; her empty place mocked him. For the first time the restaurant was reasonably full. As he left he was conscious as always of people's eyes upon him and of brief lapses of conversation at the tables he passed. The mere awareness stiffened his back and bristled his moustache. Nosy blighters. He marched out, but wearily. Returning to the cabin he wrote a note on ship's stationery:

Dear Miss Air,
I missed you at luncheon when I had hoped to apologise for what must have seemed like brusqueness earlier this morning. I had no call to vent spleen on an innocent fellow-passenger. Might you reassure a lonely old composer by permitting him to make amends?

Yrs,
Edward Elgar

He rang the service bell but no Pyce came. Instead a cabin boy stuck his cropped head around the door.

'Would you kindly take this to Miss Air? I'm afraid I don't know her cabin number.'

'Miss Hare, sir?'

'Not Hare, Air.'

'Miss 'are, sir. Right away.'

Edward gravely pressed a sixpence upon the child who disappeared and could be heard whistling his way along the deck outside. He allowed himself a pleasurable smile then once more seated himself at the table intending to continue with the microscope but falling instead into a light doze from which he awoke disgruntled. In a mood of mid-afternoon melancholy the sudden thought of going up above and parading in a boater, an old widower amid couples playing deck-quoits or flirting, was horrid. He reminded himself that there were plenty of single people, Molly herself included, to say nothing of the missionary spinsters. This thought made things no better, however. He wondered what to do. He missed the ticker-tape machines with their news from Epsom and Sandown, Thirsk and Doncaster. He missed *The Times* and the theatre reviews. He missed his dogs.

As he had gone about his rounds through darkened cabins full of reek Dr Ashe could think of nothing but the disaster which had come upon him. In all twenty years of Army life – in the sundry wanderings, postings and finally decimations of his regiment – he had never felt so lost and adrift. It was the sounds he missed as much as anything, those familiar sounds by which his inner clock was set: the scrunch of boots outside the window, the distant wails of command, the brick yards echoing to horses in their harness. And above all the bugles, hailing the sun and bidding it farewell, accompanying the flag up and down its pole, exhorting, alerting, summoning, inspiring. In this tin can amid the waves, by contrast, the only bugle call was a single note, a mockery blown by some hopeless matelot with brilliantine to invite the already overfed to yet further meals.

What had he to do with these people? True, many of them had as yet eaten very little but one could tell from the spineless way they lolled in their bunks and moaned that they were rotted with self-indulgence. It was impossible to keep the company of vermin who refused to take responsibility for themselves. At least there was comfort in knowing he had taken his own responsibility for that affair at Aldershot. Resigning his commission after so much honourable service had earned him the baffled sympathy of fellow-officers who, if they couldn't have been expected to deduce the real cause, had accepted the evasion of 'personal considerations', that stock explanation which might conceal a thousand different urgencies. Since then he had received a letter which led him to believe no further enquiry would be pursued. The military had a sixth sense where taint was concerned and his own regiment was no exception. Unruffled waters would be allowed to close seamlessly over the place where his respected head had last dropped from sight. From the Army's point of view he no longer existed.

Returning to his quarters he locked the door and poured himself a tumbler of whisky. For half an hour he sat unrelaxed at his empty table, drinking steadily and finishing the best part of half the bottle. Then he got to his feet and stripped to the waist, letting his shirt hang by its tails from the waistband of his trousers. He took out a small canvas roll of surgical instruments, the field kit he had carried in France, and selecting a scalpel clipped in a fresh blade. Then he stood in front of the mirror and examined himself minutely, angling up the lamp on the table beside him so as to bathe his upper body with light. Deep shadows were thrown in the hollows of his torso which had the flayed look of a mediaeval saint whose life was not separable from punishment. With the blade he drew a deep five-inch line high up across the left side of his chest and without pausing another in exact parallel half an inch above it. He repeated these pairs of cuts twice, moving upwards so that his work was not obscured by the blood which welled from the incisions and streamed freely down his ribs. He studied the cuts in the mirror before, apparently satisfied, pouring himself another glass of whisky which he drank off in three gulps. Then he turned back to the mirror and carefully began etching a series of vertical cuts between the parallel lines like irregularly-spaced sleepers on a railway track. It took him a minute and more and his face in the lamplight betrayed nothing as he worked. By the time he had finished his dangling shirt was spotted with blood and the waist-band on his left side sopped in it.

Laying down the scalpel Dr Ashe once more dispassionately examined his chest with its fresh grid of hatch-marks and the crimson sheen which drenched his white skin with shimmering and mesmeric beauty. In the brilliance of the electric light the colour was rich and vibrant as the juice which embodied it sank slowly downwards from the wounds. The doctor took a handful of lint, soaked it in surgical spirit and pressed it to his chest. Only then did an expression cross his face momentarily, a quick grimace, a spasm nearly of disgust. He pressed the pad still tighter then suddenly took it away. In the instant before blood sprang back to blur the pattern the filling red strokes on his skin formed the outline of the ribbons he had worn, the medals he had won: MC, DSC, the many campaign awards, the insignia of his service.

He took a fresh pad, sprinkled it this time with iodine and taped it across the wounds. Gasping almost inaudibly as he moved he cleaned up his body, put on a fresh shirt, changed his trousers, adjusted his tie in the mirror. He lit a cigarette with fingers which scarcely shook, finished both it and another tumbler of whisky, unlocked the door and went out on his rounds.

IV

Day started badly, terse with Air girl. Of course I've apologised but don't know why I shd. Then visit to engine room where the Chief Engineer's named Stanford! Can't seem to shake 'em off even in mid-Atlantic. Stainer & Mackenzie will be lurking somewhere, office-boys in Manaos probably. Engines huge, the heat & din <u>expunged</u> me – exhilarating in its way.

Looked at a sample of sea-water – some wonderful diatoms & organisms, among them Ostracods, Tunicates & Dinoflagellates. It wd. be interesting to get samples from deep water but can't imagine how. Maybe some kind of bottle with a sprung top which could be opened by a string at a measured depth?

V. perverse to be keeping a journal. The noise is all written down (long since) & most of it printed; why can't the rest be silence? But something nags. Why shd. people in their sixties find their thoughts turning always & always to childhood? Why are my dreams haunted by rivers, lost voices, sounds which can't be notated? Everything says to me 'long ago', nothing very much says 'now'. There's a horrible account of poor Schumann in his madness sitting all day feebly making lists of rivers and place-names interspersed by musical dreams. He awoke from one of these calling feverishly for MS paper since he had heard the most angelic music too beautiful for human ears. He scribbled it down while it was fading – like Tartini and his 'Devil's Trill' sonata or Coleridge and 'Kubla Khan' – and when Brahms came & read it he found an imperfect version of the slow mvt. theme of Schumann's own vln. concerto. I wept when I heard that story – couldn't help myself, it's too close to something I can't put my finger on. <u>Maybe it isn't written on the wind after all</u>, maybe we're taking <u>our own</u> dictation.

Whatever we're doing I'm certain we began it in infancy. In those few short years free of the least vestige of labour the act of vision was completed. The lifework wh. followed was merely agonising & fallacious transcription. How <u>mis-timed</u> it is, that silly reverence accorded the famous artist in his studio, the composer in his study, the poet at his table (hush! for a great work is taking shape!). For who on seeing a child poking a chrysalis with a twig or watching water flow around a stone while he plays on the river-bank could seriously suppose this very moment might be the true birth of a symphony? When I wrote to dear Nim (all those years ago) that the trees were singing my music or maybe I'd sung theirs – some such phrase – it wasn't fanciful. No doubt they do sing a different song to

−66−

each pair of ears; but those were precisely the notes which came to me as these ears heard what these eyes saw. They were what I had heard as a child down by the Severn and the Teme: the wind in the reeds & the willows, the slow slide of arterial England which at the time I idiotically supposed to be everlasting.

Miserable deception, all of it. The musical vision was so definite, the inner voice so urgent one always believed it did correspond to reality in some way – 'this I saw & knew' etc. Such were the notes, & only those notes, made by the wind passing through the trees & by the trees as the wind passed through them. Anyone who couldn't hear it was deaf or had the soul of a stone. Alas for the years it took to see why I was wrong. When Alice died dear Frank Schuster showered me with 'helpful texts' – among them a Polish mystic called Rabbi Nachmann of Bratslav (born the same year as Beethoven, I remember) & a buddhist book wh. had a neatly illustrative story. A famous Patriarch & a novice monk are on a hillside together looking down at their monastery on its crag, prayer-flags fluttering in the pure Tibetan breeze. After a bit the monk asks 'Is it the wind or the flag which moves?' to wh. the Patriarch replies 'Neither, it's the mind.' So a composer's mind is his alone & what he may hear in the wind corresponds to nothing except in himself. Ah, gross fool to expect public acclaim for private vision!

But how deceptive & swamping that certainty used to be . . . In those days I think there was no quiver of a leaf, no furl of a wing, no veiled or flashing human glance which couldn't render itself into music. I heard everything: the passing of a cloud, the passing of a waggon, the passing of a life – I cd. hear it all & still can when I manage to convince myself it's worth the trick. The smell of toast or the slicing of a black pudding (especially the ones we used to get from Moxon's, juicy, with skins that burst – pock! at a steel knifepoint); the feel of a word like 'owl' or 'slumber'; even ideas: all these things fall at once into notes, phrases, harmony, rhythm.

Why? How? It's as if there were a single raw material of all art which different people perceive with different senses, according to talent. I happen to hear it; but when a tune first comes I don't always recognise it as music straight away – I'm not quite sure what it is. Like Gerontius I'm uncertain: 'I cannot of that music rightly say/Whether I hear or touch or taste the tones.' Strange how only now do I dare admit to the private page (23 years on) that it was this passage in Newman's poem which decided me to set it. I never even dared tell poor Alice that. The dear, sweet thing was blind to all but her 'highest motives'. Yet the truth is it had nothing whatever to do with religion (& of course everybody was bound to misread it – 'stinks of incense', 'too much Mary' &c &c. Well, it was my mother who converted to Catholicism four years after she married and five years before I was born, not I. I was never a convert). It was not so much the quality of Newman's verse – I could perfectly well see at the time it was patchy – but the dramatic poetic <u>vision</u>. It was wonderfully imaginative, that idea of a freshly-detached soul being borne along without either location or time. It's never clear what he's become, with what senses he perceives things, how fast he's being impelled on his way by the 'uniform and gentle pressure'. So when (meaningless questions!) one wonders where the divvel he's got to and how long has elapsed since his death (<u>is</u> he dead?) it's a real shock to us when he hears the voices of his friends singing the Subvenite around his death-bed. It was that which really convinced me: the being in two worlds at once, the dissolution of place & time. That & the stillness, the solitariness, the cessation of everything except music – whether of angels or devils, earthly voices or lofty pines. If I immersed myself in dogma beforehand it was largely to guard against the kind of solecisms for which I shd. have been publicly pilloried (& with what glee!). That & the fact that I was still not quite decided whether I mightn't do the oratorio on Judas instead – a nice idea after all & not without its radical aspects in those stuffy days. Why a 'religious' work at all? I find myself asking with near-incredulity in 1923 in a world I share with Stravinsky, Schönberg, Ravel. Because, damn and blast it, in England at that time a big choral work was the safest way of getting a serious hearing & 'big choral work' meant a pot-pourri of biblical texts for the leather lungs of massed Yorks. spinsters. <u>That</u>'s how far behind England was musically.

So my motivation in setting 'G' had nothing to do with any personal commitment to the Church & still less was it an expression of faith (or even much interest) in the notion of survival after death. <u>But</u> it would never have done to admit it. People – individuals as well as the Great British Public – are much too dense to understand such things. You always have to toe some notional line no matter what your real views. It's odd the way publics never understand private matters, given that they after all consist of individuals, but they can't or won't. It's like a conspiracy. So the critics saddled me with Rome & the wretch Gerontius (who is after all <u>me</u> and nobody else) had to make his own way in a hostile world after the worst launching in English musical history not as a poetic hero but as the eponym of 'an oratorio'. Well they can weigh him down how they will: his wings will always lift him. There's a vast heart in him; cut him anywhere & he still bleeds. Despite his name he's a young man after all &, to these biased old ears at least, still fresh.

<u>Later</u>

The cabin boy with the aitches has just brought me a letter from Molly Air. She too appears to have a heart.

Dear Sir Edward,

If I were certain where the taffrail was I could probably say I was sketching there during luncheon; I seldom feel hungry in the sun. Your graceful apology is accepted with the alacrity it deserves. Might we not go ashore together at Funchal? I can show you what to avoid.

Most sincerely,

Molly Air

I call that generous and shall respond accordingly. Wherever Funchal might be it'll be improved by feminine company, I shd. say.

Reading through the above twaddle after a pleasant dinner marred only by the sound of a dance band somewhere not far enough away: the bit about there being a single raw material of all art strikes me still as a tenable theory but it certainly depends on how it's phrased. That day I exploded at Roger Fry & his asinine remark about all the arts being essentially the same – I think I told him that music was written on the skies to be noted down & couldn't be compared to some <u>stupid imitation</u> (I must have been thinking of those overpaid nude-lady painters like Long. Anyway it was a good lunch-time philosopher's put-down). Since then, thanks to GBS who was also present, I've come to think Fry actually meant something not much different from my own idea: he just put it badly & at an unfortunate juncture – I'd had a bellyful of hearing about the vast sums of money & honours which hack painters & popular novelists get while musicians are fobbed off with a pittance & left practically to starve. Maybe <u>au fond</u> all the arts <u>are</u> the same but they certainly don't get <u>paid</u> the same. Nor are all artists the same, not by a long chalk. One thinks of the Singing Dames Butt & Melba: solid humbug from first note to last. As for Edwin Long RA . . . The only decent thing he ever begat was the house Norman Shaw built for him & in which I lived until a few months ago. It beggared me. But then <u>I</u> don't paint naked bits of stuff & so am not paid accordingly.

<u>A propos</u> being able to 'put' anything to music: I've since remembered Donald Tovey writing to me years ago saying he knew it sounded like balderdash but he'd often caught himself actually solving some mental problem in the key of A minor where he'd failed utterly to reason it out in words. How well I understand <u>that</u>. He went on to say that somebody in Shax – Hamlet, I imagine – was inexplicable if one stopped to analyse his character but perfectly convincing if one didn't. Tovey claimed Shax achieved this by subtle artistic devices which were absolutely significant but quite beyond the reach of words & hence of analysis. Words, he said, do not represent actual ideas but only <u>particular cases</u> of ideas. The real idea goes on being in A minor just as Shax's artistic methods are closer to

being in (say) A minor than in words . . . Well of course Donald's famous for being brainy & intelleckshul. But I always can remember the gist of that letter, if only to think how ironic it makes much of his own music criticism wh. relies all too heavily on wordage, much of it purple & fanciful to a degree. Luckily nobody in Germany's read any of it or English music wd. have an even lower reputation for unseriousness than it has anyway.

Still, something in what he says rings true. In those dear old days when I used to go shopping for Alice on the bicycle (when she wd. let me out) I simply made a list in a certain key. Then all I had to do in the village shop was remember the key & the list would come back at once. I never forgot anything. Come to that, why was the hat I lost coming aboard this ship in E? I remember the very day I bought it & put it on: it sat on my head in E major & ever since then whenever I wore it the day changed key. This only sounds silly when you write it down: putting on an E major hat is after all no dafter than putting on a brown one.

There was something else, too, before going to bed – oh yes, about Gerontius. By not blabbing to people about its real origins I no doubt spared them dismay & myself no end of trouble. But one thing wh. did upset those 'in the know' was what Jaeger called the Prayer Theme. Richard Strauss told me he thought it was the precise shape of a man at prayer but I never informed him that this miraculously holy motif was originally suggested by a friend's bulldog musing about having to wear a muzzle. Alice never said a word about that: I think she actually convinced herself she didn't know. But she did. It was there in Sinclair's visitors' book at Hereford in black & white. I'm afraid people are generally rather silly about such things – going into shock on discovering that half the best bits of the 'Christmas Oratorio' were written as birthday greetings to the local Elector's wife etc, starting life as rather risqué love-duets & suchlike. It's the Great Public again. They **do not understand art** so they can't understand creativity. They really believe there's a distinction between religious & secular, poor dears. Gerontius was jolly secular. But I fear only God (doubtful) & I wot that. And now neither of us much cares.

That night as most of the passengers – including Edward – slept, the *Hildebrand* sighted a far-off lighthouse and ninety minutes later dropped anchor in Funchal harbour so that when they first came on deck in the morning they found themselves suddenly dwarfed by the threadbare mountains of Madeira seemingly at arm's length. Instead of a great emptiness of sky the drabbish steep hills with their mufflers of terraced olives bore down on top of them. Pleased (in some cases downright relieved) to see land again many nonetheless intuited a sense of displacement. Where exactly were they? What were these islands? Detached remnants of Africa? Vestiges of scenery which hinted mockingly at remembered bits of Mediterranea? Certain of those on deck tapped their hats casually on the rail while waiting for the motor launches to ferry them ashore. There was perturbation in this gesture; it expressed an imaginative *impasse* to which they had come. *If,* their musing selves insisted, *if* on the straight line between the British Isles and the mouth of the Amazon were no dry land and *if* one could leave wintry Europe and a fortnight later reach malarial tropics, what would a theoretical halfway house look like? There was no answer to this, even though a few quite enjoyed the speculation of a gradually changing sea-bed thrusting itself up in mid-Atlantic to show how far the transformations had advanced. But however they imagined the result, Madeira was not quite it. Somehow the Portuguese element was wrong, the ochre and khaki rocks amid all that blue ocean too parched. Maybe the sight of the odd parakeet might have saved things: were these not also known as the Canary Isles? Many in the speeding launches rather thought they were.

Holding his straw panama on his knees and wearing a dandyish linen jacket, silk handkerchief fluttering in breast pocket, Edward was skimmed across the dimpled surface of the harbour. Beside him sat Molly. On her head was an intrepid hat which had the air of having come between many a torrid sun and its owner's thick brown hair. It was the colour of sand and had around it a narrow ribbon of much the same tint but with a faint and mountainous line reminiscent of an effect of watered silk wandering up and down its surface. This delineated the tide-marks of sweat which had resisted all launderings. The hat's broad brim bent in the launch's breeze; the string beneath her chin was taut as she kept her head tipped back to survey the terraces with their scattering of whitewashed villas.

When they disembarked she asked: 'Are you a good tourist, Sir Edward?'

'I used to be an inveterate sight-seer, if that's the same thing.'

'It probably is if they're the same sights as everyone else's. I imagined that in your case they mightn't be.'

'Maybe one does try to bring a different mind to them.'

'Well I can tell you there isn't much in the way of sights here for people on a long journey with only a few hours to spend. There's a sort of cathedral if you like sort of cathedrals. It's got a quite pretty Moorish roof of cedarwood. More to the point, there's a restaurant I happened upon which does beautifully tender squid stewed in their own ink. You can cut them with a fork. Are you partial to squid, Sir Edward?'

'I've had them fried in Italy. I found I liked them better when they weren't called "squid": there's something unappetising about that word. Disguised as *calamari fritti*, however, they were agreeably marine. "Stewed in ink" is not an enticing description, either, for anyone who has made his living with a pen.'

'As someone who intends to make it with a brush I assure you they're enchanting. A bed of white rice and black puddles strewn with fat pink shapes like finger-stalls with collar-stiffeners in them. The colours are most eccentric.'

'Good heavens, Miss Air. If I were wearing my hat I should raise it to your stomach. There's something about the colour black I don't at all associate with food.'

'Have you never eaten black pudding, then?'

'Touché! You've hit on a great favourite of mine. Only better not tell anyone or they'll think you invented our acquaintance. Who was that gentleman you so recently described, now? Celebrated patriot, friend of Royalty, heir-presumptuous to the mastership of the King's Musick? They're not going to believe a stuffed ass like that eats black pudding. *And* comes back for seconds if there's another pint of beer to go with it.'

'My turn to cry "Touché!", Sir Edward. Please don't remind me.'

'It's already out of my mind. Not the black puddings, though. Do you know until quite recently I lived in Hampstead, which is not by any means the most deprived quarter of London. You can get most things in Hampstead, even some fairly exotic food for the various foreigners of substance who stay there from time to time. But do you think one can obtain something as stalwartly English as black pudding? I used to have to take the bus all the way down to Fleet Street and patronise a little shop which has them delivered fresh from Birmingham every week. My wife objected strenuously. She thought it was *infra dig*.'

'Which? Bus or sausage?'

'Both, I'm afraid. I was quite unrepentant. The one was a necessary economy, the other sheer pleasure. Not but what she wasn't perfectly happy to eat it herself in the old days . . . Where are we going, incidentally? Have you any idea?'

'Yes, to the top of Bella Monte. I took the liberty of buying us tickets from the Chief Steward. We get a round trip including a late breakfast at the top. Or an early luncheon.'

'That's absurd,' said Edward sharply, then, 'You're too kind. One's not used to having arrangements made by young ladies one scarcely . . . I'm a bit nonplussed.'

'But not for long,' Molly said cheerfully.

Above them the mountain obscured a good part of the blue sky. Its topmost crags seemed as near or as distant as the moon which, as a ghost of its night-time self, perversely lingered in the light of morning and balanced upon Madeira like an eroded pearl. With the herd instinct common among day-trippers their fellow-passengers, most of whom presumably had never been to Funchal before, found themselves getting gingerly into drawn-up bullock waggons.

'I can't see this getting us very far,' Edward observed as he stooped under the gay cretonne canopy and settled himself on a hard wooden seat covered in leather. 'Don't tell the gentleman up front but I think somebody has pinched his wheels.'

'Ah, there's a reason for that which you may not know. Many centuries ago a certain Teofilo was appointed first Bishop of Madeira, a young man whose conversion to Christianity had taken place while witnessing the martyrdom of St Catherine. He fetched up in Lisbon as a mendicant theologian famous for two things: his charity and his horror of wheels – for ever since that awful day he couldn't bear to see anything which reminded him of Catherine's torment.'

'He must have had a trying time crossing Europe.'

'Abominable. He walked, of course, and to drown the sound of carts and carriages on the few roads he was forced to take he used to stop, face the ditch and sing a psalm as loud as he could. You can imagine he arrived in Lisbon after an unconscionable time and quite hoarse. But what nowadays would be thought eccentricity was in those times accounted piety and he rose rapidly in the Church. When he was appointed Bishop here he was for the first time able to exercise real power in the service of his pet aversion. He simply banned all wheels on Madeira.'

With a jerk the bullock took up the slack in its harness and they set off along the cobbles, rumbling and juddering.

'This is nothing but a sled!'

'Exactly,' said Molly. 'They all are. Not a wheel among them. Oh, you'll see wheels here now and then. After all, despite the monstrous piety and conservatism of the Madeirans it *is* nearly eleven centuries since Teofilo died. But not many – you look. I believe these things are called *carros*,' she added.

'Pray excuse me,' broke in a gentle voice from the seats behind them, 'but I couldn't help overhearing your account.' Turning, they found the two spinsters from their table leaning forward. 'Good morning, Sir Edward. Good morning,' these ladies said in parenthesis. 'But,' continued the first, 'surely your version is at variance with the explanation given in Calixões?' She held up a battered red volume.

'Ah, Calixões,' said Molly, somewhat in the indulgent tone of a renowned chemist being lectured by his great-aunt on phlogiston. 'I don't believe anybody takes Calixões very seriously nowadays, not since that extraordinary hoax . . . But here we are. We have to get out here.'

The fleet of *carros* had stopped outside a rack-railway station, happening to coincide with the arrival of a funicular train consisting of half a dozen coaches of weird aspect, having been constructed at an angle corresponding to that of the gradient. Little rattly parallelograms, they drew into the platform and awaited new custom. Expressions of interest and amusement made themselves audible, mingled with one or two notes of dismay; but in the event twenty more or less resigned Britons soon found themselves seated in staggered rows being hauled upwards. As the winding-station with its quickly-suppressed images of *ad hoc* bits of wiring and loose girders fell away, so did the electrical whine of the motors until they were ascending in almost complete silence.

'It's quite like ballooning,' offered the red-cheeked explorer, Fortescue. The face which still needed a pith helmet to give it shape was babyish with pleasure. He had brought a pair of binoculars with him, Molly noticed.

Somewhere beneath them a cable transmitted a soft thrum and cogs engaged the metal teeth of the rack with no more than a crackle of grease. On either side terraces, villas and bulks of naked rock slipped away, and as they did so the passengers' spirits rose in the morning air. Gradually the town spread itself below, the harbour became a map, the *Hildebrand* – glimpsed now and then among the hydrangeas – a grey-and-white model. The warm scent of baked earth, dew and dust rose in pockets. Some late butterflies investigated the fig-trees' remaining leaves. Windings of narrow cobbled roadway disappeared beneath them, re-emerging to turn abruptly aside and fall from sight.

'It's a pity it's so late in the year,' Molly said. 'Spring must be amazingly beautiful – just look at all the plants: mimosa, hydrangeas, lilies, agapanthus, to say nothing of the things people have growing up their houses. Simply between the harbour and the station I saw bougainvillaea, wisteria, strelitzia, hibiscus and jacaranda.'

'Very *showy*,' a lady remarked.

'Even so. When I was here in June it was much clearer from the vegetation that we were passing from a hot zone to a more temperate one as we went up. For instance those fields down there behind the town were full of sugar cane and rice but by this point it's mostly grapes and wheat. I did some sketches in wash: the colour changes were wonderfully subtle.'

'You can still tell from the trees,' Edward pointed out. 'It's all palms and figs down there but it looks as if those are pines and oaks we're coming to. I wonder how high up we are?'

This had been one of those semi-public conversations which self-consciously include people who otherwise could not be excluded except by whispering. Fortescue was able to volunteer without embarrassment:

'About a thousand feet, I'd say. Give or take.'

'Is this a balloonist speaking?'

'As a matter of fact I haven't done that much ballooning, sir. But I can certainly speak as a pilot.'

'You've flown in an aeroplane?' Edward's interest was that of someone who had long ago discovered an enthusiasm for motoring and logically regarded flight as the next step.

'Many,' admitted Fortescue. 'I was in the RFC a goodish while.' Something in his tone implied recognition that war heroes were becoming unfashionable and he hardly wished to be pressed. 'The altimeters were not always reliable, you see, so we became not bad at judging height. Had to be, really. No trick to it,' he added modestly as if someone were likely to imply there were. 'Anybody could do it with a bit of practice. In any case I've cheated.' The amorphous face beamed round upon the occupants of the carriage.

'Have you been here before?' Molly asked him.

'Not a bit of it. But the guide book gives the height of this mountain as three thousand feet and while we were still on the ship I took notice of various features. This line of forest we're coming up to is about halfway, for instance. And that whitish splash that looks as if somebody's tipped paint over the cliff, that's at about two thousand feet.'

This evidently professional approach to landscape by someone claiming to be a pilot and reputed to be an explorer made Molly look at Fortescue with some attention for the first time. Suddenly the binoculars on their lanyard about his neck looked like a tool rather than a prop, and quite well-worn at that.

'You were wise to bring those,' she said. 'The view from the top is quite spectacular.'

'I never travel without 'em.'

Baby's dummy, she thought, unaccountably touched by his innocent meaty cheeks, the formless clump of hairs on his upper lip.

Roughly at the point where he had indicated the two-thousand-foot mark they reached a depressed-looking clearing in the middle of which stood a huge house of un-Madeiran aspect. Here the train halted but nobody got in or out and after a minute it started again.

'What an extraordinary house. It looks like the sort of hotel one blunders on towards nightfall in Scotland.'

'Or one of those places which advertise in the back of Ward Lock's Guide to Harrogate. You know, "Premier position. Near Moors and Gardens. Electric light throughout. Lift to all Floors".'

' "Special Suicide Suite",' put in Fortescue and went an immediate red.

'Well *really*,' said one of the spinsters, she and her companion turning away abruptly to glare out of the windows.

Despite the season the little terminus of Monte at the summit was bright with potted flowers. A uniformed official with operatic moustaches bowed to them as they disembarked and directed their attention to a nearby house where, he intimated, quite exceptional cups of chocolate and glasses of port might be had of his wife.

'Later,' they said in English and with gestures of stirring above their abdomens mimed that they had already breakfasted or maybe that the sudden ascent had destroyed all appetite. The official made several more melancholy bows and then went and watered his geraniums using a wine flask with an exaggeratedly long neck. The sun winked off the frogging on his shoulders and made pinkly translucent the ears of a motheaten tabby cat dozing on a folded copy of *O Correio*. A notice board nearby announced the height above sea level. The voices of today's visitors died away.

They straggled across a shady square which, had they been able to ignore the surrounding terrain, they might easily have supposed a well-visited Mediterranean village. But in one direction lay a gloomy pine forest in front of which a single-storey building with tall windows stood amid the sort of terraces on which tourists take tea and tell each other how lucky they are to be there.

'I say, what an abominable place,' said Edward.

'Isn't it?' Molly agreed. 'That's the – ' she consulted her ticket ' – the Chalet–Restaurant "Esplanade" in which we're entitled to eat and drink.'

'But not to be merry, I shouldn't think. How awful pines are. What's that church over there?'

'Our Lady of Something, I forget. But when I was here before it happened quite by chance to coincide with an immense *event*. The place was stuffed with bishops and sight-seers. We almost missed our boat because the trains were all full. It turned out they were cementing up the Austrian Emperor into his tomb. Charles the Somethingth – Fourth, possibly? Lots of processions, trumpets and whatnot. And about a million little brown choirboys all with cropped heads and monkeyish grins. We sat on that verandah thingy and made jokes about Catholics. Oh heavens, I suppose you're not by any chance . . . You are, aren't you? Sir Edward, I'm most . . . I mean, of *course* I shouldn't have . . .'

Much as her confusion amused him he ended it by reassuring her that he was not remotely offended. 'I daresay it *was* pretty much of a spectacle.'

'Oh it was. But even so. I'm afraid I'm always putting my foot in it like that,' she said gratefully. 'Now, we don't want breakfast yet, do we?' she turned to Fortescue and the spinsters who were a pace or two behind in the delicate manner of those who might or might not be considered part of a group. 'Let's earn it, then.'

'You've planned us some exercise?' Fortescue asked her. She thought he still had the air of a puppy eager to make amends after a noisome gaffe.

'Only a little. But having come this far it's well worth getting the view. You'd think people would be glad to stretch their legs after lying in their bunks for the best part of a week.' She glanced meaningfully towards a divergent group of fellow-passengers who were heading determinedly for the Chalet–Restaurant 'Esplanade' before she led off along a path skirting the forest of pines.

They walked uphill to where the cranium of the mountain broke through all pretence of plants and soil, a fissured plateau of baked rock meeting head-on the subtropical sun. All of a sudden they stopped being on Madeira and were instead on a point above the surface of the globe. In nearly every direction the sea stretched its crinkling sheet over the rim of the world like a drumskin on which solar rays and meteorites were falling in motionless profusion, making a great empty pattering sound they felt rather than heard. There was the sense of having been lifted out of the world, of having been extracted from it even as their memories of it as containing large and solid things such as buildings were replaced by the panorama of Funchal below, a mere map of a town on a toy planet. This majestic detachment was still further heightened by the brilliantly clear morning air, the windless expanse of blue above them and the ruffled pan of deeper blue below, neither of which elements seemed to contain them. What was more, the far-off northern port they had left behind, somewhere over many a stormy horizon together with unreal images of urban fogs and glum wintering, belonged now to a different planet and to people other than themselves.

Fortescue was studying the harbour with his glasses. Edward could see the *Hildebrand* was being joined by a rectangular vessel whose stern trailed a short white stalk of foam.

'I think we're going to take coal on,' he said around his lenses. 'It looks like some sort of lighter.'

'The Chief Engineer told me we burn about seventy tons a day, but maybe we burned more coming through that storm. This really is a splendid vantage point. I suppose you aviators get quite used to views like this.'

'Not at all, sir,' said Fortescue surprisingly. 'That is, one becomes accustomed to them but so far as I'm concerned they're never boring. Still, to get the full effect you do need that feeling of hanging in air instead of standing on an edge. You've never been up in an aeroplane I presume, sir?'

'Not yet, I'm afraid.'

'Oh, you must. It's really the only thing. You'd be amazed by how solid it is. The air, I mean to say.'

Edward thought of standing on Worcestershire Beacon in a gale, leaning against the wind, letting more and more of his weight tilt off his toes until for a fraction of a second the airstream might actually have been supporting his body like a yielding bed until he fell forward with a laugh. Oh days.

'I must make the effort,' he said half to himself.

'I really would, sir. It won't cost you much just to do a flip from some aerodrome but once you've got a taste for it there's no knowing where it'll stop. All sorts of people are taking to the air now. Someone told me there's even a titled lady in her seventies – a duchess, I think – who's learned to fly and is buying her own machine.'

'You're such a convincing salesman I can only suppose you must sell the things.'

Fortescue laughed. 'Not a bit of it. Really, I'm just enthusiastic because I've spent so much time in the cockpit.'

'I hope you'll excuse me but I believe you introduced yourself on our first evening as an explorer? Is this the latest craze, exploring by air?'

'It may become so, sir. The advantages are obvious.' And he told a story of a scheme he and an old comrade had dreamed up, to go to unmapped areas of the world and offer to carry out aerial surveying on behalf of governments. The Amazon region had seemed to them a sensible choice since so much was completely uncharted but, as the recent rubber boom had shown, there was clearly untold wealth to be had there. He had already made an exploratory visit to confirm this and now, having raised the capital in Europe, he was returning to Amazonas to put the scheme into operation. The old comrade had gone on ahead; Fortescue was following on with two machines.

'But for some reason you had to leave them behind?' hazarded Edward.

'No, they're aboard the *Hildebrand*. They're all crated up in the hold. I must say I was a bit bothered in case they got too badly shaken about by that weather. But they're both stout little buses. Johnny – that's Johnny Proctor – has got our two old riggers and fitters from service days with him and they'll have them together in a jiffy.'

'I believe you're an adventurer,' said Molly who had been listening with evident interest.

'Well I suppose it *is* a bit of a lark. But we've both sunk so much money into it now we've got to make it work or frankly we'll be on our uppers. It's a commercial proposition, all right. Regular government salary plus we can undertake work on commission for interested parties. What I mean is, we can map a river for the Brazilians but we might tell only Fry's or Cadbury's that its banks are lined with cocoa forest, what?' And though his thirtyish baby's face creased and dimpled Molly noticed a beadiness in his eyes as if behind the amiable, malleable world his outer person created as he moved through it certain hard experiences lay which had fixed all manner of edges and limits beyond which there would be no budging.

By now others of the party who had also spurned the comforts of the 'Esplanade' had followed on and were scattered across the rock. Edward, Molly, Fortescue and the two spinsters had remained loosely together and at last turned from the panorama of Funchal and its harbour towards an inland view of Madeira. They reached a point from which they could see a hillside opposite them and several hundred feet lower. This was largely covered in scrub except where vast rectangular bites had been taken from its core of ochre rock. Whatever had once been quarried here must have been exhausted or no longer worth the effort to mine since the working was quite obviously abandoned. Some rusted crane-jibs lay on its floor but all the access tracks were now covered in the ubiquitous tough bushes.

'I sketched here too,' said Molly. 'I liked those iron-coloured stains. I suppose it used to be for iron ore.'

'Now there I can be of information,' came the unexpected remark of the spinster who had earlier addressed her in the *carro*.

'Ah, you know what it is, then?'

'I do indeed. They are the worn-out workings of a cake-mine.'

Molly tried to think what substance this might be when

rendered in Portuguese, as she presumed this was. *Caïque? Queìque?* Maybe after all it was a technical English word for china clay or something.

'What did they do with this cake?' she asked, hoping for clues.

'Exported it, mainly,' said the spinster. 'It was of particularly fine quality just here. Its colour which you noted is believed by geologists to have originated from beds of clay first laid down in the Pleistocene Era. It was on that very spot over there it was first excavated in any quantity for export around the world. As a matter of fact it's your maligned Calixões we have to thank for the archival discovery that Bishop Teofilo died not as believed from apoplexy brought on by hearing a child bowl its hoop beneath his palace window but from a surfeit of Madeira cake – a substance to which he became hopelessly addicted quite late in life.'

This was delivered so precisely in the expected dreary monotone of one who imparts guide-book information that it was a moment or two before anyone could find no reason not to laugh.

'By Jove, Molly,' said Edward, wiping his eyes. 'I do believe you've been japed. And by a master-japist, too.'

Molly Air had gone a slight red at this unimagined reversal of casting. 'Well,' she said, 'I deserved that.'

' "Hats off, gentlemen, a genius!" '

'I hardly think that, Sir Edward,' said the tall lady. 'Merely someone else who tries to relieve life's awful expectedness with a little flexing of the imagination. You've no idea how dreary our two lives are shortly going to be.' She indicated her companion. 'Mrs Hammond and I do our best to keep ourselves amused, but in the interior of Ceará or Piauí that's often impossible for whole weeks at a stretch.'

If Edward was surprised by the 'Mrs' he gave no sign. 'I suppose life in the Missions can't always be as, well, fulfilling as the rest of us imagine.' Then he added, as if invoking some kind of authority, 'My own sister Dot's a nun. In fact she's a Mother Superior.'

'I think you're under some misapprehension, Sir Edward,' said Mrs Hammond. 'Dora and I are rejoining our husbands in Pará. We're just business wives, you know. Part of the little British community there, except that sometimes we go with the men on their trips to the interior. We've no connection with any mission. To be frank, we're neither of us very religious at all.'

'In that case I beg both your pardons.'

'I'm afraid, Kate, that Sir Edward looked at us, saw two dowdy creatures and drew the obvious conclusion.'

'Scarcely helped, Dora, by your choral reminiscences of yesteryear.'

'Nor by your pretence of being shocked by betting.'

These two mischievous women at once managed to produce, as if by the magic of their candour, an intimacy among the others which had that quality of appearing inevitable only now it had happened. On the way down to the 'Esplanade' Dora Bellamy said:

'I'm a prankster, Sir Edward, but not a liar. I promise you I shan't mention it again but what I said our first evening about being deeply affected by singing in *The Apostles* was utterly the truth. There. Now we should have some lime-juice or chocolate or something.'

How jocular were Britons abroad, thought Edward. Maybe it was a relief from the formalities of home or perhaps just the seeping-through of a genial contempt for the rest of the world spreading from a damaged heart, as a stain on the outside of luggage betrays an object broken within. But at the same time he knew he was being made up to by all three women and was very far from disliking it. Avoiding the bleak expanse of the chalet's terrace they went round to the garden at the back where he sat quietly at a metal table while the brilliant November sunshine fell through trellised vines patchily onto his grey hair and linen jacket. Like a cat on a newspaper he basked; but the restaurateur's wife, supervising the refreshments and covertly noting the distinction of her party's oldest member, noticed also the alertness in the way he sat which only partly concealed a remoteness in the gaze he sent at his neighbours' faces, at the calves of the serving-girl, at the sky between the leaves.

'Well, Sir Edward, are you ready for an experience?' Molly asked him.

'I'm always that.' He set down his cup.

'Good.' She led the way down through a gap in some oleanders towards the square. They found themselves at the end of a cobbled roadway much stained with grease. The thin soles of their shoes made tacky noises as they crossed it. To one side was drawn up a line of curious vehicles. They were wicker sleds of lighter design than their counterparts down in Funchal, clearly not drawn by bullocks. Nearby loitered a group of swarthy youths wearing some sort of national costume. Their thighs bulged and their bare arms were sinewy.

'Heavens,' said Edward faintly. 'D'you not think the *railway*?'

'On no account. You wanted an experience: this is one.'

The wicker creaked as they settled themselves.

'Do you mean we're going to toboggan down to the town?'

'Oh yes.'

Behind them once again sat Mrs Hammond and Mrs Bellamy.

'I say, I'm not faint-hearted, but, you know, *stopping* . . . ? Might we not shoot off the mountain?'

'Don't worry, Sir Edward, they've thought of that. Nobody's in business to kill their own customers.'

'Sweeney Todd?'

'Nonetheless, this is a much-used form of public transport. You'll enjoy it.'

A pair of buttocks appeared at Edward's ear, sheathed in crimson cloth. A spasm ran beneath, the material bulged in implausible lumps and they were off. It soon became apparent – to everyone's unexpressed relief – that this was not to be a nightmare career down a *piste* but an ungainly slither down a cobbled road at a stiff jogging pace. Once it was clear that the two young men who ran on either side were not going to let go the ropes they held and with which they steered the sled around the sharp bends the passengers relaxed and enjoyed their unusual descent. The cobbles were not too uneven and slick with repeated oilings. Now and again one of the youths reached inside for a can and, still jogging, poured a stream of oil over the upturned snout of the nearest metal runner which curved away beneath the sled. For a while the scrunching and grinding lessened.

Soon they had left solemn stretches of pines behind and had entered the lands where villas appeared momentarily behind wrought-iron gates and whitewashed walls. Sometimes they shot through a tiny tunnel as the roadway curved beneath the funicular track and for a moment the dank hole roared with the screech of iron, the slapping of feet and panting of the men. Then sunlight blazed again and the sound fell away on either side into the patches of tobacco roots and bleached maize stalks. Towards the end of the journey the Caminho became more populous with trudging peasants, water-carriers and the occasional ox. As they approached them the runners would yell.

'I like the way he shouts at 'em to go faster,' said Edward. The excitement of their hectic descent was in his voice as he half turned to include those behind.

'Do you know Portuguese, Sir Edward?' Kate asked him.

'Nary a word.'

'Well, "*Afasta!*" actually means "Get out of the way!"'

'All the same they're doing it quite quickly.'

The first roofs of the town swam up and the road tipped sharply into a last steep descent. At the same instant both men jumped onto the sled's runners as if to add their lot to a final suicidal rush. But perversely their additional weight merely slowed the thing and brought it to a perfect halt by a ticket collector wearing a crimson head-scarf. The experience was over.

'Surely the most preposterous mode of transport ever invented,' observed Edward as he climbed stiffly out. 'Tobogganing on cobbles: talk about crude. Your Bishop Whatsit has a lot to answer for.'

'Poor Teofilo,' said Molly. 'He was a troubled man. I fear his name will not outlive our visit.'

'How do you mean? He's in that guide book of Mrs Bellamy's.'

But Dora simply handed him the battered red book. It was a copy from the ship's library of Conan Doyle's *The Lost World*.

'Now do you see to what extremities of games intelligent people like ourselves are reduced?' said Kate.

Fortescue's sled had now arrived. 'I made that about four miles in twenty minutes,' he said cheerfully. 'I was just beginning to miss the twentieth century.'

'That's something I can't imagine,' Edward told him. 'I often wish I *had* missed it. In a funny way I think I probably have after all.'

This feeling intensified during the early luncheon they took together in a restaurant overlooking the harbour. Several hundred yards away the *Hildebrand* lay reassuringly at anchor, the thinnest wisp of smoke drifting from her funnel. She was due to sail at two-thirty so nobody needed divide their attention between the dishes of seafood and the clock on the wall. The mood of the table was animated. They told stories, as travellers usually do: of other times, other little adventures, other company. But even as he spoke Edward could hear the drone of some imaginary biographer describing the scene as recalled later by one of the others. 'Sir Edward, no mean raconteur himself, drew on memories of a long and varied life to the great amusement of everyone present.' What were these stories of his, many times told, if not fables of a distant self, a self who had lived forty-three years in a different century? He was nearly twice the age of anybody else at table. The things he remembered best had happened years before they were born and if dragged up into the light of present day – weighted with a little over-explanation and set adrift in this treacherous company – might they not sink down again contaminated with incomprehension? Better keep silence. The conversation turned to fairies as Fortescue, evidently neither ill-read nor unreflective for a man of action, leafed through *The Lost World* and remarked that he'd always found it odd that a 'scientific' author of Conan Doyle's character, a doctor, a man of acutely forensic imagination, should in his later years have developed a passion for photographs of fairies.

'As far as I know he's convinced the camera sees things the eye can't,' said Edward. 'If X-rays can do that – or a microscope, come to that – why might not a camera?'

'There was a witch who came through Pará last year claiming the same thing, do you remember, Kate?' asked Dora. 'That blackamoor with the French name, Madame Veyrou, Voisy, something like that.'

'Oh *her*. She claimed to be an ectoplasmist. One took a photograph of her in a trance and when it was developed the plate showed all this white stuff coming out of her mouth. It looked like butter-muslin to me.'

'Of course it was a *trick*; but it was quite well done for a fake medium. Still, she did cure some child's sickness in a séance.'

'The Aylings' little boy? She didn't have to fake a thing, the child did it for her. It was no more sick than we are.'

'However,' continued Edward, 'I won't allow that Sir Arthur Conan Doyle is a cheap fraud. I've met him and he's as straight a man as ever there was. So how do you explain the fairies in the photographs?'

'Have you seen the pictures, sir?' asked Fortescue.

'Well, not the actual photographs, maybe. Copies. But in some reputable source – a magazine or something.'

'One thing always strikes me about those sorts of photographs,' said Molly, 'as also about the ghosts people claim they've seen. Why is it they always look as they're *expected* to look? Conan Doyle's fairies, for instance. I've seen pictures of them too and they're all wearing Kate Greenaway costumes. Why? Are there fashions in the fairy world? Why weren't they all in miniature suits of armour, or woad? Or stark naked but for a moleskin *cache-sexe*? I think it's significant that Edwardian photographs of Edwardian gardens should show fairies wearing idealised Edwardian children's costumes.'

They were drinking a light Portuguese red wine of the kind which makes the English think of sunny holidays abroad but which is not strong enough to remind them of mid-afternoon headaches and lassitudes of Calvinist guilt. It was just the sort of speculative conversation Edward had once delighted in and for an instant an unstoppable sense of good times past welled up and flowed over him so that he half expected to see old faces, his little daughter still impatient to leave the table and climb back on Gaetano the mule, the sunlight outside to be Italian. But there were only the faces of four near-strangers, his fellow-countrymen abroad. A weary passion came to him that postwar scepticism should not have everything its own way.

'I have a theory,' he heard his own voice saying with pompous defiance, 'that the human imagination is far more powerful than is convenient to admit. I believe that in certain circumstances the mind of the photographer might well impress its imagery onto the collodion surface of a film. We may not yet have any scientific way of proving how this happens, nor indeed that it does. But it seems to me a much more rational approach than assuming automatically that men like Doyle must either be deluded or lying in their teeth. Besides, nobody need be surprised when the images he captures conform to the imagination of the times.'

This was so clearly, even fiercely, delivered the others were evidently impressed.

'Now that's an interesting theory,' said Fortescue. Strangely, he had not taken off his binoculars when he sat down but had merely tucked his napkin behind their eyepieces. As he ate they stirred slightly behind the fall of white linen. 'I'll tell you why. When we were in France I flew for a time with a squadron doing photo-recces: photographic reconnaissance, you know. We'd fly behind the enemy's lines and take pictures from the air of various strategic points and then our experts would try and decipher what they meant. Of course the Germans were doing the same to us so we all had to become more or less tricksters. There's quite an art in camouflage but there's an even greater one in hoaxing. For example, if it becomes necessary to advance some troops over open ground while being essential they're not seen one can tie bushes to their backs and tell them to freeze each time a machine comes over.'

'The Birnam Wood principle,' said Edward.

'Exactly. That's camouflage. But supposing you needed to give the enemy the *impression* you were advancing forces into a certain sector but without deploying the troops which you anyway may not have? You get bushes and dot them about the landscape but after the dawn recce's gone over you move them all slightly and add a few. Next time the photographs show fake bushes on the move and with a bit of luck they'll mistake them for troops. That's hoaxing.'

'Rather ingenious,' said Kate. 'I never knew that sort of thing went on.'

'Oh Lord yes. I once helped to build an entire British airfield with a squadron of FE 2b's out of cardboard and plywood. We had one or two old buses beyond repair and parked them with their engines ticking over for the sake of realism, even some brave souls walking about. We called it Honeypot Squadron. It was a lure, you see.'

'And did it work?'

'Oh, it worked. It brought over a whole circus who'd been giving us hell but this time we had a couple of squadrons waiting in the sun.' There was now no trace of boyish enthusiasm in Fortescue's eyes. Absently he used his fork to prise open the mouth of his fish and examine its teeth. 'It was a carve-up. But anyway, to return to the subject,' he pushed shut the unresisting mouth, 'I was merely meaning to say that I can never look at a photograph without wondering what's been arranged, and why. But even in those unromantic times there were some strange occasions. For instance, a pilot could fly over a dead wood and take pictures which later showed a lot of mounted troops sheltering. Then another pilot would walk in with a picture taken of the same wood at much the same time and show not a man anywhere. That happened once at Bapaume and we never did get to the bottom of it. There was nowhere for all those men to have gone, unobserved, in five minutes. And we took that wood a day later after a lot of unnecessary shelling and there wasn't even a foxhole in it, let alone a tunnel. So where did those men go? Nobody knows to this day.'

'Maybe they were ghosts,' said Dora.

'Don't worry, that was suggested,' Fortescue said perfectly seriously. 'A lot of men including quite high-ranking officers managed to convince themselves that they were the ghosts of a squadron of cavalry which had been caught in a gas attack in that wood two years before. It was late on in the war by then and far easier to believe in such things. There was nothing rational left about any of it. So if Sir Edward's theory is correct perhaps the first pilot, knowing at the back of his mind of the gas attack, somehow projected onto the photographic plate an image of what he *imagined* might be there, even though he actually *saw* an empty wood.'

The effect of this account from a somewhat unexpected source was to throw Kate and Dora onto the defensive.

'You're in danger of ruining the gaiety,' Dora told him with mock severity. 'Awfully morbid.'

'Just history,' said Fortescue. 'Just history.' And he too looked up as if half expecting to see old faces.

Edward was evidently much moved. 'The horses,' he murmured. 'The poor ghost horses.' It came to Molly that the tears which suddenly stood in his eyes were shed for something other, had been almost relieved to find so ready a pretext. For the first time she was touched by him, wondering at the source of an abundant emotion which in its turn had had the power to move others. What else was art if not this contagious sensibility? Equally she felt the incongruousness of this man, once apparently on hearty terms with a dead king and now being wrenched into the company of very ordinary strangers in an unfamiliar world by the mere circumstance of having survived long enough.

After a moment's withdrawal Edward rallied, however. Resuming the theme of fairies he told them he had once written some music for an adaptation of Algernon Blackwood's *Prisoner in Fairyland*.

'Not a title which gripped me with enthusiasm,' he said, 'given that this was in 1915 at about the time of the events Mr Fortescue was relating, and given that a good many people had sons who were even then prisoners in Germany. The thing was for children, of course, and they re-named it *The Starlight Express*. Still, Algie Blackwood's a good sort. I don't quite know what I expected when I first met him; in my experience writers are often a pretty rum bunch – except for Doyle, of course. I suppose I vaguely thought he might go on rather a lot about wands and toadstools but actually he said "A pint of something would go down nicely" and told me how Black Jester, who won the St Leger in 1914, had been entirely reared on dried milk. Imagine, dried milk *by the gallon*. They steeped his mash in it. Well, for an author he struck me as being a normal sort of fellow but I fear I made a more eccentric impression on him.'

'Eccentric, Sir Edward?' It seemed incredible that anyone should think such a thing about someone who looked so like a denizen of the Royal Enclosure at Ascot.

'It seems so. Because of a toad I was carrying in Hampstead. It was in the butcher's. No,' he said, 'I haven't got Gallic tastes. I was buying two chops but I found difficulty in getting my change out because I had this toad in a handkerchief. So I set it down on the counter momentarily although this did cause a good deal of *squeakage* among the butcher's female patrons. Then a voice said "Ah, Edward, I see you've got your Sunday roast with you but who are the chops for?" and it was Algie Blackwood. I explained I'd been for a walk and had come upon these two boys with the toad and since I like toads and this one seemed unhappy in their company I bought it off them for twopence and was on my way back to Severn House to release it in the garden. Sort of thing anyone might have done, except that Algie happened into the middle of the story. So there and then I told him I'd decided to name it after him in honour of the occasion and in due course into the garden Algernon went. But I'm afraid the story got about, rather, and people started to think I was pretty much off my head. The butcher, especially, became noticeably cool although I didn't mind that since he was a most inferior sort of butcher: wouldn't even sell black puddings. The best comment came from Jack Littleton at Novello's. He just said "H'm. *Toad and Verklärung*" which I think's quite witty from one's own publisher who'd give his right arm to be publishing Strauss as well.'

There was considerable laughter at this but on the way back to the ship it occurred to him it was likely nobody at the table had had the least idea of what he was talking about. There was nothing like people's failure to understand a reference which could so give one the feeling of having already stepped into a coffin whose lid they were purposefully nailing down bit by bit in small sections. Each day one's own understanding of the world became more partial, the view a little darker. Yet only the occupant knew how astonishingly clear had become his vision of what was left. The clarity was one thing, the astonishment was for its lateness.

Back aboard the *Hildebrand* Edward lay in the cool of his cabin and allowed himself to fall into doleful rumination brought on by the morning's activities and the wine he had drunk. The business about fairies hadn't helped, either; had let a vague disquiet edge in. It wasn't that the new world of the Bright Young Things with all their extravagance and awesome silliness was so much more rational than the old, rather that a whole culture had become outmoded. A world ruled by Lyddite and phosgene and 'Archie' would have made short shrift of Mrs Doasyouwouldbedoneby, while Peter Pan would have had his own troubles in the trenches. Trying to look at it through modern eyes he could quite well see the ridiculousness of it all; but then surely it had never been more than a way in which people of a stolid race living in a stolid time had dealt with the whole uneasy business of childhood and, well, of the imagination, the poetic dream. True, the mode of expressing the vividness and anarchy of an infant's vision might have degenerated a bit since Wordsworth's day but . . . Or maybe . . . Who could blame those authors like Barrie and Algie Blackwood for doggedly holding out against the horrid tide of materialism, to say nothing of all those psychologists banging on about how the thoughts of children are really unspeakable? Modern grown-ups were indeed wumbled; and if regrettably they were no longer to be unwumbled by anointings with holy water or fairy-dust or star-dust then . . .

Into his drifting mind came snatches of the private language he and Alice had written to each other in the form of jottings, notes in each other's margins, a language which if brought out into the light of day *coram publico* would frankly appear as baby-talk. It was insane, this black world. How could 'Pease wite more dis booful music' now lie beneath the inscription *Fortiter et Fide*? All too easily. He closed his eyes on such things, tears welling from beneath his lids, almost in exasperation at what was the whole of him and would not let him go, only to awake with a small jump and discover that two whole hours had elapsed. He had expected to find it mid-afternoon at the latest and the ship back at sea with Madeira a diminishing smudge intermittent behind a flapping Red Ensign. But when Steward Pyce came in as requested at four-thirty with a cup of tea the floor was not quivering with the power of Chief Stanford's engines.

'Are we not under way, Steward?'

'I'm afraid not, sir. There's been a slight delay. Something to do with one of our fresh-water tanks, sir. The Captain assures us we'll leave by five-thirty at the latest.'

Edward remembered something he had meant to do earlier but forgotten. The delay in starting was a bit of luck. 'In that case would you mind very much getting me another bucket of sea-water, Pyce?'

'Sea-water sir. Of course. But if it's from the bows again I'm afraid I shall have to do it without your assistance: Captain Maddrell was quite firm about ship's regulations, sir. Strictly speaking I shouldn't have taken you so far forrard last time.'

'Well, I'm sorry if I got you into any trouble.'

The man has some imagination after all, thought Pyce. Few passengers in his experience would have bothered to draw such a conclusion. A not very strong feeling of indulgence for this old fellow allowed that, barmy or not, he was probably a decent enough stick.

'I'd like it from the stern,' said the stick. 'Assuming we're anchored head on into the tide or current?'

'Very well sir; the stern it is. A whole bucket or just your hip-flask, sir?'

'The hip-flask. Wait a moment.'

His passenger took the flask from the desk where it stood among the mysterious wooden boxes, went to the wash-stand in the bathroom and could be heard rinsing it out thoroughly before returning and handing it over.

'I'm much obliged.'

'My pleasure sir. Before we sail, sir.'

'Should I not be here kindly leave it on the desk.'

Despite his relayed assurances it turned out to be not until seven o'clock that Captain Maddrell finally weighed anchor and sent a single abrupt C like a shell into the town of Funchal, its echoes rolling back from the facets of the mountain, the rocky slopes, the woods and crevasses which rose high into the dusk above it. The evening was not quite warm. The passengers hugged themselves at the rail as they watched a battered tug slew the *Hildebrand*'s head round so she faced 2,200 miles of empty ocean and nine landless days. The top of the island was cinnabar in the last light of a sun which had long fallen beneath their horizon. Edward was on deck with his cane and boater. He cut a dapper figure at the rail, standing a little apart or – Molly thought as she joined him – stood a little apart from.

'I suppose captains never feel as we do each time they leave,' he said as the bodegas of the waterfront slowly revolved and passed astern. 'I'm never unaffected by departures.'

'Nor me. The funny thing is I haven't travelled very much by ship except across the Channel and the trip last year, but sailing out of a port on an evening like this I feel I already have a lifetime of leave-takings and journeyings behind me. Memories of things which never happened: how are they possible?'

'It's the melancholy that's familiar. That always did seem ancient because one could never remember a time without it.'

She abandoned her undiscriminating gaze to turn her head and stare sharply at the side of his face. 'Would you describe yourself as a melancholy person, Sir Edward?'

'Good Lord yes,' he said in surprise. 'Wouldn't you describe yourself as one? I've never met an English person who was even slightly thoughtful who wasn't a bit of a melancholic.'

'You're not happy, then?'

'That has nothing to do with it. One may be very happily melancholic: it has its own delights, as Sir Thomas Browne and Robert Burton well knew. But as it happens, no, I'm not happy. Nor can I think of a single reason why I might be. My wife is dead, my friends are dead, my music is dead. Only I, inconveniently, remain alive. I shall continue to be so for an undisclosed length of time and for no discernible purpose whatever except that I've got to provide some idiotic music for a damnfool occasion at Wembley next April. That in itself is hardly an adequate reason for prolonging someone's life. With any luck there may turn out to be a Supreme Being who agrees, but I know it's unlikely. Not for nothing is he familiar as the Arch-Jester.'

Somewhere far off, borne to them through a large metal duct like the horn of a gramophone bolted to the deck there came the sound of a bell and at once the engines' beat increased. The boards began to vibrate under their feet and foam slid past the ship's side with a rinsing hiss.

'You're silent,' he said and she thought crossly that there was satisfaction in his voice.

'What is there for me to say? I wouldn't presume to try and talk you out of your view of your own life even if I thought I might succeed. I'd gain nothing but a deserved rebuff.'

'Do I strike you as so very prickly?'

Had he been thirty years younger Molly thought she might have identified a flirtatiousness in this question. But it was not in the least teasing nor even anxious, merely an enquiry of fact. The idea that he should care to know left a taste in her mind identical to the one which had provoked her outspokenness a couple of days before. There was something faintly disgusting about so famous and – in worldly view – so successful a man still insisting on having everything on his own terms: something of the child which devours the world it dominates. The self-pity was quite bleak enough to be acceptable, even to transcend itself. But it was odious to retreat behind inviolate grandeur or hooded withdrawal while reserving the right to emerge suddenly and demand assessment from a comparative stranger – more particularly as she was certain he would never normally dream of doing such a thing. She had never known the habitually reserved break their habit without seeming to surprise themselves, and this she found particularly distasteful. In fact the experience of nursing in France during the last year of the war had changed her irrevocably. The juvenile, undifferentiated kindness towards her fellow-men with which she had gone had been abraded – or at least refined – into something she valued enough not to bestow indiscriminately. Like many other nurses or professionals whose work is among suffering people she had acquired a fine recognition of the often modest symptoms of courage. Equally, she had an impatient category of her own: what she called 'DBB' or downright bad behaviour. She had coined this term herself, partly because she found she needed it and partly as a satirical comment on the despised pseudo-medical diagnosis of 'LMF'. Now, five years later, Molly would never have dreamed of accusing anybody, no matter what the provocation, of lacking in moral fibre; but at this moment it did occur to her that Sir Edward Elgar was indeed capable of downright bad behaviour.

Declining to answer his question she said instead: 'My steward told me this ship was delayed because of a drinking-water problem.'

It was Edward's turn to look sideways at his companion staring down at the waters of Funchal harbour. Eventually he said, 'So did mine.'

'Well, I ran into Dr Ashe, the ship's doctor – have you met him? Looks like a vulture and is wonderfully indiscreet. The whole story's bunkum. The truth is exactly the reverse: the problem which delayed us all was quite precisely not caused by drinking water.'

'What then?'

'Good old drinking alcohol. It appears a few of our passengers, so relieved at having weathered the storm, went ashore to celebrate being alive with Madeira's most famous export.'

'Not cake?'

'Not cake. They went to ground in somebody's bodega at about ten this morning and the Captain had to send a party of crew-men with an officer to comb the dives of Funchal like a shore patrol looking for delinquent sailors. Dr Ashe said they were found at about three o'clock but they all wanted carrying.'

'My goodness,' said Edward with a suggestion of admiration. 'Pie-eyed on madeira for five hours. I hope the doctor has a good headache remedy aboard. Conditions down in Steerage may become a little unsavoury, too.'

'They were all First Class passengers.'

'Really? We're turning out rather a lively lot, in that case. I wonder who they are? Presumably no-one at our table. What the Varsity types call "bloods", I expect.'

'And what I'd call drunks.'

'You object, of course.'

'Not on moral grounds; possibly on aesthetic. I'd call them drunks simply because they were drunk.' Molly looked at him with great directness. 'I don't object just because I'm a woman, if that's what you're thinking.'

Edward, who had indeed been thinking that, said 'It's silly our fencing like this.'

'Quite. Incidentally, I did want to say that I completely agreed with what you said at luncheon. I mean your theory about photographing fairies.'

'It was just an idea. I'm not at all sure I believe it myself, you know. But all of a sudden I couldn't bear to let this hateful century get away with it once again – not without putting up some resistance. Nothing is avowed to exist nowadays unless it can be bought or sold or measured by scientists. Why should artists have to acknowledge the complete supremacy of materialism? Must everything mysterious be exploded or all unaccountable things explained away? And if so, what's gained? Plain men drudging in a world of plain things. That's not the world I know and it's one I've no wish to know.'

The distant bell rang again and the engines further increased their speed. The sound was suddenly reflected from behind and both turned to look across the deck towards the opposite rail beyond which the mole guarding the harbour entrance was sliding by only a few yards away. There were no old men and boys with rod and line around the squat stone lighthouse at the end. Instead a lone cat was sitting with its back to the ship, staring out to sea. The animal's posture at once made it memorable: its motionless attention to the horizon was so complete that a seven-thousand-ton liner passing within yards was in another universe, a shadow crossing behind muslin. The cat ignored the *Hildebrand* and her two hundred souls, not with disdain but with a profound distraction. It sped past in unmoving meditation and diminished astern. As the distance and twilight increased Edward during the next few minutes stared back, with difficulty separating the receding lighthouse from intervening masts and davits to discern at its foot the black fur dot. Soon there was nothing of Funchal but a winking beam from the base of an indigo bulk sprinkled with lights. The moon which had been poised above the island that morning had not yet risen but in the limitless blank of unruffled turquoise sky the stars were coming out.

'There's no getting used to it,' said Edward. 'The beauty of this earth and its animals, and the barbarous wasteland man makes of it all. I don't know why people aren't more *astonished* by beauty. You must paint your jungle pictures with astonishment, Molly. As long as you put something of your own heart into them they'll be exceptional.'

'I certainly want to be original in the way I do them.'

'Yes, of course. Well, remember what Ruskin said: "Originality is not newness, it is genuineness".'

'Did he say that?'

'I seem to remember he did. An academic musician called Henry Hadow was fond of quoting it and he was a man of genuine unoriginality.'

'You're not fond of academics.'

'I suppose some are all right. But finally it's down to the heart and not the head. What's the point of having so much knowledge and technique if it dissipates in cabals and rivalries and lectures?'

Molly was struck by his vehemence. There was something so unsophisticated and raw but at the same time confident in what he said that with surprise – as if she had not realised it until that moment – she found herself thinking 'The man actually *is* an artist throughout.' She was impressed by the idea of someone in what she still thought of as an uncertain and marginal line of business being so used to his own idea of himself. It was even exhilarating to hear somebody take for granted that living a creative life was not something which had to be accounted for. At this period her ideal was acquiring enough stature in her art that she would never have to be bluff or apologetic or furtive about it: no modest ambition for a single Englishwoman even in those enlightened days of partial franchise. Edward had with great casualness just displayed the very confidence she herself yearned for and her envy made him again remote and distinguished in her eyes. She no longer even thought of him as a man but as a person who had lived his talent and suffered in consequence. As if he had read this envy he said:

'You can't be in much doubt yourself. Even nowadays no young woman takes herself off alone to paint the Amazon jungle without being very certain of something.'

'That's no doubt how it looks but it's not at all how it feels, I promise you. I wouldn't presume to compare our talents but weren't there moments at the beginning when you, well, had doubts? Did you never despair just once or twice? Even after what I assume was exceptional promise at college?'

'Doubts? Despair? My dear girl, I've never been without 'em. At this moment I doubt a single thing I've done was worth doing and I despair of a life thrown away on something nobody needs or wants. As for my college, I'm a graduate *summa cum laude* of a cramped flat above a music shop in Worcester. The first time I ever had anything to do with a university was when I made the appalling mistake at the age of forty-eight of accepting a professorship at Birmingham. I needed the money. Disastrous. I never did loathe anything so much. Oh, and I'm forgetting Cambridge gave me some footling doctorate or something a few years earlier. I'm sure Birmingham couldn't have made its offer had I not already got some letters after my name. Otherwise I contrived to keep myself remarkably unspotted and unstained by academic influence. I was far too busy writing music and trying to feed myself.'

On the basis of their short acquaintance Molly was unable to know how brilliantly he had pitched his description, so exactly did it console her for her own lack of academy training and so precisely did it conjure up the fierce independence of wayward genius. But even he might not have said whom this version of events was designed to impress since he himself believed it a little more deeply at each re-telling. Not that it was untrue; it was merely economical with the truth. But Molly had lived in the world for longer than most students.

'Even so,' she said, 'technique has to be learned.'

'Of course it has. How else but by example? From my earliest boyhood I read every score I could lay my hands on, I played and sang in groups and chamber orchestras without number. I spent every last penny on train fares to London to hear concerts at the Crystal Palace and I was still coughing yellow fog out of my lungs days later. I took violin lessons; I gave violin lessons; I wrote cotillions and quadrilles for a lunatic asylum. Year after year it went, penny-pinching in the provinces. Doubts? Despair? My father wanted me to be a lawyer, you know, and I actually started in one of those offices with high stools. But I soon stopped that, unlike Chabrier who I gather qualified and practised, brave fellow. You ask about doubts and despair when I rejected the respectable career urged on me by my tradesman father in order to be a damned musician with cracked boots and a teaching suit which was more invisible mending than it was cloth.

'And in all those miserable years not one person gave me a single shred of support or encouragement. Not one person. And my advice to you, Miss Air, is to expect nothing from anybody. An artist is on his own. He's stuck up a tower preaching to pigs, no matter that now and then they'll pretend to listen and even to applaud. But don't be deceived. They soon get tired of rattling their trotters at you and wander off to find someone more diverting. After that they'd cut you down as soon as look at you.'

This last sentence was added with lowered voice as if he were talking more to himself. Confused as she was by the violence it implied Molly hardly liked to pursue it. In any case a steward in a white uniform took that moment to emerge on deck from a companionway and blow a brightly-polished B♭ on a brass bugle.

'We'd better dress. We're late.'

'Oh, hang all clothes,' he said to the passing sea. Like a small boy chafing at being put into his Sunday best, she thought, while observing the paradox of his obviously liking to be well groomed to the point of nattiness.

When they came back on deck after dinner it was clear that the day's visit to Madeira had sanctioned a change in the atmosphere aboard the *Hildebrand*. The passengers were in evident quest of the night life whose imagining had enlivened the gloom of their autumns. As far as they were concerned a formal promise had been made the moment their cash had been exchanged for a ticket. They now roamed the ship expecting its fulfilment and enviously presuming it in the various couples talking in low voices at the rail or in pools of shadow. But it was altogether too early in the voyage to think of disconsolation and they drifted towards the ballroom from which came the muffled and lively strains of Tommy Hawtree's Melodeers. Edward scarcely felt like turning in yet: his afternoon's sleep had taken the edge off his weariness and he detected the beginnings of that second wind which, when he was in London, increasingly took him on lonely rounds of indiscriminate theatre-going or kept him chatting in the smoke rooms of his various clubs until his mouth was rank with pipes and his brain whirled with the names of horses.

'Come on everybody, it's spring,' said Dora Bellamy's voice behind them. 'We allow no moping here.'

'Quite right too,' said Edward. 'What do you propose?'

Dora dropped her voice confidingly. 'I hear tell of a lively little game starting up below. For those who like a flutter now and then. Only don't tell Kate, Sir Edward. As you already know, her views on gambling are irreproachable and fiercely held.'

'They certainly are,' said Kate from the dark behind her. 'Never follow an even number by an uneven with two digits.'

'Very sound advice too,' said Edward. 'I never go twice on a red.'

'I say, the gentleman's a sport. Give him a gasper, Dora.'

'Not for me. But by all means go ahead. We'll follow you shortly.'

Kate and Dora drifted unsteadily away trailing cigarette smoke.

'They're rather awful, aren't they?' said Molly.

'Frightful. I like them quite a lot. I don't believe they care very much what anybody thinks and I always find that endearing. Though I must say I can't imagine what their husbands are like.'

'If they have husbands.'

It had never occurred to Edward to question their acquaintances' self-description. 'Golly,' he said. And then, 'Golly.'

'Oh, I'm sure they have. In any case I don't care either.'

Since they were last on deck the sky had darkened into true night. The starfields sprawled in brilliant prodigality, traversed by the running-lights on the *Hildebrand*'s masts and gaped at by the sooty O of her funnel. No further trace showed of the islands they had recently left behind them. The ship was alone and –infinitesimal in the night and the faint sounds of revelry only made it the smaller. The stars' brightness defined the surface of the ocean beyond the dim yellow cocoon spun by deck-lamps and portholes.

' "The sun has gone, the tide of stars is setting all our way; the Pleiades call softly to Orion as nightly they have called these million years." '

He spoke so quietly that he was finished before she realised he was quoting, not addressing her, not addressing anybody.

'That's beautiful.'

'It is. Surprising, really, amid all that twaddle. It's from the old *Starlight Express*. About the only memorable thing in it including, some might think, the music.'

Nevertheless it was the music he heard as he watched the stars, music which had first come to him as a boy and had been written down in pencil for a childhood play under the elderly title *The Wand of Youth*. How those tunes had recurred! Throughout his life they had come back, first in full orchestral guise then once more for pit orchestra in a wartime theatre. And still they haunted him and offered themselves as little mines which had the air of refusing to be abandoned and from which things of value might yet be dug. Two hours later as he undressed for bed he heard again the cadence at the words 'nightly they have called these million years' and thought of that incomprehensible gap which was no gap at all and could never separate him from that far-off self who had first heard the notes and in time had turned them into his second Suite's 'The Little Bells'. He sat on the edge of the bed fiddling absently with studs. There was a spot of port on his shirt-front.

'What was it all for?' he murmured. 'What rot it was . . . Dear old rot.' He wiped his eyes on his sleeve. 'Oh, damn it all.'

V

Of <u>course</u> Edwardian fairies wore Edwardian costume. My trees sang me music of my time, not plainsong or organum or snippets of the 'Pastoral' sym. Being of your time means making everything in the world yours for as long as you're in it. It may once have belonged to Beethoven but it belongs to me now. Belonged.

We've left Madeira (yesterday) and are reportedly facing more than a week's blank ocean. Staring at the sea – as after breakfast just now – makes one banally reflective. I found myself thinking that eight or nine days without land is quite a long time in these days of steam. But even as recently as Conrad's (and my) youth it was obviously possible to be becalmed on some ocean for a month or two without the sight of anything more solid than clouds at dawn and dusk. First the unease of being so deserted by the wind, then panic as fresh water needed rationing, then listlessness & torpor. (<u>Meeresstille</u>. I love the sound of that word.) Long before their month was up the sailors must have begun to wonder whether land any longer existed or whether it hadn't been some kind of communal dream or folk legend. Even now aboard the old 'Hildebrand' the reality of England is beginning to seem hazy, faintly in doubt. It still has a solid inner presence but then so does anything imagined & lived with for years. There may after all be no external counterpart to the England we all carry within us. Maybe the ship will arrive back at the right co-ordinates for Merseyside and – sail straight on over vacant waters. It was a myth after all. I think we've no confidence in things we don't constantly touch or see & even then they all the time suggest something else. It's a shifting wasteland, this world, & necessarily viewed from another. Just as the Patriarch said, the <u>mind</u> moves. So at the moment England no longer exists for me. (I manifestly don't exist for <u>it</u>.)

Quite enjoyed Madeira & have at any rate become better acquainted with some of my fellow-travellers. It appears I was wrong about <u>everybody</u> that first evening. Mrs (Miss?) Bellamy & Mrs (Miss?) Hammond turn out to be racy while Fortescue seems neither cad nor buffoon. Each in his/her own way – I include Molly – is to some extent an

<u>adventurer</u>. I like that (so different from the members of one's clubs to say nothing of those damned musical asses who keep pestering) tho' it does make me feel old . . . I suppose I <u>am</u> old, hang it all, until I'm by myself when I become pretty much ten or twelve again. Talk about keeping faith. There are some things one can't betray even if one wanted.

<u>Meeresstille</u> . . . How that word brings it all back tho' not really with pain. If I'd had a leg cut off in 1884 I'd not now be able to remember the anguish with much acuity nearly 40 yrs later, only much-revised memories of pain. Even tho' we never saw each other again I did feel a pang 15 yrs. afterwards when I heard from Stämpfli that Lena was married & had left Europe. By then of course I'd got over being turned down, not least because I'd since been accepted by dear Alice; but it did seem the final lopping-off of my painful twenties. Well, putting it into music was as good a way as any of burying an unwanted past & it was a happy accident I was actually writing Enigma vars at the time. An even happier was being able to use Mary Trefusis as the alibi for Lena's var even tho' it really didn't bear close scrutiny. However the dolts swallowed it whole & even Alice never twigged despite my saying that the asterisks at the head of no. 13 stood for the name of a lady who was on a sea voyage at the time of composition & Mary palpably wasn't. She <u>was</u>, though, later that same year when that brother of hers was appointed Governor of NSW & she went off to Australia with him. So of course it wasn't the engines of <u>her</u> ship I heard as it rumbled eastwards across the ocean but those of Lena's as they had carried her away for good many months earlier & in quite the other direction. In any case I wdn't have written a var for Mary as at that very moment I was dedicating my 3 Characteristic Pieces to her. Nor does anyone seem to have bothered to notice that all the other vars have names/initials so why wdn't I have put Mary's? Everyone who knew us also knew there cdn't possibly be anything mysteriously romantic – it's absurd. As for the idea that if I <u>had</u> intended putting her initials I'd have made one of the asterisks stand for her title – that's downright vulgar. It suggests that had I – in a moment when my brain had turned to addle – decided to dedicate a var mysteriously to Dame Clara Butt I'd have put ***!

I think the whole thing started when people saw my sketches for no. 13 headed 'L' (I ask you, imagine using a working-title of 'Lady' or 'Lygon' for a friend like Mary!). Then when we were dickering with the Finale Jaeger with his huntsman's eye must have looked at one of my original drafts & spotted that I was thinking of working in some of 'LML' at that time. Well, I was: but it was Lena meine Liebe I was going to work into the summing-up of my own var. But it didn't quite go & anyway I'd given her a close enough place to me by putting her own var right next to mine. This neatly satisfied various proprieties: Alice first, me & Alice last

& Lena penultimate. The anguish may have long gone but I'm very glad the mystification has lasted so well. It's part of the advantage of calling something Enigma: the amateur sleuth straightway ignores all verifiable fact such as chronology. If one obligingly puts a ring through his nose one can lead him into the most implausible territory. It's splendid to behold!

Even the <u>Meeresstille</u> quotation . . . True, nobody's likely to know that this was the Overture to the Leipzig Conservatoire concert the afternoon Lena & I first met. But a few with a knowledge of German might have thought that the usual English translation (Calm sea & prosperous voyage) is, if not inaccurate, misleading. <u>Meeresstille</u> isn't just a calm sea: it's a desolate menacing becalming as per the Ancient Mariner – the slow intro. – followed by the hopeful lyricism of the happy onward journey (wh. God knows I wished her). How much I wished it her is plain enough since it's the prosperous voyage bit I quoted from rather than the becalming. But those are the reasons for the quotation: our first meeting, our shared enthusiasm for Mendelssohn, his own connection with Leipzig, the significance of it having been an overture for both of us . . . And of course her going away did make me sad with old memories so the orchestral light in which I quoted an otherwise lyrical extract is mournful with hints of flat abandonment & shot with unease. Of course it matters not a jot at this late stage, any of it; but it's funny the wilful way the same amateur sleuths will ignore the evidence of their own ears, mis-read & mis-hear Mendelssohn so as to uphold a shaky alibi for me. Gawd bless 'em!

<u>Later</u>

Made some good slides before lunch. Sample taken from Funchal harbour as we lay at anchor yesterday. Quite a plentiful crop of the plankton I've already seen but almost every drop I looked at was <u>swamped</u> with <u>E. coli</u>! Either they're normally there (drains!) or we aboard the 'Hildebrand' were flushing unmentionables into the Madeirans' water. Perhaps if I run into this Dr Ashe of Molly's I'll ask what he thinks. There's something of a ghoul about the man's appearance – seems a funny choice for a cruise doctor & suspect he has a <u>past</u>. Never did I think everyone on board wd. have one too, still less that within a week I shd. be slightly privy to several. Strange how briefly being ship-mates together turns total strangers into confidants practically overnight. Even the most reticent souls throw caution to the winds (some of the <u>conversations</u> I've overheard, esp. among the younger element!). Why is this? I return to my theory: England's no longer real to anyone aboard so anything they say is equally unreal & will never be accountable. H'm. We shall see.

Over the rail postprandially (excellent word) I thought some more about the amateur sleuths who from time to time have sniffed me over. I expect they'll give up now – they've done their sleuthing & got it all wrong but everyone's happy with their version so they can move on to some more fashionable composer. It's wonderful how much they've missed – all those initials in the chorus of Devils in <u>Gerontius</u>! – & heaps more little encodings à la Schumann. Well, they're just part of the crowd who constantly write about music – talk & <u>talk</u> & <u>talk</u> about it – almost none of whom are performers & still fewer composers. Whom do they think they're addressing? And about what? Music is what it <u>says</u> & it says what it is through sounds & not the written word. Most of those who prate about music are nincompoops, which isn't to be wondered at since most people are that anyway. But they're often musical illiterates, which is intolerable. They're illiterates in the sense that while they may know all the right terms & technical flummery they're ignorant of what's being <u>said</u>. They don't understand – or even appear much to like – the language & what it expresses so they waffle on about the grammar instead. I except Shaw from this accusation. His politics may be benighted & many of his plays wrong-headed to a degree but not only is he the kindest man who ever stepped, he understands & <u>feels</u> music. He alone among contemporary critics acknowledges that composers & musicians <u>think</u>, but that they do so in A minor & not in words. He alone wdn't be puzzled by watching an orchestral rehearsal where we stop & start & clarify whole passages with often scarcely a word spoken. That's how professionals communicate when they're attuned. I grunt, I mutter, I draw a waggled curve in the air at the violas: <u>they</u> know what I mean. 'Too <u>h'm</u>,' I expect I say, leaving out the adjective or adverb. A disappointed 'Twenty-eight' will re-start them at that cue but this time I draw the bassoon line in the air & lo! out it comes. Sublime dictation. Shaw knows; the rest are asses & as far as I'm concerned can go & re-bury themselves in the nearest library with Hadow. The concert hall's got far too much to do with the heart for them.

Pleased to discover that 'RMS Hildebrand' yields 'Brindled Marsh'. This must surely be the name of one of those minor moths which fall into one's lamp at night. <u>Check South on return.</u>

The unfamiliarity of shipboard days and the torrent of air through which they forged greatly affected Edward's awareness of the slipping away of time, which for some years he had pretended to welcome both in public and private. 'Trivial pursuits' or 'masterly inactivity' were the phrases he indifferently offered when people asked him what he was up to nowadays. It had become a habit as he sat on the edge of his bed at night, letting his fingers undo his tie with the minimal skill of fifty years, to say – half to assert his own bleakness and half to harrow the shades of any listeners: '*One* more day I shan't have to get through.' Even a diary bristling with engagements (if he let it) represented no proper curriculum but only diversions for day-to-day indulging: luncheons, dinners, outings to the Races, conducting his own works up and down the country, having the vet over for the dogs, attending Three Choirs Festivals. Forward momentum had ceased; what remained was the temporarily eternal present to be bought off.

But that was on dry land. It soon became plain that it was different on board ship because no matter how one frittered or filled the days one was willy-nilly going somewhere. Over and above the lassitudes of chatter and the empty cries of bugles there was a steady progress carrying on independently and on one's own behalf. There were constant reminders of it in the purposeful life of officers and crew glimpsed now and then; in the endless banner of smoke and smuts unravelling from the funnel; in the liquid tumulus which raised itself glassily and followed the ship at an unvarying distance of fifty yards. Future ports of call took on the significance of destinations. 'When we reach Pará,' a husband could be overheard promising his wife as they strolled past. Or, 'Just wait till we get to Manaos.' But to Edward Pará and Manaos were as Wednesday and Thursday. Somewhere ahead lay Sunday, Liverpool again, and the resumption of the habits and patterns which brought him to his bed each night yawning and saying, Well, that was one November the twenty-fifth he'd never have to re-live. Meanwhile in the *Hildebrand*'s bar and smoke room, on its bridge now empty of Mr Mushet's dour presence, beneath its awnings and sightless in its deck chairs turned to the unvarying expanses hurrying by, Edward recognised that a ship was no place to escape being directionless and neither might strangers allay anxieties of loss.

Earlier that year he had written to Compton Mackenzie about how he took no more interest in music, observing that the secret of happiness for an artist when he grew old was to have a passion which could take the place of his art. This was by way of explaining his new hobby. He went on to say he had discovered the joy diatoms could give him and that the miraculous world of beauty under the ocean as revealed by the microscope was beyond music. Now he kept Steward Pyce to a routine of gathering a daily sample, from this side of the ship or the other, from the bows and from the stern. After several days' conscientious work with Dowdy's *A Pathologist's Commoner Micro-organisms* he had made his deductions. He resolved to visit Dr Ashe with the perfectly valid excuse of insomnia since he had been sleeping badly since leaving Madeira.

He found the doctor in a cabin disguised as a consulting room, in acrid contemplation from the swivel chair behind a desk of the ceiling fan. This gentleman did not precisely spring to his feet at his appearance but levered his angular form grudgingly upright, both hands on the blotter. In Edward's recent experience this was a surprising enough departure from the deferential attitude of the ship's personnel; he was still further taken aback by the question the doctor shot at him.

'Have you come for an operation, Sir Edward?'

'An operation? That is, well, no, not so far as I know.'

'I'm sorry to hear it. I'm getting most infernally bored. Take a chair, sir. Do you know, I had a woman in here not half an hour ago who couldn't get her necklace off?' With a bony finger he tapped his own shirt-front. 'Royal Army Medical Corps. Qualified at Guy's and served in France where we cut off the limbs of young men by candlelight. And this . . . this *creature* wanted me to help her out of her jewellery. I sent her to the Quartermaster. Told her he had some cable shears which were just the ticket. What?'

'Indeed,' said Edward weakly.

'Can't stand frauds. Never could. Put my teeth on edge.'

He was regretting he had ever come, especially on such a trivial pretext. Dr Ashe, although probably only in his forties and hence a good twenty years Edward's junior, had that ability to make one wish to please him – even to placate – which went far beyond any ordinary social recognition of disparate status and in doing so trivialised the very idea. Edward suddenly wished he were quite ill. 'At least you must have been kept pretty busy the first few days.'

'If, sir, by "busy" you mean endlessly traipsing about from one cabin reeking of sal volatile to another then yes, I was. We must have walked miles, my assistant and I. Normally I imagine one can expect a few bona fide injuries in rough weather: scalded cooks, stokers who fall off ladders, skulls laid open, that sort of thing. But this time nothing. Nothing but puddles of vomit on the carpet and people with too much money lying around moaning they were going to die. Not soon enough for me. What?'

'Pardon me if I remark that you're beginning to strike me as an odd sort of doctor for a cruise liner.'

'Odd, am I?' Unexpectedly the doctor's lower face opened a brief and mirthless cavern. 'You're right, sir. I don't fit at all. This is my first trip and, DV, it'll be my last. Already I've a yearning for dry land. Biggest mistake I ever made, resigning my commission. Fact is I've made a balls-up of things . . . What did you say you'd come about, sir?'

If the confession and the doctor's manner had left Edward disquieted, this sudden question with its overtones of *Punch* jokes and bar-room stories made him wonder whether the unusual mode were not perhaps a form of humour designed to see if one were worth bothering with. Well, two could play at that game.

'I didn't say I'd come about anything. However, since you ask, are you any good at amputations?'

Dr Ashe's raptor's eyes brightened momentarily. 'Top-hole. Anything in particular?'

'Shall we say it's of a trichological nature?'

A short silence. 'You want a damned haircut, sir?' Abruptly he sat down. Then he grinned again and opened a drawer.

'You're a card, Sir Edward. I do believe you like a bit of a prank yourself from time to time.' He produced a bottle. 'Would you care for a snifter, sir? Unless you're worried about the yard-arm?'

'To be honest I'm not sure I'd know a yard-arm if I saw one. But I don't mind a spot.' Why was he all at once so sapped of energy as to allow himself to get drawn further into complicity with this dubious man?

'I'm afraid it's madeira,' the doctor was saying, 'but I'm assured it's a good one and it's what people round these parts drink any time of day or night.' He glanced at the porthole. 'When I say these parts of course . . .' He poured two tumblers with much steadiness. 'Got it off a drunk,' said Dr Ashe, handing one to Edward.

'Ah, I heard about the drunks from Miss Air. Grateful patients, were they?'

'They weren't patients at all. Regular topers, all of 'em. Know all about the morning after. Not the sort to go running to doctor with a headache. Back to the bar for them, hair of the dog. What?

Go on, what did you really come about? I'm not bad at doctoring provided I can stand the patient, you know.'

'I'm a bad patient if I like the doctor. I pretend to be well just to oblige him. I came with a moan so I'll keep it to myself.' He caught a sudden, shrewd gaze from opposite.

'Just as you please.'

'On the other hand you might tell me about *E. coli.*'

'*E. coli*? What did you want to know? We're all riddled with 'em. Micro-organism of the lower alimentary tract not advisable to introduce into the upper.'

'Does sea-water kill them?'

'No. That's why bathers sometimes get sick on beaches near towns.'

'That partly explains why Funchal harbour's full of rod-shaped bacteria.'

'I can't say I'm surprised. How do you know?'

'I took a sample and looked at it through my microscope. I was looking for diatoms and things but these bacilli just took over.'

'You have a microscope with you, Sir Edward? I didn't know you were a bacteriologist as well.'

'Oh I'm not. Just an amateur. You must have done a bit yourself.'

'Not since student days. Forgotten the lot. No, it's interesting for another reason which I'll tell you if you can keep a secret.'

'Depends on the secret.'

'If you like a joke, then. This is quite funny but it'll spoil everything if you get miffed. You know your steward? He thinks you're off your head.'

Edward bristled. 'Pyce? Dash his infernal cheek! He came and told you that?'

'He did. But before you get exercised let me ask you, has he ever seen your microscope?'

'What? I suppose he might have done. But only in its case, I believe.'

'Does he know what it is?'

'I don't imagine he does, no. I may have referred to "my instruments" or something like that, though.'

'Hah. This is rich. The man's convinced you have trombones in your cabin trunk and that you need sea-water to wash them in. Or to give them to drink, I forget which.'

'*Trombones?*'

'Well, you are a famous musician. And having asked around I gather the fellow has a bit of a history of getting bees in his bonnet about his passengers. Not over-bright, you know. There was apparently a most odd episode involving an American illusionist a few trips ago.'

'Oh I say.' And suddenly Edward began laughing and could scarcely stop. 'Yes. That *is* . . . Ah,' he sat back and dabbed at a trickle of madeira on his chin. 'If I read you aright you're thinking a little fun might be had at the good Pyce's expense, is that it?'

'It would be more entertaining than coming clean, wouldn't it? But only if you feel like a bit of amusement. What?'

Not many months earlier Edward and an elderly boyhood friend had roamed the streets of Worcester for a whole afternoon playing 'Beaver' again as they had half a century before. Gripped by the infectious absurdity of beard-spotting they had worked themselves into a fit of near-hysteria. In pain from the effort of preserving a grave demeanour, scoring competitively in undertones, they had both exploded simultaneously on catching sight of a treble-score: a full, rich red beard sailing majestically down Lich Street. Their joint shout had caused heads to turn in time to witness the spectacle of two immensely distinguished men leaning helplessly against a wall by St Michael's, tears streaming down their cheeks. 'Japey in excelsis,' Edward had commented on a postcard to his friend the next day. '*Japissimo*. As of yore. Wot think'ee?'

The conspiracy he and Dr Ashe now hatched was trivial enough: merely to prolong the misunderstanding as far as possible. He undertook to play up while the doctor promised to listen with due gravity to any more of Steward Pyce's alarmed solicitations of professional advice. It was a measure of each man's peculiar desperation that neither thought the enterprise tinged with extremity. Later when recounting the whole thing to Molly on deck Edward was astonished by the account he heard himself giving. That a ship's doctor should admit within minutes to a celebrated passenger that he despised his job and had ruined his life was bizarre in itself; it was stranger still that at the time and under the influence of the man's curious force Edward, instead of going to the Captain and remonstrating, had stayed to connive at a prank.

Molly was troubled but said nothing, only laughed uneasily into the wind as it flashed invisibly by. She was by now beginning to feel like one of the few people aboard who knew where they were going, what they were doing, why. She alone was not to be swept up into the common ennui, the dancing to all hours, the shrieks of the young, the elderly moping and jesting. Knowing she was not herself even slightly eccentric she was equally certain Edward wasn't either. On the other hand the doctor had from the beginning struck her as quite mad. She had come upon him on the second day out being lurched as she herself was from side to side in a corridor, preceded by his red-moustached orderly. As one of the few passengers on their feet she had given him a sympathetic smile, greeting him with the observation that he and his orderly must already be tired.

'Indeed I am,' Dr Ashe replied, bracing himself against the mahogany handrail and letting his assistant go on out of earshot. 'Of my dratted orderly. He hasn't a clue. Frankly the man couldn't give an enema to a brown-hatter. What?'

Five years had suddenly rolled back on themselves: she at once recognised the crude terminology, the manner of its delivery, something in the way the men held themselves. 'He's military,' Molly thought. 'They both are. He's an Army doctor.' As in Edward's case the episode was so completely inappropriate, not least in its ferocity, that it was only later she had understood by how much it exceeded all bounds.

Since leaving Madeira she had spent much of each morning studying Portuguese, at first on deck but then in her cabin. It had not taken her long to discover that up in the sunshine the claims on her attention were too many and too strong. Quite apart from the hypnotic view of shifting water which drew her eyes from the page as effectively as though she were being stared at, the nature of a foreign vocabulary was such as to make one progress slowly. Perhaps a minute to read half a dozen new words and then five minutes' repeating them to the horizon which, when one next looked at one's watch, turned out to be half an hour's daydreaming with not a single word memorised. In any case a single young woman sitting by herself in a deck chair with a book on her lap from which her attention was constantly straying acted like a lure to the drones who buzzed about the deck in blazers and white flannels. These tried a variety of approaches whose ingenuity would often have been entertaining had she wished to be entertained. A few had taken the trouble to discover her name;

of those only one in five resisted making a pun or some reference to it. One young man, very short and sprite-like and undeniably good-looking had simply bounced up and said 'I think I should tell you, Miss, that I'm a roaring cad,' and bounced away again. An hour later he barged into her as she was coming down the stairs and he was going up. 'See what I mean?' he said and whizzed on up.

Accordingly she held herself to a set routine of three hours' study in her cabin after breakfast, like one facing an imminent examination. This was no hardship: she was accustomed to a disciplined life and besides, she had been preparing for this trip ever since arriving back in Liverpool from her previous one. Not that she had spent the year systematically learning Portuguese. She had taken a job as a nanny to supplement what savings she still had and the children and their family had exhausted her to the point where her only thought on most nights was to crawl into bed. Her days off had been spent shopping in the local town and – in one or two rare instances – painting in the grounds of her employers' Sussex mansion.

But if she had not acquired much book-learning she had been preparing herself mentally for the exile she was pleasurably storing up for herself. She had seen the Amazon and was as one who has glimpsed the Grail. There was indeed a purposefulness about her throughout that year reminiscent of someone about to set out on a crusade. She put her affairs in order; she wrote an unfaltering letter to Hugh Ogden telling him that her mind was made up; she broke the news to her parents. Her mother wept, her father was angry, her elder brother told her she was one of nature's spinsters and a daubing spinster at that. She had herself wept, but in the empty Ladies Only compartment of the train taking her back to Sussex, angry for this little display of drama she was suddenly too weary to prevent, knowing as she cried that generally speaking people weep only when they can be seen but that of course this did not preclude their being their own audience. Not *one* of them, she thought miserably to herself, not *one* of them said a word of encouragement. Not one of them even cared to know why I'm doing it. Still less did it cross anybody's mind that it might actually be rather an interesting thing to go and paint a famous and distant forest.

And at that moment, somewhere in the neighbourhood of Haywards Heath, she perceived her whole history in a flash as one continuous chain of other people's objections. From preferring science to the violin at school, through nursing training and her demand to be sent to France, to her increasing determination to paint and travel: all this had been in the teeth of every possible discouragement including threats like her own brother's disguised as prediction. And once this clean perception had come to her it was amazingly followed by a swift happiness as at bursting out of a tunnel and finding a tranquil landscape spread out on either side. That was how things were, it no longer constituted a problem; she was on her own. She had emerged at Hassocks singing like the blackbirds in the elder sprays which overhung the platform, pleased to find the children had come to greet her in the pony and trap.

In the end she and her two charges had become quite attached to one another and when her departure day came she was sorry to be leaving, while knowing that as soon as the carriage door closed on her she would not be at all sorry to have left. Suddenly the imminence of her great trip had made her afraid and for an instant she was like someone hesitating to leave a warm bed in a freezing dawn. But in the event it was an easy transition and she had sat on the station forecourt with twenty minutes to spare drawing a funny picture in each of the children's autograph books. For Alastair she drew 'Pony and Trap', which showed a puzzled-looking horse sniffing a set mousetrap complete with a piece of cheese. ('But does it go off and catch his nose?' demanded the child. 'Wait and see,' she had told him. 'One day you might open your book and find it has'.) For Hetty, who climbed anything she could, Molly drew 'Horse and Rider': a caricature of Hetty herself, pigtails flying, mounted on the clothes horse which often stood by the nursery fender. 'If I keep looking,' said Hetty, 'do I fall off?' 'Probably not,' said Molly, getting out with her hat box, 'but I expect you will if you keep climbing.' Once or twice while learning Portuguese aboard the *Hildebrand* she would glance up and think of the children and smile without missing them. They were pleasant little images while more puzzling concerns swiftly overlaid them. 'Why on earth do they need *two* verbs "To Be"?' she murmured to her cabin walls. 'Surely one is quite sufficient?'

Several cabins away the adventurous Fortescue could also now and then be found, similarly engaged with preparations for his aerial surveys. He worked largely on the eau-de-Nil carpet since the writing table provided by Booth's for their passengers was genteelly proportioned and his linen-backed maps overhung it like altar cloths. So he studied their exotic tapestries on the floor, on his knees, rulers and pencils and dividers strewn across mysterious terrains. More than ever as he drew his light lines and made notes in an exercise book he resembled a schoolboy, tongue emerging beneath the moustache as he frowned in concentration. Now and then he sat back on his heels and took up an ivory slide-rule which he then let fall with his hands to his lap. 'A hundred gallons, near as dammit,' he softly addressed the legs of the desk. 'Call it a hundred and twenty . . . safe side . . . we'll need two caches in that sector . . . one hour each way . . .'

The logistical problem was clear enough: how to fly a slow, methodical grid pattern over areas which lacked not only fuel but even clearings in which to land. Other than a dirt strip on the outskirts of Manaos itself the only reliable landing areas for a thousand miles were the rivers themselves. Accordingly he had brought pontoons for his aeroplanes but had not yet been able to test them to find out whether the machines would unstick with a full load of aviation spirit in the additional tanks he had fitted. Then, of course, a floating log or half-submerged alligator . . . The possibilities for disaster were without number. And every disaster, over and above its physical threat of injury or death, carried with it the sure penalty of bankruptcy. He sighed; but it was only the equivalent of the involuntary grunt a man makes when lifting a heavy weight. Neither resigned nor daunted Fortescue and his friend Johnny Proctor had lived the kind of lives in which such were familiar terms, to the extent that all forms of speculation could be subordinated to the proper making of plans. Altimeters were accurately set, a full kit of tools carried.

When not in his cabin he was often in the ship's library trying like Molly to learn Portuguese or browsing through the few books devoted to the area in the 'Geography and Exploration' section. *Secret Rites of the Amazon Tribes* soon provided him with an abundance of excellent reasons, in addition to those he already had, for not wishing to crash-land in the jungle. *An Economic and Regional Geography of South America*, on the other hand, told him nothing despite its title's sweeping omniscience. 'By far the greater part of the Amazonas region remains wholly unexplored by white man, and it is to be doubted whether the tribes known to inhabit certain riparian zones have any systematic knowledge of their region's topography, still less the desire or ability to assess that region's possible economic value.' The map of Amazonas included in this unhelpful chapter was even blanker than his large-scale flying maps which, for all their own areas of white, did at least have patches of local detail supplied piecemeal from the reports of other pilots, recent expeditions and the like.

Fortescue replaced the book and took down another entitled *Where Day Breaks Never*. This was an excitable little work purporting to be the account of an expedition which had started down the Madeira River and then wandered off along one of its tributaries, the Aripuana, more or less due south of Manaos. It was not clear what the members of this expedition had thought they were doing. They appeared to spend most of their time making endless trouble for themselves and anyone else they encountered, from capsizing the canoe containing their only medical supplies to skirmishing with Indians 'whose hostility was, however, not proof against our trusty Winchesters which soon knocked the fight out of them and left their ramshackle village more peaceful, no doubt, than at any time since its construction.' As he skimmed the pages he seriously wondered whether the whole account had been invented in a quiet house in Berkshire: it was too suspiciously a compendium of every explorer's tale, its sensationalism too studied. The only interesting thing he found in it was the identification of a remote range of mountains almost on the Bolivian border as those which Colonel Fawcett had photographed in 1908. It was this photograph Conan Doyle had seen and which had suggested to him his story *The Lost World*. Fortescue noted this chiefly as a coincidence; the unexpected recurrence of the topic of Conan Doyle and photographs so soon after their luncheon in Madeira was curious. There was nothing else to be learned from a book like that, however, so he opened his Portuguese grammar instead.

Edward also spent time in his cabin, either at his microscope or writing his Journal. Otherwise he roamed the ship, something of a lonely figure, a look on his face both inward and slightly expectant as if somebody he had known might come around the corner or straighten up from the rail next to him.

Once Captain Maddrell asked him whether he was making the journey out of interest or in order to visit someone. Edward had told him he was badly in need of inspiration, citing the forthcoming Empire Exhibition at Wembley for which he had at least to write a March and possibly more besides. The Captain put at his disposal a bare day cabin which he claimed he never used and which, unlike Edward's own, had outside it a small private section of deck and rail where he might escape social pressures whenever he wished. Edward accepted this offer gratefully and soon was spending daily hours in a deck-chair beneath the shade of the port wing of the bridge, staring out over the ocean with a manuscript notebook and propelling-pencil on his lap.

And there, as it often had, the sight and sound of water in motion began to produce its familiar effects. Great things had come to him from the voices of the Severn, the Teme, the Wye and many other English rivers. The Arno and the Tiber had added their note to *In the South*; the Rhine had spoken to him of his devotion to Schumann and the mainstream of the German classics. It did not occur to him to wonder whether this late journey to see the greatest river in the world contained a measure of longing, even of desperation; he simply lost himself in the dazzle of scud before his eyes. It raced along the base of the dove-grey iron wall but even a few yards out from the ship's side slowed and thinned into lattices and marblings which, effervescing themselves into nothing, briefly mantled the purple sea with whites and greens. It fled and fled; it fell behind and became wake; its ripples dissipated. The staring eyes saw nothing, but the impression of passage leaped vividly through them into the mind. He began to hear things in the motion. Even from the rumble of engines beneath the water-line rose suggestive pitches, voices, notes. His fingers tightened on the pencil. There was as yet no tune, but the lively space for one was being created.

How many times over the years, working late into the night in order to meet some rehearsal deadline or a scheduled first performance, had he not gone to bed and been unable to sleep for the insistence of these very spaces? There were often no tunes, only this clamorous framework into which marvellous music might be fitted: an immanence of rhythm, a sense of paragraphs, blocks of feeling and a glimpse of a shape two blank pages ahead unmistakably in his hand but as yet unreadable. And ever since he could remember, a flow of water could also create this ache and expectancy, this melancholy engagement with everything of him which mattered. Here were no human faces, no loved voices, no thoughts. Those could be allowed to intrude later, if need be, to domesticate or make poignant raw inspiration. Later on could come the title, the affectionate dedication or the quoted stanza by way of preface, all the scholarly jokes, concealed anagrams and word-play which put a literary gloss on abstract sounds. But at this earliest moment there was no contamination, only the pure and murmurous emptiness which encased itself and shone. And as an exhausted bell-jar in a sunny laboratory draws water into itself and begins to fill, so the old composer's hand at last and of its own accord began to write.

He sketched in short score, which is to say on two staves as if for piano. But the sounds he heard were not those of the piano, a workaday instrument of limited tonal possibilities which interested him scarcely at all. *Ob.* he jotted above the top line at one point, then *Hn.* Already at this moment of the first sketch he placed the hairpins of crescendos and diminuendos, the characteristic tenutos over notes he wanted stressed, the detailed dynamics which always were as much a part of what he heard as the notes themselves. On impulse he added a third stave above the other two halfway down the page and scrawled *Tenor* above it: there was suddenly the sound of a voice but he could not hear the words. The atmosphere in which it sang was quite clear to him, however. The voice fell upon an immense hush, a pristine emptiness in which light was steadily growing. Lost in this breathless dawn, yet central to it, was the suggestion of a figure – maybe raised on some sort of pillar – whose isolation both created the emptiness and was created by it. It was a *desert* landscape which filled the aural horizon. The unsleeping figure was not greeting the dawn: his tingling declamation seemed concerned with something else. But what? Unexpectedly, somewhere beneath his tower's base, a silver propelling-pencil wrote a short motif and added *Solo Tpt.*

Edward sat back, gradually understanding what it was he had heard. That trumpet motif seemed familiar . . . Of course! The Shofar call from *The Apostles* which he had once thought of carrying over to the planned oratorio *The Last Judgement.* He read through again what he had just written, hearing the full orchestral sound rise from the grey pencil-marks, the tenor soloist soaring above. The line of the voice had something in it akin to Mary's great aria

'The Sun Goeth Down' in *The Kingdom*, but in place of that scena's ravishment was a strange chill. Empty pianissimo harp chords, widely spaced and plucked all at once rather than spread as arpeggios, were placed against oboes above and *muted* trombones below. Somewhere in that space vibrated a desolation he had never quite written before.

'I say,' he murmured, shivering as if something malign had risen from the scud alongside and briefly blocked the sun. 'I wonder what *that* is? I say . . .' He recognised at once that it was authentic. Nobody knew better than he the devices which came to him most readily – and which he was most powerless to stop – when inspiration had thinned or dried up altogether. He had not needed the damned critics to remind him of such things, like that puppy in the *Pall Mall Gazette* who had written 'It is as difficult for Elgar to leave a sequence as it is for a bicycle to leave the tram lines.' That had stung. But this – he looked again at the sketch on his knees – had not a sequence in it, not a hint of a *nobilmente* tune. What it did have was the unmistakable Elgarian note. Where it had come from all of a sudden he had no idea – from the water itself, maybe – but it had done so without his having to turn to the dog-eared and much-thumbed sketch-books of his youth. That in itself was heartening. It was obviously no good for this Wembley march nonsense, but while it lasted it was a definite resurgence of a once-familiar thing.

Years ago he had written to his Malvern architect friend Troyte Griffith that something 'took him back to boyhood's daze'. In the letter the 'daze' had been a mere homonym, a pun, a fanciful mis-spelling such as the Victorians loved and which had peppered the letters of men like Edward Lear: familiar words in fantastic guise (such as that painter's succulent Mediterranean phyggs). But in its unconscious garb the daze of boyhood had been real enough. It had come to him as he lay on his stomach on a drifting punt, fingers trailing sunlit water, dreaming open-eyed as his directionless craft nudged the hoof-pocked shallows beneath the bank and slowly swung its other end out into the stream, setting him off again now facing the other way. Backwards or forwards, who knew? It was the tiniest details which stole into the mind and stayed: the brilliant green flecks of duckweed now captured and towed along in the still inch of water next to the wooden hull, half-adhering to the amber varnish . . . The daze of wind on top of the Malvern hills when the clouds paced their own shadows across the counties whose quilt of fields retained its pattern of mediaeval shapes. The fleeting bruises of shade across that gentle landscape were a daze: the high melancholy of what cannot be grasped or ever stopped. The sense of height was a daze: the exalted roaring of the sky poured through him and filled him . . . Walking home through lanes little more than sunken paths between towering creamy plates of umbelliferae, drowsy with pollen and bees. Dazed with the feeling of incommensurable things and with the prospects of success which must surely attend anyone pierced by such thrills. And finally the daze of sound in the organ loft as his inadequate fingers tried to re-create what he had heard. River, hill and lane: they ran like water through his mind and left behind on scattered sheets of manuscript crooked rivulets of notes which glittered like mud-flats draining in the sun. Why were there no great English composers, at least not since Purcell? Was the German countryside really so much better? For surely it could only be that which determined the quality of a nation's music. Very well then; he would see.

But the overweening self quickly forgets its nation. The creative urge does not march beneath a flag although it may from time to time astutely invoke its shade. Edward's England became not quite anybody else's. Now and then people thought they recognised themselves and their landscape in it as crowds might glimpse their own reflections, faithfully distorted, in the polished paintwork of a State coach as it passed or in the glassy lacquer of a monarch's hearse. The cheers sounded; the handkerchiefs fluttered and fell; then almost immediately there was nothing to see but a little dust in the air and nothing to think but that something of moment had passed them by, something which left their heads ringing and a slight desire to weep. It was not England which had passed in its disguise but Edward, whose dreams were of his countryside and not of their country.

And he had written his landscape down as it had come to him and where he had found it. But bit by bit what seemed a rich spaciousness had begun to reveal aspects of monotony. Surely his entire imagined world could not be voiced by that single note of elegiac lyricism? No: there was plenty of briskness of a healthy outdoor sort on which he set, perhaps, an exaggerated value as if grateful for a plausible defence against accusations of unseemly emotionalism. But over the years, with that self-assessment which thorough artists often carry out whose brutality far outstrips any critic's candour, the thought had come in secret: My emotional range is limited. Impossible to confide in Alice. Her job as she saw it from the beginning had been to take a stern line with self-doubt. For her, success was a matter of course and greatness not marginally less so. A genius could walk undeferentially with the shades of Wagner and Brahms. Edward had reviewed in his head the voluminous works of Wagner and Brahms and found a reassuring uniformity of tone in all of them.

But something had begun to change for him a year or two before the war – from the moment, in fact, that Alice had deemed it time to make a second, victorious assault on the capital and they had bought 'Kelston' in Hampstead (which he had promptly re-named Severn House). The telephone rang; bills came; people came; the war came. On the increasingly rare occasions he managed to obtain access to his private landscape he found it parched: it supplied little and most of that he had seen before. A modern art-form provided him with a horrid image. On one of his earliest visits to the cinema he watched a sequence which included two funny men in a compartment of an American train. It was only after a minute he noticed with a jump that the scenery beyond the carriage window was recurring. He was at first amused by the adroit trick; then he was overtaken by an oppressive despair which confounded him completely and spoiled the rest of the film. The image of an endless strip of backcloth being rolled round and round by men in shirt-sleeves standing on packing-cases behind it returned to him as many times.

He was not a man to bear desertion without having to announce loudly how glad he was at last to be free. Of course there was no private landscape. The music-makers and the dreamers of dreams could finally wake up to the poisonous Eden in which they had so foolishly laboured and to the whore Music who had led them so long by the nose. This Doll Tearsheet of a muse, who capered to fashion and the pit, hoisted her skirts so her audiences drank odours and howled for more – more jigs and waltzes and quadrilles and salon tunes and now apparently for something called the Charleston. Well, he wanted no part of it, washed his hands of it with the air of a man who compulsively rinses them after merely glimpsing something unclean on the floor . . .

This wretched man, this man of exquisite sensibility

masquerading as fit company for bloodstock fanciers: how could there not now come to him the troubling shade of his dead wife? Had she not for thirty-one years sedulously urged her beloved Edu to cavort with the whore? Had she not firmly detached his fingers from test-tubes, kite-strings, handlebars, steering-wheels, golf-clubs in order to place them once more around his pen? Worse, had Alice not herself faithlessly slipped away, deserting him when he was stranded well past the zenith of popular acclaim and in a world far beyond any he loved or recognised? Precious, dishevelling treason! No wonder he could not have said how he viewed the rusting gate which had finally slammed on his lost domain. Was it a glare or a gaze of longing he sent into that land which lay beyond the barricades, whose trees he could still glimpse with between them the wistful glitter of river? And if it was longing after all, how much more easily placated was the world from which he gazed if he changed that longing into disgust!

Yet now aboard the *Hildebrand*, really without trying very hard, a hand that was his had sketched a page or two of its own volition. It was a hand which had written virtually nothing since it put the last notes to the Cello concerto in 1919, nine months before Alice's death. Yet somewhere in mid-Atlantic amid the hypnotic dazzle of his passage something old had stirred and the hand, itself full of an old cunning, had responded.

The years had depressed him too firmly to allow anything as crudely doomed as excitement but he did find himself looking forward to luncheon. He screwed back his pencil and glanced at his watch. It was ten past three. For a moment he was put out but the feeling was swiftly replaced by one of pleasure. The unnoticed passage of time was authenticating; it reminded him of many years ago.

VI

Began a scribble (?what?) this morning. Perhaps after all the 'spark of that which has consumed me' did leave something, a final bleak ember. V. spare but good & potentially big. Not the opera, tho'. Perh. pt. 3 of trilogy. I know I long since rejected him but Judas does still haunt me now & then. There's something in that tragic & maligned figure which makes him full of heart. I believe I really gave up The Last Judgement because the idea bored the living daylights out of me. But poor Judas – I still think Archbp.

Whately got him right. Surely Judas had no idea that he might actually betray Jesus by what he did because he was convinced of his Lord's miraculous power. He was certain that Jesus wd. use this power to prevent his own arrest & arraignment, thereby convincing both the Jews & Romans that he was truly King & not of this earth. This makes him devastatingly <u>human</u>, a proper tragic figure instead of the accepted symbol of cynical greed & betrayal. His remorse & suicide wd. be a real musical challenge – a scene of immense potential power – as he realised that the awfulness of what he had done was due to a failure of <u>thought</u> & not of <u>heart</u>. He had presumed to anticipate the Son of Man, but the ways of Heaven were disastrously not his. There were to be no magic tricks or chicanery to bring about the Kingdom . . . In any case at this moment it's enough for me to be thinking of a few cramped notes again even if they don't lead anywhere & even if they did make me miss lunch. I'm damn well not going to miss dinner. As I write this sentence I'm dressed & waiting for the First Trump.

So of course he sat in vain the following morning on his borrowed patch of deck, notebook and pencil to hand. The same blinding scud raced past; the same harmonics from the engines hummed in every bolt and plate of the *Hildebrand*, quivered up through his thin leather soles. But today the constant rush of water spoke of impatience, of a hurry to arrive, while the subliminal tones of machinery sang of a cheerless age carrying him off beyond anywhere he wanted to be. Neither did reading his sketch help re-create the mood which had conceived it. It was bleak, certainly; but was it really anything he hadn't already said years ago in one form or another? Parts of the biography of a character who kept on cropping up disguised variously as a man with friends to depict, a dying ancient, a soul on a passionate pilgrimage, a dreamer of dreams. A mysterious figure on a pillar would slip easily enough into that canon. It was true that a tone of stark nihilism would be new if it remained untempered by melancholy, but it was not clear to him how he could sustain that for very long. He was a man to whose eyes the tears sprang naturally; nobody that placable and moody could keep up indefinitely an unblinking desolation. Sooner or later a heart would have to beat. And besides, if nihilism and desolation were to be his new bailiwick there was no ignoring how the battlefields of Europe, still treeless and littered with shards of bone, had usurped that space with a directness far more terrible than anything he could hope to achieve.

Meanwhile the unspeaking sea rushed away sternwards. What solace was imaginable for this lack of purpose? The frisky heart still beat, the soul had died. Lose yourself, he said silently as he stood up and tucked away his propelling-pencil. Theatres, dogs, clubs, motor-tours round old haunts, races. There's plenty to do: lose yourself. Look at these blank horizons concealing even blanker continents. Are you not already lost?

But when he thought nobody was looking he laid an ear to the after-mast and heard the voice of the wind exactly as it sounded in the telegraph poles in the lanes around Kempsey. Their voice was constant, neither rising nor falling with the gusts which shook the grasses at their foot, coming from close at hand and infinitely far away. The mast, too, ignored the buffets of tropic air the bows and bridge threw over their shoulders. It spoke instead in the long paragraphs of trade-winds as if the ship itself were tuned to catch the underlying music of this sphere. On the way back to his cabin he thought of another story which had caught his fancy in that buddhist-book Frank had sent him. Well – not really a story at all, more a snippet of dialogue between the inevitable monk and someone called Unmon. It went as follows:

Monk: What happens when the leaves are falling, and the trees are bare?
Unmon: The golden wind, revealed.

Tommy-rot, of course. Yet in the next-to-nothing this exchange contained there was maybe enough to catch at the mind as it slithered through, and just for that instant one thought one saw the wind . . . Similarly with masts and telegraph poles, he mused as he let himself into his cabin: for a moment one had the impression of a *something*, the least and most banal of whose manifestations was mere blowing.

He was surprised to find Steward Pyce standing by the table in the act of polishing the silver hip-flask with a yellow duster.

'Please excuse me, Sir Edward,' he said, setting down the flask and pocketing the rag. 'I've just obtained your sample for you and finding you were out I took the liberty of leaving it.'

'Oh. Yes, I see. Thank you, Pyce. Where's it from this time?'

'The bows, sir. As requested.'

It only then caught Edward's eye that he had left his microscope out of its case on the writing table where he had been using it for an hour after breakfast. He had not even slipped its cover over it. Well, he thought, *that* cat's out of the bag.

'I didn't know you were a man of science as well, Sir Edward. Pardon my saying.'

'May I not be if I wish?'

'Of course, sir. I only meant, well, a composer of music's a bit different from, well . . .'

'Do you know of the Russian composer Borodin?'

'No, Sir Edward, can't say as I do.'

'He's an excellent composer who earns his living as a chemist. I believe he's Professor of Chemistry at St Petersburg and has text-books to his name which are standard reference works. Just because one's a composer it doesn't mean one has to be a dunce at everything else. Nor, for that matter, does it mean that when one's not actually composing music one has nothing else to do and no other life.'

The Steward looked astutely at the microscope as though he had only just noticed it. 'In a manner of speaking, sir, you work with two kinds of instruments, then?'

'Rather wittily put, Pyce. Good afternoon.'

('Bleeding *microscopes*,' the Steward said later to Hempson in the Linen Store, 'who'd ever've thought it?'

'Might easily've been trombones with this lot,' said Hempson darkly.

'True enough. But what does a composer on holiday want with a microscope? Up the Amazon? I ask you. And looking at ruddy sea-water. Sometimes I reckon you and me're the only sane ones aboard this ship, Hemp. That new doctor now, Ashe . . . To think I tried to tip him the wink about one of my own passengers. Crikey!')

In token of the latitude sunset that evening was of a tropical unrestraint. Alone on refulgent tinfoil RMS *Hildebrand*, the Brin-dled Marsh, the minor moth, headed for several minutes directly at the settling orange ball as though to be drawn down over the horizon by its dazzle. The ship's insect passage amid splendours of immensity presented itself as though to an ascending eye which, taking in more and more of the wrinkled metal across which it crawled, lost belief in the very existence of the microscopic beings it contained.

Yet they were there, and busy. Some steered on the bridge, others laboured deep below in a timeless hot clamour uncaring of setting or rising suns. Some in spotless jackets were arranging wine-glasses upside down on white linen, some were playing musical instruments quietly for people drinking cocktails on the after-deck. Many were dressing for dinner: the outward-bound travellers wishing their lightweight suits did not smell quite so pungently of camphor, the tourists who would be returning self-conscious of the obvious newness of their clothes. Several people were kissing; two waiters were making love in a locked pantry. An aviator past his first youth was talking to a lady painter just quitting hers. An English composer was in animated conversation about a stables in Newmarket with two red-nosed men, one of whom wore the tiny ribbon of a decoration in his lapel. Two middle-aged ladies were finishing a rubber of whist: they had been playing since three o'clock that afternoon. Their male partners had initially done all the laughing and exclaiming while the ladies had throughout played as if against one another alone, with steely affection.

As it inched its way across the globe this insect – which was due to cross the Equator the next day – shed a trail of sound which streamed behind it and thinned out over its wake. Engines and laughter and the clatter of crockery; exclamations and discreet gasps; saxophones and the hum of a hundred conversations. And in a small room near the Library, the modulations of a lady giving an audience of six her recollections of missionary work in Peru. These sounds leaked from porthole and hatchway, boomed from ventilation ducts, filtered through jalousies and blew off the decks like dust, swirling away past the Red Ensign on the stern and carrying with them the crack of that flag's material. A small fraction of this audible smoke contained the Captain's observation to one of his officers on the bridge: 'Aye, they're a restless lot this trip. Not the usual "out-and-backers", Ned,' referring presumably to the passengers at his own table, only one of whom was booked to return. 'That Elgar, now. Seems a bit down. Surprised he didn't fix himself up with a companion before he came, famous chappie like that.'

'A bit of stuff, you mean?'

'Inelegantly put, Ned, but yes. A floozy.'

'Well, he still can, can't he? There're enough on board.' An even tinier fraction of noise was contributed by the empty madeira bottle which rolled from under Dr Ashe's arm off the edge of his desk and broke on the rim of a stout metal wastepaper bin as his orderly tried to raise him and get him to his bunk.

And before long the sun had outrun the little moth and left it still crawling across a benighted ocean. But soon enough it put on lights and transformed itself into a glow-worm which twinkled in the middle of nowhere, for as long as nowhere took to pass, leaving behind it in addition to its fume of sound several dozen empty magnums of champagne variously bobbing and sinking amid a scatter of unravelling cigar butts. For an era of horror and attrition was behind and an age of whoopee had dawned. (How the Melodeers twiddled and thumped!) Much later that night the aviator told the lady painter, who was leaning against a davit, that the brilliant white star she was looking at was not Sirius at all but – since it was in Orion – Betelgeuse. The lady painter replied that she was glad to hear it since she happened to know a poem about Betelgeuse, part of which went (and she spoke it softly in the voice which is used for decks of ships at night in the middle of nowhere):

> On Betelgeuse
> the gold leaves hang in golden aisles
> for twice a hundred million miles
> and twice a hundred million years
> they golden hang, and nothing stirs
> on Betelgeuse.

And the aviator was canny enough to guess that whatever else it was about it was not Betelgeuse. So he refrained from pointing out that Betelgeuse was actually a star believed to be three times hotter than our own sun, an inferno in which were assuredly no leaves, golden or otherwise. Instead he leaned towards the davit and slipped his arm around her waist, saying nothing at all but gently touching his moustache (once, twice) with the other hand.

Whatever eye it could have been, seeing the little *Hildebrand* from far enough away to observe it only as a glowing speck whose motion amid all that nothingness was barely apparent, it might have reflected on the oddness of that ship's monthly passing – now one way and now the other, year after year. Who besides labourers and fortune-hunters (which two categories might well include office-boys and businessmen) was it ferrying between Britain and Brazil? Who were these chatterers with so many changes of clothes who danced and played and drank their way across the ocean and back again, leaving bottles in their wake? For every day portholes opened and glass rained into the sea: wine, gin, brilliantine and ink; Shippam's paste and Bovril; chlorodyne and scent. Most contained dregs and air. Now and then one with a tight stopper held a safely untraceable obscene message or mock cry for help. For that matter what were the circumstances in which a pair of ladies' shoes, a clarinet and a hundredweight of Devon butter plopped into the swirling cavitations of the twin bronze screws and vanished for ever? What were these loungers in deck-chairs, these players of deck-quoits and shuffleboard, these readers and flirters thinking to do by coming all this way in order to steam between walls of jungle into the centre of a continent about whose very position on the globe many were quite unsure? 'Get away from it all,' was the stock answer people generally give who habitually take as much as they can of it with them. 'A change of scenery,' a lost and demoralised old composer had explained to his daughter when she asked what he hoped to find: the change of scenery commonly believed to procure a change of heart, regeneration.

The shipboard ritual staged at the moment of crossing the Equator and repeated each voyage was both comprehensible and absurd to Edward when he watched it for a short while next morning. It was the first time he himself had ever crossed the Equator, come to that, but he hardly expected to feel very different and neither did he. The freakish pantomime involved Captain Maddrell receiving aboard King Neptune and his Oceanic Court and several passengers – presumably volunteers – were given haircuts and ducked, thereby becoming initiated into something called The Ancient Order of Shellbacks.

Half of Edward knew what was happening and inwardly applauded this evidence of reassuring British eccentricity. The other half pretended disdainfully not to know, forgetting his own extended fancy-dress role as the pirate Nanty Ewart which he had once played with a friend's three sons. This fantasy had been sustained for some time and had involved skirmishing with wooden swords in the shrubbery wearing a piratical head-scarf and with curtain-rings in his ears, as well as writing letters to his 'crew' away at school in pastiche seventeenth-century English. 'All harmless enough,' several onlookers said as they watched the *Hildebrand*'s Purser in spirit-gummed beard, tattered green robes and a trident. 'What jolly fun.' But probably none of them were quite sure why they thought so nor, if dressing up were such a sterling part of the national character, exactly what necessary act was being performed. Afterwards everybody trooped down to luncheon in high communal spirits like participants in a sport whose unwritten rules are never infringed and which no foreigner will ever hope to understand.

Tomorrow evening Pará. Next day the Amazon. Soon Kate and Dora and several other passengers would step down the gangway onto the lip of a continent and be swallowed up whole. Edward noted the change of atmosphere in the ship as soon as the Equator had been dealt with. Something was ending, something else about to begin. He spent the afternoon, notebook on lap, staring towards the invisible mass of land which on a despairing rainy day he had on impulse made his temporary destination. Why not? he asked the equable ocean across whose surface flying fish skittered from the onrush of the *Hildebrand*'s hull. Why not keep inventing destinations? Spend whole years in deck chairs voyaging across one ocean or another to places which have no particular existence beyond their names and varying skylines? The time would fill itself, the clock cease to matter and be replaced by an arcane system of ship's bells. There would be good eating and drinking and an endless succession of convivial strangers, none of whom – God willing – would know anything about music. There would be diverting things to do in ports of call: weird conveyances (had he not just tobogganed down a mountain four hundred miles off the coast of Africa?), peculiar foods, extravagant customs . . .

And suddenly he realised how horrid the entire notion was; that he didn't in the least want any of those things, that he wished at this very minute more than anything else to be walking the lanes of Worcestershire or sitting beside the Severn or the Teme. Never mind that it was late November and probably wet and cold. He saw a thousand pictures of his rivers in all weathers and none was unfriendly, none without its pleasurable echo. Even the saddest and most sodden afternoon had its charm, the hat left off to spite the doctor's orders, hair plastered with rain, coat heavy, dog soaked but everything rinsed through by whatever it was in immemorial weather which dissolved foolishness and brought one always to the essential things of a life. The thoughts, the continuities and all that made a clutch of years look whole, even the smoke from a cottager's chimney or the wraith of a smouldering bonfire on the other side of a hedge (since wood-smoke was the incense of nostalgia): such things lay as solid as a range of hills behind mist. This was known terrain and had been walked and walked and yet could still surprise with an aspect never glimpsed before, then in sunlight, now in rain. What for this running to the ends of the earth? What had the ends of the earth ever done for him? They were no *more* mysterious than the planet's ghost whose sad perpetual strain could be heard by laying an ear to the splintery wood of a telegraph pole. Certainly they could be no less known than the patterns of starlings which arranged themselves across wintry skies over fields and spinneys: boiling clouds of ex-reptiles descending on and then deserting no particular tree, taking with them their single garbled tune.

More than this, the spinneys and the lanes and the cottages had about them faces and incidents and glimpses of incidents. Somebody's hands in bright sun twirling as they wound in a kite-string; a muddy hem of skirts ascending before the eyes as someone was handed up into a carriage; a dog rolling down the bank into the River Wye. The echoes of mouths now stuffed with soil; the echo of the strange four-note whistle he had invented to announce at the gate his arrival home and which had found its way into *Enigma*; the echoes of an existence. What did the blank and dazzled equatorial ocean know of such sounds? Across which raw continent did another Severn flow? In desperation a life might be abandoned, jettisoned over the rail of a ship as unwanted on the remaining voyage; but it could scarcely be sought elsewhere, still less transplanted. He recalled a visit he and Alice had made to Capri early in 1907 during which they had visited Axel Munthe whose English neighbour had just spent twenty years of his life trying to create a Home Counties garden around his white and shuttered villa. They had sat one afternoon in mild sunshine amid lavender bushes which were the wrong species, being a little too tough and spiky rather than soft and blousy, looking across lawns which ended in blue space. The greenhouse was subtly the wrong shape, the roof being a fraction too steeply pitched. The rockery and sundial were perfect. Since everybody knew they were sitting in Capri there had seemed little point to this painstaking fake but their host glowed. 'All the pleasures of an English garden without the awful weather,' he said. ('All the pleasures of the English vice without the law,' Edward remarked later, having been introduced to a 'gardener's boy' who was as much an actor as the garden was a set.)

The hand holding the propelling-pencil made a few meaningless marks in the margin of the notebook while the eyes remained fixed on the sea. What *had* it been for? Again and again this stupid question. On his side there had been the power of his intentions. For several years such clarity of vision, such unerring setting down that it was his proud and very nearly truthful boast that he never needed to alter a note when he first heard an orchestra play what he had written. And on the other side had come immense acclaim, and not by any means principally from England. It was the Germans who had first recognised him: men like Hans Richter and Richard Strauss who first used the unqualified word 'genius'. At long last Henry Purcell had found a successor; England's musical renaissance had arrived . . .

For some years the accolades had grown, from people whistling in the street to the King knighting him and going to the Races with him. Nor had it taken long, either. In 1899, the year of the first unequivocal masterpiece, *Enigma*, ten of his compositions were played at Queen Victoria's command in the private chapel at Windsor. Within five years he was Sir Edward Elgar, within thirteen he had completed practically all his important works. In that brief span he had walked with kings and had been cheered by crowds, but more to the point had been praised and befriended by fellow-artists and composers from all over the world. He was discreetly mobbed and indiscreetly swooned over. Distinguished people he had never met wrote him expressions of their deepest gratitude. He was everywhere made much of. The only thing he was not given much of was money; but between them his closest friends patched and hired him through a succession of suits marking his honours, and Alice moved him through a series of ever grander houses. This went on until even the lack of money had seemed unimportant beside the lack of silence.

But what nature of a triumph had it been which led to this: an ageing man in a deck chair four thousand miles from home in a desolate waste of sea-water, almost-empty notebook on his knees, a single rented berth down below? Baffling that it all could have drained away and left such nothingness. The glory had been real, the love and affection in his life quite genuine. What he had written he had written whether they played it or not and whether those who had once thought it worthy to stand beside Beethoven had given way to those who now cried 'Pompenstance!' and derided what they called Edwardianism.

But the ones who thus dismissed his music, was not their injustice exceeded only by their ignorance? For his marches had merely been the bread-and-butter music of their day, and their day was not even his own. Strange indeed how the first dozen years of the century were now almost wilfully mis-remembered. Even those who should recall them perfectly well looked back as to a lost antediluvian land of innocence and plenty. Another of the war's abominable mischiefs. Not only had it ruined the world after it but it had falsified the one before.

Very slowly his hand wrote the figures '44' in the margin of the notebook. 'I was forty-four when the Queen died,' he told the ocean inaudibly. 'I'm *not* an Edwardian.' And because he had worked as he did there was a sense in which he had already written his life's work before the century ever turned. The ideas had come in their profusion in boyhood, in the Seventies and Eighties and Nineties, filling notebook after notebook with jottings, fragments and themes. It was only when he turned them into finished works that the praise had come, but by then the original inspirations had often been in his mind for twenty years. He was a Victorian in heart, spirit, essence.

The passion of this internal monologue must have remained undimmed for some hours. At dinner, in response to an unwitting 'Ah, those were the days, eh?' from Captain Maddrell apropos the prewar popularity of Booth's South America run, Edward replied with a churlish 'Oh no they weren't.'

'I only meant, Sir Edward . . .'

'In no sense were they "the days". I sometimes think people must be suffering from collective amnesia, or whatever it is these alienists call it. Does nobody here remember that feeling of being on a butter-slide?' He glared belligerently around the table.

'Well, politics were sometimes a little unsettled,' ventured Kate, 'but then aren't they always?'

Edward fixed her as he listed the unsettlements and their

gravity: Tariff Reform, the rise of Union power and Socialism, the demands of women for emancipation and the Vote, the decline of Britain as a manufacturing country and – as if those weren't enough – Home Rule in Ireland. 'Were we really supposed to let a band of Fenian yahoos simply annex a part of Great Britain? In 1914, at any rate, it was a monstrous piece of treason. And though as a matter of principle I think artists and musicians ought to hold themselves aloof from being used in political affairs I did indeed join with Kipling and Lord Roberts in signing the British Covenant to support Carson in Ulster. But it wasn't a pleasure by any means, for all that a lot of powerful people told us it was our duty to sign and set an example. In any case if that's your idea of a golden era in the nation's history you may well have considered the War a minor skirmish when it came.'

Hoping perhaps to divert attention from the dubious taste of this remark while trying to pacify his distinguished guest the Captain mildly asked 'Might you explain to us, sir, your theory of the decline of Britain as a manufacturer? I was under the impression that as a trading nation we were second to none. At least, at that time.'

'Unfortunately we were second to several even by the time the old Queen died. It's just something the British go on refusing to believe with their normal ostrich-like behaviour, but it's nevertheless true.' And he maintained at some length that the real turning-point in the country's fortunes – the moment when decline had inexorably set in – was when those nations on whom Britain had stolen a march with her industrial revolution caught up and passed her. Somewhere around the 1870s, he guessed, when the German steel industry began producing more steel or foreign exporters started to eat into Britain's dominance and capture her erstwhile markets.

Mulling it over afterwards in his cabin, where he had retreated, he thought how there had probably been an actual instant – a sunny morning in May, perhaps, while he was demonstrating the fingering of a violin passage to some schoolgirl in the music-room of The Mount in Great Malvern – when a contract was signed in Essen or Brussels or even New York which, all unbeknownst, had toppled Britain over into descent. Of course there was a long ironic lag. Imperceptible at first beneath the global pageantry of Empire, the slide gathered speed as the century expired. But those with feeling had already felt it: the sensation of something drawing to a close, the hollowness of hymns, the hubris of 'never, never, never' bawled out as if at a party in full swing but held in one of those new-fangled lifts going down, down, down. It was intuited well before Kipling wrote 'Recessional' so that the general celebrations in 1900, pivoting as they did around Victoria's near-mystical survival, were nonetheless shot through with national unease.

And as with a nation so with an individual, he thought. When public acclaim finally grew and gave an artist his due he might already have passed – one sunny morning in May – some quiet internal zenith, a calamitous instant which went unrecognised amid the din of recognition. Maybe he himself had intuited it, too, with that stabbing 'They don't want any more' as the OM was conferred, as purple descended, as audiences rose. That was the reality of popular esteem, of course. By its very nature it was always premature or too late. There was finally not the slightest connection between the public's trumpetings and the private soul, nor could there ever be.

Thirty feet away and a deck lower Dora Bellamy and Kate Hammond were having one of several celebratory rounds of drinks to mark the last night of their voyage. They shared them with certain acquaintances, one of whom was wondering what life at the Captain's table was like with so famous a man as Elgar among the company. Kate was still smarting.

'I can tell you – it's like dining with a time-bomb,' she said. 'It's up to you to guess when it's due to go off.'

'He *is* a genius,' said her friend emolliently.

'A bloody rude one.'

'You have wide experience of the type, of course,' said Dora. 'But as far as I'm concerned he's a genius and that's that. It's funny – you know I mentioned I'd sung at the first performance of *The Apostles*?'

'You did let it drop once. Or twice.'

'Well,' continued Dora unperturbed, 'we saw him a bit during the last rehearsals and then at the actual performance, of course, but we none of us got any closer to him than between this table and . . .' she looked around the confines of steel bulkheads disguised as fumed oak panelling '. . . golly, I should imagine the bridge. You know how big those concert halls are and the chorus was stuck up on tiers on either side of the organ console and beneath us was the entire orchestra and then Sir Edward on a little podium with a brass handrail. I mean to say, *miles* away. But what's funny about it is that he hasn't changed at all even though it's twenty years ago. Of course he looks older – grey hair and a bit stouter and so on – but as soon as we all sat down to dinner our first evening aboard I recognised him.'

'Astonishing,' said Kate. 'The man's probably never been photographed more than twenty thousand times and even I, who am tone deaf and wouldn't greatly mind if I never heard another note of music, even *I* had heard of Sir Edward Elgar VC, KCVO and Bar, Master of the King's Own Mounted Sackbuts.'

'Kate, darling, you know that wasn't exactly what I meant, don't you, sweetness? It's the gin,' she confided to the others in dramatically lowered voice. 'Have you noticed how obtuse it makes certain people? What I meant, Katie dear, is that I recognised his *presence* at once. He never said much at all during those rehearsals – he just sort of smouldered and now and again clapped a hand to his brow when someone did something silly. Actually I rather think he once turned his back on the lot of us when we missed an entry and various people had to trot up to pacify him and turn him round.'

'That part at least sounds like our passenger,' Kate said.

'But that isn't the part I mean. When the actual performance was going well and we all had that feeling, you know? – as if nobody can put a foot wrong? – he was extraordinary. That little figure on the podium in the distance looked *apart* in some way but at the same time we realised he was controlling the lot of us. We were all completely in his service and for as long as we could give ourselves up to his spirit or his musical vision or whatever it was the whole thing became absolutely *magnetic*. By the end we all felt exalted, too. Personally I never slept a wink that night. And from then until the other day I never clapped eyes on him. Yet when we were introduced it was that odd quality which hit me at once and even after so long I remembered it. I can't explain it better than that.'

'I'll allow he has a certain something about him,' admitted Kate, 'but in all honesty I don't know whether that isn't just because I know who he is. One's unfairly disposed to detect all sorts of qualities in the famous simply because they're famous, while all they might actually have done was invent a mutton extract for a South Polar expedition.'

'Exactly,' said an Acquaintance. 'Or dissolve a wife or two in a bath of acid.'

'One thing you can say about him – he looks like nobody's idea of a composer.'

'I suppose not,' said Dora. 'But I'm not sure how a composer *should* look. That Beethovenesque romantic hero – you know, tousled hair, wind-tattered cloak, shaking his fist at lightning and generally living in squalor – that would frankly look pretty silly in Nineteen twenty-three, wouldn't it?'

'Granted. But even so you don't expect him to look like a retired general full of equine anecdotes about linseed oil and skimmed milk and ante-post betting.'

Dora said: 'I still don't think there's any point in applying ordinary standards of behaviour to completely extraordinary people. Look at all that music he's given the world which they'll still be playing long after we're forgotten. You can teach even quite stupid children to say please and thank-you and hold doors open for ladies and generally ape being a good little social animal, but who can you train to write *The Dream of Gerontius* or even *Land of Hope and Glory?*'

'I still think it hurts nobody to be moderately polite.'

'Dora's got a point,' said another Acquaintance who had so far not spoken. 'Surely a genius is someone whose gift is so commanding, so overwhelming that there's no space or energy left over for bothering with niceties. Most of the geniuses one can think of were pretty odd in one way or another. You'd have said they were half crazy if they hadn't been writing or painting or composing works which were obviously of greater importance than the unconventional private life of the man who created them. Look at van Gogh.'

For a while they looked at van Gogh while on the deck above them the genius who had caused all this tipsy speculation snored slightly in the well-appointed steel box he had rented. Beside him on the bunkside table stood a ribbed blue bottle containing a sleeping draught formulated especially for him by a retired Royal Physician. Edward had been much taken by the man's having invented it originally to give the King's horses in order to render them docile before travelling by rail. His own supply was somewhat weaker, perhaps, and taken in smaller quantities; but he was quite content to entrust himself to a medicine with so reassuring a pedigree.

While his passengers were thus variously engaged Captain Maddrell was earnestly in conversation with the Purser who, at this late hour, had brought him disturbing news.

'As I say, she's distraught. Frankly, between you and me she's pretty tiddly and something tells me she mightn't have said anything about it had she not been. What do we do?'

'Let's get it straight. Did she actually accuse the doctor of anything worse than foul language?'

'I suppose not, if "worse" means you're thinking of what I'm thinking.'

'I am,' said the Captain.

'In that case, no. She says she called him with a legitimate complaint – won't specify what it was and of course I didn't ask – but it was sudden enough to warrant attention at eight o'clock in the evening. She absolutely agrees it was an inconvenient time but she says bodies are inconvenient things and anyway what the hell are doctors paid for?'

'She sounds a forthright sort of lady.'

'Indeed. My impression is that drunk or not she's very much to the point and hardly the sort to invent things. Anyway it's such an unlikely thing to invent, isn't it? You and I know from bitter experience that some women will accuse doctors of the most awful indecencies when it turns out to be utter nonsense and the poor wretch is like as not ruined even though cleared. But this time it's nothing like that. She simply claims he swore at her and then laughed. It was his attitude which upset her as much as the language, apparently. She says she can overlook brusqueness if a doctor's first-rate; what she can't overlook is his refusing to take her symptoms seriously. She claims he said – among other things – that he would only consider treating her if she agreed to immediate surgery.'

'Good God. The man's a lunatic. I've never heard . . . But go on.'

'That's it.'

The Captain thought for a moment. 'No witnesses, of course.'

'One assumes not.'

'I'll see the lady now and then I'll see the bloody doctor.'

'It'll have to wait till morning. She's gone to bed.'

'A thousand times I've wished Bill Barnard hadn't retired. This is the thousand and first.'

'What a man. Next layover I'm for going down to – Godalming, isn't it? – just to shake him by the hand. This Ashe is a non-starter. Odd, though: he came with the highest references.'

'Of course he did, he'd hardly be working for Booth's if he hadn't. But Bill was ex-Army too. You couldn't wish for a greater contrast. Well, I must admit Ashe didn't strike me any too favourably when I first saw him but it's not for me to say who I sail with. It's not me who's employing him, after all. I can damn well have him off my ship after this, though. It's incredible. His first trip and everything. Man hasn't been on board more than a fortnight. As far as I'm concerned he walks the plank at Pará.'

'Better if we could hold out until Manaos. We might be able to filch a medic from the Iquitos run.'

'Mr Gates, the voice of reason.'

Next morning Edward woke early; the draught of horse-dope had given him many hours of dreamless sleep. After breakfast, which he took practically alone, he went up on deck to find the sea had changed. No longer was it the purple which would lighten to deep blue as the sun rose to set aglow its uppermost sixty feet. It was now a yellowish-green colour ridged with small waves which slapped at the *Hildebrand*'s forefoot as if she had been a yacht changing tack before an oncoming tide. The sight filled him with the disquiet of estuaries. But an even more convincing sign of change was the smell of the wind. The crispness of pure ocean breath was overlaid now by a soft reek of rot: the exhalation of a hundred million arboreal lungs, the thrilling perfume of the tropics full of unknown oils bled off untold golden leaves by a heavy sun. It was the scent inseparable from torrential distillations of water and the river had carried it faithfully like a familiar far out into the Atlantic where at a dishevelled boundary each passed into a larger diluent.

'Your first sight of Brazil, sir?' It was Pyce with a starched white cloth over one forearm in mid-bustle between points of dutiful activity.

And only then did Edward look properly at the horizon and notice the low stain between sea and sky.

'So that's it, is it?'

'That's Brazil, sir. Unless the Captain's made an error.'

'Of course.'

'An error of course.' For a peculiar instant the two men nearly smiled at one another. 'But he never has yet, sir. In any case you can smell it. Can't mistake a smell like that. The land you can see over there'll be Mary-Jo island. It's right in the mouth of the Amazon and they say it's about a hundred and seventy miles across.'

'That's a whacking big island.'

'It's a whacking big place, Brazil. Never got used to it myself and I've made this trip dozens of times in the last five years. This water here, sir? 'T'isn't sea-water, you know. That's fresh water, Amazon water. You can drink it. In fact a bit further on's the place where all the ships take on fresh water, including us. It's pure Amazon water we'll be drinking from now until Liverpool. They tell me it's still drinkable two hundred miles out to sea but I can't say I've tried.'

'Good heavens . . . I say, Steward, can you get me some?'

'Thought you'd say that, sir. I already have.' And from the pocket concealed by the napkin he drew out the hip-flask.

'You deserve a medal, Pyce. A small one.'

'I've got one of those, sir. They gave me one a few years back.' And he excused himself and walked away up the deck leaving Edward holding the flask at a loss for words. Cheeky the man undoubtedly was. And yet . . . Probably he *had* served with honour: why mightn't he have done so? And yes indeed, probably anybody would prefer a half-sovereign to a medal.

('I can't eat my bloody sword,' he had said to Alice in a rage not long after he had been knighted, 'though I may yet have to fall on it if I can't pay the bills. Who gives a fig for honours? What I need is cash, cash, cash. You pack me off to Court with my underwear in holes, my waistcoat slit up the back and my borrowed shoes with fabulous silver buckles a size too small. Every inch a gentleman, every foot a penance.' But this minor *bon mot*, popping out as it did without the least volition, had made him laugh and Alice as well, even though she was the daughter of a Major-General, and for several minutes they had both howled helplessly at the irony of the whole stupid business.)

He spent an hour or two with his microscope after first trying a drop of water on the tip of his tongue. To his surprise it was indeed sweet. And placing one slide after another under his instrument and lighting them with the strengthening sun he made out the diatoms and protozoa peculiar to fresh water. He much lamented not having his chemistry apparatus with him since he might have done a series of tests to determine the exact percentage of sodium chloride. After all, he thought, the man who'd gone to the trouble of taking out a patent on an apparatus for making hydrogen sulphide could certainly have managed *that* without relying on text-books.

He still had difficulty believing that even a river as monstrous as the Amazon could impress itself on the Atlantic Ocean. He had done his desultory reading in the Library: had read the section of the geography book headed 'Facts and Figures Pertaining to the World's Greatest River', had noted that at certain points it was so wide that one bank was invisible from the other, had deliberately not memorised the incomprehensible cubic mass of pure water which allegedly flooded out every second. But that was always the problem with facts and figures: they never made anything more comprehensible, merely tinged wonder with boredom.

When he went back up on deck it was mid-morning and the passengers were disporting themselves in the usual manner while radiating a feeling of being only half attentive to the rope rings they were tossing at the distant peg or to the nearly-finished books they had to return to the ship's library before disembarking. People kept glancing up as if by magic the vista of approaching coastline might have given way in the last five minutes to a harbour bar, a jetty, a waterfront. Ladies could be seen asking themselves how they might recognise the last reasonable moment, when it came, for slipping down and doing their hair once more. Yet it was not until early afternoon that on the eastern horizon an indistinct row of buildings appeared which was the town of Pará. By then the yellow–green water through which the *Hildebrand* glided was free of the long oceanic swells which had marked much of her recent passage. The oncoming ridges of water defining the meeting of river and sea had likewise been left behind. Here the surface was merely ruffled in places as light punches of hot wind dabbed locally at it among the blue- and crimson-sailed fishing boats they passed with waving arms and wordless hails.

Beside him at the rail Molly appeared, her face transfigured.

'You're pleased to be back. That much one can tell,' he said.

'It's the smell. I haven't smelt this for over a year and it brings it all back like nothing else. What it says to me is that I haven't made a mistake . . . Isn't it funny how easy it is to imagine places one knows and loves, to see people and things in immense detail, to hear exactly the sound of a familiar clock or a particular door opening, and yet to be almost incapable of imagining smells? Why is that, do you think? It can't be that they're less significant, at least not for me because smelling something again brings everything else back in a rush . . . Pará's not very inspiring from here, is it? But at the moment I love it. Did you know it had another name? It's sometimes called Belém, which is Portuguese for Bethlehem.'

Her excited talk eased the images past his eyes. How had he imagined this continent? He hadn't, to be truthful. One morning in a distant land which he felt he knew to the point of exhaustion he had quite deliberately selected a terra incognita. It was precisely because it had conjured up nothing in his mind's eye more specific than a wilderness of trees concealing unknown mysteries that he had chosen Amazonia in preference to – for example – the Greek islands or the road to Mandalay. So now the muddy, unimposing skyline of Pará whose principal buildings, even at this distance, bore the Portuguese stamp familiar from Madeira filled him with neither surprise nor disappointment.

'Did you know there was a sizeable English colony here?' Molly was saying.

'I'd rather gathered as much from our prankster friends. Business people, one would imagine, like their presumed husbands.'

'Their poor, poor husbands . . . Wouldn't you like to meet them?'

'I would have done once. But in an odd sort of way my curiosity for how the rest of the world gets by has ebbed rather in the last few years. To be honest I no longer care very much. But I would wish them all well if I were the wishing sort. Do you know, I may not even get off here.'

'Not get off? It's a long way to come not to get off.'

'No, it's really only a long way to come, which is why I came. You get off.'

'Oh I shall. I know Forty wants to' (he had no difficulty guessing the identity of 'Forty'). 'It's not a particularly exciting place except it's the gateway to the Amazon and that's quite exciting enough for me. It's wonderfully informal. You'd be shocked.'

'Do you find me easily shocked?'

'Well, disconcerted perhaps. Not actually shocked.'

'I should hope not. There aren't many thoughts one doesn't have in a long life. In any case, when in Rome and so on. What is it one does when in Pará?'

'Oh, for instance if you called on someone in the English colony here it would be thought perfectly in order if the lady of the house received you herself, asked you to take off your coat and sit with her in the drawing room in your shirt-sleeves.'

'Deeply scandalous. But eminently sensible in this sort of climate.'

'If you're a good friend and go to someone's house the first thing they'll say is "Here's the peg and there's the bath". They always say that here. It's like a greeting.'

' "Here's the peg and there's the bath"?'

'Yes. Hang up your coat and have a nice cool shower before coming and talking. It's a real courtesy.'

'Sounds charming. But I can see it might be open to mis-construction were you to try and introduce the habit in England. Not that a lot of one's guests wouldn't be the better for a good tubbing.'

'Gracious, Sir Edward, you must know some grimy people.'

'I certainly used to. Academics mostly. I think it's the dust they pick up from living in libraries. Cobwebs and so on. Decayed thought. Most contaminating.'

'Maybe by the end of this trip you'll find yourself wanting to come and live here.'

Edward watched the slow glide of small but imposing buildings through the masts and rigging of moored ships. The *Hildebrand* had lost way: throughout their conversation he had heard intermittent bells being rung deep underfoot.

'Dammit, it's too late for that,' he said. 'Ten years ago, maybe . . . But then what would have been the point? One doesn't up sticks and move half across the globe just because they dress informally. After all, I've spent as much of my life as I could in what my wife used to call "gardening clothes". It wasn't enough, of course. My God, the things she used to insist on my wearing. She once tried to make me buy a bicycling suit for bicycling. Never heard such nonsense. Whenever I wanted to go for a ride I used to have to hide my old grid in a hedge down the lane and creep out and leap on it when she wasn't looking. She was worried about the neighbours. What neighbours?' An extraordinary sorrow suddenly weighted his face into lines and Molly saw his eyes fill with tears. 'Silly old girl. And if there *had* been any they wouldn't have been trying to write *The Dream of Gerontius*. What did it matter?'

And before she could divert him with tales of the lightweight, jazzily-striped pyjama jackets in which Englishmen in Pará nowadays received visitors of either sex, and of the white duck trousers and cotton shirts both groom and host had been wearing at a wedding reception she had attended, Edward turned abruptly and left her looking at the chipped stucco façade of the Customs House. He went below and let himself into his cabin. Compared with the past the territory of the present, as exemplified by the town beyond the *Hildebrand's* rail, was as null as cloud. But as the sounds of mooring came in with pinkish evening light through the open portholes he resolved at least to send a postcard to what little remained of the solid in his life and wrote a couple to Carice and a friend of the 'am being wonderfully well looked after' variety. Reassured by Molly's account of sartorial licence he went up on deck in his lightest jacket, prepared after all for a gloomy foray ashore.

But when he reached the outer fringes of the crowd of passengers eager to rush down the gangway like – as he observed to a bystander – First Class rather than Steerage sheep, he was taken up by Molly and Fortescue while Kate and Dora came to say goodbye.

'The parting of the ways, Sir Edward.' Kate extended a white-gloved hand. 'I'm sorry it was so short.'

'I, on the other hand, feel our acquaintance stretches back to nineteen hundred and three,' said Dora, 'and I'm even sorrier than she is that you're going on and we're getting off. There're heaps of people here who'll be dying to meet you when they know. The entire English colony will turn out and put up flags. You'll have no end of a grand time in Chapco Virado and São Jeronimo. That is, if you want one,' she added.

And all the while she was speaking he felt something ebbing out of her and Kate. Whatever assumptions he had made on the basis of a shared table, a shared class, a day on Madeira and many conversations, they were now seen to fit with a looseness which increased by the minute the two ladies who stood in mauve hats on the brink of the unknown town containing their homes. He had been disconcerted by the confidence and oddity of their humour as he always was by people who were sure of themselves. But the ebbing continued as they made their way fairly regally off the ship. He could not help noticing ungallantly how thick their ankles were above the strap shoes; nor that by the time they reached the quay – where they were both embraced with evident warmth by two very swarthy plump gentlemen – Kate and Dora had lost all claims to identity.

'*Well*,' said Molly, who had been watching with equal fascination. '*They* weren't going to invite us to their houses, were they?'

'You'd thought they might, too?'

'Of course. Or at least they might have said it was impossible for them to be hospitable the first evening of their arrival so how about tomorrow? We're going to be here three days. Even the offer of somebody reliable to show us Pará. Most extraordinary. And those men who met them.'

'Is one to assume those are the husbands?'

'They looked to me like mestizo cabbies.'

'You warned me that Pará was informal,' said Edward, 'but you never said it was customary for taxi drivers to embrace their fares.'

'I've much to learn,' Molly told him. 'It's one of the reasons I came back, after all. Now, Forty and I have already been here so if you'd let us be your guides we can give you a first taste of South America. Or at least help you post your cards.'

And so saying she took them and dropped them straight into a red steel post box welded to a nearby bulkhead, explaining they would be sorted and stamped aboard the *Hildebrand* and passed straight to the captain of a Booth's steamer bound in the opposite direction, that being the quickest possible way. 'The Brazilian post office will only try to get them on the same ship when they've sorted them, but they'll probably miss it.'

Almost as soon as his feet touched the quay the listlessness induced by the vacant, estuarine approach to the town and its impression of being a settlement on the low coast of nowhere, fell away. It was indeed difficult after two weeks at sea to dispel the feeling that he was in a maritime port, for here the River Pará was thirty miles wide and its far bank not to be seen. Once beyond the quay and in Frei Caetano Brandão gardens, strolling on rubbery legs through tropical vegetation in concentric gravel rings about the bishop's statue, they heard through the strange leaves and festooned trees the sounds of a large town. The unmistakable grinding of tram-wheels reached them, the clanging of bells, the voices of a hundred thousand inhabitants coming back to life after the heat of the tropical day.

'It's the legs,' said Fortescue. 'That's what makes everything so unreal. The ground keeps tilting. It does that after bumpy flying.'

'I hadn't expected to find trams here,' said Edward.

'Then you'll be impressed that they've also got newspapers in both morning and evening editions.'

'The existence of gossip here impresses me less than that of tramways.'

Gently, like convalescents, they made their way towards the Praça da Republica which Molly claimed was the social hub of the town after nightfall. Despite the shops and stalls lit by electricity and naphtha flares; despite the broad, cobbled avenues with their polished steel tramlines leading off to the residential suburbs of São Jeronimo and Nazareth; despite every evidence of civic bustle, Edward was conscious of nothing so much as the jungle at his back. The Governor's Palace, the Cathedral, the various private mansions they passed were all tethered by creepers to the surrounding earth. Unlikely blossoms hung about their columns while every bush twinkled with fireflies. In consequence he was even more struck by the classical grandeur of the buildings they passed. It seemed to him evidence of a commendable sense of priorities that the Brazilians should have put up such an imposing stone theatre, for example. Reading the bills with Molly's assistance he gathered it was not permanently open as it would have been in London but received periodic visits from touring players, troupes, foreign opera companies. Towards Christmas, he saw, a French ensemble of which he had never heard was to give a series of concerts which included Berlioz's oratorio *L'enfance du Christ*.

Edward, having changed some money with the Purser beforehand, insisted that the others be his guests that night for, as he explained, once they reached Manaos they would doubtless become busy with their own affairs to the exclusion of social convenience.

'It's very good of you, sir,' said Fortescue. 'But I should hardly wish you to dine me under the false impression that I'll be spending my first fortnight in Manaos too busy with rigging and fitting even to eat. There's a limit to what can be done in a day's work on a dirt airfield on the outskirts of a tropical town. When we knock off we knock off.'

'The night cometh when no man may work?'

'Absolutely. Nothing to say he can't have a drink and a square meal.'

They were daunted by the prospect of the English Club, so evidently the focal point of the colony. Already through the lighted windows half shrouded in leaves several of the *Hildebrand*'s passengers could be recognised. They chose instead the restaurant of the Grand Hotel, set on the boulevard beneath a glass-and-ironwork canopy, and from here they watched the passers-by and tried to guess their racial origins.

'I think as colonisers the Portuguese must have been as unlike us as it's possible to get,' observed Molly. 'They evidently had no taboo on marrying into the local population and, what's more, neither does anybody else who comes here.'

'Except the British,' said Fortescue.

'Except the British. Although it looks as if Kate and Dora might be breaking the mould . . . Why do you think it is? I don't really understand this thing about racial purity,' she confessed. 'Personally I find this mixture of Indian and Portuguese and Italian and negro and everything else makes for a very handsome colouring.' And indeed Edward was himself aware of remarkable skin tones beneath the mothy glare of the electroliers, of the light striking dusty bronze glints from heads of hair by no means a uniform tropical black.

The food was good, the chilled Portuguese rosé excellent, the human stream diverting. Edward experienced it all like one behind layers of plate glass. There was about the street a peculiar lack of that stridency which he had found so much a feature of Naples and Smyrna. Pará was lively and in some way unrestrained, yet the soft hot night blunted the acuteness of sound by absorbing it into the folds of its curtain.

The description Molly gave, piecemeal and graphic, of the economic disaster which not so long ago had hit Manaos and Pará with the collapse of the rubber trade seemed to him likewise to apply not to the people passing at his elbow but to another population altogether. Surely nobody he could see was in any way connected with world-famous Pará rubber. The beggars, stall-holders, matrons with their children, the tram-drivers, potential drama-lovers examining the bills posted on the columns of the theatre – all seemed to have lives which bore no relation to the market fluctuations of a commodity. Molly's information that after the initial slump the region's fortunes had been partly retrieved by substituting cocoa and Brazil nuts as its chief exports remained for him information. He was left with his diner's view of lives immeasurably removed from his own being lived in a place he had never been able to imagine.

Afterwards he insisted on walking back alone to the ship while Molly and Fortescue went off to the Bosque. He had given them dinner: that was what could be reasonably expected of an older companion. Beyond that there was no intercession between his memories and their prospects. A great horned beetle cracked into an electrolier and fell stunned at his feet. He turned it onto its front with the ferrule of his cane. 'Buzz off,' he told it kindly, 'otherwise you'll get squidged.' Somewhat to his surprise it did spread its black shards and drone heavily upwards into the lights.

VII

We seem to have crossed the Atlantic. At all events I dined tonight on dry land somewhere or other. Everybody assures me it's a place called Pará & certainly the props (newspapers & playbills in Portuguese, peculiar trams, beetles, lianas, fireflies etc) seem calculated to give the illusion of being in Brazil. Rather more convincingly Pyce assures me Captain Maddrell has never yet made a navigational error – at least not of the size required to miss a continent. I'm forced to conclude that this apparent seaside town by which we've moored is the very riverside city for which we've been heading.

I'm English; or I'm European. I'm used to boundaries. I love those maps of English counties with their age-old lines of demarcation wiggling along the middle of a river or following a line of hills or skirting the non-existent property of some long defunct Duchy. Thus the counties have acquired distinct characters of their own. Everyone knows exactly where Worcestershire ends and Shropshire begins, even where there are no signs. Since this journey began, however, certainties of that kind have been more than a little eroded. First there was Madeira – neither Europe nor Africa. Then there was the Equator, a notional fence whose mythic position had to be celebrated by mummers. Next I awoke to find the ship far out to sea but afloat on fresh river-water. And finally I've dined tonight surrounded by human tides whose racial distinctions are every bit as blurred. In short everything in this part of the world is intent on flowing into everything else. Matters haven't been clarified by the ridiculous disembarking of Kate & Dora. Who <u>were</u> they? No-one seems to know. They were whisked away by dumpy little dagoes to every sign of mutual satisfaction. They were rather splendid & I'd begun to like their peculiar double act. The journey home <u>is</u> going to be lonely.

Very early next day Edward walked off the ship into a morning full of pastels. Out in the roads and in the port itself the ships' paintwork and liveries shone against a pale blue wash of sky. Each rope and mast stood out with dense clarity in air which sparkled with its saturation of water molecules. The ropes mooring the *Hildebrand* wore metal cones, their open bells facing the quay, to fend off the large black rats which could be seen everywhere burrowing into piles of litter or browsing along the stretches of muddy foreshore strewn with vegetable waste.

He had not drunk so much as a cup of coffee yet, had woken full of energy which translated itself while he was dressing into a sudden desire to breakfast ashore. Having first asked directions he made the short stroll into Old Pará whose narrow streets of coloured colonial houses were filled with oblique sunlight. He bought a copy of *O Jornal do Pará* out of curiosity and found a café where, indicating that he would have the same as his neighbour, he was served with hot bread and a cup of thick strong chocolate. With surprise he noticed the paper's date: it was the first of December.

As he read slowly but – thanks to Latin and Italian – not wholly uncomprehendingly through the headlines a feeling suffused him out of nowhere which made him look away at the pavement with filling eyes. It was a sensation he hadn't had for scores of years, from so far back he couldn't associate it with any particular event but could only identify it happily, sadly, as that of being *young*. The brightness of the morning sunlight outside, the pungent and unexpected taste of the chocolate, the crackle of foreign newsprint between his hands, the ancient street whose houses and passers-by he could not have assigned to any definite corner of the globe – all of them started the ghost of that excitement at finding oneself alive and free which can suddenly break like day in the foreign ports of one's youth with promises of endless enchanting occurrence.

Then the unfairness of so clear a revisitation shook him with pain. Ghosts of the past self had no business sliding back out of hiding after decades of absence, cheerfully untouched by the tolls and ravages of a lived life. It was a cruel trick which just for a moment had dangled the jauntiness of twenty-six before the man of sixty-six. Not that his life in those days had been so very light-hearted, either: painfully in love with Lena, more than a little poor, many years from recognition. But those are quite usual conditions at twenty-six. Beneath them lie all sorts of energetic tides and all manner of surges which suddenly leap out of ambush in a foreign café early one morning. (Thus a cat will without apparent reason break its purposeful step to pat the air and frisk among shadows.)

The memory of this feeling persisted as he wandered back towards the river. An infrequent tram screeched slowly past trailing an electrical smell of ozone and the scent of whetted knives from binding brake shoes. At the glassless windows (fitted, however, with oilskin blinds which could be lowered in down-pours) were men in brilliant white shirt-sleeves on their way from their suburbs to banks and offices and godowns, many holding folded handkerchiefs delicately to their moustaches to keep out the dust, others lightly fanning themselves with newspapers. Several of them disembarked at an imposing bank or bourse from whose pediment a lopsided spray of flame-coloured blossoms trailed from the cleft in which it had taken root. The effect of this brilliant weed was artlessly to add a seductiveness to the cracked temple of mammon which dominated the mango-lined boulevard as coquett-ishly as any Latin beauty with a carnation over one ear. It served also to remind that this was a *vegetable* town, a town owing its existence and prosperity to sap and lignum, to nuts and fruits and juices. Beyond the last tram-stop began a continent's-width of vegetation stretching clear to the Andes. Down at the wharves stirred a forest of dead trees and lianas: the masts and rigging of the river-steamers, fishing smacks, liners, cargo and tramp vessels without which Pará would swiftly languish and return to the jungle. In every crack in each wall something had taken root. The very pavements bunched and heaved around the mangoes as if a primaeval creature were patiently surfacing. In the gardens he passed were scarcely any bare patches of soil except here and there where a gardener in cotton trousers and sunhat had begun his day's labour, the sweat already glistening on his mahogany torso as he deployed his hoe without evident haste.

The remembered sense of being young now manifested itself in a different way. All of a sudden there came the conviction that he had not after all done anything yet. It was not that what he had done was of little account, not quite the glum modesty which had once made him say that setting any of his work beside a single Beethoven symphony put him in the position of a tinker surveying the Forth Bridge. It was maybe more akin to whatever had made Beethoven himself on his death-bed remark how funny it was that it now seemed to him he'd scarcely ever written a note. Nobody could say if Beethoven had meant this literally or whether confronting eternity he felt his whole output was an insignificance.

In Edward's case, though, it was literal. Amid this lethargic, alien bustle in a tropical city which had no doubt never heard of Gerontius he could hardly recall the composer he'd once impersonated. On what, then, had that twenty-six-year-old's energy been expended in the intervening forty years? Only the echoes of great troubles and turmoils and upsets reached him now. Not a note written but whole hinterlands of emotion drained, tributary joining tributary until there was the impression of the sound of many waters, of a general sliding, of being a perilous bystander on a quayside watching a great river in spate, the turgid yellow swirls mere inches beneath his feet.

Yet the very impersonality of a morning in Pará came to his rescue: the cheerful activity, the strangeness, the passers-by stopping at a vendor's fronded stall to drink glasses of deep red fluid or eat brown slabs of compressed jam. What did it matter? He had done nothing. There was nothing to do. No matter how hard one worked there was nothing to be done. Rounding a corner he came face to face with Captain Maddrell and the Purser, resplendent in whites so pressed they appeared to have been cut from metal sheet. Caps off, straw hat lifted, good days given. He? Back to the ship. They? To Booth's offices. Good-bye, good-byé. The formality and decorousness cheered him as he boarded the *Hildebrand*: they were part of this morning's weird energy, of people doing things in harsh sunlight as though they nearly mattered. He rang for Steward Pyce.

'I'll be using the Captain's day cabin for a little,' he said. 'I should like a pitcher of something cold to keep me company. A soft drink.'

'*Guaraná*,' said the Steward promptly. 'When in Brazil, sir, do as the Brazilians. It's wonderfully refreshing. I'll bring you some at once.'

And no sooner had Edward pulled the Captain's deck-chair to the rail where it could command a view of the wharf, the Customs House and the godown roofs with intermittent glimpses of white town and dark green vegetation than Pyce appeared with a tall jug at whose rim chunks of ice rang clear chimes. It was full of the reddish-brown liquid he had earlier seen drunk in the street. He sipped gingerly at the glass he was handed and then drank more deeply.

'I say, Steward, that hits the spot. What marvellous stuff. What did you say it was called?'

'*Guaraná*, sir. The Indians here drink it for dysentery, beg pardon, Sir Edward. But as you can see if it's aerated it's really very refreshing. Practically everyone here in Amazonia drinks it.'

'But what is it?'

'Seeds, sir, of the *guaraná* plant. The natives dry them in the sun and roast them a bit and then grind them up into paste. You just add water and sugar to the paste.'

'Well I'm damned. And you say it's medicinal?'

'Dr Barnard – he was our last ship's doctor, sir – he found it in the British Pharma-coopia so it must be all right.'

'You seem very knowledgeable, Pyce,' said Edward as he offered his glass to be refilled.

'I've been making this run some years, sir, haven't I. It's the sort of thing passengers like to know. I've even seen the Indians actually making the paste. It's quite interesting how clever they are in their own way, seeing as how they're savages. They were making models in this paste, little birds and snakes and alligators and things, then smoking them over a fire. That's the way it travels best, apparently. You can buy it like that in Manaos. Many people take some home as a souvenir but it's very hard to grate once it's been baked. The Indians here use a fish's tongue.'

'A what?'

'It's the local file, sir. Comes from the tongue of a fish whose name I can't recall offhand – '

'Thank God for that.'

'– but we sometimes trawl for it with spinners over the poop. Largest freshwater fish in the world, sir. Three hundred pounds, the biggest we've ever caught. The galley didn't half curse.'

'And the tongue, Pyce?'

'It's like a file, sir, as I say. They dry it and grate up their *guaraná* with it. I don't know any more about *guaraná* than that,' added the Steward disarmingly.

'It's more than enough,' Edward told him with a smile. 'You may return in an hour or two with a fresh supply. If I develop, ah, dysentery as a result I shall know whom to hold responsible.'

From his borrowed deck chair he sipped and watched, sipped and watched. The sun climbed swiftly, leaching out of the town beyond the rail a variety of scents and stenches. From the open warehouse doors along the quayside drifted rich aromatics: hot jute bags of peppercorns, cocoa-beans stewing under corrugated iron, sacks of manioc *farinha*, sawn tropical hardwood exhaling resin and the spice of unlit cigars. The mud on the foreshore popped and hissed as it dried; the mats of decaying jetsam, impregnated with the town's ordure, heaved gently as the rats in their interiors released a myriad trapped perfumes which drifted almost visibly across the wharves. In the clear blue funnel of sky above the town a loose cone of vultures revolved slowly. Low down in the ship's side a gangplank led straight into one of the holds and up it half-naked navvies were disappearing with sacks on their backs directly beneath where Edward sat, iced *guaraná* in hand. It glittered. The people glittered, the town glowed and stank, the huge fecundity of its setting overwhelmed him.

From his watch he decided it would now be about four-thirty on a winter's afternoon back in England. Perversely he superimposed a familiar scene onto the dazzling quayside before him. An English village – none he could identify – drifted before his eyes. The sun was just setting, the rest of the sky a deep turquoise against which the gilded weathercock on the church tower was a blackish stencil. The air smelt like early frost and spent gunpowder. For the past hour, he thought, woodpigeons had been wheeling in across the plough behind the vicarage to roost in the overgrown thorn hedges into whose high and tangled thickets they were still vanishing. In the village store opposite the church the lamps had long been lit. Each time its door opened or closed a clear bell pinged a note audible from the village hall. A few homing villagers trudged by on bicycles with lamps leaving the reek of acetylene and carbide.

But where was the observer, was Edward himself at this very instant? Many thousands of miles away with the blazing December sun almost directly overhead in a blue sky where vultures swirled lethargically, sipping an exotic drink and with a river beneath him containing logs and great armoured fish and flakes of gold. And for that moment he was content. He did not miss the immemorial English scene as he had a few days earlier while gazing at an empty ocean. With the glitter of this moment filling his ears and eyes and nose the far-off country which rose up in his mind (with its muted colours and spare sounds, with its church clocks and shop-door bells and its autumnal twilights falling soft as pigeons over thatched and peg-tiled roofs) engendered in him no nostalgia at all but only a traitorous happiness at being free of it all.

In at the distant pair of dock gates turned a couple of imposing white figures who, as they neared the ship, became the Captain and the Purser. As he watched them vanish beneath the scuppers where his line of sight ended he caught a glimpse of Mr Maddrell's face under the stubby visor of his cap. It was wearing the intransigent expression of someone not used to being crossed by either fortune or design. The officers had just been told by their company that there was no way of replacing Dr Ashe without delaying the *Hildebrand* indefinitely. There was no other English doctor in port suitable for the post. Dr Ashe would have to serve at least until the ship called back at Pará. It was only a matter of two or three weeks and by that time a feasible substitute would surely have been found.

'Two or three weeks,' the Captain had been saying as they walked along the quay, both men's eyes busy with details of the *Hildebrand*'s moorings, gangway awnings and paintwork. 'We've hardly been gone that time and the fellow's already done incalculable damage. Imagine what he might get up to on this next leg, Gatesy. Well, if anything else happens I'll have him in irons. He can hold his surgery in the forepeak.'

'He'd certainly be the soberer.'

The Captain marched a few steps. 'Aha, that's the size of it, is it? I didn't know. I think, Gatesy, we've both been at sea long enough not to remember a good few men who needed a bottle to hand and I must say some of 'em seemed none the worse for it. I recall a First Officer who went on a bender once a month, regular as clockwork. Useless for twenty-four hours. But by God he was a fine seaman the rest of the time. Couldn't get through a day without a bottle of rum inside him but you'd never have known it.'

'What became of him?'

'Oh, he went down somewhere. *Titanic? Empress of Ireland?* One of those, I think. I hope he had a skinful when he went.'

'I've a feeling our own doctor isn't in that category.'

'Me too. Funny, isn't it? You can tell. Three sheets in the wind. Chin up, Gatesy, we've had worse aboard than a Bones who's off his rocker.'

'All passengers, Mr Maddrell. They were all passengers.'

On a sweltering afternoon the *Hildebrand* slipped her moorings, saluted town and inhabitants with its customary C and steamed away. Edward, a pitcher of *guaraná* half empty by his side, watched Pará quickly turn back into a waterfront, then become a mere coastal settlement. But from far across the opening yellow–green expanse of water the loose cone of vultures continued to be visible as it turned and turned its black particles many thousands of feet up into the blue air above the invisible town.

From then on the ship remained in sight of a shore which appeared now at hand, now at several miles' distance, sometimes on the left when Edward glanced up and sometimes on the right. He lost track of the days and all sense of their navigational progress. He spent some time on the bridge where he often found a Brazilian counterpart to Mr Mushet, for all vessels of any draught had to take a pilot on board for certain infamous stretches since the Amazon was constantly shifting its shoals and sandbanks, and channels long in use might silt up within a matter of days. But most of the time he spent in the Captain's deck-chair from where he watched the slow drift astern of a practically unbroken expanse of rain forest.

Shortly before entering the Amazon proper they reached the Narrows, a stretch of a hundred and thirty miles of islands and islets, each with its tuft of virgin forest, which in places reduced the navigable channel to a rapid current barely two hundred yards wide. The river was now yellow–brown, the islands green. Each bend the ship rounded disclosed a new scene whose components were generally the same but whose details struck him afresh. There were trees such as he had never imagined. It was one thing to talk of venerable old oaks in England, but the venerable old trees in Amazonas would have made an English oak look like a toadstool. In places the forest canopy stood well over two hundred feet high and several species of tree had roots like flying buttresses: great triangular slabs of wood which from far enough away took on an architectural gracefulness. From the branches of these giants hung all manner of lianas and creepers like tethers to prevent the tree's growing any further into the sky. Everywhere the sun beat in bright dapples: on the feather fronds of the assai palm, on the plumes of the *miriti*, on a myriad stalks and sprays. The light fell in sheets, drenching the burnished river and striking sudden red gleams of sandstone as if the recent erosion by floods were revealing still-molten magma welling up from the planet's core. Elsewhere in the creeks and *igarapés* which led off namelessly into the jungle and in the glades which opened beneath the canopy the darkness was startling in its density.

But if this forest stood like some illimitable sculpture in wood, intermittently lit and polished, there was much that was in motion. Across the seething water from one islet to another flew macaws and parrots, their apparent absence of neck making them blunt-headed as moths or owls. Kingfishers skimmed like bolts of electricity from a rotten trunk on an island to a flowering shrub on another shore. The *Hildebrand*'s passing disturbed ducks and egrets, the dull mechanical sound of her engines was given back by the walls of vegetation. And off it all blew the smell of the forest's glands: the oils and gums, the orchids and fungi, wild peppers and spices and gaseous decay. If the sight was both entrancing and sobering (since it reminded all aboard of their insignificance in the middle of such wild immensities) the smell was chilling in its primaeval purity. It told of aeons, of geological eras, of incomprehensible stretches of time. It was unmistakably the smell of the planet before man ever set foot on it, while dinosaurs still browsed and coal was being laid down. It, too, announced that nineteen twenty-three was nothing, the fraction of a second, a ring in a tree-trunk. It breathed into each passenger the seductive perfume of futility. And as often in such cases a few responded by experiencing the piercing pleasure of melancholy, being those curious souls who are reassured by reminders of their own annihilation. Among them was Edward, who for many hours would sit watching the details stream past him until they merged into a continent, an unknown and unknowable land across whose surface would flit images from his own past, the incidents of a life, emotions wearing mortals' faces. It became a dream: the watcher in the deck-chair, the vegetation, the memories which slid about between. Only the sun seemed real, and then only as the source of the bright daze in which alone such a pageant might take place.

At times a detail would briefly emerge from the dream like a snag, unravelling a thread of his attention: a scent, an alligator on a sandbar, the cry of a bird. Once or twice he even resumed jotting quavers and crotchets on the pad he held, for although if anyone had asked him he would have said music was dead (viewing a landscape inimical to art and innocent of mankind's cultural tomfooleries) something came insistently to him in dribs and drabs which out of a lifetime's habit he could only notate. The unknown figure on its tower proceeded with its wordless song but the context was still unclear. A solitary scena, maybe, or – he looked up with a start – part of a Mass? *A Mass of Life* suggested itself at the very moment he crossly told himself that Delius had already thought of that. But a *secular* oratorio or Mass might be the answer. It would offer opportunities for many of the effects with which he had first made his mark: dazzling passages for full orchestra, grand choral blazes, *a cappella* numbers with the sketchiest accompaniment, quiet meditations for a soloist with maybe a single gracile obbligato instrument (oboe? clarinet?) winding its figurations in the manner of Bach but in the mode of Elgar . . . He laid aside his pad and propelling-pencil. No, this was quite definitely not going to be the third part of the trilogy. That project was dead. *The Apostles* and *The Kingdom* hadn't worked in terms of popularity, he could now admit it. They contained much of his own favourite music but they lacked that inner dramatic compulsion which made *Gerontius* so electrifying. What was that phrase Beethoven had used about his op. 22 piano sonata? *Hat sich gewaschen.* How he recognised that tone of proud assurance, of absolute knowledge that what he had just finished worked and was first-rate. It seemed a long time since he himself had felt the same certainty, an elation which made one almost ribald, content to describe one's new work with a piece of offhanded or heavy humour like Brahms referring to the massive second movement of his Bb piano concerto as 'a little wisp of a scherzo'. Well, *Gerontius hatte sich gewaschen*, the oratorios hadn't: they'd all too obviously been texts set to music. So forget about Judgements and Judases; he didn't believe in the one and the human drama of the other was too contrived. Archbishop Whately's version was a nice idea but it was literary and brought with it a mustiness of ancient heresy which no longer mattered.

This figure on the tower whom he still couldn't see with any clarity – it had possibilities. It had sprung from his mind and not from some book and came accompanied by a fragment of music which, for all it was aching and bleak, had a distinct freshness. Who was it? Zoroaster? Irritating that Richard Strauss had done him even if for orchestra alone. Whoever this was had renounced the world – or had been deserted by it – but what was left was positively no idyll. This was no Worcestershire lad who preferred dreaming among the bullrushes; this was somebody with no memories in the midst of a naked reality . . . He gave up. Sooner or later the picture would become clearer or simply fade away as so often before.

During the first day or so of the voyage upriver – which is to say from the Narrows to the tiny settlement of Monte Alegre – the majority of the *Hildebrand*'s passengers spent much time at the rail simply watching the panorama as it passed. Whether at dawn with the ghostly layers of mist arising with water-birds or at noon with its steep heat or at nightfall with its fireflies and monkey-cries, the Amazon seemed to fulfil most people's dreams of the exotic and untamed. Then gradually they began to tire of what they saw as the repetitive scenery, the unbroken walls of jungle, the impression that the ship was eternally rounding the same bend to disclose two islands on the right no bigger than tennis-courts with a large grey heron on each. Surely they had seen them only an hour ago, as well as that group of huts on the bank standing on spindly legs with motionless figures watching apathetically as the ship went by?

'*Caboclos*,' Steward Pyce informed anyone who asked. 'Half-breed rubber gatherers. Half-Indian, half-Portuguese. A miserable lot.' He was a fund of facts.

Bit by bit people drifted away from the rail back to their cards, drinking, backgammon, knitting. (Several women were implacably knitting layettes for babies back home as they had recently knitted socks for the Boys at the Front. These would have the distinction of having been made south of the Equator and up the Amazon. By such things were local reputations enhanced.)

After the Narrows, which effectively separated the great Island of Marajó from the main body of Brazil, the *Hildebrand* turned west into the main stream of the Amazon proper. And now the banks on either side retreated as if some threshold had been crossed. The ship was more generally in midstream than not and often well over half a mile of tawny water flowed between it and the nearer bank. There were fewer of the *caboclos'* huts, too, and the line of jungle seemed darker and still more unbroken. Once over this threshold Edward was astonished by the one thing he had never expected to be impressive: the sky. As the banks diverged everything broadened and fell away leaving enormous spaces overhead. This sky would have struck any sensitive traveller by its vastness and the majesty of its cloudscapes. It was quite unlike the celebrated skies of East Anglia or of the Dutch landscape masters. Those had a quality of luminous emptiness even when filled with clouds and they lacked completely the energy of the Amazon skies. To Edward the clouds over Holland or Suffolk always gave the impression of having drifted in from elsewhere and, provided he watched for long enough, would eventually drift out again unchanged as beyond the edges of an invisible picture frame.

But here it was clear to him that the appalling forest they had entered was exhaling the sky even as it slept. A million square miles of this organism's lungs were sending up pillowy tons of moisture, convections of breath, megawatts of energy. Because the movement of these cloud-masses was so noticeable they gave the sky an extraordinary quality of height which the gentler, more static skies of northern Europe lacked even when flecked with wisps of uttermost cirrus. Here, prodigies of cauliflowers, sacks and cities boiled up and up, turning in upon themselves with wild shifts of colour and texture, dark bruisings, frosty streaks, reaching far overhead to where, at noon and in the late afternoons especially, massive thunderstorms would take place at altitudes so high that not a whisper of sound reached the ears nor drop of rain struck the *Hildebrand's* decks. From cloud-mass to cloud-mass the vivid lightnings crazed, sometimes running from a single point like trickles of liquid down each side of the sky. People held their breath. Nothing. The silence unnerved them: it was not natural. The cathartic order of steamy heat relieved by a violent thunderstorm was withheld. The lightning whirled and jabbed in silence, the steamy heat persisted.

At dusk the colours were stupendous and again the sensitive among the passengers had no doubt that this was how the primaeval skies of the planet would have been. An enormous orange sun, swelling as it fell to the surface of the forest, would set ahead of the ship and flare the river into molten substances across which birds skimmed. Hoatzins, with their wispy crests and peculiar breastbones more like pterodactyls than birds, flapped in silence away from the river heading towards their private lost worlds. The extreme tranquillity seemed even to mute the sound of Chief Stanford's engines and the steady rush of water became louder. The dawns, too, were calculated to make any observer think of pre-history although not many were up in time to notice since most had found sleep difficult on account of the heat and still lay like logs with pads across their foreheads soaked in long-evaporated cologne.

VIII

In Amazonas at any rate it's easy to believe Time's ever-rolling stream flows backwards. We're being borne into pre-history. It helps one's memory – not just for the details but the atmosphere (sounds/smells/tastes) – of one's own past.

The real awfulness of becoming an 'official' & public figure is that by a long series of lies, biographical evasions, over-simple explanations for people who don't understand artists – one gradually falsifies one's own life. I look at these stupendous clouds now in a way which reminds me how little I've properly observed the sky for years despite my insistence to everyone (& myself) on my 'outdoor' habits. This afternoon I watched a bronze and vermilion city paved with pearl pass across the 'Hildebrand''s bows for the best part of half an hour. Just like a child I walked its dissolving streets, entered alleys as they formed, climbed a hillock which overlooked a palace until suddenly the palace began overlooking the hillock. I subsided with bridges and was wafted to fraying pinnacles. I burst painlessly through mushy ramparts. And all the time there was that sound – why not call it sound? – a sense of inaudible music which accompanies such things & is heard as tho' beneath the open windows of a veiled mansion. It always was like that except once the music wd. make itself properly heard. Now it reminds me sadly of how I felt & so for a moment I forget I'm supposed to be an old master & become an apprentice once more, all ears & full of <u>longing</u>.

How at any age can one make any sort of decent terms with this longing? At fifteen one did it by thinking those marvellous tunes would – as soon as the 'craft' had been 'lerned' – fit together into sthg. which had never before been done. One carried them about like a collection of diamonds sewn into a traveller's belt for use when the exact needy moment arrived. But after enough years next to the skin they began to feel like uncomfortable liabilities, likely to be losing their value through some vagary of the marketplace. (The longing, however, persisted undulled.) As for the diamonds . . . That damned Trio of P&C no. 1 – when the King asked me how I'd dreamed up such a 'corker of a tune' (HM's phrase) – I told him quite truthfully I'd been carrying it around for twenty years, which puts it at 1880ish. I can't remember its genesis, of course – maybe it was sawing wood or perh. the rhythm of an exultant tramp up the Sugar Loaf. Or maybe it was what the clouds were moving to one afternoon as I lay flat on my back in a field. But when I was actually orchestrating the march in 1901 I remember writing to Nim saying sthg. like 'Gosh, man, what a tune I've got in my head' as if it had just dropped on me that afternoon. But of course it hadn't – an excellent example of an implied fib. It was simply time to 'go public' with an old diamond so I was just being a good salesman to give Novello's <u>& myself</u> confidence.

Well, 1880, those <u>were</u> good days for music-making. To read the asses now you'd think I'd spent the time walking around like Beethoven in those Lyser sketches, hands behind back, frock coat billowing, furrowed brow raised 4square to heaven, trying to work out a way of putting England on the musical map of Europe. Too silly. <u>England</u>. I didn't care a hoot about 'England' – who at that age wants to bother himself with his own nation? – there was only this marvellous landscape into wh. I'd been born & wh. <u>exuded</u> music. Schumann, Dvořák, Tschaik., they'd all of them looked around at their own landscapes & then written <u>themselves</u>. They hadn't the least interest in writing 'German' or 'Bohemian' or 'Russian' music. As Schumann himself said: 'Being a man, and humane, is much more than being a German and Germanic.' I read and played them all – especially Schumann. No mistaking what they were about.

Like many of the others Edward himself found the heat at night made it hard to sleep. When he wrote an entry in his Journal his forearm stuck to the page. He was pleasantly surprised by the absence of mosquitoes since he had heard the adage repeated as a litany by even the least experienced travellers aboard: 'Behind every leaf an insect; in every flower at least one ant.' He lay on his bunk with the light off. A muted glow penetrated the curtains from the shelter deck outside. Footsteps and voices passed now and then. At a great distance the band was intermittently audible until midnight. The faint sounds seemed to reach him from across millennia, now as if he were overhearing the last revels in Babylon, now as if they were fragments of something more mysterious. He remembered the Piper at the Gates of Dawn in *The Wind in the Willows*, whole passages of which he knew practically by heart. How had the Rat put it? 'Dance-music – the lilting sort that runs on without a stop – but with words in it, too – it passes into words and out of them again – I catch them at intervals – then it is dance-music once more, and then nothing but the reeds' soft thin whispering.'

He roused himself enough to pad into the bathroom, drink copious draughts of water and swallow a dose from his blue bottle. Bit by bit the potion which quietened horses lulled him and sent him into a sleep deep enough for a sudden commotion at three in the morning to wake him to a drifting, semi-conscious state which precluded curiosity. Far away a bell was clanging, the engines' massive purr changed to a shudder. Steel creaked. Footsteps ran down carpets outside and drummed on naked iron overhead. Maybe there were shouts, too, but Edward was waiting for the purring to begin again and consciousness ebbed away.

Going to breakfast the next morning he met the Purser and it was not until the man greeted him and trusted he hadn't been disturbed by the noise during the night that he dimly remembered having been woken.

'The fact is, Sir Edward, there was a tragedy last night.' The Purser had a discoloured look about him and his voice was low as if he were entrusting a true version of events to a senior man who would know better than to pass it on to juniors. 'Dr Ashe has gone.'

'How do you mean, gone?'

'I know it's incredible but he simply jumped overboard and vanished. Quite by chance he was seen by two of the people you share your table with – Miss Air and Mr Fortescue. I believe you know them both?'

'Certainly I do. I'd think they, if anyone aboard, would make admirable witnesses. What happened?'

'Just that,' said the Purser, who kept glancing aside at the floor as if fresh consequences were only just striking him. 'They were up on deck, looking at the stars and so on – you know. They noticed Dr Ashe come past but assume he didn't see them since they were in the shadow of some davits. But they saw his face in the deck-lights and swear he didn't look crazed or drunk in any way. He moved off down the deck about twenty feet away, climbed over the rail and simply dropped into the river. They were so astonished it took them a few seconds to react. Of course we stopped and made a thorough search with every light we could muster but the wretched fellow was gone.'

'Good God. How do you reckon his chances?'

'Slim, frankly. We were a good couple of cables – that is, about three-quarters of a mile from the nearest bank and the current was treacherous enough to deter the Captain from prolonging the search. I expect you've gathered, sir, that Captain Maddrell's not a man who deters easily but when it comes to the safety of his ship and the passengers, well.'

The Purser left it there but the unspoken verdict was clear. Nobody walked deliberately overboard in the middle of the night, sure of being unobserved, without wishing to do away with himself. The doctor would not have surfaced. Whatever the alligators or piranhas had left might fetch up on a sandbar or bump against the rotting stilts of a *caboclo*'s hut, but the mortal Dr Ashe had undoubtedly ceased.

Molly and Fortescue were not at breakfast. He assumed they were in their cabins, too shaken by what they had witnessed to feel like eating. Indeed as he took his seat he found his own appetite had vanished and drank a cup of coffee in a sort of solemnity while thinking back on his meeting with the unfortunate doctor. The more he thought about it the more uneasy he became. There had been something indelicate about that conversation and their schoolboyish pact. Underneath the doctor's manner, he now saw, had run a current of murkiness, destructive and desperate. Yes, and he himself had . . . During these reflections he became aware the ship had stopped and through a nearby window he could see an olive-skinned man in a uniform climb over the rail. Not a pilot, he thought, and shortly afterwards Molly and Fortescue appeared with the Captain and all four moved out of sight. But the ship remained hove-to for barely ten minutes and as she got under way once more he caught a glimpse of the official's cutter heading back towards a settlement on the bank trailing a white plume of smoke above its curling wake.

The news travelled quickly around the ship, gathering lurid details as it went. The orderly with the red moustache was so distraught he had to be sedated in his quarters. A hasty search was made of the passengers for a qualified doctor and two retired family practitioners were unearthed who, together with a nurse on the *Hildebrand*'s crew and Molly Air herself, would probably prove equal to most medical emergencies. There was also a vet who had practised in Africa.

The incident had clearly enraged the Captain. He stayed away from his table and was only occasionally seen, dark-faced, about the ship. That morning he appeared in his own day cabin after knocking.

'I'm sorry to disturb you, Sir Edward.'

'My dear fellow, this is your cabin.'

'I gather the Purser told you about last night's little episode?'

'He did, yes. I can only say I'm extremely sorry. A tragic business.'

'It's that all right, but I really came to apologise to you. Puts the Company in the devil of a position. However one sympathises with the wretched – with the poor man, his act has caused endless . . . Do I make myself clear? I suppose not.' And Captain Maddrell went to glare at the river.

'Did he leave any indication? A note?'

'Not a thing. No, it's obvious he had deep-rooted problems about whose nature I should frankly not care to speculate. The point is he should never have been taken on: the man was quite unstable. Turns out he was rude and aggressive towards some of our passengers. *His own patients*,' the Captain thumped the rail. 'That's what I can't forgive . . . I trust he was never rude to you, Sir Edward?'

'I can't say I ever had reason to consult him as a patient,' said Edward guardedly. 'I've been as right as a trivet so far. But I did chat to him on a couple of occasions and I must admit he did strike me as oddish. For a doctor he certainly had an unconventional manner. I seem to have reached the age, though, when I sometimes find unconventional people more tolerable than the right-thinking herd.'

'Very liberal of you sir, I'm sure,' said the Captain bitterly. 'However, I fear that as far as the Company and its doctors are concerned we set the highest possible value on propriety. I'm sorry the poor devil was off his chump but that's no excuse for gross dereliction of professional standards and nothing whatever can excuse the sheer cowardice of such an act. Taking one's own life ...' The Captain inspected the glittering waters with honest incredulity before simply shaking his head once abruptly like a dog trying to dislodge something in its ear and leaving.

Edward was obscurely surprised by the Captain's reaction which struck him as being at odds with his expressions of concern a week or so previously over the fate of the migrant workers he was taking to Brazil. Of course there was every difference between the evils which beset humanity and the private problems of a man who was thought to have let himself down, but ... Strangely it was Fortescue who seemed the most upset, who with that last glimpse had read in the doctor's face an untroubled casualness. 'Like somebody boarding a bus,' was all he would say, but he said it repeatedly. 'Like somebody boarding a bus.'

For the rest of that week much of the ship's gossip had to do with Dr Ashe's presumed suicide and sensational reasons were promoted by bored topers claiming inside information. Several passengers, all of them women, admitted to having had the most extraordinary consultations with him and several outrageous *bons mots* circulated as authentic Asheisms. Young men with polished hair would gleefully pick up the carving knife and fork to tackle the cold buffet (which was now set out at luncheon in place of the table d'hôte) with a curt 'What d'you want cut off?' to their lady friends, evoking peals of laughter. The roaring cad who had kept bouncing into Molly, leaving a little Guerlain on the air, giggled a lot with his friends and snatches of their conversation could from time to time be heard rising like acrid thistledown above the hum of the restaurant. 'Ah, Lady Bugloss. Those little lumps around your neck. What? Going to have to remove 'em.' 'Oh no, Doctor, they're my pearls. Over my dead body.' 'Happy to oblige, m'Lady. What?' The Captain, chancing to be present, ground his teeth.

But although Dr Ashe's dramatic passing became itself swept away – since once Manaos was reached there were plenty of new things to gossip about – it did leave behind a legend which endured. On four subsequent trips, the last being in 1929, passengers reported seeing a man step overboard in the middle of the night. It was always at the same spot in the river and on each occasion the ship stopped and searched without finding anything. The man was always identically described, wearing the same clothes and with the same cadaverous face. The fifth and final sighting occurred in the early Thirties aboard the *Hilary*, the *Hildebrand*'s new sister ship (the original *Hilary* having been sunk in 1917).

Such phenomena lay in the future, however. The incident upset Edward for reasons he could not have confided to the Captain. The memory of having colluded with the Doctor was something he preferred not to dwell on and his guilt extended to wondering anxiously whether before he vanished the man might not mischievously have told Steward Pyce of their little plot. Did Pyce know? It was a question which bothered him in a minor way until the end of the voyage.

And why had he not interceded on the dead man's behalf when Maddrell had charged him with cowardice? Maybe there was such a thing as cowardice in war; but if a man were at war with himself and lost, why might that despairing act not be seen as both dignified and brave? No-one could ever know what went on in another man's mind, nor could they presume to judge another's mental suffering. It had always struck him as the final horror that attempted suicide was a criminal offence and if the person trying to do away with himself failed and was physically saved he was likely to face prosecution and even imprisonment, a prospect which seemed cold-bloodedly designed merely to ensure that any further attempt would be more efficiently executed.

He had no difficulty in remembering the passages in his own life when he had seriously thought about killing himself. The nearest he had come to it had not, strangely, been after the greater disillusionment set in during the lowest points of the war or after Alice's death. It had been at the turn of the century, following the infamous fiasco of the Birmingham première of *Gerontius* when the fate of his art seemed perfectly reflected in the accounts he drew up for Jaeger which showed a net loss of £21 in getting *Cockaigne* performed by the Philharmonic Society who had commissioned it. He had also reckoned that, to date, *Enigma* had earned him £2. 9. 11d. There was no future for a musician in England. The pigs weren't interested in proper music and that was that . . . He entered a pact with himself that if he failed to make a go of some other kind of profession, then rather than making an abject return to teaching he would kill himself despite the appalling stigma for his family. Composition was so obviously a dead end in England he would have done with it and go into trade. Without telling anybody he wrote to a coal company in Malvern and on one of his visits to London walked through the very city streets he had just set so splendidly to music to knock on the door of a brokerage firm whose name he had come across.

Staring now at a *pao d'arco* tree on the distant bank whose brilliant yellow flowers provided a dab of colour amid the sombre green he could not even manage an ironic smile at the recollection. He had presented himself as Edgar Wardle, the sleight effacement of his own name having given him a moment's grim pleasure in the train, but it was immediately clear that whatever name he had gone under he would not have been employed. They had been polite, even respectful, but firm. What it boiled down to was that at forty-four he was far too old to be taken on in any capacity since he came without evidence of employment in other brokerage houses. At that age a gentleman would long since have aspired to a seat in the Boardroom . . . On the instant Edgar Wardle vanished and in his stead a penurious composer went out down the front steps. He lacked even the energy to look up at the heavy ironwork arms holding between them a white glass globe which at night no doubt sent a gaseous beacon of brokerage hope across the tangling sea of City traffic.

Perhaps the most painful of Alice's relics were her diaries which since her death he had opened once or twice at random and then miserably closed after reading a line or two. An entry he had found dated from this time in 1901. She had confided to the page an awful anxiety that he would actually carry out what were obviously almost daily threats. That immediate crisis had eventually passed. Less than three years later he was Sir Edward Elgar – still rat-poor, but even at the time he must have recognised that the chances would have been slender indeed of his having become Sir Edgar Wardle, plutocrat, in the same short span.

IX

If at some future date I shd. chance to re-read this balderdash & wonder why it looks as though I have wept on it the answer is – SWEAT. Pyce knowingly informs me that it's wonderfully cool at present aboard this ship on account of the effects of bowling along at however-many-miles-an-hour-it-is over water. I shd. just wait until we tie up in Manaos, he says with ill-concealed glee. He still brings me samples daily so I can't grumble. Despite its colour the river appears remarkably clean under the microscope. Virtually no bacteria, only a certain amount of suspended vegetable matter. This morning I spilled the last of my eosin, damn & blast. I suppose there might be a supply in Manaos; I'll have to make up to a scientist. I shd. have bought a trunkload of glass beads/trinkets/test-tubes.

On a flat morning (yesterday) I found in the library & read Richard Jefferies' novel 'After London'. Good idea – viz, after some unspecified disaster London's wiped out, most of southern England's beneath a gigantic lake, jungle & jungle law are everywhere taking over & making a green & unpleasant land. Hard to imagine what cd. possibly bring about a disaster of such magnitude – socially, that is; after the recent war we none of us need to be convinced about man's technical destructive powers . . . (How the images still haunt one: that Belgian town reduced to acres of rubble-heaps neatly gridded with cobbled streets which a ragged man is sweeping.)

But here I keep looking up at that fecundity, the blind burgeon of it all & am chilled. Maybe this is a vision of where we're heading, steadily at Full Steam Ahead into a new Dark Age. I think it is my own country on this boat; England on its long voyage backwards to oblivion. What was that unguarded phrase I used to describe the Ab Sym? 'Massive hope in the future'? H'm. That's a goner at any rate. The young ladies aboard twitter, the young men prance (some of 'em). They foxtrot & charleston & tango to all hours without a care in the world. My contemporaries drink & snooze & lay down all the laws they never obeyed themselves. Almost no-one seems overwhelmed by what we're sailing into. An ex-Indian Army man (Cuthbertson?) fetched up at the rail beside me this afternoon, looked long & blinkingly through b-&-s fumes at the distant prospect & said with memorable aplomb: 'Gad sir, can't see the trees for the wood,' but then went & ruined what was probably the first witticism of a lifetime by adding, 'Should be the other way around, that.'

Finally I suppose there's good reason for despair. The 'massive hope in the future' did after all refer as much to my own career as to anything more general since the concerns of Humanity at large seemed less pressing (I bet that never crossed Walford Davies' mind, tho' – not that it was intended to). But now after the best part of a generation has been reduced to bonemeal what do we see all around but ineffable mediocrity. Nobody any longer has the least idea of the solid, the noble, the hard-won. Everything must be easy, palatable, undemanding & preferably dusted over with jiggy little jazz-noises. Where are men's aspirations now? Why are they all so scared of the least difficulty? That dreary sniveller Beecham, not content fourteen years ago with having cut the Sym to $\frac{1}{2}$ hr (when he cd. be induced to play the thing at all) still cuts the malign influence out of Sym II, apparently. Someone must have held a gun to his fat head to make him include the thing in one of his progs. A little too raw for poor Bowdler-Beecham, I suppose. Oh Edward what a stupid doltish ass you've been to waste your life on the idea that art – in its small way – can make the least difference to things. The greater the art the less it has to say to the mediocre & there's no getting around it. The human race will just go on stumbling blindly across an endless battlefield 'cos it don't really mind physical pain & destruction: it's thinking & being moved & having to change it can't bear. So it deals with art by guzzling down the sugar & imagining any bitter lumps are the artist's culinary oversights, evidence of Homer nodding in his chef's hat. Of course the public's greatest revenge is not to ignore a work of art, nor even to amend it like Beecham but to turn it into a classic. Those great works conceived on the edge of darkness are most easily tamed by being made classics because almost by definition classics don't disturb. You can no longer see classics (the 'Mona Lisa') or hear them (Beethoven's 5th & 9th). What was it that professor said recently of 'Jude the Obscure'? 'Some of us will feel he rather overdoes the gloom.' Perfect. An astonishing & painful work of the imagination reduced by some rancid little twerp to an offence against good taste by not being cheerful enough. That's England all over & above all when dealing with its own artists. Good taste, fair play & the amateurish reign supreme. Anything really great or awkward or uncongenial is simply beyond the British capacity to cope. Imagine 'King Lear' being published today – the field-day of the Mediocracy: 'Repulsively violent', 'Dreadfully depressing', 'Unrelieved gloom', 'Quite absurd'.

Not that the great British Public haven't been set by the ears of late, what with some of the modern noises being chucked at it. I can certainly remember the furore of Schoenberg's 'Five Orchestral Pieces' when they got their first perf. at the Proms in 1912. It was the British equivalent of the Paris première of Stravinsky's 'Rite of Spring' the following year. I never heard it myself, being otherwise occupied, but it was clear that neither players nor audience knew what had hit them. Ernest Newman wrote sthg. about the work being so destitute of meaning the audience laughed audibly all through the performance & hissed vigorously at the end, while 'The Times' said it was like a poem in Tibetan which made me laugh drains. Since then one has heard a good deal more of Herr Schönberg & while I still don't know any of his music & have not much desire to I do think he writes sympathetically in his own defence. He's caustic & intransigent & I'm quite old enough to like that in an artist, especially when that artist says congenial & sensible things such as he wishes he were as popular as Tschaikovsky only rather better & that people ought to forget everything they've heard about his music & just listen to it. I recognise that. I read somewhere that he claims every note he writes conforms to the logic of the heart & I like that too. No accidents, just accidentals. Well, while his 'Orchestral Pieces' were being done for the first time so were the Music Makers up in B'ham and they were from the heart, too.

Later

How wonderfully bad-tempered I've become! Re-reading the above I come across apoplectic phrases like 'dreary sniveller' & 'ineffable mediocrity'. But how else other than in private rant can one sound off about anything as blithely unstoppable as a new Age? Things really have changed from top to bottom, even one's oldest friends are not immune to rot setting in. Those awful people Frank Schuster seems to have around him nowadays – his new 'set' – oh, it's not like it was in the dear old days at Bray. Even The Hut isn't the same – full of Bright Young Things or whatever they call themselves, all of them things, some of them young & none of 'em bright. Frank keeps on introducing a series of more or less dubious youths as his 'nephews' – he must be an uncle 80 times over – am I a fool? Does he really think I don't know & if so can he imagine I care a jot? I suspect it was that which poor Alice didn't like about him, he was too luxurious & exotic for her, Chosen Race & wealthy & – in that single respect – not comme il faut. But he was – is – the gentlest, kindest of men, has always championed me & was as instrumental as anyone in getting me into 'Society' when I needed someone in influential circles to pay some attention or I wd. have gone off & shot myself in despair.

But even 'Society' seems all to have changed now. The Court of those days is no more, all the dear King's racy bohemians & Jews & wits, all those Keppels & Sassoons – proper Europeans with a love of the arts & good gossip & decent horseflesh gone. And to think I used to complain of their philistinism! Now look at it – the grey, lifeless mediocrity of the Windsors – purged of the last thing vibrant or funny. The House of Windsor – how that says it all. With a stroke of the pen Saxe-Coburg is transformed for reasons of patriotic embarrassment into Windsor. Why not Reading? Why not The House of Molesey? (Why not Philistia-on-Thames?) At any rate Europe has given way to the Home Counties and it shows. Dull, bourgeois propriety & they say the Prince of Wales's brother's virtually a cretin. The rumour now is the King wants to do away with the Mastership – imagine, that ancient post of Master of the King's Musick abolished overnight. I'd take the wretched thing if only to keep it alive tho' God knows it's at its last gasp under the dead hand of Parratt. An organist. For pity's sake. But doing away with the post – it's very revealing about the new Britain & its sense of priorities. I don't think.

At present we're steaming placidly under an inverted bowl of seething meteorology. I've never seen cloudscapes like these (Molly says triumphantly that this is what she came for & now will I believe her? and Fortescue eyes them with the proper awe of somebody who's shortly going to be flying through them). It's a most extraordinary effect they create – ab origine – & one sees fairly commonplace things as for the first time, or at least shorn of their associations. There was a breathtaking rainbow after luncheon: an unbroken arch planted in the jungle & filling much of the sky. I waited for the associations to come, for the delicate melancholies wh. follow summer storms in England when the sun breaks out again & lights up a line of elms & a silver-white church spire against purple–black sky & a rainbow suggests itself – smiles breaking through tears &c – and the whole thing becomes too watercolourist for words . . . Nothing. None of it here. Just the elements at play, just primordial physics. Most refreshing in its way tho' I don't think I'd care to live with it, never being quite sure if it was a vision of the past or the future but certain in either case that the hand of man was nowhere to be seen. Fortescue, who is the hand of man in person, tells me there's sthg. in America called 'Skywriting' when they go up in aeroplanes & write messages across the sky in smoke. He says it's terribly difficult since unless you're very skilful your own 'prop-wash' rubs out the letters as you make them. Seeing the rainbow today he said that it was theoretically possible to go up and write the word 'Rainbow' in giant letters in an arch in an otherwise rainbowless sky (say in the middle of a cloudless summer's day). Personally I can't see the point but it did strike me as an unexpectedly original & imaginative thing for him to have dreamed up. I asked if it wd. be possible to write a line of music in smoke & showed him what it wd. entail but he thought by the time one had flown back & forth drawing five parallel lines everything wd. have run together & doing uprights & dots on top of that completely impossible. I informed him that it was nothing of the sort – that I'd written all my music in smoke & that it was fast blowing away.

Later still

Smoke or not the Music Makers still left a wound. It's better than anyone knows about the apartness of the artist but all they can find to say is that it's a pot-pourri of self-quotations, as if I'd run out of inspiration & concocted a potboiler from the scattered corpses of previous works. They laugh knowingly when they catch Handel at it as if he were an unscrupulous old rogue, so I get tarred with the same brush. Oh bitter, bitter. I lived with MM on & off from about 1903 and it was <u>most carefully</u> constructed using relatively few quotations (& always reworked). Perhaps what people don't like is it's autobiographical & they simply don't like ME. I wrote out my soul in the Vln conc., Sym II & the Music Makers & I can't disguise it, why shd. I? Maybe they don't like O'Shaughnessy & maybe it isn't a brilliant poem but if they're too brilliant they don't set well. Look at the rot Schubert set so wonderfully. In this case though O'S expressed perfectly in the first 6 lines that sense of the artist's loneliness which is what the 'Enigma' theme was doing in 1898. I therefore couldn't have done better than use my own music again – oh the memory of that feeling was so <u>intense</u> – nor in 1912 cd. I not feel the bitter truth of the Tasso quotation I'd put on the full score of 'Enigma' 14 yrs earlier. 'Bramo assai, poco spero, nulla chieggio'. I <u>had</u> longed for much, I <u>had</u> hoped for little, I <u>had</u> asked for nothing – and got it!!

The pretty settlement of Santarem was reached at the mouth of the Tapajós whose waters, the pure dark green of molten bottle-glass, flowed out into the tawny flood of the Amazon but refused to mix. Instead the entire surface of the confluence became mottled with bi-coloured whirlpools, an effect which delighted Molly although she said sadly that it could hardly be painted since no-one in Europe would believe it.

They were past the halfway point between Pará and Manaos. From now on the Amazon became as exotic as anyone aboard the *Hildebrand* could have wished. Anything edible thrown over the side was generally taken within a few seconds by creatures from below which defied identification. Enough was generally glimpsed to send a frisson through the more nervous: a flash of scaly plates, a vast armoured head, prognathous jaws, teeth. Some of the fish were immense, as could be seen when they rolled leisurely out of the ship's path exposing for a moment a grey–green flank the length of a scraped pig.

Great butterflies drifted across the river and over the decks drawing small gatherings of onlookers wherever they randomly alighted on a straw hat, an awning, the edge of a sticky glass. They flew away again with that tropical flight so different from the fluttering of European species: the few flat strokes and then the wobbling glide carrying them off across the surface of the water where they might settle on the emerald raft of an uprooted tree, sharing it perhaps with a motionless jewelled bird until both had flowed away astern. At night the lighted decks attracted even huger moths, some of which were the size of wrens but with colour and figurings as brilliant as those birds were dowdy. This time their presence was usually announced by squeaks of dismay and a rush for head-scarves. Edward would stand at the rail, often with an immense night creature perched on his lapel or his sleeve, its folded or shimmering wings leaving all manner of gorgeous dusts on the creamy linen. At this he would gaze fondly until it flew away, murmuring 'I say you *are* a beauty' or 'They've dressed you up to look more fearsome than you are.'

Once the ship stopped for an hour opposite a tiny settlement which from midstream was no more than a handful of orange oil flares, the only lights on a dark continent. A pilot had to be picked up and because of silt banks the ship stood off and dropped anchor while the transfer was made in a *bataloe*. Without the sound of water along her plates and with her engines quiet the *Hildebrand* was suddenly at the centre of emptiness. Standing at the rail on the side away from the settlement Edward could see practically nothing, there being no moon, except where soundless flashes lit the horizon or from closer overhead gave a mauvish impression of dark and endless vegetation. For the first time strange calls became audible from the distant bank. Behind the mechanical frogs and the sizzle of tree crickets came cries which, had he been his own ancestor, would have bristled his pelt the length of his spine. The screams – of jaguar? monkey? of hunter? prey? – had that curious hollowness of jungle sounds which appear to be simultaneously the cry and its echo. It was easy to believe that the density of the vegetation and the night which stuffed its chinks conducted sound as effectively as water, so that these howls and lonely barks might be coming from boundless distances, the night air like a membrane bringing him news of savageries beyond the horizon. Suddenly the ship felt very small and frail anchored there in the middle of it all with water on either side as meagre insulation. The conviction came over him again that this voyage he was making was a journey backwards in time; what remained to be resolved was how much of that time was bounded by his own few decades. What lay all around was elemental and pagan: it was in no way gentle. Here there was no kindly-eyed Pan like a Victorian uncle with shaggy thighs and hooves who would cradle small lost river-creatures as in Kenneth Grahame's animistic vision.

'You can't write out of nothingness,' he murmured at the water, the pink–blue flashes, the screaming wilderness. 'You have to write out of a culture. Without men there is no art, no hearts to be touched, no eyes to weep. There are only cells.' Even so, he thought briefly of his own creature on a tower and wondered what dawn it was witnessing, leaved in hectic crimson. He was glad when a shudder through his soles announced the quickening of the engines and the ship's eventual getting under way, unaware (until he went below to better-lit regions) that the temporary pall of coal-smoke drooping heavily in the windless air over one rail like a lock of greasy black hair had left his linen jacket encrusted with smuts.

After the settlement of Obidos they passed over the deepest point in the Amazon so far known. The figure of one hundred and twenty feet was known also to Steward Pyce who circulated with the news, generally being thanked for his pains. But people were less intrigued by fact than they were by rumour. It was learned that they would shortly be passing an island on which was supposed to be a lost city. The very phrase echoed with mystery and adventure and indeed figured prominently in the titles of several books in the ship's library. There was speculation as to how a city might come to be lost in the first place, it sounding more like a case of remarkable carelessness rather than anything more dynamic.

'Surely there's a stock historical scene,' said Edward; 'when a wounded man on a wounded horse drags himself back inside the shattered ramparts and says "All is lost! The city is lost! Flee for your li . . ." and an arrow takes him plumb in the wishbone.'

'Oh, lost in *that* sense. I hadn't thought of it like that, not actually *sacked*.'

'You can see why – at least from an adventure-novelist's viewpoint. There's got to be a treasure and there's got to be a mystery. Neither of those can survive a really decent sacking.'

'More than that, there's got to be a more or less intact city.' Fortescue revealed himself as no stranger to the genre. 'The whole point is the place must look as though everybody woke up on a

Tuesday morning and said "This is the dullest town in the whole of South America. I'm off" and simply left. Then after a few months the jungle moved back in and a year or two later nobody could have found the place even if they'd looked for it.'

'But why wouldn't they have taken their treasure with them?' asked Molly.

'That's easy,' said Edward who was entering the spirit of this fictive city. 'The people did take their treasure with them but since they were poor it didn't amount to more than a few personal belongings. A retirement clock, a cigar-cutter, Aunt Ada's amber necklace. That sort of thing. The real treasure belonged to the priests: vast golden idols, ingots of green Amazonian gold, silver, unknown minerals and gems of hypnotic beauty and enormous weight. But how could they carry them? The people had already left and they themselves were hopelessly weakened by years of debauchery and excess compounded by a monotonous diet of human hearts. They had to abandon it all where it lay and hurry crossly after their departed congregations in flapping white robes and jaguar-teeth necklaces. But they got hardly any distance before falling prey to deadly orchids whose scent alone lured men to screaming dooms, and anacondas whose glowing yellow eyes swayed thirty feet above them on necks of such sickening girth that the priests died of fright even as the huge jaws opened and a sticky rain of venom sprinkled their grinning faces.'

'Enough!' cried Molly. 'More than enough! It's quite obvious you could have made an excellent living as an adventure writer had you not been a composer.'

'Much better. And don't imagine the irony escapes me.'

Interested passengers scanned various lumps of land they passed but few of these appeared large enough to conceal a city. Shortly after Parintins they noticed various bifurcations in the main stream, many of which seemed to be substantial rivers in their own right. It was not until Edward was shown a chart on the bridge that he appreciated how the next one hundred and sixty miles of left-hand bank represented the northern 'coast' of the gigantic Tupinambarama Island which had claims to be the world's largest river island. Even Fortescue, when Edward pointed this out, stopped scanning the distant shore with his binoculars as if hoping to glimpse a white gleam of hitherto-unnoticed temple among the myriad acres of foliage.

A few pink and white *barracas* standing in a clearing announced Itacoatiara. It was hard to imagine that such a small gathering of sheds and bungalows should be the entrepôt for the entire Madeira River which joined the Amazon eighty miles further on. The Madeira led off south-west through some of the world's least-known territory towards the Mato Grosso and Bolivia and uncharted headwaters in the far Andes. The very sight of the confluence was enough to intensify Edward's sense of the unimaginably remote, piling as it did the additionally undiscovered on the already undiscovered. It was extraordinary to think of men four or five hundred miles up that river looking not upstream to Porto Velho but wistfully back to this shanty-town of Itacoatiara as marking the nearest real link with the outside world.

And suddenly nearly four days had gone by since they left Pará and they had nearly reached their destination. There was a sense of people surreptitiously stretching themselves as after an overlong sermon, ready to get to their feet and feel what it was like to be on the ground in the heart of this jungle which had accompanied them unbroken every one of the thousand and forty-two miles from the sea. Molly and Fortescue were clearly excited and relieved their apprehension by saying well, if it didn't 'work out' at least there was a regular steamer service back to England. Since they were neither of them the sort to permit themselves an easy return from anything on which they had set their hearts it intensified Edward's sense of imminent desertion. It was not hard to imagine disasters that were less possibilities than likelihoods: Molly's wasting fever and irreversible decline up a tributary in a bungalow ticking with termites; Fortescue's crash-landing leaving him with a broken leg, a Webley revolver and six rounds.

At twilight on the evening before their arrival he chanced to be on deck at a moment when the ship's course took her to within fifty yards of the bank. He was thinking of the fragment of work he had achieved: all too little in three weeks to justify his celebrating the Muse's return. Happening to glance up he was immobilised by what he saw. On the bank was a small clearing and in the centre of the clearing stood a vast pole which on closer inspection was the trunk of a dead tree, most of whose branches had broken off into stubs. At the top of this pole stood a figure – undoubtedly a human figure – dressed in a white robe and appearing to stare out across the river, across the thousand-mile jungle to where the sun was setting.

It was absurd, solemn, so unexpected in its congruence with his own reflections that he felt his heart actually pause. The ship went on. The motionless, rapt figure stared and stared and passed from sight as the forest swallowed the clearing in its general dusk.

What vision was this? He was withdrawn at dinner and later embarked on an anguished night which soaked him in heat, plunging him in and out of insomnia and mild delirium until the two states became indistinguishable. There was no narrative, only a repeated motif of being on a series of journeys all of which left him stranded, alone and defenceless, in a variety of threatening land-scapes. The word Somnaa echoed through these slept places: a native location, the name of a planet (for one of his journeys was on a deserted forest world circling an unknown golden star), a potion which had to be sought and taken to restore things. He would regain consciousness enough to find himself sitting on the edge of his bed drinking avidly from the water-bottle. In his last remem-bered bout of troubled slumber he was under threat of death in the lost city of Osmana at the hands of a Samoan witch-doctor or high priest wearing a necklace of jaguar's teeth and girt about with monkey pelts and shrunken heads on strings. This man was offering Edward two gourds, one of which contained *mosaná*, a lethal poison prepared from the urine of temple bats, and the other which was empty. The terms were that if Edward were lucky enough to choose the empty gourd he must mime drinking the contents as if it were the *mosaná* and keep up the pretence by apparently dying in convulsions. This was to convince the audience, a hostile priesthood who were not in on the subterfuge. The high priest was supposed to be secretly on his side but Edward had heard too much about witch-doctors to be fooled. He knew the stories of perfectly healthy people dying simply because a witch-doctor had told them they would. He therefore suspected that in carrying out the mime he would be playing into this barbaric prankster's hands; at some point he would willy-nilly begin believ-ing in the inevitability of his own death and so die.

When at first light Steward Pyce came in with a cup of tea he found his distinguished passenger half off the bed, flannel pyjama top rucked up under his arms and exposing a waxy white torso shiny with sweat and with some sparse grey hairs around the nipples. Edward, ragingly thirsty, scalded his mouth on the tea. Reaching for the water-bottle at his bedside he found it full to the brim, clearly untouched since the previous evening.

'When do we reach this damned place?'

'At about ten this morning, Sir Edward,' said the Steward who was pottering attentively. 'Did we pass a bad night, sir?'

'I don't know yet. It's too soon to tell if I *have* passed it.'

'Definitely you have, sir. It's a beautiful morning. Amazon's given birth. That's the ship's cat, sir.'

'Good name. Is she particularly big, then?'

'Less so now, sir.'

'Do you know, Pyce,' said Edward, putting down his teacup and passing a sodden handkerchief over his head and face, 'if you spell Amazon with an "s" instead of a "z" and jumble the letters around they'll spell Manaos?'

Evidently he had not known. He went impassively out leaving a faint smell of brilliantine on the air. As Edward finished his tea he began idly jumbling the same letters afresh in his head until they soon began to bring back uncomfortable flashes of the night he had just spent.

'I've enjoyed this trip,' he said on deck after breakfast. 'I suppose I ought to say I *am* enjoying it since for me it's not yet even half over. It's been wonderful to get completely away.'

'You've not done much work, then?' Molly asked.

'Certainly not. Why should I? I'm sixty-six and I've *done* a lot of work. I don't have to go on doing it until I drop in my tracks. Look how much else there is to do –' and he waved a hand at the sheets of sunlight lying elastically on the broad river ahead as if showing an inheriting son his future dominions.

'Of course,' said Molly apologetically. 'I only meant, well, a few days ago you mentioned you were sketching something.'

'Oh, just an idea now and then. A germ. A glimmering. Something might be made of it one day. Nothing serious. You, on the other hand, have been working quite hard I suspect. When you're not downstairs boning up on Portuguese or Tupí or – what was that language you said everyone gets by with here? *lingua geral?* – you're up on deck quietly sketching away. I admire that. Our friend Fortescue, too. I imagine he's also done quite a bit of homework in his own quiet way.'

'He has, yes.'

Edward looked at her. 'He strikes me as an admirable young man.'

'So he does me,' she said to the passing water which was now beginning once more to take on the marbled appearance of two immiscible liquids swirling in eddies of contrasting colour. The *Hildebrand* had reached the confluence of the Amazon and the Rio Negro. The black waters from the north, stained with the soil acids of the Guiana Shield, contrasted weirdly with the yellow–green Amazon which was already lighter here than it had been lower down because of the silt-laden white-water tributaries which poured into it from the west. The ship ploughed across this treacherous expanse of what seemed sinister oils before deserting the Amazon for the final nine miles of its outward journey.

'That's the way I'll be going shortly,' she said, pointing to the great stream they had left, to Iquitos and the Andes and the far Pacific Ocean.

'You're not scared?'

'Of course. But fascinated. The one's supposed to cancel out the other.'

'It does with me,' he agreed drily. 'The question is, which?'

Molly laughed. 'But when you've been *longing* for something?'

'Ah. Longing. I understand that all right. Look,' he fumbled in a side pocket and produced his silver propelling-pencil, 'I'd like you to have this. Go on, take it. Not very grand, I'm afraid. Just a memento.'

She knew the more she demurred the gruffer he would become. 'I'm honoured, Sir Edward. I'll always keep it. Thank you very much. I don't quite know . . .' and she somewhat bemusedly read the inscription on its side: *To Edward Elgar from his friends in the L.O.S.* 'Surely this is a very personal thing?'

'Of course it is. What on earth would be the point in my giving it you otherwise? The man who ran the Liverpool Orchestral Society was the truest friend I ever had, Alfred Rodewald. That was the year he died – twenty years ago now practically to the day. Well, one can't go on forever looking back. Take it – it's not a bad one. It's done me well.' And he turned away and walked off leaving her staring at the nearer of a pair of stone lighthouses falling astern.

Suddenly in sunlight across an expanse of water Manaos rose up as a sizeable town, all white houses and towers. The trees and vegetation which split up the red of its tiled roofs appeared by contrast a brighter green than the surrounding forest. As they approached with a blare of C which lost itself over the waters and rebounded feebly from the low red earth cliffs the passengers lining the *Hildebrand*'s decks could make out individual features. Dominating everything with civic extravagance was the dome of the Opera House glittering in its topee of blue and gold Alsatian tiles. On the foreshore a series of floating wharves supported an extensive shanty-town of dilapidated huts in addition to cranes and the monster hardware associated with modern commerce. It seemed altogether extraordinary to find a city of this size so remotely situated; the decrepit dwellings merely emphasised the mercantile solidity of the buildings behind.

And now the movement of people became apparent on the distant dockside: men in white shirts, women with parasols, gathering to wait in the shade of sheds and godowns for these visitors from another world. Edward stood largely unmoved watching the frenzied muster of tattered children with trays around their necks, the silver winking of ice-cream carts. Drifting round in the thermals over the town the inevitable cloud of *urubus* circled, sifting with their slitted nostrils the rich boiling of metropolitan odours for the delirious perfume of carrion. And now names were sliding across his vision, names in bold capitals over the warehouses: BOOTH STEAMSHIP COMPANY LTD, JOAQUIM SOARES and, on a pair of huge white doors in a blue matching that of the sky, the great legend PUSSELS CRONIFER GmbH.

*　　*　　*

Frau von Pussels had been posting a notice on the board in the cool lobby of the Schiller Institute when she heard the C announcing the *Hildebrand*'s arrival. '*Donnerstag*,' she said to herself, glancing up at the rest of the cards and announcements tucked symmetrically behind the lattice of ribbon which criss-crossed the baize board, '*schon gut.*' Elsewhere – very far away – there were clocks and calendars. In Manaos there were boats and seasons, in addition to the daily thunderstorm at ten past noon.

In the five years since her husband had died Frau von Pussels had taken to spending most of her time in the Institute she had helped found thirty years previously and which she had effectively run ever since. She preferred it to her own house, an overlarge .modern villa built at the expense of her husband's parent company

—176—

in Hamburg in a style thought suitable for the founder–manager of a mercantile concern which nowadays had five other branches in South America. She found the villa soulless and – although she would never have said so – in most awful taste. It was prettily sited on a knoll overlooking the river but she liked none of the views inside the house itself. Additionally, the architect had installed some new system designed to cool the air without overhead fans. This mechanism was concealed under the floors and despite his assurances that it would be completely silent it rumbled faintly, making ornaments buzz on polished tables and giving one the impression of being on board ship. Nor, as far as she could determine, did it make the house a single degree cooler; but since she was embarking on her fourth decade here she had long since grown acclimatised and it made little difference to her whether the system worked or not.

The premises which housed the Schiller Institute were by contrast quite old, having been built by one of the earlier Portuguese settlers. The house was large and dark but to her mind not at all gloomy. Rather, it was sombre and fragrant, being lined with dusky forest woods of immense weight and hardness. The waxed floorboards in the hallway near where she was standing were each a metre across and lay like sheets of a fabulous glowing metal, creakless and so close that a playing card might not be inserted between them. From the half-open door of the salon came the repetitive sounds of the Nepomuceno boy quietly tuning the Institute's tropicalised Bösendorfer. A shaft of brilliant Brazilian sunlight lay across the hall and from the shrubbery outside the front door came the faint sounds of tussling birds. She gave one of those involuntary little sighs which, once sighed, made her wonder whether perhaps she had forgotten to breathe for the last five minutes. She realised she was quite happy – no, that was absurd at sixty-two with a dead husband and a dead son – unexpectedly contented would be a better way of putting it. Everyone knew human lives petered out, but here in this stout house on foreign soil there was every evidence of a culture which would outlive. Here were busts of Schiller and Goethe, of Beethoven, Leibnitz and Bach; here was a library; here were the tones of a piano being brought up to scratch for tonight's recital. And here – she glanced once more at the board to make quite sure all the cards were straight – were the talks and slide-shows and lectures by residents with particular skills and by visitors of distinction and accomplishment. It was all a small and proper part of the only thing which finally mattered: the handing-on of a tradition, the transmission of civilisation.

The notice she had just posted was for one of the Reverend Miles Moss's popular talks which he often gave when passing through Manaos. The Reverend Moss was the Anglican Chaplain on the Amazon with a parish stretching two thousand miles from Pará to Porto Velho. His real distinction, however, lay in his enthusiastic moth-hunting. He was at present in Manaos and had told her he had just discovered three new varieties of hawk-moth, one of them in a garden not a hundred yards from the Institute. He was witty, eccentric, charming in a fashion which made her feel something lopsided in him to which she was attracted. She had insisted on his speaking before he quit town to return to Pará in time for Christmas at the end of a month's parochial duties upriver. The Reverend Moss was above all one of those gifted professional amateurs the English seemed to produce in such numbers; he was a considerable authority and in international entomological circles was held in the highest regard. His own collection was magnificent, his work – which from time to time was published by Lord Rothschild – systematic and pioneering. He was also an exhibitor at London's Royal Academy. What could better symbolise the passing-on of European civilisation than taxonomy itself? Classify, classify, classify; that was the painstaking but ultimately sure way of making sense of the natural universe. Things proceeded, the unknown became known, the darkness retreated.

Such were not, of course, Frau von Pussels' actual thoughts as she approved the neatness of the notice board. They were the basis of a rationale which underpinned her dedication to the Institute and its principles and indeed her public person here in this remote enclave. She had long been the wife of Otto von Pussels and a pillar of Manaos's cultural life. She was now the widow von Pussels who, once she had emerged from mourning, could beat no retreat. In any case she had nowhere to go unless it were back to an unfamiliar Germany defeated by war and humiliated by treaty in one of whose anonymous military graveyards lay the remains of their son Eusebius. No, there was no retreating. But the sheer barbarousness of the war had undercut everything, including her own confidence in the civilisation she loved. The machineries of mass destruction had been unprecedented yet there had been scarcely any hesitation in using them. The ethical humanism of centuries, the flower of European culture, had stood wiltingly by while on all sides men climbed into cockpits and tanks and submarines, threw poison chemicals at each other, shredded nature and human beings with impartiality. If Frau von Pussels was not alone in having lost some of her faith she was equally in the company of all those who re-asserted the values of their battered civilisation. She was gently, indomitably marked by that human tendency which, seeing how nearly a building was toppled, praises it for having been so soundly constructed; but she had come perilously close to blaming it for the inherent weakness which almost overthrew it.

Young Nepomuceno had practically finished. He was now vamping in various keys the tunes which only piano-tuners play: pieces seemingly passed on by rote through a guild, since no tuner she had ever met was any sort of pianist. As she passed the doorway, which exhaled a scent of pot-pourri and the mildewed felting inside the opened Bösendorfer, she again experienced a tingle of pleasure at the calm and purposefulness of it. Here in the middle of however many million square kilometres of jungle, dotted with naked savages still occupied with blowpipes and shrinking each others' heads, a cultivated young man had just tuned a very beautiful musical instrument on which later that evening an Italian girl was to play Scarlatti, Mendelssohn, Schumann and Busoni. It was going on. It was proceeding. The darkness would have to take a further step backwards.

In at the front door, catching her in a white blast of light at the foot of the grand staircase, came Raymundo the messenger boy. Raymundo, a handsome *mestiço* lad in his teens with glittery black eyes, had various duties about the Institute in reward for which he was fed and clothed and given a converted pigeon-loft to live in. This was an airy den of which he was greatly proud and for two years he had been showing the kitchen girls the rooftop panorama it afforded of the town. One of his duties was to go down to the dockside and obtain a passenger list of every sizeable ship which visited Manaos. He offered one now, the pages very white in his brown hand.

'Our latest visitors?' Frau von Pussels asked him in *lingua geral*. 'You're a good boy, Raymundo.'

'It's the *Hildebrand, senhora.*'

'I know it is. I ought to recognise its hooter by now.' She took the list with that pleasurable anticipation such things give in out-of-the-way places. Now and then people one knew turned up unexpectedly, but more often there were visitors whose names were familiar and who could be persuaded to give a talk, a lantern-slide show, a recital. She had a considerable knowledge of who was who in the arts and sciences of the Western world and in turn had herself become a minor celebrity whose name was widely known as that of a person one could not leave Manaos without visiting. Now she smoothed out the sheets of the *Hildebrand*'s passenger list and froze, one shoe caught in a puddle of light on the tread of the first stair. There was a long silence.

'*Es musste passieren,*' she said half aloud.

'*Senhora?*'

Realising she had been staring through the boy she smiled and shook her head, dismissing him. She scanned the rest of the list but there were no other names she knew. Her foot in its light-puddle turned slowly and as slowly rose to the tread above as if leaving glue. In the empty space where it had been the mineral flecks in the white marble sparkled like exploding particles of dust. She went up to her office and opened the shutters enough to permit the energetic half-light of an excluded tropic day to bring the room and its furnishings to life. Sitting at her desk she wrote a careful letter in English on the Institute's headed writing-paper.

Dear Sir Edward,

News of your arrival has just reached me via the grapevine which, in places such as this, operates with the efficient self-interest of an isolated community greedy for contacts with the 'movers and shakers' of the world outside.

In any event, welcome to Manaos. Since as a long-term resident here I am certain this is your first visit I wonder if you would permit me to offer my services in the capacity of a guide? From the rubric at the head of this somewhat bombastic stationery you will see that I hold some small position in what are loosely called 'cultural circles' here. But lest this conjure up for you the image of an earnest harridan with spectacles a-glitter with artistic fervour let me assure you that my late husband was a commerçant of not merely local standing and that one way and another access to virtually any door in these parts is guaranteed.

Whether or not you care to avail yourself of this private offer of mine,
might I anyway in my official capacity humbly request that you find a
moment to pay our Institute a visit? You would be doing us a great
honour and not least because internationally-celebrated artists are few
and far between in these parts nowadays. You would also discover that
our library here has a not inconsiderable section of Elgariana as
evidence of a longstanding admiration for your music and yourself.

Respectfully yours,
Magdalena von Pussels

She laid down her pen and re-read what she had written. Too
effusive? Certainly it was a bit wordy, a bit long. Too much about
her own and her husband's credentials? And might not the tone –
beneath the conventional phrases – be construed as slightly
informal? That piece of self-mockery about the harridan, for
example. There was also the quotation from O'Shaughnessy
which maybe hinted at too intimate a knowledge . . . Above all,
why *hadn't* she the courage to identify herself? She took up her pen,
poised it to delete, expunge, alter, re-write entirely. Instead she
addressed an envelope, folded the letter with a sigh and sealed it. It
was too difficult. She could have written twenty versions but there
was no single correct or even plausible way to write to a man one
had not seen for forty years but whose career one had followed
score by score, magazine article by magazine article, month-old
press cutting by month-old press cutting.

Downstairs in the hall she met the Nepomuceno boy just leaving
with his little leather roll of tuning forks and keys.

'It sounded very sweet to me,' she said. 'Are you happy?'

'With the tuning . . . As good as I am able . . . But the action . . .
Several notes were slow and sticky. The climate, you see. French
chalk . . . Now . . . '

She had long grown accustomed to the young man's peculiar
speech which one might have taken for hopeless diffidence until
one noticed his gaze which never left the face of the person he was
addressing. She had decided it was more a boredom with the effort
required to compose whole sentences. Once the meat had been
expressed the remains of the thought was allowed to run off. She
had no idea what would become of him. Of his intelligence there
was no doubt. He had an excellent ear but practically no musical
talent. On the other hand Professor Almeirim spoke of him as a

mathematical genius but one whose numerical arguments proceeded in much the same way as his verbal, something which might well disqualify him from serious consideration by the University of Rio de Janeiro's Mathematics Department where his application was already lodged. Still, budding genius or brilliant dunce there was no reason why he might not at the age of nineteen be required to act as an errand-boy, so instead of summoning Raymundo once more from kitchen regions or pigeon-loft Frau von Pussels handed him her letter.

'I'm sure you wouldn't mind slipping down with this,' she said firmly. 'It's rather important that it reaches the ship within the hour if possible and Raymundo . . .' she let the thought trail away in the young man's own style.

'Certainly, Frau von Pussels. You can rely . . . I hope the recital . . .'

The front door opened and closed with a silent blare of light. Somewhere in distant regions the kitchen staff could be heard preparing the refreshments the Institute served in the garden to anybody who cared to drop in to use the library, read a German newspaper or simply chat over a cup of chocolate. She went into the salon through a drift of dust-motes, a beautiful spacious room stretching the depth of the house half filled with rows of jacaranda-wood chairs. She walked its length smelling polish and pot-pourri as well as an odour of burnt jam which drifted robustly in through the net curtains of a pair of French windows standing ajar behind the piano. The *goiabada* or guava jelly the kitchens habitually made just as habitually burned: it was now one of a lexicon of familiar Institute smells of which she had grown fond. Her own villa, by contrast, contained scarcely a single smell of the least emotional significance for her. Its rumbling machineries sometimes contributed a faint oily aroma which only added to the illusion of being on board ship.

She sat down on the leather-quilted piano stool and lifted the keyboard's lid. The sight of it diffused over her a resonant happiness. The inlaid florid signature had a certain Austrian exuberance as if to say 'I, Ludwig Bösendorfer, in my little factory here in Vienna, have created a work of art. There – I sign it *thus*, with a proud flourish. Now, my unknown performer, the rest is up to you.' Passing a fingertip over the letters she could detect scarcely a variation in the silky veneer. Even twenty-five years of equatorial humidity had found neither crack nor swelling to exploit. Now that her letter to Edward was out of her hands she regretted acting with such dispatch. Strangely, she had never envisaged what had actually happened. She had often conceived of going back to Europe for some reason, retiring there maybe, of sending him a letter of condolence on the death of Lady Elgar (instantly rejected as being too pointed, not to say downright threatening), of making an anonymous pilgrimage to some concert or festival where he was conducting. Certainly her imaginings had always included a moment of mutual recognition. But whatever her fantasy it had always depended on her taking the initiative. It had never occurred to her that in all innocence of this being her home (of that she was sure) he might one day fetch up on her threshold as a tourist. Had she taken more time to consider, she now perceived, how very easy it would have been simply to avoid him for the duration of his stay – to have lain low for a few days behind the walls of her mercantile villa and the disguise of her mercantile name.

Still, she was too old to dwell on such things. It was done now. Either he would come or he wouldn't, either they would meet or not. And if they didn't, then his happening briefly to share the same small town many thousands of miles from Europe was merely a curious irony such as Fate occasionally supplied in impish mood, a way of pointing up four decades of estrangement between two people before each went to a widely-distant grave.

She brushed both palms over her thighs and began to play the second of Schumann's *Davidsbündler* dances. It was what she had played when the news of Eusebius's death had reached her, and she had done so with the unopened letter on the music stand as though she were playing the text she had no need of reading. The letter from her surviving sister, with whom she had so little communication that she vaguely knew the handwriting before she could identify it, had exuded an unmistakable aura of next-of-kin. Besides, no letter from Germany in late 1917 could possibly have brought good news. And so she had played without stopping to wonder what to play for an occasion she had long awaited. Later, having done with more conventional ways of expressing loss, she wondered at so unhesitant a choice. As a formally-trained pianist she had, after all, more than three hundred years of keyboard music from which to choose. Why not Bach? Mozart? Almost any Beethoven slow movement? But instead what had come foremost to her fingers was this haunted piece of romanticism, full equally of longing and the loss which engenders it, and with that air of not trying to console which is its own consolation. Beginning on a wayward harmony, the music transcended mere wistfulness by suggesting to the inner ear even after the final cadence that it was still going on endlessly, forever slanted away from resolution.

This short piece she now played without self-indulgence as to rubato, letting the dreamy, faraway quality of the writing do its own work. The notes rang softly in the wood-cased room. Presences came and went: Eusebius, who had himself loved it; Otto, who hadn't. Behind them the years stretched back to Leipzig where she had studied at the Conservatoire, full of ambition to become the Clara Schumann of her day. And behind even such evanescent ghosts of the personal past the great tradition of European culture stood, that magic mountain from which this gem had been chipped. It bulked in the room as in her life. It was as if most days when the roosters woke her in the villa she left her netted bed and went to the opened windows and saw, rising majestically from the still-benighted stain of forest stretching to every horizon, this huge and singular alp. It imprinted its splendour on the landscape of dawn, drawing the eye up the dark pyramid of its foothills towards the peak from whose glittering snows the wind drew a plume of ice crystals like smoke across the pale blue sky. Sometimes the mountain was there when she looked again; often it vanished completely for weeks or even months as if worn out by having to transcend so inimical a climate, so unpromising a place. It was a reassuring vision; it was poignant. It had been many years before she finally accepted that she would only ever be able to look at it: she would never herself tread even its lowest slopes and gaze out with a unique view. This realisation had been a source of abject despondency, then of sadness, and led finally to a judgement – neither resigned nor bitter – that things were as they were and that it was more to the point to run a Schiller Institute in an outpost which craved culture than to keep up the pretence of failed genius in perpetual exile. Brisk as she was accustomed to be with herself, Frau von Pussels was honest enough to wonder whether it was still possible for her to be betrayed by what had once been a marked tendency towards *Schwärmerei*, a certain girlishness of admiration for anyone she suspected of being able to see for themselves the view from the magic mountain.

Often since her husband's death it had been supposed she might leave Manaos and return to Germany although no-one had been so tasteless as actually to presume it to her face. Yet she had spent half her lifetime here and everything she read and heard about Europe led her to imagine she would find little left that was familiar. The Germans – and the English too, for that matter – had a saying which in effect ran: 'You've made your bed, now lie in it' which was always meant punitively. Yet in the last thirty years she had been making a bed here which she accepted would also be her death-bed and she was perfectly content to lie in something she had prepared with care and which fitted her comfortably. It was not the moment for a lumpy mattress amid the wreckage of the land of her birth.

Not that by contrast with Europe Brazil itself had remained hearteningly unchanged. The whole of the Amazon region, and Manaos in particular, had seen a heyday arrive and depart. To that heyday she owed the last three decades of her life. Without it her husband would never have been tempted to pull up his Hanseatic roots and re-plant himself in the scalding red laterite of the South American jungle. Without it, too, she herself would have had no Schiller Institute, no thriving cultural court. This was Brazil, not California or Australia. She had seen pictures of the ghost towns which had once been centres of gold rushes or various other mad scrambles for mineral wealth (she was a little vague about what it was they mined in Australia) and despite contemporary accounts of prodigious fortunes and booming local economies there appeared to remain little now but a single main street in the middle of nowhere, a sad splintery line of wooden shacks through whose sagging doorways many hundreds of pungent men had once been carried or thrown in the last stages of mortal injury and inebriation. Amazonas, by contrast, was a land where a living was even more hazardously earned on the edges of a primaeval abyss of bites, stings, fevers, poisons and murderous slavery into which anyone might topple at any time and vanish without headstone. Yet on every cartload of the sticky black footballs of *borracha* latex creaking and rumbling down to the wharf at Manaos the Government had levied a tax of twenty percent with which it built O Teatro do Amazonas, now ubiquitously known as the Opera House. The souls of the town's inhabitants no doubt dwelt in the shadow of its Cathedral but their lives were lived in the radiance shed by the dome of the Opera House with its gilded tiles.

'Look,' this splendid and preposterous building said to them as it winked and flashed amid the endless forests like a Fabergé egg on a football pitch, 'I am no ornament, I am central to life. Without art, without music, there is nothing. Without civilisation the sun shines only on the backs of greedy men grubbing endlessly for gold. Without culture they leave hovels and a wasteland, a Klondyke from which the survivors stagger away with what wealth they can carry, as truly impoverished as when they arrived.'

For Manaos was a marvellous, romantic *idea*, and this was what she loved – perhaps even more now it was in its first evident stages of decay. An Opera House seating sixteen hundred people (many of them in four tiers of boxes decorated with cherubs and angels) in the middle of the world's most trackless jungle: how could that idea be resisted? And some of the best-known figures in the performing arts had made no attempt to resist, sailing up the Amazon with their tiaras and entourages, impresarios with snapping black moustaches and boxes holding collapsible opera hats. Tetrazzini, Melba, Melchior, Caruso, Gigli, Rubinstein, the Ballet Russe . . . all had come and sung and played and danced and even – in the case of Villa-Lobos – composed here. Sarah Bernhardt had played Phèdre. Yet not the least of the place's oddities, as Frau von Pussels took pleasure in reflecting, was that in all her years here she could not recall a single performance of an opera. Instead the musical lions and grandees made the pilgrimage to give recitals, for as an experience it was unforgettable, salutary in a way in which commuting between state opera-houses in Dresden, Berlin, Vienna, Paris and Milan was not. In Europe's capitals the performers vied to keep their careers in as dazzling a shine as possible; here they could play the messianic role of bearing a brave, raw flame into prehistoric night. They soon found it did no harm to their careers, either, to add Manaos to the list of places where they had triumphed. To have taken Copenhagen by storm would probably have been just as within their powers but it lacked *glamour*. In 1901 an American big-game hunter variously named as Blenker and Blanket had ascended the dome of the Opera House and shot an *onça* prowling the nearest outskirts of town. By 1923 it would have been necessary to go to the last stop on the tramway to be able to get a clear shot at a jaguar, but even now there was no part of the town further than twenty minutes' walk from aboriginal and unexplored jungle.

About such a place – one which Frau von Pussels knew stone by stone – there was more than a hint of dignified decline. As the eyebrows of elderly aristocrats might gradually show a tendency towards bushiness or their ears and noses to sprout odd tufts of hair, so were the colonial mansions beginning to betray their age and circumstances, albeit without real shabbiness as yet. Their gardens were for ever on the point of rampage. Speckles of jungle had begun breaking out here and there across town, swags of greenery bursting through stucco façades. On the roof of the tramway's main shed orchids grew and power failures were becoming more frequent so that passengers were sometimes trapped inside their stalled machines for the duration of the midday downpour. After dusk all the street-lights would suddenly go out and passers-by would pick their way carefully along pavements full of tilted flagstones and potholes by the intermittent lightning-bursts of a silent storm far overhead. When the electroliers came back on they revealed, sauntering out of a tropical night full of obstacles such as dead curs and the legs of beggars, beautifully dressed ladies and gentlemen arm-in-arm, raising their straw hats to one another or stopping to point out a passage in the evening newspapers they carried in one gloved hand.

About all this there was nothing resembling the deluge which had so recently swept away much of Old Europe. From the viewpoint of an overseas observer the writing was on the wall there – or on such walls as were still standing. Here by contrast the walls sprouted nothing more prophetic than mango suckers, and the business community cheerfully speculated about the next boom which would restore the region's fortunes as if there were some law common to nature and commerce which provided that all glory, once departed, must return. Only at times was the Director of the Schiller Institute overtaken by a certainty that something was unstoppably ending. But when she thought more carefully about what it might be she was always faced with her own ungainsayables: her son, her husband, her life. By the mere virtue of having lived into her seventh decade, Magdalena von Pussels was herself inexorably declining. Beside that the temporary ups and downs of a local economy seemed as repairable as masonry.

When she had finished playing she closed the lid of the piano and stood up. The music hanging in the air continued to speak of irresolution. If she no longer actively missed the first twenty-five years of her life with their endless concert-going and music-making, her marriage and uprooting still occasionally seemed to have set off an unnatural silence. It was presumably to be expected that the friends of her youth should mostly have dropped away until she now did no more than exchange one or two dutiful letters at Christmas-time. But the suddenly-materialised ghost of Edward was another matter, for his career had been as vivid to her as if she had watched it from an adjacent room instead of from so many thousand miles away.

From their first meeting in Leipzig in 1883 he had dazzled and exasperated her early twenties and, it had turned out, he was fated to remain for her as a beloved paradigm of the young artist plodding his lonely way up the sunless side of the magic mountain. Yet at the time she had believed she was also making the same ascent, unimpressed by the uniformly gloomy view and puzzled by how uncompanionable it was. Eventually it had been she who ended the relationship, her *amour propre* wounded by his refusal to pay at least as much court to her genius as she did to his. Later that same year she had gone to England for a two months' return visit when he had taken lodgings for her in Worcester. On his home ground she had wondered at his strange mixture of childishness and ruthless self-sufficiency which she could all too easily see might characterise genius. It was something she conspicuously lacked herself; and the more she reasonably insisted on her daily three hours' piano practice the more it seemed to be asserting a hollowness. Edward had been amiably indulgent, which made it worse. He was not fond of the piano as an instrument and once told her it was a useful tool to keep in a vestry. Finally, genius had to be creative in some way: even Clara Schumann had written her own music and, what was more, in the face of her husband's.

The walks with Edward up on the Malvern hills and down by the river were perfectly memorable for ebullient conversations inexplicably broken off when she would glance at him and know she no longer existed. There were rumpled pieces of manuscript paper in his pockets, some of which had bars showing every evidence of having been scrawled behind the tree where he was supposed to be answering a call of nature. Even at a distance of nearly forty years Magdalena experienced afresh the feel of his company, that gawky young man with legs whose thinness could be inferred through his trousers and the brown hair he always seemed to be combing with water. She had never before or since met precisely his blend of chronic self-doubt and arrogance, especially not allied with all sorts of exuberant high spirits. For a short while she had been happier than she would have thought likely; and in this tropical room so far removed from the original scene saw again a slicing of light off varnished oars, a swan drift by with a single black web tucked up across its back. The sadness which followed this vision had less to do with lost opportunities than it did with the mere ability to look back forty years to a sunlight which was not imagined.

Raymundo pushed open the door of the salon but remained diffidently on the threshold as if uncertain from the silence whether she were still in the room.

'It's about the bush.'

'Bush, Raymundo? Oh yes, I'd forgotten to tell João. I've heard it's arriving on the fifteenth, that's Saturday week, so you and he will arrange to meet the boat and bring it back then, please. It is to go in the hall like last year's but this time if it's too tall will you make certain João cuts an appropriate amount off the bottom rather than the top? It looked most peculiar.'

'*Sim senhora*. But that was because . . .'

'I quite remember what I said then and I was wrong. It was a mistake. I don't wish to repeat it.'

The boy disappeared leaving a flash of dark eyes on the air behind him, but it was not one of comprehension. To somebody born within horizons filled with nothing but trees it must have seemed eccentric indeed to bring a single Christmas tree in a ship from a distant country. It had been beyond Magdalena's patience to explain either the Weimar Republic or its idea that the battered Germanic spirit might be inspirationally nursed back to health by means of national symbols. In the *Ministerium* in Berlin someone had conceived the image of exiles gathering in embassies and cultural missions across the world to sing '*O Tannenbaum*' as if from the glary African or South American sky outside heavy snow were really falling on shivering Germans hurrying in for *Glühwein* and gingerbread. The tree they had sent last year arrived in Manaos scarcely three weeks after it had last sighed to the winter winds of the Black Forest. It was in perfect condition, beautifully packed in a long deal box like some monstrous cigar. Only when João the gardener had come to unpack it was it found to be three feet too tall for any room in the house. It had been her idea not to cut off the bottom since she entertained a fancy of re-planting it in the garden after the festivities were over. It had seemed scandalous to bring a living tree all that way merely to bundle it up as firewood, and it intrigued her to imagine it taking root in so alien a habitat.

The roots had been left and the top pollarded instead so the tree ended flatly like a bottle-brush. This had been more or less disguised by artful tapering but it was not an aesthetic success for all its popularity with visitors. João had carted it off and dropped it into a hole in an obscure corner of the garden. To everyone's surprise it had not died at once but quite the contrary had begun growing at an amazing rate, putting out shoots and sprigs for a period of several months. Then just as suddenly, as if drained by this unnatural spring, it had wilted and gone brown, its spears etiolated as wild asparagus. João had dug it up again and it did indeed play its part in the burning of several batches of the Institute's guava jelly.

She glanced again towards the notice board on her way back upstairs and could not help visualising a large announcement that Sir Edward Elgar, world-renowned composer of *Der Traum des Gerontius* and *Enigma-Variationen*, would be here in person to address the Institute. Remarkable as the Reverend Miles Moss's work was in its own way her notice of his lecture now seemed a painful reflection of the trivialities which measured out Manaos's year, to say nothing of her own life. When one encountered the real thing, she told the marble stairs beneath her ascending tread, there was no mistaking it or its way of humbling the common round. And all at once on entering the Library she began to feel afraid. What had she done? And with what appalling temerity? How could she presume a link between herself and this famous man after a gap of forty years? There could be nothing left of that boy with the wet furrows in his quiff and the bony wrists which endearingly had made all his sleeves appear a half-inch too short, as if at twenty-six he were still growing. From that summer onwards their ways had diverged, his on his lonely and distinctive trail up the mountain, hers to marriage with a Lübeck merchant who had a penchant for 'intellectual' girls. In that long meantime of a life's work he had been taken up by royalty, had known and been admired by Richard Strauss, Paderewski, Hans Richter,

Fauré, Kreisler, Chaliapin, Siegfried Wagner . . . the list of fellow-immortals was endless. In that same meantime she had been a wife and a mother, not displeased to shine a bit on evenings when obliged to play hostess for Otto to Brazilian Government officials keen to court Pussels Cronifer GmbH and its influential trade links. Otto's solidity, as well as his slight resemblance to Bismarck, had implied long-term power more convincing than that of the *nouveaux riches* rubber barons with their slaves and shenanigans and fountains which sprayed claret. And after dinner the guests were impressed and charmed when their hostess allowed herself to be persuaded to the piano and played with accomplishment and feeling, if to their private taste a little severely.

She suddenly glimpsed herself as exactly that creature she had just now claimed not to be in her letter: an earnest clutcher in a torrid backwater of the cuffs and hems of visiting Parnassians. What more humiliating in its way than that the shelves in the bay between the Library's two great windows should be devoted entirely to Edward? For years with the help of a network of cultural spies in Europe she had built up a comprehensive collection of books, articles, and cuttings about him. Here were reviews, programmes, gramophone records (on most of which he himself was conducting) and as many editions of each score as she could lay hands on. As she looked at it all in the half-light of the jalousied shutters she could think only that those few feet of shelving represented a distance which could not be measured, and that to pretend otherwise was an impertinence.

By mid-morning she had attended to the various light duties which fell to her. In the present season they mostly concerned arrangements for various Christmas festivities. She then found herself doing something she had almost never done. She wrote a note to the Institute's Secretary, who generally spent the mornings at home, to the effect that she was suffering an attack of migraine which regrettably would prevent her attending tonight's recital. Magdalena felt sorry for the Italian pianist, a sweetly pretty girl who had come out with the escort of a female cousin to visit relatives and had consented to put together a programme at short notice. The indisposition of the Institute's Director would be regretted on all sides but it would in no way affect the concert's success. Nevertheless she wrote a second note, this one to the girl herself, apologising for her inevitable absence and wishing her luck. Then, handing Raymundo both envelopes, she returned home through the glaring streets, already finding it easy to play the part of a sufferer (for her conscience always exacted the penalty of a touch of the malady she was claiming). If she appeared to be made a little unsteady by the sun, a little carefully enclosed by the shade her parasol cast, and if there was an unaccustomed paleness in her greetings, it was in response to a feeling across the temples which might yet turn into the migraine attack she had never in her life had. By the time she reached the road which gave access to the Villa Mirabelle, Magdalena von Pussels had indeed the makings of a bona fide headache.

The high whitewashed walls and wrought-iron gateway were planted squarely across the end of the road, saying to the visitor exactly what Herr von Pussels had said to the architect: This is one street which goes no further. When he had bought the lot there had been some vague idea that the road – which in those days petered out in a waste of vines and scrub – might eventually curve around so that the slight eminence on which it was built would afford a view over the port area. Herr von Pussels, with the help of an assiduously-purchased majority of the town council, had put a stop to that. The road would indeed continue, but as his private drive. It would not curve around to the left but continue straight ahead through the gates before dipping down to the right. Here, just over the brow of the knoll, the view was away from the town, across the river and out over the endless forest undulating to the violet horizon. There was something decisive in this plan's exclusion from the panorama of the least sign of human existence unless one considered as such a barely-visible handful of greyish shacks on the far shore and the various craft which drifted like twigs about the river. The villa faced the future, there was no doubt of that. It was not intimidated by the prospect but looked out with confidence across a continent which would in due course be tamed by trade. At the bottom of the knoll the grounds, which were not very extensive, ended at the water's edge and a small *igarapé* seeped at right angles into the main stream, marking the other boundary.

Magdalena reached the shelter of her verandah the requisite two minutes before the midday storm, which betokened an inner clock made accurate by years of habit. Tumults of cloud throbbed and piled and prodigious blue voltages made the furniture in the suddenly dark house leap out of its shadows. The jungle, the river, the grounds outside disappeared behind a grey pelt of water. Amid enormous noises she went calmly about the house removing her gloves, examining an envelope on a side table, going upstairs to change. By the time she had done so, her brow cool with eau de cologne, the clouds had been knocked into fragments by their own violence and were hurrying off to re-group over some other horizon, leaving an innocent sky beneath which steam was beginning to rise from paved surfaces.

After her maid had served her a light *almôço* in the dining room she announced she was not at home to callers and would spend the rest of the day in the pavilion where she would like tea brought later. Taking dark glasses and a volume of Heine Magdalena walked down the now steaming grass to the spinney of jacaranda which concealed the pavilion. This was her favourite spot on the entire premises. Being a little lower than the house its view over the Rio Negro was less dominant, and since it was also further round the edge of the knoll one could, by walking a few steps, just glimpse between the trunks of some *carnaúba* palms the outermost *favelas* and hovels of Manaos's floating docks. It occurred to her that if she tried really hard she might even pick out the varnished masts of the *Hildebrand*, but she made no attempt to do so from the same impulse which had taken her two safe streets away from the waterfront on her journey home.

She was upset at being upset, puzzled and resentful of herself for being so easily reduced to indecision by a shock. Maybe there was no-one of any age who was not susceptible to the unforeseen arrival on a wharf of a person from the past, but it hardly helped to be reminded of it. In any case Edward was not precisely a person from the past. He filled several shelves in the Library which grew a fraction with nearly every mail packet. However, she had noticed that the new material was steadily becoming slighter and there was of late a tone in the few articles which mentioned him suggesting that as far as England was concerned its national composer was safely dead. The critics, many of whom she recognised as being comparatively young men eager to establish their names, implied that while they conceded he was the dominant figure of the so-called English musical renaissance this had occurred so long ago now that he ought to be content with his canonisation and let serious attention turn to newer music written in the abrasive idiom of the times.

Such articles would make her gesture impatiently, sucking in her breath at each heretical liberty; but this role of champion hid within it an obscure and illicit relief. She could deal with the idea of a master who had earned his acclaim and vanished up the mountain, becoming a surname on the programmes clutched by posterity's audiences. But the unheralded appearance of the Cello Concerto three years previously – and the arrival of the score in Manaos – had shaken her. It seemed unfair or not quite right that a man so obviously past his prime should suddenly produce an original work of great emotional power which would, without a moment's hesitation, join the canon of Haydn, Schumann, Dvořák and Tschaikowsky. What was least comforting was that he could achieve this without being part of any tradition; and this was what the music critics themselves most disliked. Unable to assign Edward to any useful category they more and more wrote of him with slight distaste as a maverick. 'An aloof figure', 'A lone but unignorable example', they said. 'Neither teacher nor leader nor guide', they complained, going on to write of a dedicated artist with a self-regarding singleness of aim. Well, she herself could vouch for the self-regard.

The sky above her bower had by now returned to a mid-afternoon normality. The massive parade of clouds drifted on and on full of subtleties of colour and implied stillnesses. On distant undulations of the forest, within the range of a watcher's eyes but still unmarked on any map, their passing shadows moved: prints of nothingness sliding over acres of sun. It was so exactly the eternal view from this pavilion that Magdalena no longer thought in terms of clouds and shadows but of an ever-changing texture. The entire thing stretching from the tips of her shoes to the horizon was a living entity, twitching and shedding and breathing like the hide of a sleeping animal. It never looked the same twice; it always looked identical. Now her mind had been so painfully jarred it easily produced the memory of a similar effect she and Edward had remarked on a walk in the English hills that long-ago August. They had stood at the top of a down, she rather out of breath and trying to pick burrs from her long dress, and watched the clouds drawing their shadows across the mild fields below. That had been gentle, pastoral. It had been a time for quoting poetry – at least, for Edward to quote poetry: something about being meatless and moneyless on Malvern hills which she took to be an elegant way of apologising for having forgotten to buy her luncheon.

And once up on those hills, what had her host wanted to do? He had produced a roll of sticks and cloth, which she had until then supposed to be some kind of collapsible stool brought in case she should feel tired, and assembled it into a large kite. Getting this aloft with its rattling tail of newspaper screws had involved his running round and round in his braces, staring up at the string he held so that he twice stepped on his cap and jacket thrown onto the grass and once nearly knocked her over. It was that afternoon which had marked a turning-point. She told him it was all very well giving himself today the airs and graces of a dazzling future, but it was hardly consistent to expect her to collude while she was forced to witness displays of a complete want of seriousness. He had fallen silent, grumpily like a chastened schoolboy, before insisting that kite-flying *was* serious, certainly a good deal more serious than Hanon's bilgey exercises for piano virtuosity.

'Bilge? What is bilge? How unfair you are, Edward. And do you not have violin exercises so one day you can go back to Adolphe Pollitzer and say, "There. Nothing more you can teach me. I will tomorrow pack my bags and study with Ysaÿe"?'

'No. I've given up all idea of a career as a violinist. And even if I hadn't I certainly wouldn't be wasting my time doing boring old exercises on a perfect kite-flying day with a very pretty girl for company.'

'*How* unfair you are, Edward.'

'Oh, can't you feel it, Lena? Today's a day on which tunes are made. Exercises aren't for people with tunes in their heads.'

And such things kept coming back as she stared out, forty years later, across Amazonas until her *mestiça* maid brought tea on a tray, a glass of *guaraná* and a Japanese fan. Later that evening she moved restlessly about the villa, going from room to room picking up and putting down again silver-framed photographs of her husband and son. Moths and other insects of the night outside drummed against the mesh screens. She lifted the piano lid, played a C while standing up, put the lid down again.

She dozed fitfully that night, falling into a heavy sleep shortly before dawn. Her maid woke her at the customary early hour, however, enquiring after her headache, and she took a glass of lime-juice over to the windows. There in the fresh light of morning stood the mountain, blotting out a large part of everything. Its upper snows glittered, its pinnacle was pure and uncompromising. It told her nothing she did not already sadly know, but it did so with calm insistence. She was here and it was there and in between lay a gulf into which protests and negotiations and recriminations fell and dissolved. They could never reach the mountain but would fade from inanition and irrelevance even as they were vehemently yelled. The miraculous alp had simply sailed up in the night once more and dropped anchor in her back garden. The rays of light fled in a scatter from its prisms and leaped right round the world. Three toucans with bills like lumps of yellow timber flew out of the jacaranda thicket and, with the sunlight gleaming off their wings, passed through the heart of the mountain and diminished away over the river. Magdalena followed their whirring dots until they merged with the debris in her retinas and lost themselves in Brazil.

Reaching the Institute half an hour earlier than her custom, as one who has made a complete recovery, she found no letter on Booth Line stationery waiting for her. The piano recital had been a great success, she gathered; she expressed pleasure. The Reverend Moss would come round later for a brief word; she said how charmed she would be. Up in her office she sat at the desk and heard the papery whirrings of a moth trapped between a window pane and a blind. The flutterings grew more frenzied as the heat rose and presently, after a few spasms, stopped altogether. Still she sat on. He had never received her letter. He had received her letter but thought it just another piece of importuning by a local dignitary. He had received her letter and found it offensive. He had not guessed her identity. He *had* guessed her identity and . . . and was thinking about it. Altogether it took quite a long time before she was able to tell herself to stop behaving like some idiot schoolgirl, snatch up her green parasol with a crawling sensation in her stomach and hurry off down to the wharf.

A spotless cream panama hat moved slowly along a shady avenue, flashing as it left the pools of mango shade and passed through patches of sunlight. At almost the same level beside it progressed a sand-coloured, broad-brimmed floppy hat with a silk band faintly sweat-stained. The faces beneath each – military-moustached and fading English rose – still bore the pallor of a sunless autumn a hemisphere away.

Molly had said: 'There isn't a boat leaving for Iquitos inside week. Until then I'm sure we'll keep bumping into each other. suppose now I'm finally here I don't have to be in a hurry to leave.

Edward had said: 'At all events you'd like to see youn; Fortescue airborne?'

'And maybe even Sir Edward Elgar safely embarked on hi: voyage home to where he belongs.'

'Ah, my dear, I don't belong anywhere nowadays. According tc popular wisdom home is where the heart is and I seem to have mislaid mine.'

'You may find it again in Manaos,' she laughed. 'It seems to be one of those places where hearts inexplicably whizz about. I lost mine here a year and a half ago and I'm not sure I mightn't be on the verge of doing so again.'

In one pocket of his linen jacket Edward had a sheaf of letters, all unopened. They had been delivered in ones and twos to the *Hildebrand* throughout the previous day as the news of his presence aboard ran through the English colony, the civic and cultural circles and, he suspected from the aspect of several of the envelopes, missionary and charity elements as well.

'Shan't open any of 'em,' he had said, and Molly could not be sure whether he were genuinely irritated or secretly pleased by this attention. 'I came here for a holiday. It's exactly this sort of thing one wishes to get away from at all costs.'

'Twenty-four pounds.'

'Twenty-four? I'm paying twenty-six pounds seventeen and eightpence each way. That's monstrous. Did you really pay only twenty-four? We ate at the same table and reached Manaos at the same instant . . . Twenty-*four*.'

'You've never seen my cabin. It's not a de luxe Stateroom or whatever yours is called. Besides, I don't have a private steward.'

'I'm sure I don't either. He's very fly, is Mr Pyce. I believe I share him with half the ship. Once or twice he's answered my bell admirably disguised as an idiot boy of sixteen . . . Just look at these. Hounded about the globe. Don't ever become famous, Molly, it's the death of everything.'

'What have you got? "The Britannia Club", "*A Câmera Comércio do Manaos*", "*O Pais*", "*As Notícias*" – those two sound like papers, don't they?'

And before that day was out two Brazilian reporters had come trotting up the gangway together, scowling at one another and each trying to find Sir Eduardo's cabin first. He went to ground on the Captain's patch of private deck, drinking iced *guaraná* and wondering why, now that he had at last reached this legendary place, he didn't quite feel up to going straight ashore. It crossed his mind that it would be amusing, having come all this way, never to set foot in Manaos but to remain aboard the *Hildebrand* for the entire five days of its stay, looking at the town over the rim of an ice-cooled glass. He might even start a fashion. Next year he could go to Samarkand or Timbuctoo and turn back on reaching the outskirts. Thus he would make a late name for himself as an eccentric traveller who had once been an inveterate sight-seer but who now could not abide arrivals.

But on this following morning Molly had persuaded him to stroll through the town, at least to see the Opera House and have an ice-cream. And suddenly there had seemed nothing else to do. Fortescue had been met the previous day by an ebullient man in late youth, undoubtedly the old comrade Johnny Proctor. These two had spent much time supervising the swinging ashore of large crates which emerged from the holds looking pale and raw, criss-crossed with stencilled admonishments which none of the Brazilian stevedores could surely have read. Chartair Ltd, consisting of Fortescue, Johnny, the crates and two monkey-like men who had about them a bristling air of Scots stubbornness which might have passed for loyalty, disappeared in a series of ramshackle vehicles towards an alleged airfield on the outskirts. Everybody else on board had gone ashore and the company of the ship's cat, while agreeable, seemed too studiedly poignant.

Molly was explaining that the slabs of dark jam on sale at a stall were guava jelly, and pointing out that a sign reading '*pudim*' sort of meant 'pudding' but of a quite un-English genre, when Edward became aware of a woman staring at him. She was imposing, probably in her late fifties or early sixties, with greying hair. She held a parasol which shaded her face so he could not read it but the impression her whole figure gave was of someone long used to feeling confident. When she spoke it was with a faint accent he unthinkingly assumed to be Portuguese.

'Have I the honour of addressing Sir Edward Elgar?'

'I doubt it'll do you much honour, madam,' he ungraciously

said after a moment's hesitation, 'but yes.' His voice had taken on a gruffness Molly had come to recognise as that of displeasure at being put out. He was clearly not a man who relished the effort of having to rise to an occasion.

It was the stranger's turn to hesitate. 'I . . . Please forgive me for intruding on you both like this – ' her dark eyes took in Molly but her face remained turned to Edward. 'I am . . . You may perhaps have received a letter of me, from me. I heard you had arrived and at once I wrote. But . . . '

'A letter? Ah. Now you come to remind me I do have some letters with me. They, ah, arrived but my steward put them on one side where I'm afraid I didn't see them.' Like a child discovered he felt in his pocket and produced the sheaf of envelopes. 'I was just about to read them, you see, over a cup of coffee somewhere.'

'Of course, Sir Edward; I wouldn't have dreamed . . . Yes, there is mine you're holding.'

'This one? The, um, Schiller Institute?'

'Yes, exactly. I . . . I am Magdalena von Pussels. I was waiting . . . but you will read it when you read it, Sir Edward. Please not now,' she motioned with a gloved hand to prevent his opening it on the spot. 'At your leisure, I beg. Introductions in the street like this are not convenient. I ask the forgiveness of both of you.'

The fraction by which she inclined her parasol and upper spine before sweeping away made him place her on the spot as being German even before his mind had had time to recall the suggestive name she had left.

'I say.' He was looking after the green parasol as it sailed steadily off above the dark Brazilian heads. 'Now *there's* a character.'

'You don't know her?'

'Never clapped eyes on her in my life.'

'How strange. I had the impression she knew you.'

'Oh, I expect she's seen a photograph in a magazine or something. I'm afraid it happens all the time. Once one's face becomes familiar complete strangers imagine they know one. As I said before, pray it never happens to you.'

He dismissed the incident and, resuming their stroll, began to take evident pleasure in the variety of small surprises the town sprang on him. He said he had not expected to see so much civic ironwork a thousand miles up the Amazon – lamp-posts, balconies, fountains and the like – and certainly not stamped with the names of Scotch foundries.

'Somehow one never thinks of Britain as having exported elegant things,' he murmured. 'Why is that? Why shouldn't we? But I believe our reputation is for sturdy functionalism. Those new cranes down at the docks are all from England, I noticed as we passed. They're perfectly hideous and I suppose will last a hundred years, highly efficient and perfectly hideous to the end. But look at that lamp-post – it's really rather something, isn't it? I thought only the Italians could do that. Have you seen Bologna? The *Corso*'s so grand, we've nothing like it in England. But apparently we could have if only we imported Scotch lamp-posts to replace those mass-produced metropolitan horrors they keep planting in London. The problem with the English is they're not a race which sets much store by aesthetic values. They mistrust such things because they smack of flightiness and pleasure. I wonder if it isn't also a kind of laziness . . . ? By Jove!'

For they had reached the Opera House standing in its piazza, a creation with pink-washed walls likely to remind any English visitor of nothing so much as blancmange. The interior into which they passed hardly lessened the impression of a confection. Edward and Molly stood in the foyer surrounded by gold draperies, tall Sèvres vases on plinths and pillars of marble in various shades of coral and cream such as he had last seen outside the *botteghe* of funerary masons in Carrara. The same style extended exuberantly through the jacaranda-wood doors into the auditorium itself. Inside among the cherubim and angels it was dim and cool, a lofty rococo temple echoing not to the tremulous vibrato of Tetrazzini but to the cries of several budgerigar-like birds which had somehow got in. A gentleman in torn shorts and straw hat was sweeping the top of an upright piano with a long broom in one corner of the orchestra pit.

'What a place to conduct in,' Edward was saying. 'It's so wonderfully bizarre. When one has made all the jokes and poked all the fun the solid fact remains that here we have a people for whom music is central to life. Remember the theatre in Pará? That's grand too. I admire it. It even makes me feel jealous. Had the English as a race been as musical as the Brazilians then composing for them wouldn't have been such an ungrateful business. Anything to do with music in England's an uphill struggle from first to last. I always wanted to write an opera, you know. Still do.'

'Really? Have you got a subject – or is it a libretto?'

'More or less. But I keep getting disheartened. Nobody wants that sort of stuff nowadays, not there at any rate. All they want is cinema shows and Jazz and sport. Look what happened to poor old Stanford when he tried to write opera. For the English it's Gilbert and Sullivan or nothing. Or, of course, *The Beggar's Opera.* Have you seen the Nigel Playfair revival? It's splendidly improper and amusing, just a jingle of songs really, but it's the perfect proof of how radically unmusical the English are. Their imagination never runs beyond burlesque. In our own way I'm afraid we're barbarians. That woman who spoke to us just now? The Schiller Institute? Good example. I bet we could scour Manaos all day without finding a Shakespeare Institute. The arts simply aren't a living part of us.'

'Surely you exaggerate slightly? We've some marvellous writers and painters. As well as the odd composer.'

'Yes, and look how they had to suffer for it. Penury and neglect for a lifetime and then being turned into classics as soon as they're safely dead.'

His voice had joined the insistence of the budgerigars inside the dome and Molly realised she had once again provoked a piece of autobiographical vehemence. She steered him out of the building and they left it echoing with grievance. The sunlit piazza, the grand trees trailing aerial roots like Krakens surfacing, blotted away this brief mood.

'I'm holding you up,' he said at last.

'No you're not. I haven't much to do until my boat leaves except I'm tempted to come up and paint this lost temple one day. There are a few places worth a visit after the Opera House but not many. The Cathedral's a possibility and I can recommend the Public Library. Apart from being a nice building it's got the prettiest double staircase in iron which looks as light as a feather. Glasgow again, I seem to remember. There's the English Club and of course the Schiller Institute, wherever that is. But really apart from those sorts of things life in Manaos seems to be principally a matter of little launch-trips up and down river. There are lots of tiny resorts with bathing-boxes and bungalows where people can go and fish for their lunches. The Purser's got outings laid on, I think. For me the real attraction of the place is its oddness. I like all this civic splendour on the edges of nothing, and the decay, and the newspapers and the trams and the modern docks all covered with river-mud and naked children. I like taking the tram out to Flores which is still really in the jungle.'

'A tram in the jungle? That sounds interesting. Flores, you say? What's there?'

'Nothing. A restaurant. It's wonderful fun having dinner. Oh, we should go. I'll try and detach Forty from his airfield one night, shall I?'

'I'd quite like to see the airfield.'

'I bet he'd take you up if you wanted. Why don't you?'

'Ah, he'll have better things to do than fuss around pandering to fogeys . . . D'you think he would?'

They stopped at a café and Edward read his letters. 'Did you know they had a racecourse here?' he asked. 'Somebody must have found out about my weakness. This is the Secretary of the Club – an Englishman, apparently – inviting me out to the "hippodrome" hoping I might care to view some racing, Brazilian-style. He says here it's, what, "capital entertainment even if not exactly run under Jockey Club rules. Sometimes there are fatalities." That sounds quite sprightly. I wonder if he means horses or riders? I hope not the horses . . . I do like this word, *hipódromo*. Now, ah, the Schiller Institute. Of course, let's see . . .'

But there was something about Frau von Pussels' letter which seemed to throw him into a clouded thoughtfulness and he said nothing beyond a muttered 'No shortage of guides, I see,' which gave Molly a pang of indignation. Later they lunched at the Britannia Club where they found a good many of their fellow-passengers. Edward was visibly irritated by the effect of his unannounced arrival. The Club Secretary bustled up, evidently having been dragged away from a drink in order to greet this celebrity, but neither quite knew what to say to the other and Edward was left with a feeling of being over-dressed and stuffy. From cool rooms in the background came a good deal of laughter and the men were mostly in shirt-sleeves. The food was acceptable but an uncomforting silence fell as they entered the dining room. Neither he nor Molly was sorry to leave.

Returning to his cabin for a brief siesta he found, laid on his desk next to the microscope, another Schiller Institute envelope. 'Damn, damn, damn,' he said under his breath. Was there no end to this harrying? But he sat on the edge of the bed and opened it resignedly.

Dear Sir Edward,
    I am extremely sorry we happened to bump into each other like that this morning. Since you were already carrying my letter it must appear to you as if I am pestering.
    Please accept my assurance that I am not. But as you evidently did not recognise me I cannot bring myself to remain silent and watch you sail away again in a matter of days. Nearly forty years have passed (and left you looking magnificent, I must say). Might we not salute them if only for half an hour? For some reason I badly wish to know if you remember the last piece of music we played together in Worcester.
                              Truly yours,
             Lena (Magdalena von Pussels)

And it hit him like an attack of some vital organ midway between heart and head: her eyes, that voice, her carriage as she had walked away down the street. All were Lena's, disguised by nothing but time itself and her long absence from his thoughts. The more he considered them the more he remembered her and the less he could imagine not having seen it at once, not even in her handwriting, not even though she now spoke almost faultless English. In this of all places . . . How could he have expected that half-thought, disgruntled act of booking a passage to lead to his past arising like vapour from the Amazon jungle and massing over his head? Once one had reached a certain age there was evidently no place on earth whose neutrality was guaranteed. The entire planet was peopled with ghosts. Even the most alien of its terrains might exude them, the most preposterous place quicken thoughts and memories. Perhaps one had to be young in order to travel, for it could be diverting and adventuresome only so long as there was no past to press. The older one became the less possible it was any longer to travel in that sense: the exterior globe was increasingly displaced by an interior lifetime. It would be an act of great purity to be able to jettison that deadweight of memory and travel at the end of one's life as if seeing for the first time just clouds, just a forest, just a great river. He knew he would never achieve that purity; there was something relentless about the way in which he felt himself contaminated. It was as if his very culture demanded it.

He lay back on the bed. Once the shock had begun to diminish his initial dismay was displaced by an amicable curiosity. Might it not be interesting to find out what her life had been? Two elderly people would scarcely wish to embroil themselves in anything more emotionally muddying than peaceable recollections of another world, one distant enough to have left nothing but an afterglow, maybe a fondness, surely the comradeliness of survivors. Besides, so far as he was concerned he had – he reminded himself as if addressing her – done her more than justice, all things considered. He had twined her into some of his earliest successes – *Enigma*, for example – even though doing so had written her a little more irrevocably out of his life. She had lingered for many years after her abrupt departure as The Girl, the unmarried bride such as a young man would have chosen for himself. But she had commenced her gradual fade from the moment the woman he actually married began taking control of his creativity. The one Girl was squeezed out by the one Woman, then by several women – ladies, even, with titles and influence at Court. The team of Edward and Alice had assumed dominion over English music of the century's first decade even though that music had its roots in a past which pre-dated their first meeting, one which contained Lena as well as pre-dating her too.

There could be no harm now in seeing what had become of her. In any case, what else was there to do here? Somehow he felt he had already absorbed Manaos – it was like Pará only more so – and Molly's description of its attractions had suggested only a momentary quaintness. Since he had no interest in bathing and picnic excursions he had a matter of four days left to get through before the *Hildebrand* cast off and began her downstream voyage. It occurred to him that had one of his boyhood friends like Hubert Leicester been there they might have celebrated finding themselves up the Amazon by swimming in it as they had once swum in rowdy groups in the Severn and Teme. In those days country boys had swum naked and he could quite see it would be essential to find a secluded spot. However, from his observation seclusion was one of the things the region was richest in. And think what a *jape* it would be . . .

On impulse he snatched up his hat and cane and, having asked directions, walked down the gangway and set off for the Schiller Institute. This building, when he found it, almost bore out Molly's guess that it might be worth seeing. It was an imposing but not very large old house set back from the rumbling avenue by walled grounds with ironwork gates. As he approached the front door he thought for a moment there was evidence of crime or mishap partly concealed by a bush of garish flowers: a single brown leg emerged at an angle, the sole of its foot palely gleaming. But as he walked on he could see it belonged to a sleeping Brazilian lying crosswise in a hammock slung very low between two trees in deep shade. He rang the bell and after a moment the door opened and there stood the lady who had addressed him in the street that morning.

'You came,' she said in evident pleasure. 'Oh, I'm so glad.'

'Your letter left me little choice, as you intended. Good heavens Lena . . . What a long, long, time,' and they grasped one another's forearms uncertainly. 'Ah,' said Edward after a moment, 'I thought I'd stumbled on the scene of a dramatic crime.' He indicated the shrubbery. 'That fellow looked dead to me: I could only see his feet.'

She followed his gaze and laughed. 'That's our gardener João. I sincerely hope he's not dead since only he knows how to put up our Christmas tree. But please, please come in, Edward. I'm going to call you Edward, you see: that's how you were. The "Sir" is somebody else.'

'I'm afraid it is. I often fear it's what I've become.'

'Well, we've all acquired our stage names, it was inevitable. See? I'm Frau von Pussels, the widow of a merchant and the director of an institute. But my memory is excellent. And *do* you remember what it was we played?'

'I rather think it was a sonata by Rubinstein. I'd guess the one in G.'

'*Ach!* There's nothing wrong with your memory either. Imagine, thirty-nine years.' She had led the way automatically into the salon as if this were her private house. Now she walked to the piano, threw up the lid and, still standing, played the sonata's opening few bars, turning her head to watch him with a smile which anticipated his delighted recognition. But he only remained as if turned in wood before saying 'Terrible rot really.' She closed the lid, perplexed, even deflated.

'I suppose one might outgrow Rubinstein,' she said.

'I'm afraid I've outgrown music, Lena. It no longer gives me any pleasure.'

'Oh Edward, you haven't changed. It's incredible. I can still hear you saying how boring it is playing the violin instead of flying a kite.'

'Did I say that? It shows how wise I was at such an early age. It also shows I'm nothing if not consistent. Now you must tell me about yourself. Who was Herr von Pussels? I seem to have heard the name even though I know it's on your letters.'

'Unfortunately it's almost the first thing one sees of Manaos from the river. You have entered part of the far-flung empire of Pussels Cronifer GmbH.'

'That was the name. It's all over town. Who or what is Cronifer?'

'A Swiss.'

Edward made a barking sound which caused a momentary hum within the Bösendorfer. 'Perfect! A bearer of watches. A man with time on his hands.'

'Oh! He was very hard-working, he had no time for anything. He was here in the early days but his family have since gone back to Zürich. There's no shortage of Cronifers there. But I'm the last von Pussels now that our son is dead, and of course I'm not a genuine one. Another empire on its last legs, you see. It may survive as a name but it will gradually be taken over by managers. Family concerns don't last, do they? Even if circumstances allow one to pass on the name the children seldom inherit that energy which founded the firm. How could they? Their laps are full of fruit. They don't have to clear a patch of jungle and plant the orchard as their grandparents did.'

'Would your son have been an exception?'

'Eusebius? He was not interested in fruit. He was a child. I don't know what he was interested in and neither did he. Sometimes it was music and sometimes it was going to dig up Troy with Schliemann and sometimes it was duelling and sometimes it was learning to drive a motor car. My God, Edward, what did we do, our generation? We killed off our own children before they even knew who they were. And now look: Babylon, Nineveh, Troy, Egypt. Germany.'

'England too. We've all had the same thought.'

'Well, so we have. Of course. And of course it doesn't help. Come upstairs at least, sit down, we'll drink a glass of something. Are you yet familiar with our *guaraná*? Excellent.' She rang a bell. A maid met them at the bottom of the marble staircase and Lena gave her orders before they went up. An imposing halfway landing was lit by a window framed in dark-leaved creepers bobbled with flowers or fruit like brilliant yellow beads. In this patch of light stood a plinth with a large bronze bust on it.

'Our Founder?' suggested Edward.

'How irreverent you English are about culture! Now and then I admire it rather. It looks so like courage in the face of immortality.'

'Not a bit of it. It's temerity born of pure ignorance.' With the fond gesture of one habitually kind to dogs he patted Schiller's laurelled head as he passed. Observing this at the edge of her vision Lena smiled in self-satisfaction like one who has correctly solved a crossword puzzle clue.

'Still the same Edward. Oh, don't worry; I shan't patronise you. I'm far too happy to see you again, you know.'

'It *has* been a goodish time. Rather a lot seems to have happened since those days but whenever I try to remember exactly what, I can't come up with enough to fill the gap. One got married, one did some work, one survived. Don't ask me what it was all for, though.'

'Very well. But I must ask what it is you're doing here? I was amazed, *ich war volkommen baff* when I heard you had arrived in Manaos,' She had led the way into her office and Edward sat down creakingly on a wicker chaise longue, his hat and cane on the floor beside him. 'Shall I tell you the first thing which crossed my mind?'

'You probably don't need to.'

'No. It was only for half a second. I knew it was stupid as soon as it had been thought. You truly didn't know I was here.'

'Truly not, Lena. I heard from what-was-his-name, Stämpfli, that you'd finished at Leipzig but after that I more or less lost touch until a letter turned up from him in 1899 to say you were married and had left Europe.'

'And in 1886 you met your own future wife, in any case.'

'You're a good deal better informed about me than I am about you. Why don't you tell me why I came here?'

'Don't you know, Edward?'

'I'm by no means certain. Come to that I'm not absolutely clear as to why I've done any particular thing these last three years.'

'I was so sad for you when I heard about Lady Alice, Edward. What can I say? A person of considerable gifts.' The small solecism hung about the room with the flavour of conventional piety, so she added: 'We have here in our library a copy of her novel, as well as an excellent translation she made of *Ritter Glück*.'

'She wrote the novel before she met me,' he began, only at that moment the maid came in with *guaraná* and little cakes and said something to her employer in a low voice. Lena motioned her to wait.

'I'm dreadfully sorry, Edward, but it seems I must deal with an interruption. A countryman of yours is downstairs and I need to have a quick word with him about a talk he's giving us. Would you mind very much if I went down for two minutes only? I could ask him to call back but he is very busy as well as being amiable and esteemed.'

'Of course not, Lena . . . What makes him esteemed?'

'Maybe that depends on who one is. Some are impressed by his work as a priest since he's the English Chaplain here in Amazonas – surely Anglicanism's largest parish. For others he's simply one of the world's best amateur entomologists. It's about moths that he will address us.'

'Sounds an odd sort of fellow. Why don't you show him up here, unless you wish to be private?'

'Oh Edward, he would be most honoured to meet you.'

'Just so long as he doesn't want to talk about music.'

'Why should he?' Her tone had a sharpness which in the next moment vanished as she turned to the maid. In due course the Reverend Miles Moss was shown in.

'Mr Moss,' said Lena, going forward to greet him. 'Thank you for coming. May I present to you a very old – one might say long-lost – friend of mine who unexpectedly arrived on the *Hildebrand* yesterday? Sir Edward Elgar, the Reverend Miles Moss.'

'Honoured, sir, honoured,' said the entomologist, shaking hands with Edward as he rose. 'Frau von Pussels is always introducing me to her distinguished guests but this time she has surpassed herself. Welcome to our Green Hell, sir.'

'Is that what people call it?'

'Oh yes, and much more besides. Of course it's paradise for me as a moth-man. I suppose you aren't a fellow-sufferer? An obsession I fear has reached in me the proportions of a vice, a positive vice. I have to be increasingly on my guard lest my real duties become neglected. Remember Chaucer, sir, and his corrupt prelate? "I rekke nevere, whan that they been beryed, Though that hir soules goon a-blakeberyed!'"? I sometimes find myself in danger of going a-mothing at the expense of my scattered flock's spiritual welfare. Most regrettable,' and he gave a little chirrup and bounced on the soles of his feet.

'I like moths,' said Edward cautiously when the Reverend Moss paused for breath. 'But I couldn't describe myself as a moth-man. Bit more of a dog-man and a horse-man, I suppose. Yes, I like moths well enough. I don't swat 'em. Talking of which, maybe you can tell me something. I was going to look it up in South when I got home. Is there a moth called the Brindled Marsh?'

'Brindled Marsh? Oh dear, I've become so out of touch with the British lepidoptera. After a time all those fanciful names start to sound interchangeable, don't they? Least Carpets and Smoky Wainscots, Grizzled Skippers and Silvery Arches. To say nothing of a Muslin Footman. I mean to say, jolly easy to imagine a Grizzled Footman with Fallen Arches, what? No, let me see. Brindled Marsh. Why yes, I believe there is such a thing. Why?'

'Nothing really, just a silly thing I discovered. It's an anagram of "RMS *Hildebrand*".'

The Reverend Moss thought for a moment, his head on one side. 'By Jove, so it is. Clever, that. Dear old *Hildebrand*. The number of times I've watched her come and go. Like clockwork, if a good deal noisier. As a matter of fact I saw you sail past the other evening, Sir Edward. Well, perhaps not you personally although I can't be certain of that. I was too far away. Actually, I was up a tree.'

'Up a tree?'

'Exactly. I was waiting for nightfall. I was just about to light my lamps when I heard the ship coming. You can hear the rumble of engines for miles across water, you know.'

And suddenly Edward saw again the white-robed figure standing at the top of an immensely tall dead tree on the river-bank, facing the setting sun in hieratic pose. 'I say, was that you dressed all in white?'

'There, you did see me. How embarrassing. In such a way, my dear Magdalena, one acquires a perfectly undeserved reputation for wild eccentricity. A middle-aged Englishman a hundred feet up a tree in the middle of the Amazon jungle at dusk, wearing a newly-laundered surplice. Oho. What are we to make of *that* before we send out sharpish for the nearest alienist? But like many a person before me caught red-handed I can explain everything. I'm on the trail of what I believe is an unknown species of the Sphingidae – hawk-moths, you know, Sir Edward. A very weird creature indeed, very weird, since if I'm not mistaken it has trained itself to suck the blood of animals.'

'A vampire moth, you mean? That's downright sinister.'

'Precisely. I have all sorts of evidence I won't bore you with at this moment since it's what I'm supposed to be talking about to this Institute shortly. But in brief he's the devil to pin down – ha! pin down, that's exactly what I have in mind,' and he bounced with pleasure. 'He never seems to come below sixty feet or so. I presume you know, Sir Edward, that there are different layers of jungle canopy, each with its distinct flora and fauna? You didn't? But yes indeed. The majority of the creatures which live in those aerial worlds never come to earth at all and consequently we remain in sad ignorance of life up there. I now believe this fellow is one such denizen and it therefore behoves the lepidopterist to leave earth and track him down in his inconvenient habitat. One tries with a number of lures, sugaring and the like, but you happened to see me as I was about to stand there in dazzling white beneath three powerful pressure-lamps and tempt him with my blood. It's a very hot pursuit,' he added mildly, as if mere discomfort were hardly worth recording.

'Goodness,' said Edward, impressed.

'I know,' agreed Lena. 'He tells us these things and people in his lectures can scarcely believe them. Think of the other sorts of insects he attracts up there which sting and pester, to say nothing of tree snakes and poison spiders and all manner of horrors.'

'Frau von Pussels exaggerates, of course,' Miles Moss said in deprecation, and at that moment Edward noticed how scarred were the backs of his brown unpriestly hands. 'From time to time one gets unwelcome visitors, of course, but really when trying to juggle with nets and killing-bottles the greatest danger is the simple one of falling out of the tree. I've done that many times but up to now I've bounced,' he said, doing so. 'But you must excuse all this chat. I'm not used to such famous company and I've a tendency to blather. I really came to tell you the title of my talk, Magdalena, and confirm the date. Thursday at seven, we agreed? I'm calling it "Three hitherto unknown hawk-moths". I had hoped the vampire would be a fourth but I had no luck the other night so it will have to wait.'

While Lena made notes Edward asked, 'How did you get back to Manaos so quickly?'

'Ah, that's sharp of you, sir. I'm lucky enough to have the use of a little steam launch loaned me whenever I come here by one of my wealthier parishioners. It's really too kind. The boat is very fast and being of shallow draught can be driven with much more recklessness than a liner like the *Hildebrand*. I overtook you somewhat after midnight, you know. I'd only been down there for the day. Oh dear, I really must go. I do hope we can meet before you go away again, Sir Edward. We could do a swap.'

'What had you in mind?'

'Your news for my gossip, at the very least. There are heaps of things I'd like to know about what's happening in England at the moment and even if I can't interest you in the petty scandals of northern Brazil there are always some strange tales in circulation wholly unlike anything you might hear in the Home Counties. Though of course your own voyage here furnished one of the most mystifying and sad episodes I've heard in ages.'

'Ah, poor Dr Ashe you mean?'

'Yes. A wretched business. The banks of the river from Pará to Iquitos are no doubt buzzing with the news at this very moment.'

'I have heard nothing of this?' said Lena.

'The *Hildebrand*'s doctor,' explained Edward. '*Nil nisi bonum* and all that, but he was a rum sort of chap from the outset. Jumped overboard in the dead of night after we left Pará. Suicide, apparently.'

'How awful!'

'Yes. In a funny way I liked what I'd seen of him, too. Very direct and outspoken. Ex-Army, so perhaps that explains it.'

'I've yet to speak with Captain Maddrell but maybe we should hold a short memorial service here. There's frankly no chance that his, er, body will turn up – not in these parts. And had he reached the shore alive I'd have heard by now: that sort of news travels faster than the swiftest launch around here – don't ask me how. Poor unhappy man. What an eventful voyage you must have had.'

'Oh, he was not the only intriguing character on board. We also had a most colourful pair of ladies who got off in Pará. If they're members of your far-flung congregation you maybe know them? Dora Bellamy and Kate Hammond?'

'Know them? My dear Sir Edward, everybody knows them.

They're famous in these parts. I dare say even a little *infamous*, for although it's scarcely part of my vocation to go about spreading calumnies they themselves would be deeply flattered to hear me ascribe a certain notoriety to their reputations. They're splendidly quick-witted as I'm sure you discovered.'

'Oh, is that all you're prepared to say?'

'For the present yes, since I must fly. I shall leave you, sir, on that tantalising note. Maybe, Magdalena, if it's agreeable to Sir Edward we might have dinner together after my talk?'

'I should like that,' Edward told him and it was clear to her that whatever it was he responded to in the Reverend Moss it had the ability to fetch him out of himself. 'I want awesome scandals and horrid tales. I wish to be diverted and be-sinistered.'

'It's a tall order, Sir Edward, but we'll do our best. And now I'm off to buy – amongst other things – a quantity of cyanide,' and the door closed behind the Anglican Chaplain on the Amazon.

'You never did tell me why you came,' said Lena at length.

'That's because I don't know myself. Oh, some friends of mine did the trip a while back and praised Booth's and the scenery. They had a nice time, in short. I was having a rotten time and I wanted above all to avoid Christmas, which I most cordially detest, and I suddenly remembered their cruise. The Amazon – why not? Though I nearly went up the Nile. Ever since the Tutankhamun discovery it's been at the back of my mind to see the Valley of the Kings but – I don't know. I suppose I thought it would be intolerably hot and stark. I wanted comfort, I'm afraid. One has grown old.'

'All the time you speak as if you've had a sad life, Edward.'

'Haven't you?'

'No.' She said this consideringly, as if it were something which had not occurred to her before. 'I don't believe I have. I don't think of it like that. There have been sad things, awful things. But much of the time I've enjoyed myself.'

'Even here?'

'Why not even here? I'm not an exile, you know. When I met Otto and we were married I was prepared for anything. He was so full of energy I wanted to go anywhere with him. You see by then I'd finally accepted what you had once so kindly tried to tell me: that I was not a genius.'

'I'm sure I never said anything of the sort.'

'Of course you did, Edward. You couldn't help it because *you* were one. You were right to be impatient with my delusions.'

'My dear Lena, I remember you as a first-rate pianist. Very likely you had the makings of a great pianist but I was not a reliable judge. As you probably recall, the piano's not an instrument dear to me. People scurry about it more or less adroitly and I'm afraid I miss the finer points. What is true is that it's fearsomely difficult to make a career as a soloist, especially on an instrument as commonly played as the piano. God knows the violin's no easier as I found to my own cost. I've no doubt we could neither of us have made satisfactory solo careers.'

'No. That was not my difficulty, Edward; it was that I so clearly lacked something else which you had. Of course I can quite see now this was my own problem and not yours, but at the time . . .'

'At the time. Oh, there were good things in those days, weren't there? Remember that first concert in Leipzig? How wet we were from the rain?'

'*Doch!* And the first piece in the programme was a Mendelssohn overture, *Meeresstille und glückliche Fahrt,* and you turned to me and said in German "Out of the rain and into the sea" and it made me laugh so.'

'I expect my awful German was the funny part. It doesn't sound very witty to me.'

'Not now, no. It was the time.'

'Did you ever hear of a piece I once wrote called the *Enigma Variations?*'

'Edward! How absurd you are! Do you think you're talking to the wife of a *caboclo?* It's enraging.'

'Oh, sorry. Anyway there's a quotation in it from *Meeresstille,* if you remember. I'm sure now it was no accident.' Even as he made this noncommittal evasion he felt it as a physical lurch, as abrupt as a horse baulking at a hedge, a shying-away from anything more headlong which might lead to unknown tracts of rough country. 'Odd how such little things go round and round in the mind until they pop up from nowhere years later.'

'Come here, Edward, I want to show you something.'

She led the way outside across the passage to the Library, the timber of whose joinered floor gleamed like a sheet of oiled iron in the light from the windows. The room itself disseminated a smell of beeswax and frangipani.

'It would make a splendid club, you know,' he said as he surveyed the shelves of books and the clock ticking on the mantelpiece. 'If you allowed smoking and had some decent sporting prints on the wall.'

But she was not to be provoked. She went serenely over to a group of shelves and said 'There!'

'Very nice.'

'No, Edward, but you must *look* at them. You don't know what is here.'

He went forward and scanned the shelves in silence which he suddenly broke with small exclamations. 'Good Lord!' 'I say!' '*That* old thing!' 'Well, really!' 'Well really,' he said again, 'you have been to a lot of trouble. Or somebody has. Time *must* hang heavy out here.'

'What do you mean?' But she already knew she had made a mistake and that in all probability there would be no way of undoing it.

'I mean imagine the waste of energy. All this time you've been *collecting* me.'

He had never before seen such a gathering-together of his works and of things concerning his works, his life. Or rather, he had; and he had supposed Alice to be the only person in the world thus to have filed away everything. He had hated it but was never able to dissuade her. It smacked to him of hagiology. There was something infinitely distasteful about the thought of anyone dogging his footsteps with a pan and brush, as it were, gathering up with eager impartiality a symphony, a grocery bill, a yellowed review, a letter, his nail-clippings. He was diminished by it even as he felt she had demeaned herself. Had she not written poetry? Evidently the man of flesh had not been enough. Why had he never been allowed to get away with merely (merely!) being a composer? But no, it had also been his daily duty to connive at the creation of his own legend, at the erection of some ridiculous monument to himself constructed from torn scraps of paper, a broken favourite pen, interviews he wished he'd never given: a jumble of the ephemeral and the lasting which mocked both. He'd never understood it even as he grudgingly recognised it as one more of the terms she created for disciplining his moody and vagrant Muse. Thus had she tried to temper his dartings between apathy and excitement, between months of inertia and burstings of energy, and on days of precious sunshine had kept him in his study. Edward the intermittently industrious had been swept up in the Elgar industry and was carried along helplessly by it to meet head-on the incoming bills as they poured across his desk.

'It's damned *cheek*!' he heard himself say, his voice all but lost in the spacious library. Then louder, 'You had no right, Lena.'

Surprising herself, she remained calm. She had never dreamed he might one day see what she had so painstakingly assembled but now that he had she felt not the slightest cause for shame. 'I had a perfect right, Edward. I have merely been doing what any decent librarian would do – and, I'm sure, has been doing across Europe and America and everywhere else.'

'There's no privacy, none.'

She realised belatedly that he was not really addressing her at all, that the vehemence in his words was left over from another time and another place. 'You'll find nothing private here I assure you, Edward. Nothing. All that is here is public property and has been printed and issued. There are no letters, no personal things. I'm sorry if our collection gives offence but you're a famous composer and your music is now public property. That is the price of fame.'

Somehow her words quietened his alarm. With the unfamiliar cries of brilliant birds which rolled and twirled in the vines outside the window he felt an unexpected drifting-in of an earlier mood which had reminded him both reassuringly and gloomily that something essential remained untouched, unassuaged, unexpressed by an entire lifetime's work. He looked again at the shelves of material: a corpus, a cadaver. What had this fossil past to do with him? Whom did these Jurassic strata concern?

'Well, it's silly to quarrel over such nonsense. I suppose I should be congratulating you, Lena. As a librarian you've evidently spared no pains. There's stuff here I'd long forgotten about.' And as if to make amends he drew out a part-song and glanced through it. 'My God, what utter rot! I've vague memories of having sweated blood to finish this and I don't believe it made me a penny piece. But that goes for pretty much everything else you've got here.'

He put it back but not before she had glimpsed the attribution of the text. She was perfectly certain he had not been describing his wife's poetry. How that woman posed a challenge to the conscientious Elgarian! An apparent spinster of forty had swept a struggling, unknown composer of nearly thirty-two to the altar of the Brompton Oratory. Or was it the other way about? She, finally, was the greatest enigma of them all. Lena could sense her puzzling ghost even here, standing at the shoulder of this peculiar man. Was it through her or despite her that he appeared to remain so identifiably the youth she remembered from Leipzig and Worcester days?

'*What* a strange place,' he was saying. He had moved to a window and was looking out. 'All the way up the Amazon to find what I most wanted to leave behind.'

'I'm sorry.'

'Oh, it's not your fault, Lena. Just circumstances. Fate. The business of Fate is mockery rather than tragedy, and I feel mocked. Let's talk about old times, we'll be on safer ground. Or maybe not . . . Do you think I should come to your moth-man's lecture?'

'Of course, unless you have something better to do. He's very entertaining. He liked you, you know; he really meant for us to have dinner together afterwards. Are you free?'

'Yes, I suppose I must be. Anyway I like the idea. Perhaps he can chill my blood.'

'Then we shall dine the day after tomorrow. Forgive me, Edward, if I . . . That young lady you were with this morning. Should I invite her too?'

'She's merely a fellow-passenger. She gets off here so I don't suppose I'll be seeing much more of her. She's an artist. Name of Molly Air.'

'An artist? Oh, I should meet her.'

'I shouldn't think she's very famous at present, she's just starting. But she's interesting and estimable and undoubtedly *serious*. She's come to paint the Amazon.'

'Unusual. And she's single too? You shall introduce us, Edward. I insist.'

'I do admire you, you know, maintaining your cultural outpost.'

'Do you? Well, I too am serious. You and I have both felt the world shudder. At all costs civilisation must be handed on.'

'Must it? If you remember, it was that civilisation which caused the shudder in the first place. It was kings and kaisers who fought the war, not Brazilian Indians. I couldn't believe it was happening. It made everything horrible beyond belief. I loved Germany and the Germans yet practically overnight one had to treat them as an enemy. Incredible. It was the Germans who'd been my greatest friends and champions. They recognised *Gerontius* when the English were still turning up their noses at it. How could I suddenly repudiate Hans Richter and Richard Strauss or publicly despise the country of Brahms, Wagner, Schumann, Beethoven, Bach . . . my God, the list is endless.'

'Of course, Edward. That's what wars do. They are wholly insane.'

'Half my close friends were German or of German and Jewish descent. Frank Schuster, August Jaeger, Alfred Rodewald, Henry Ettling. Brodsky at Manchester. Fred Kalisch the critic. Friends of Brahms and Strauss and Tschaikowsky and Fauré . . . Is an artist to shut himself away like some sort of national hermit? To this day I believe it counted against me. After the general braying about how I was supposed to epitomise England – whatever that meant – there were some filthy little innuendoes about my keeping the company of Huns. You must excuse me, Lena, but you've no idea the beastliness of some of our press. There is in England a disgusting fake patriot they've just jailed for fraud called Bottomley who ran a rag called *John Bull* . . . Oh Lena, you've no idea. That war killed everything.'

'You suppose I don't know? It killed my *son*, Edward. Your reputation has survived. And do you imagine we too didn't have a popular press of our own just as full of hate and lies? Even out here the . . . the mud and the stink of it came. So what now can we do but try and repair this civilisation so such things cannot be again? Do you think I didn't come under criticism even out here in the middle of the jungle? That in our *echt deutsches Schiller-Institut* I was keeping so much music of Edward Elgar, British nationalist composer? I was telling people "Listen – only listen: he has great things to say even to us Germans who already have so many famous voices." And if that was true in September was it suddenly to become a lie in October? No. Nobody comes with honour from such things.'

She had spoken with such a crescendo of passion he was shaken out of his own mesmerism, perhaps not by the sting of her reminder but by her accent's decay and incoherence. Harsh words between old people in a quiet library, not directed at each other's head but hanging above like an evil smoke. It was enough to remind him of a characteristic which he had shed from the bland image he retained of her memory: that she had always been as forceful as he. And for the first time he could clearly recall her attraction, a pungency of temperament when her age and sex had most presumed demureness and self-effacement. This sudden reminder of how she had been in the streets of Leipzig and on the hills near Worcester bumped up against the next forty years which he had lived – it now felt – within a penumbra of correct behaviour and then the long shadow of habit.

'Well, we're not at war still.'

'We? *Us*, you mean? Oh Edward, I'm . . . I must apologise. It's so difficult. So much time has gone by and yet . . . I have to remember I'm talking to a man whose *biography* is on these shelves. I last remember you as a boy, a young man, and now . . . a biography.'

'And I'm not even dead, you mean.'

'No,' she laughed. 'Not that. But all those *facts*: your life, our friendship – why not be truthful and call it our romance? – all of it doesn't really count, not against what you've done.'

For it was strange, she thought, how easily when talking to certain artists or reading their biographies one forgot the greatness of their art. One might read about Schumann, for instance, and his life at once degenerated into a pathetic domestic tally of hypochondria and misery. 'Towards March,' one might read, 'these depressions and aural disturbances intensified to the point where Robert was consulting Dr Carus almost daily leaving little time or energy to spare for composition. Nevertheless he managed to fulfil his commission on time and the Gewandhaus Orchestra began rehearsals. But almost at once it became apparent that Clara was pregnant again with their sixth child and simultaneously his old alarming symptoms began to re-appear . . . ' For a time we'd been thinking, yes, the usual human problems; we'd even begun to feel slightly superior since our own were not as a rule so doom-laden. But then we suddenly returned to our senses: that 'commission' was the *Manfred* Overture – or the piano concerto or whatever – one of the masterpieces of nineteenth-century music. The saga of an artist's life was on the whole an irrelevance and the public's voyeuristic interest in the circumstances of creativity so easily and vulgarly overshadowed the creations themselves.

In the silence he watched from the window the clouds in the

huge Amazonian sky which seemed to cast never a shadow into the garden below. Two *urubus* were just visible in the alley which ran beneath one wall of the grounds. Ugly, verminous-looking creatures like turkeys with mange, they were tearing at a dark lump of something, bouncing and sidling before the approach of a gaunt dog. There ought to be some way out, was the idea which filled his mind. There ought to be some way of shucking off this longing for ancient times and grieving for the present and expecting from the future at least an unspecific truce. It was no longer clear where one lived nor from what one drew sustenance.

'What a strange place,' he only said once more.

'It is and it isn't. If you look at everything like the travellers' guides do then it's nothing but contrasts: the modern port, the aboriginal huts; the Opera House, the open sewers; the trams, the bony horses; the newspapers, the illiteracy . . . That's how they go on. But the more one sees of Brazil and countries like it the less strange such things seem, the more ordinary. I don't understand why everybody thinks Progress must be instant and uniform. Anyone can see differences, they don't have to make them significant by calling them contrasts. Did not Ruskin look at your Industrial Revolution and complain that the railways had filled every green valley with belching smoke? Yes, I'm sure it was Ruskin.'

'My dear Lena, I didn't mean . . . When I said "strange" I was thinking of rather a different thing. But it doesn't matter. *Is* there anything particular I should do or see while I'm here?'

'There are trips. You might go to the Tarumã Falls but they're really only worth seeing in June and July after the rainy season. It's quite dramatic – not the Falls themselves, they're ordinary – but when the Amazon floods the water here rises forty feet and the Tarumã Forest is drowned. One must go by rowboat through alleys between the tops of the trees . . . What else? You could see the giant lilies at Solimões: I believe they're called *Victoria Regina* lilies so you might feel a patriotic urge to visit them? No? Then there's bathing in Chapéo Virado at Mosqueira.'

'I don't know. None of those sounds . . . '

'Or we have here in Manaos, believe it or not, a museum of coins which is the world's fifth largest.'

'Only the coins in my pocket have ever held any interest for me.'

'Or you could stay here and talk to me.'

* * *

But within half an hour he had taken himself off to the *Hildebrand* where he made a mistaken attempt at a Journal entry. He soon crossed out the three lines he had written and rang the bell for Pyce. It was high time for something sensible and down-to-earth: time for a closer look at the river-water in which the ship floated.

The *Hildebrand* meanwhile had taken on the aspect of a hotel. Of the passengers who had not already disembarked most were away all day on various trips and diversions; and of those some had even engaged a room ashore for a few days. Molly Air was still living aboard in a lingering fashion and Edward presumed she had come to an arrangement with the Purser, retaining her cabin for a *per diem* consideration until her berth was needed. He half wished she would suddenly vanish. He didn't want to witness any erosion of her determination, nor the process by which the clarity of plans laid in the subdued light of England began to cast ominous shadows under a tropical glare. In such ways did simple grand designs for a life fetch up against the world's small hard edges. He had no doubt her need to make economies was pressing; he was also sure that her determination to push on to Iquitos had been made shakier and more fateful by the unforeseen Fortescue and his presence in Manaos. Now and again a low mooing could be heard from behind the town. This would rise to a distant bellow and then fall abruptly to a moan before stopping altogether. Molly, who happened to be on deck with Edward during one of these moments of animal agony said proudly, 'That's Forty.'

'I wondered what it was. Is he testing his machines?'

'Only their engines. Tomorrow they'll fly them. Why don't you come and watch?'

So next morning they took a tram to the outskirts and walked down a dirt road to where, across a cleared expanse of ground, a distant white pole stood with a wind-sock on it. The road was potted with the half-evaporated puddles of yesterday's rains. From the mud at their edges thick clusters of white butterflies rose in clouds around the walkers as they passed.

'It's not like this in Worcestershire,' said Edward good-humouredly, dashing butterflies from his face and endeavouring to sweep a forward path with his cane. But they were distracted from the insects by a sudden howling and in the distance a bright yellow biplane took off, banked steeply and made a circuit of the field, coming back low along the road over their heads.

'Oh I say!' Edward had his face to the sky, the single hind wing of a butterfly stuck unnoticed to the sweat on his temple beneath the panama hat.

'Isn't he wonderful?' shrieked Molly into the din as the machine passed over them trailing a cool draught which smelt of burnt castor oil. The wings waggled briefly in salutation before the aircraft landed and jolted to a stop two hundred yards off. It remained stationary for a moment, the propeller ticking over and flashing in the sun before it revved abruptly and cantered once more into the air. This time the pilot put his machine through some more strenuous paces and Molly and Edward had long since reached the modest club house when it taxied up. The engine stopped, the racket died and Fortescue jumped down, his face dark with burnt oil except for the outline of the goggles he swung in one hand. His hair was blown flat.

'Hullo old girl,' he said, 'Sir Edward. Come to watch the fun?' He was wearing a battered leather flying jacket done up to the neck with a lump at its chest. As he spoke he opened it, allowing his binoculars to swing loose.

'What's the view like from up there?' asked Edward.

'Grandish. One can see the occasional tree. But I wasn't paying a lot of attention, I'm afraid. At this stage we're just testing to see if the crates have been put together with all the bits in the right order. Up to now we haven't had much time for sight-seeing though we've definitely noticed the odd hazard peculiar to these parts. The Rio Negro's the most deceptive piece of water I've ever flown over. From up there it's like a sheet of black glass. Impossible to judge your height unless there's a boat below leaving a decent wake. Otherwise it'd be all too easy to fly straight in. There're these damned vultures into the bargain.'

'What happens if you fly into one?' asked Molly, looking hard at the plane behind him.

'Depends where it hits and when. If it smashed your prop. just after take-off it would be a bit tricky. I did hit a swan once, up over Cambrai. It was pretty messy. Some of it stuck in the radiator but most ended up in the cockpit with me and my observer.'

On the hard-standing beside the club house an engine started and a second biplane – this one painted light blue – taxied a few yards before opening up to full throttle and taking off. A low storm of dust and pebbles swept back towards the onlookers.

'There goes Johnny.' The two simian riggers were standing outside, oily hands on hips, watching the plane's progress. A small dark puff formed behind it transiently and after a second or two they all heard the note of the engine blip before picking up again. 'Bit of dirt there, I'd say,' observed Fortescue as Johnny completed his circuit and landed. 'Now, Sir Edward, I was going to insist on taking you up for a flip, give you a taste, you know.'

'Oh I say.' Edward swallowed nervously.

'But I'm very sorry to tell you I can't. The local brass won't hear of it.'

Edward's disappointment was manifest. 'Surely the authorities in a place like this can't be too punctilious? I mean, a couple of bob in the right pocket . . . ?'

'You might think so and in most parts of this continent I daresay you'd be right. But the Brazilians seem to be particularly sensitive about aviation. They say they gave us a government licence to do aerial surveys and aerial surveys is what we can do. Giving joy-rides, even free ones, breaks the conditions of our contract. They're quite surprisingly strict for a place stuck out in the middle of nowhere like this.'

'Maybe that's the reason,' said Molly.

'No doubt. At any rate they insist on our filing flight-plans before we fly, though I don't imagine they've got much in the way of search-parties laid on. The whole thing seems to be connected with national honour somehow. They're very put out because the Americans claim to have invented flying – the Wright brothers and all that. They say Brazil did it first, chap called Santos-Dumont. Don't ask me.'

'Well never mind. You surely mustn't dream of risking your livelihood just to get me into the air. I don't believe I'm dressed for the part in any case.'

'He won't even take *me* up,' said Molly consolingly.

But Edward was allowed to examine the aircraft and then to sit in the cockpit of Fortescue's yellow machine. It hadn't occurred to him that a pilot could see so little: the view ahead was of struts, wires, exhaust manifolds and an enormous propeller all pointing up into the sky.

'How on earth do you steer the thing when you can't see the ground?' he asked. Molly was struck by the incongruity of the composer's grey head peering nervously over the leather-rimmed edge of the cockpit as if he expected the machine to spring into life of its own accord and carry him helplessly off. She had to turn away to conceal her smile.

'You look over the edge until you're moving fast enough to get her tail up. It's only a few yards. Once the tail's up the forward view's pretty fair; you'd be surprised.' Fortescue was standing on a stirrup, holding a strut and looking down at him. 'I know it seems like a glorified kite but you'd be amazed how strong all this becomes when it's loaded. All these stays and everything are stressed for flight, for the wings to support the weight of the machine in the air. On the ground the whole thing just sags with gravity. Have you ever sailed, Sir Edward? Well, it's quite like a sailing-boat. When the wind puts everything under tension the boat suddenly becomes alive.'

But Edward was thinking more of his kites, how limply on the ground they lay like mere ideas for flight but how, once tacking up the sky, the wind put heart into them, tautened them, made them dart and sing. He was helped down from the cockpit and after a *guaraná* in the club house set off back to town with Molly. Once again they passed through the clouds of butterflies and once again Fortescue circled overhead. But long after he was back on board the *Hildebrand* Edward could remember as the morning's strongest impression the smell inside the cockpit of high-octane aviation spirit, castor oil and cellulose dope. If the twentieth century had an incense which was not solely that of exploded cordite then maybe this was it. Certainly for the space of half an hour it had quickened his blood.

'Be careful,' he said to Molly, but fondly.

'My friends, Sir Edward?'

'My dear, I wouldn't presume,' he told her with genuine alarm. 'I simply mean your work. It's what chemists call the Litmus Test. Either your work comes first because it has to, or it doesn't. Either you're an artist, or . . . or . . . '

'Or I'm a fake?'

'Not at all. I meant something entirely honourable. Dilettante? Amateur? But those have the wrong connotations. Nobody has to *be* anything. Perhaps Molly Air is going to be someone who *also* paints pictures. And why not? I myself also used to compose music. Hard to believe, of course, about a decrepit globe-trotter with a microscope and a new-found interest in flying machines. We should all be different things at different times in our lives.'

But Molly took away with her to her own cabin a morose feeling of admonishment which it suited her for quite some time to believe came wholly from her disgruntled companion.

The next evening Edward joined perhaps thirty people, half of them British residents, for the Reverend Moss's lecture at the Schiller Institute. He had already been introduced to some of the community's elders, had lunched at the Consulate, dined at the Club. He was not sure of any of their names. They were more or less portly, more or less gaunt, showing to a greater or smaller degree the effects of long exposure to fever and gin. Of the two the fever appeared to have left a lesser mark except maybe for a certain shadow about the eyes which the fanciful might suppose to be mortal awareness. But they all, even the women, carried with them a bluff joviality, an aura of soldiering on.

They were clearly disconcerted by the sudden appearance in their midst of Sir Edward Elgar. It was one thing to glimpse a stout foreigner promenading the streets of Manaos with a retinue, glossy mustachios and an ice-cream suit and be told reverently that the fellow in question was a world-famous Italian tenor. It only confirmed their notions of foreigners and music. But it was another thing entirely to find this soldierly gentleman who could have passed for a sporting peer drinking brandy and soda in their club and talking about the recent flat-racing season, when in most of their minds he was vaguely associated with Royalty and State occasions. Had King George himself stumped in from the jungle and asked their opinion of the last Cesarewitch they could scarcely have been put less at their ease. Besides, many thought, surely Elgar was dead? The composer? But he plainly wasn't. He was here as large as life, sitting next to the German woman who ran the place. Bygones be bygones, of course, but it was all distinctly strange. As Vera Reynolds often remarked, one of the peculiar things about living in Manaos was that one never knew *who* was going to turn up. Each time a ship like the *Hildebrand* docked it decanted the oddest selection of people onto the streets and – frankly – into certain bedrooms now and then. If one lived in Calcutta or Rangoon or Singapore one could predict pretty much the types who would wash up from time to time: they varied little. But here . . . 'Well of course, that's what gives us the advantage over the Empire set,' Vera had pointed out. 'We commercials are so much more cosmopolitan, don't you think, or don't you? Far less *insular*, I always say.'

If Edward had supposed that an hour's talk about three hitherto unknown hawk-moths was going to be boring he was agreeably mistaken. The Reverend Moss was an excellent public speaker, unlike most preachers he had ever heard. He made a narrative of each discovery, an adventure of the hunting-trips which took him with muslin net and killing-jar into realms where most white men would venture only after a good deal of fuss and preparation and girt about with bandoliers. The hero of each story, somehow, was always the moth: a good sport who had put up a spirited run to evade detection and capture for so long. The prey was worthier far than the hunter. Whereupon the Chaplain handed round a series of airtight display boxes through whose glass lids his audience could see each specimen on its little cork Calvary. When it was over and everyone had shaken hands and said what first-class entertainment it had been (while of course transcending mere entertainment) Lena took Edward and her speaker aside.

'You are my guests now. We shall go and have dinner. Not another word, please.'

A horse-drawn *caleça* took them rattling down the cobbled main streets and then more silently but lurchingly through unmade side roads where the wheels squelched through puddles and piles of vegetable matter. They rejoined a narrow paved road down whose centre a pair of steel tram-lines gleamed in the moon. In a short while these stopped at a wooden shed. After a further fifty yards of slight descent Edward could see the building for which they were evidently heading, since it was lit by electricity. The mere fact that there was electricity available but that the houses and huts they were passing leaked only chinks of candlelight or the glow of oil lamps suggested they were in a poor quarter of town.

' "O Caboclo",' said Miles Moss. 'How very nice. Some time since I was here.'

'This isn't a place called Flores, is it?'

'That's right. How did you know, sir?'

'Just something I'd heard. I must have remembered the name.' But now he felt a jab of guilt: this was where he had half agreed to dine with Molly and Fortescue. The gharry stopped and they all got out and turned into the garden which had electric globes concealed about the shrubbery. These, by emphasising the darkness their light could not disperse, had the effect of making the surrounding vegetation press closely inwards. At once the Reverend Moss left the short path and began peering quizzically at the insects which whirled about each bulb. For a moment he looked a very English and parsonical figure, an elderly gentleman in a cottage garden examining a neighbour's bees or roses. Edward felt sadly remote from the generation which roared about the sky in the heady scent of castor oil and cellulose dope. Three people past middle age dining in the shadow of their hobbies, he thought as he followed them in.

If he withdrew a little in the early stages of the meal it was probably not noticed since Miles Moss talked with much animation while orders were given and things brought – such as the obligatory sifter of manioc flour and a tall electric fan on a stand. Both the Chaplain's talking like an old friend and the glances of Lena (who after all was one) contributed to a feeling of disloyalty – disloyalty to a shade, to an era. Lena looked more at him than she did at the Chaplain, but there was something within him which rebelled against conniving at intimacy, against piling up betrayal. Besides, there was the heap of years which lay like a jagged Andean range between that time and this.

'You were going to tell me about Dora Bellamy and Kate Hammond,' he said when the wine had begun working and had brought him back to the surface.

'Ah. Oh dear. I was slightly hoping you might not have remembered. My calling is rather against gossip. Or at least against bearing false witness.'

'Bear a true one, then.'

'I suppose the matter seems so well known. The fact is, Sir Edward, those remarkable ladies are . . . Might I enquire if you ever played cards with them?'

'No. They asked me once or twice and I nearly did but something cropped up to prevent it.'

'Perhaps then unless you're a very expert player it was just as well.'

'Oh? Good, are they?'

'I'm told they make an extremely comfortable living out of it.'

'Good Lord. Professional gamblers? That's rather rich. What a prize pair!'

'They work the boats, as I believe the saying is. This is one of the more lucrative cruise runs: many of the passengers between Europe and South America are people of some substance, and once away from land . . . Well, I'm sure I don't need to tell you.'

'Aren't the shipping lines wise to them?'

'I should imagine so. But I'm told they quite often resort to disguises and assumed names. Really, one can't help admiring their nerve, or ingenuity, or whatever it takes. Of course it's infernal cheek, but all the same.'

'Would they be married to those gentlemen we saw greeting them in Pará?'

'Not English?'

'Not remotely.'

'In that case yes. You undoubtedly saw Felipe and Wanderley. A very amiable pair, I believe. Rogues, in all probability, but what of that? This isn't England. As a matter of fact Kate and Dora and their respective husbands are well liked in Pará, even by the community. They're beyond the pale, of course, but the pale here is by no means as fixed or as distant as it would be back home. They're known to be good company and extremely kind and both ladies are after all well-spoken and educated. Some dislike them for exactly that reason, of course – backsliders and traitors and all that sort of thing. But mostly – well, we're very relaxed here in Brazil as I'm sure you've gathered and it rubs off even on the British.'

'I'm honoured to have met them. Though I must say I'm glad not to have lost my shirt to them. We composers are decidedly not in your category of people of substance.'

'Do let me ask you about music in England, Sir Edward. I feel so out of touch here and so much must be happening. Does this fellow Stravinsky carry much weight there? From all accounts it's rather barbaric stuff he writes.'

But Edward's gaze had become distant. 'You'll have to forgive me,' he said. 'I'm afraid I can't tell you anything. I haven't been following things of that sort at all. Actually I've no further interest in music – haven't had for years.'

The Chaplain put down his fork in amazement. 'No interest?' he said. 'I don't . . . I can't quite follow you, sir. You can't have *lost* interest in music.'

'Well I have,' Edward told him shortly. 'I presume one may get bored with what one has slaved at for decades? I've done with all that kind of thing. It can't be so very difficult to comprehend. After all, it's hardly unknown for priests to lose their faith as they get older and start to look at things differently. There suddenly seems to be so much else.'

If the Reverend Moss was shocked by the sudden truculence he gave no sign. To Lena's evident relief he merely said 'Of course if you feel that way, Sir Edward, I perfectly understand. It must be tiresome if one is very famous always being expected to allow perfect strangers to pick one's brains about one's speciality. Please forgive me.'

But Edward seemed unable to let the matter rest. 'The point I'm trying to make, sir, is that it's no longer my speciality. Never was. Merely a way of making a living – a dashed bad one, as it turned out. I bitterly regret having wasted so much of my time in so futile an enterprise. The entire British public as well as my friends tried by their attitude to warn me but I stupidly refused to heed them. My own fault, of course. Everyone was perfectly content to go on with their favourite diet of Sullivan and polkas and I had to stand up like a damn fool and offer them symphonies and suchlike. Well, they quite properly turned their noses up.'

Even so the Chaplain was equal to this, evidently having realised that Edward's abrupt change of mood had little to do with a dinner table in Manaos. 'In that case Sir Edward I wonder if I could interest you in another road to immortality?'

This was so unexpected Edward broke his fixed gaze and looked up in surprise. 'You're proposing to convert me?' He even smiled.

'No thought was further from my mind,' admitted the Chaplain, also amused. 'No, I was wondering about naming my new moths. One gets tired of seeing *Mossii* tacked onto the poor devils. Mightn't *Elgarii* look well? Or *Edwardii?*'

The crisis was past. 'I'd feel a fraud,' said Edward. 'Not my discovery.'

'It wouldn't have to be. An association is all that's necessary.'

Edward was mustering graciousness, evidently mollified. 'I'm sorry you should have dragged up that musical stuff. Now if only you'd asked me about *microscopy* . . . '

'Ah, you're a microscopist, sir? Had I but known. What I'd dearly love to be able to do is examine the scales from the wings of my specimens and devise a way of making them into photographic slides for my lectures. Have you ever seen scales under magnification? No? Oh, they're the most beautiful things; like snowflakes, no two ever seem identical. Alas, I've no instrument of my own.'

'I have one on board the *Hildebrand*.'

'I say, have you really? You don't suppose I . . . I mightn't come on board for half an hour before you leave?'

Edward was now expansiveness itself. 'My dear fellow, of course. Spend as long as you want. Bring all the specimens you need. I shall be fascinated. Frankly, I look forward to it. This is a most interesting place and people have been – *are* being – most charming, but to tell the truth I'm not sure how to fill the time. It would be less of a problem were one here for a month, but a day or two – it's too short for anything other than a kind of frustrated inertia.'

Lena observed how carefully he avoided looking at her, heard the evasion behind his clubbish enthusiasm. 'Let them,' she thought resignedly. 'Let them look at their moths together like a couple of schoolboys.' But something not unlike rage or tears welled immediately up with the thought that it would be unimaginably absurd were she and Edward merely to wave to one another in two days' time as to a friend going by in a train. Why wasn't everyone equally desperate to make some kind of sense of it all before it was too late? To gather up such loose ends as could still be gathered? To make as much peace as could still be made with a former self and its ghosts? Might it not solace at least some of the spectres of 'if only' which she feared might be attendant on the end? No matter how messy and misshapen one's life the grave would always be a perfect fit. Damn the man, safe on his magic mountain, blustering on about moths. She smiled and ate and smiled while her two guests discussed the problems of photography.

'There's a doctor here,' Miles Moss was saying, 'who thinks the absence of sunstroke in this region is connected with the low actinic value of light which makes photographing natural things so difficult. There's no need to have any truck with the usual sort of hampering gear for one's own protection: no green veils and smoked glasses and spinal pads, not even a cork helmet. But in quite moderate undergrowth I find I need an exposure of five or six seconds with a really low stop on the aperture to get any decent result, while in the jungle proper one really needs to double such values. It's rare indeed that an insect will hold still for that long when there's a lens pointing at it from a foot or two away, to say nothing of a perspiring Englishman trying not to breathe. As for one's camera outfits, they all have to be cased in watertight mahogany lined with tin and the films themselves done up in tins and sealed with waterproof plaster. It's a bit of a performance carrying all that around, especially since I like to work alone . . . '

Eventually desserts arrived, among which the by-now-not-unexpected slabs of sticky brown guava preserve. Edward essayed a delicate inroad on one corner with his spoon. 'You promised to chill my blood,' he reminded.

'I'm not sure I can guarantee that,' Miles Moss said. 'It depends if you want the usual traveller's tales from the depths of Green Hell, that sort of thing. Giant anacondas. Piranhas stripping the flesh off infants in the time it takes their mothers to wash them in the river so that when they lift them out the child is a gleaming white skeleton from the thorax down.'

'Good Lord,' said Edward, glancing in alarm towards Lena. But she was evidently inured to such things. 'The mothers in these parts must be remarkably unobservant. Deafish, too.' Lena went on eating her *goiabada* with a slight smile.

'Or,' continued the Chaplain, 'would you prefer a genuinely mysterious tale which none of us out here has ever quite fathomed? Ah, then I shall let you judge for yourself,' he said with the happy decisiveness of one allowed to embark on a story. 'It concerns *power* of one kind and another, principally that of the white man and that of the Indian. You have to remember the events took place at a time when the rubber barons here were still living lives of quite unbelievable extravagance and exemplifying an attitude which permeated down to the most ignominious European, even those who were penniless. Magdalena is of course better qualified than I to describe how things were twenty years ago – I only arrived in Pará in 1911 from three years in Lima – but even in those days one grew accustomed to tales of the freakish luxuries of Manaos.

'We'd all heard how the Customs House was made in England and shipped out here in pieces for re-assembly, how every last cobblestone had likewise been imported. But the spectacle of tycoons trying to out-do one another in extravagance was of a different order. It was like Babylon, I assure you. Men literally did feed their dogs caviar and water their gardens with champagne. In fact it was the sight of gardeners at dusk walking to and fro with watering-cans of the stuff which once made an entire garden party break into spontaneous applause and induced one of the guests to order a yacht with solid gold deck-fittings.

'You're going to say that's a vulgar and limited kind of power but reasonably harmless. Unfortunately, though, it all too often goes hand in hand with an arrogance which sets at naught human life itself. There are certain names which are still feared here, men who have long since departed with their profits. Paulo da Silva Leite, for example, was a trading baron who simply exterminated whole tribes of Indians practically on whim. He used to punish recalcitrant workers by firing them from cannons, you know. And Nicholas Suarez virtually wiped out the Karipunas after his brother was murdered. It was said he had ten million acres of rubber lands and once monopolised all traffic on the Madeira River. Exactly,' Miles Moss said, watching Edward's face. 'Ten million acres. And you think certain estates in England are on the large size.

'In any case such was – and I'm afraid still is in certain parts – the arrogance of the white man's greed and power. That's all by way of introduction to place events in some sort of perspective, you understand. Magdalena is familiar with the story so she knows whom it actually concerns, but for the fellow's own sake I shall give him a pseudonym. For our purposes, then, we'll call him Major Blackham, from which it is not pertinent to conclude his real name is Whiteham or anything of that sort.' The moth-man smiled at him, the draught from the fan on its tall stand lifting his hair gently. 'Major Blackham was a parishioner of mine not long ago.'

'That disguises him pretty well, with your parish.'

'Quite. Now then, the Major was out here at a venture in search of the usual kind of thing: a bit of excitement, maybe some big game, a lost temple or two, the bones of an expedition, a way of making money. Not, shall we say, an over-scrupulous sort of man but probably not much worse than hundreds of others here like him of all nationalities. Anyway, he fell in with a Brazilian Army officer who was stationed in one of those tiny river ports run by the Indian Service. The Indian Service, I should tell you, is an admirable idea of the Brazilians' though its work is much hampered by lack of funds and the sheer size and inaccessibility of the terrain. Its duties are primarily to mediate between warring tribes of Indians and protect them from merciless exploitation and wholesale slaughter, to say nothing of the theft of their tribal lands by outsiders.

'In any case Major Blackham and this Brazilian hit it off like billy-oh. The Brazilian was stuck upriver, utterly bored, his small squad of troops was becoming demoralised with inactivity and fever, when one day they came upon a truly vast forest of *castanheiros-do-pará*, which are Brazil nut trees or *Bertholletia excelsa* if one wishes to be botanically pedantic. I don't know if you're familiar with how the nuts grow, Sir Edward? No reason why you should be – no, well, each fruit contains between fifteen and thirty nuts and weighs up to four pounds, so they're a tidy size. What makes them particularly convenient is that when they're ripe they simply fall to the ground. Then it's comparatively easy to collect them up by boat since the terrain the trees favour is usually criss-crossed by *igarapés* – creeks, you know.

'The problem with this forest they'd found was that it lay across the dividing line which separated the territories of two tribes who were traditionally at each others' throats, the Ga-Tuparú and the Coimbé. The Brazilian officer and Major Blackham between them hatched a plot which involved using the troops to annex the entire Brazil nut forest under the pretence of creating a no-man's land between the warring factions, and then to share the proceeds of their newly-created private estate. One day they went in force and to their surprise found much of the forest already settled by the Ga-Tuparú although small areas were under Coimbé control. They had thought it uninhabited, you see. There followed a series of nasty little engagements during which they took quite a large Ga-Tuparú village. They killed a great many villagers – some say as many as a hundred – and confiscated all the Indians' plantations. That was quite bad enough but they took captives as well whom they forced to work as slave labour, gathering nuts indiscriminately in territory that had formerly belonged to the Coimbé. People didn't like this at all when the story got out since the Brazilians quite rightly congratulate themselves on their so-called Golden Law which outlawed slavery. That's not to say it doesn't still go on, I'm afraid, but they find it harder to overlook when the slavers are foreign. I suppose one sees their point.

'For a month or two everything proceeded according to plan. The nuts were sent downriver and sold and the two conspirators began to make some quite substantial sums. But then things began to go wrong. One day the Brazilian was shot with an arrow which was evidently poisoned with something especially horrible in place of the usual curare, which generally kills swiftly, since he suffered the most protracted convulsions, hallucinations and creeping paralysis. It took the wretched man a week to die and witnesses said his agonies were remarkable – and this in a country which tends to the phlegmatic about such things. Even though it's unfortunately not uncommon in these parts that a white man is shot by an Indian arrow – many have never seen whites before and are mortally afraid – there were other odd aspects. Firstly, the arrow itself could not be identified as belonging to any known tribe in that region. It was quite unlike those made by either the Coimbé or the Ga-Tuparú. Secondly, it took the officer vertically down through the top of the shoulder right beside the neck –' Miles Moss tapped his own shoulder where he might have worn an epaulette. 'At the time he was standing a long way off the nearest cover and it would in any case have been a remarkable shot even from close range; imagine calculating such a steep arc of fire for so narrow a target. Of course I know perfectly well that certain tribes habitually use such a technique, but hardly from so far away. A witness was heard to say that it was more as though the arrow had literally dropped out of the blue.

'Well, Major Blackham was disturbed by this but at the same time took consolation in the fact that without the Brazilian his own portion of the profit from their nut scheme would now be so much the larger. A junior officer took charge of the troops and business went on as usual. They built two *barracas* on the site of the Indian village for storing the nuts and for accommodation while burning the rest of the huts to prevent the Indians filtering back. Generally the Major slept alone in one of these sheds with the nuts while in the other were the native troops who took it in turns to guard a sort of stockade where their captives lived. One morning Major Blackham awoke to find something terrible and at the same time completely incredible.'

Here the Reverend Moss paused for a sip of wine and a mouthful of the *goiabada* which, like that of his listeners, had lain largely untouched ever since he had embarked on his story. So intent had Edward become, he found himself watching even as the narrator put the spoon in his mouth, chewed, swallowed.

'What he found,' the Chaplain resumed at the end of a pause judged to perfection, 'was that the Brazilians' *barraca* had been crushed during the night by a gigantic tree. Actually, it was not crushed so much as obliterated. The Major of course climbed among the branches to see if he could find any survivors but it was soon plain from the presence of flies and the *urubus* gathering overhead that the thirty or so men lay in the ruins beneath this enormous trunk. You'll have seen some of the trees round here, Sir Edward, so you'll realise I'm not describing anything on the lines of a big English elm or horse chestnut. I'm talking of something which had stood fully two hundred feet high and through the base of whose trunk one could have driven a motor car. It was then, of course, that the real horror dawned on him – which was that there had been no tree of that description standing at the edge of the clearing, certainly not within a couple of hundred yards. Neither had he heard a sound during the night and it was inconceivable that a thing that size could have fallen in silence. But not only that. He soon noticed that the tree hadn't rotted, nor had it even been sawn. *It had snapped.*'

'Snapped?'

The priest nodded. 'I doubt if there exists a piece of machinery anywhere in the world capable of snapping that monster as if it had been a pencil and assuredly not up a remote tributary in the Amazon rain forest. The same goes for a machine capable of lifting it, complete with its branches and everything. Once again someone observed later that it was as if the tree had simply fallen out of the sky.

'This time the Major panicked. He was after all left alone in the clearing with an impossible event and the remains of thirty men, to say nothing of the ghosts of the villagers they had killed. The Indian slaves had disappeared, you see; their stockade was empty and the men on guard never found. Blackham got to his canoe and paddled for all he was worth back to the settlement where he told his story. But nothing would keep him there. He pressed on downstream to the next township, engaged boatmen, pushed on some more. He reached the main river, the Tapajós, and still kept on. He was heading for Santarém just as fast as he could for he now believed himself a marked man. He felt weighed down by an awful heaviness. What made his terror worse was that every now and then when he stopped at a settlement an Indian would catch sight of him and set up a great cry while pointing at something apparently a foot or two above his head. Whatever it was these people thought they saw was not clear, and by no means every Indian could see it – or if they did they gave no sign. But they all reacted when they saw the pointing and heard the word being shouted.'

'What was the word?' Edward asked, thinking he had detected the signs of another dramatic pause in the Chaplain's narrative and wishing to forestall it. The Reverend Moss looked at the stem of his glass as he twirled it absently between forefinger and thumb. Then he said quietly but with intensity:

' *"The Squatter"*. That was what they were shouting. *"He carries the Squatter"*.'

And yes – Edward felt a coldness pass over his entire body which was not to do with the breeze from the fan. 'The Squatter?' It was unexpectedly sinister.

'The Squatter. When Major Blackham finally arrived in San-tarém he was in a terrible state, in a high fever and babbling. That was where I first came upon him. I happened to be visiting – on my way back to Pará – when I was told that an Englishman had reached town a few days before in a condition which suggested a priest as much as a doctor. Of course one had heard that before and it usually means by the time one has arrived the poor wretch is beyond the help of either. But I went and found him full of quinine and largely recovered from the fever: very weak, maybe, but perfectly lucid. He told me the whole sorry tale and ended up by saying he knew it sounded ridiculous but was I licensed to perform exorcisms? I said well, yes, I supposed I was – I believed there was a form of service and as an ordained priest I could conduct it but it was rarely used nowadays and was frankly not something I wished to undertake at all lightly.

' "Lightly?" he said. "My God, Padré, believe me, there's no lightness left in my life – however much remains of *that*. I'm haunted. I know it now. A curse has been put on me for what I did and I'm afraid there's no power great enough to remove it. I'm a doomed man."

' "You mustn't say that," I told him seriously, "still less believe it since the Devil himself was vanquished by the love of Our Lord Jesus Christ and by His grace I can call down that power to your defence. There is no evil can withstand it, but it has to be asked for in all humility and with absolute and complete contrition for your deeds." Whereupon he said yes, he would make a proper confession and added he was in such a state of mortal fear and anguish that saying he was sorry for his dreadful crimes would probably sound facetiously in God's ears as a ludicrous under-statement. Naturally I reassured him that God was not given to mirth at a sinner's expense and then asked him what made him so certain he was haunted literally, rather than figuratively by his conscience.

' "Don't ask me to describe it, Padré," he pleaded. "Just believe me – it's there. Oh, oh, how lucky Agassiz and the others were! Things fell on them and they died, but what has settled on me is a far worse horror, a . . . a *sitting* on my shoulders. I can't actually see it but I have – glimpsed – ah – " he was rolling his head from side to side on the pillow as he spoke, sweat pouring off him and with his eyes round open as if fearing to close them and see again what it was he'd caught sight of. "It's an *oppression*. Here, pull me up, see for yourself." I put my hands beneath his arms to help the poor man into a sitting position – his body was a furnace, I could feel my face glowing with the heat he radiated – and do you know, he weighed twice what I'd imagined he would. "You feel it too?" he said, watching my face and nodding. "Yes; you know. You know now I'm not making it up. Some of the Indians can see . . . can see what it is that squats on me."

'I told him to compose himself while I went and fetched certain necessities and that I would be back at once to carry out the exorcism. And when I turned and looked back at him from the doorway, propped up on a pillow and leaning back against the whitewashed wall – just for a second, for an instant's imagining, I thought I saw the thing which was *roosting* on him . . . '

The Reverend Moss's eyes darted quickly to one side as if he had seen something at the verandah windows open to the night. Involuntarily Edward looked as well and between the other tables and diners glimpsed a bat, no, a huge moth sailing along towards them with that flat, tropical glide. Maybe the Chaplain, long acclimatised to such things, could see what was bound to happen but Edward didn't and was still watching as the moth floated into the mild vacuum behind the fan and was sucked into it with a soft *ping!*

Immediately their table was swept by a small storm of frag-ments. Putting a hand to his cheek he felt what appeared to be ointment. Opposite him the lepidopterist's shirt glistened with smears of seeming egg yolk. On the *goiabada* jelly in front of Lena a hairy insect leg flexed itself once or twice. Long afterwards Edward had the clear memory, accompanied by a definite measure of pride, that not one of them gave a single cry of disgust although such cries broke from the table behind them, for the moth had been a large and juicy one. The Reverend Moss was peering sadly at the smears and tatters.

'*Agrippina*,' he said. 'What a shame. Funny: they're not all that easy to catch. I say, I don't know about you two but it's rather put me off my food.'

'It's certainly put itself *on* mine,' said Edward, wiping his cheek and shirt-front with a napkin. 'A little moth goes a long way, a bigger even further.'

Lena pushed her plate a decisive half inch towards the centre of the table as waiters converged on them. 'We should go home,' she said. 'It has spoilt dinner and the story. As you remember, this was my affair, Mr Moss, so if you'd be good enough to pay I shall reimburse you as soon as we are outside.'

'Oh dear, oh dear.'

Once outside they engaged another *caleça* and set off for town. Beside him in the darkness Edward heard the sound of paper rustling. The punctilious whisper filled him at once with pity for her.

'I must say, until that wretched insect came into our lives it was a most enjoyable dinner. I thank you both most sincerely for an occasion I'm not likely to forget.' The night ambled by with its squares and rectangles of flickering orange glows. 'But I say, Mr Moss, you can't leave us in suspense like this. What happened to the Major?'

'Oh, I don't know,' came with a deprecating laugh from the dark. 'Anything you like. I hadn't got that far.'

'You mean . . . you mean you were making it up?' Edward sounded aggrieved.

'I was under the impression you wanted a mysterious tale for the dinner table. I'm sorry if it fell short of expectation.'

'It was absolutely gripping as far as it went. Do you mean all that business about disguising his name and everything . . . ? Lena! Had you or hadn't you heard it before? Was it true?'

'Oh, perfectly.'

'Put it this way, sir,' said the Reverend Moss. 'Let's say yes, there once was a man haunted by his past and yes, I did perform an exorcism in Santarém. The person concerned, Major Blackham if you like, was convinced of a horrible incubus and was certain it was useless to get on the first ship back to England to escape his curse. He knew he would only carry it with him. It couldn't be outrun; it had to be induced to leave him by one means or another.'

'Well, and did you induce it?'

'I most truly believe so. Something . . . happened during the exorcism which, since it involves sacred matters, I'm not in a position to divulge. Such rites, involving as they do the innermost matters of a man's soul, are not to be used as fodder for anecdotes. However, yes, I'm convinced that whatever it was – the Squatter – left Major Blackham's shoulders and returned whence it had been summoned. I can tell you seriously, sir, that I don't believe it's ever to be found here in Brazil rather than anywhere else in the universe. Whatever home it has is nowhere as friendly as an earthly jungle; no.'

'And the Major? What became of him?'

'He returned to England in due course, I'd guess what novelists call a changed man.'

'Under a changed name, it seems.'

'Exactly. To be truthful I've quite lost touch and am not sorry to have done so. There was something contaminating about – but here we are.' They had reached the wharf. Before them lay the *Hildebrand*, her elegant hull pierced with lit portholes. 'Well, Sir Edward, may I ask if your kind offer still stands for tomorrow? I would understand if you felt you'd already had rather too detailed a look at the local lepidoptera.'

'Absolutely not. Come tomorrow morning as convenient. The earlier the better. I don't suppose, Lena, you'd be free later in the day?' The bulk of the ship which blocked off the view of the river, glittering with lights and evidently alive as it was, spoke of imminent endings.

'Of course, Edward. How can you ask? Do important things happen every day in Manaos?'

From the top of the gangway he watched them drive away. Far above the bellows hood of their *caleça* the vast notice in glimmering capitals sang out over the ship, across the river, across Brazil itself: 'Pussels Cronifer GmbH'. Only when he had actually got into bed did a thought which had been gradually forming suddenly articulate itself with shocking distinctness. Had Lena's late husband been one of those mercantile barons of inconceivable wealth whose marble palace was built on the proceeds of brutality and slave labour? A veritable Marchcroft Manor of Amazonas? Impossible to imagine somebody of Lena's fineness of soul condoning either the vulgar or the atrocious. Yet what darkness did these primitive jungles exhale which might not in time infiltrate a man's best nature? There again, sterling fellows like Miles Moss appeared quite uninfiltrated. And so one would hope (thought Edward to himself as he dozed off); son of the vicar of Windermere, native of Birkenhead, ex-member of the Leeds Clergy School . . . Assuredly the down-to-earth quality of that background was proof against all manifestations of sinister waywardness . . . He slept.

But that night the lights of the Villa Mirabelle shone for many hours, casting their rectangles onto the dew-laden grass outside and bringing insects thudding and rustling at the mesh screens which guarded the open doors and windows. Lena played to herself as she still did sometimes, more frequently of late since her husband's death. The sounds of the Viennese classics flew out past the reflecting eyes and quivering wings, drifted down to the pavilion in its spinney of jacaranda and reached in faint tones the slipping waters of the Rio Negro. The music spoke to her not of any past, not even of her own; it was simply something immutable, something which had always been there, which had sustained and would sustain her passage through the world. She no more thought of student days and her dazzled aspirations at the Conservatoire – not even with Edward's presence in town to evoke that precise period – than she remembered learning to walk. She played to calm an immense and present anger whose very incoherence was a source of distress to her. In consequence she did not play very well, having only half a mind for the music. Her eyes read the notes or her fingers remembered them. Had she been knitting she would not have dropped a stitch; but between the patterns formed by her hands and the raging conversations in her head would have been no connection.

No apparent connection, certainly. Except that as she played on, the music's orderliness gradually gave shape to her rage and bit by bit this fury, which seemed squatted on by the accumulated weight of forty years' rumination, at last moulded itself into simple outrage at the unfairness of his victory – or better, of his victoriousness. How dare a man enjoy worldly success yet court sympathy by pretending to have failed, all the while basking in the implied virtue of self-deprecation? It was too much; no, it was downright gross. It was difficult to give anybody their correct measure of public recognition while keeping back enough affection still to be privately touched by them, and Edward expected – *demanded* – that this difficulty be overcome. For he was above all one of those men who simultaneously yearn for praise and despise it, whose desire for approval is implacable even as they reserve the right to belittle their admirers' qualifications to bestow it. As Lena's fingers played to an audience of moths she furiously addressed a figure, an Edward who looked neither quite like the young man she had known nor the elderly gentleman with whom she had just dined.

'You're a baby, Edward, you always were. A brilliant baby, a genius baby; but a baby in your clamour for attention, attention, attention. And you always got it, too, although it suits you now to pretend otherwise. All your venom about no-one ever taking any interest in your music, that bitterness with which you allege that had you had the least encouragement you could have composed *Caractacus* ten years earlier: it's all the invention of a baby.

'How do I know about that? Well, dear Edward, not only did I once know you rather well and see you on your home ground but I have spies in Europe who have always kept me informed. There! Be shocked if you will. Talk about traitors within your own camp and the rest of that silly rhetoric. You'll never know who they were, who they are. Some of your favourite Germans, I'm afraid. But it's further evidence that right from your cradle you had people interested in everything you said or wrote or did, from your mother onwards. Far from letting your music emerge unsuspected from behind a garret door to make its way painfully in an indifferent world, you made very sure that everybody was privy to each step in its creation.

'It's not very gallant to say I lie . . . Then I shall simply be more gallant and say you've conveniently forgotten how you collared anyone who would listen and make them stand beside the piano to hear your latest big tune or your musical impressions of a bulldog swimming as you fumbled your way towards a complete work. Especially women, Edward, if you'll remember; especially women. You always did have a string of admiring females in tow, didn't you? Beginning of course with your mother and ending . . . and not *quite* ending with your wife. They were vouchsafed glimpses of your creations in exchange for adulation which you accepted serenely or with temper tantrums according to your mood. The point is that no-one minded. On the contrary they felt privileged, flattered, overwhelmed, just as they were by your long walks which might turn out jaunty and funny or morose and confessional, full of your dreams for the future – as if we didn't also have one or two dreams of our own.

'So what emerged from all this? What but that classic myth of the romantic artist – the lonely dreamer of the reed-beds taking dictation from the wind, young Ted Elgar up from Worcester whose genius was for ever being snubbed and thwarted by some upper-crust musical establishment in Cambridge and London? But it remains a myth, Edward. Oh, there was probably enough truth in it to make it worthwhile embroidering a little; but you embroidered a lot. Publicly, too. Remember that interview you gave in *Strand Magazine* back in 1904? Certainly – I have a copy here in our remarkable library. You claimed to have written wind quintets as a youth during the morning services in St George's at which you played the organ, and then to have performed them later the same day at the Leicesters'. Entire wind quintets, Edward, thrown off during the sermon? We might have believed it of Mozart, but not of young Ted Elgar the famous slow starter who for a good few years hardly finished a single piece of substance he started. Of course I'm not saying those weren't years of great musical fertility, that you weren't sketching ideas which later became most if not all of your major works. What I am saying is that put that way it didn't sound quite portentous enough for you, not quite enough like Florestan and . . . and Eusebius triumphing over the Philistines. No. So you went beyond embellishment. You invented a myth for yourself in which you, at least, believed fervently. But I'm afraid those of us back then who saw at first hand your uncertainty, your nervous prostrations, your tyrannical slightedness, your mysterious illnesses – we were under no illusions.

'But the one thing which of course made it all possible for us was that you so clearly had genius in you. I'd never met it before in its raw state and nor have I since, but it was as unmistakable as it was unfocussed. Contrary to what you prefer to believe even people who disliked your music could perceive it, which was not guaranteed to make them like you any better. For those of us who loved you it was precisely what saved the whole thing because it gave us the stamina to see how funny and affectionate you were underneath the touchiness.

'Why do I speak like this? Perhaps because I've watched – all right, *spied on*, then – your life from afar for so many years I've earned the right to intimacy. Perhaps because I'm shocked to see you so dreadfully unhappy at a time when you might be sad but tranquil, even contented. You don't at all like the person you've become, this person you've created for yourself, because in your heart you know he never existed. There once was a deeply sensitive, intelligent child, an artist to his fingertips, and he was a dreamer of dreams. But it took him many years to find his proper voice, which he found neither earlier nor later than he should have done. Unfortunately he never could accept that simple fact because it conflicted with the desire of the baby in him to have from the very first the adulation due a genius. So he largely invented the enmities, the machinations, the cabals, misunderstandings, snobberies and the rest as a palatable way of explaining to himself why the symphonies weren't pouring from his pen as they had from Haydn's and Mozart's at a far younger age and faced as they were with even worse penury and social ignominy.

'But . . . no, I'm afraid I've not finished yet. There's another aspect to your unhappiness, one connected with us poor women in your life and especially with Alice . . . Of course I dare speak about her – don't be pompous. Lady Elgar is as much public property as Sir Edward. For genius or not, you actually needed us and especially her in order to function as a composer. Oh, not for our hugs and kisses; not for tremulous encounters in summer-houses while the sounds of croquet drifted through the shrubbery from distant lawns. It was for something far less romantic, more basic than that, more . . . babyish, I suppose. Dear Edward – it was because of *that* I resolved not to see you again. Quite simply, I didn't want to become your mother. But Alice – well, Time's wingèd chariot was bearing down behind her in a way which made it all the more possible and right. She was exactly what you needed: an older woman who believed utterly in you. To make doubly sure, she had good reasons of her own for wanting your success: she badly needed to be able to cock a snook at all her horrid snobbish relatives for marrying beneath her – as they saw it. And your success is what she got. She made you work when you

－242－

didn't want to and she praised practically every note you wrote. She ruled your life and she ruled your bar-lines. Suddenly it all came right. Triumph. *Enigma, Gerontius, The Apostles, The Kingdom* . . .

'Ah, but we're still conniving at your myth, aren't we? Our version suggests that Alice stepped into your life, took over the running of it and almost at once your now unfettered genius was free to take off. But it still wasn't ready, was it? Nearly ten years went by before *Enigma*. Ten more years finding your way until you yourself were over forty, working through your *Froissart* overture and all those oratorios. What were they, now? *The Black Knight* and *Lux Christi* and *King Olaf* and *The Banner of St George* and *Caractacus* – heavens, one might say one detected a curious obsession with chivalry and its silly lance. Can it be the pure-hearted young Edward riding valiantly out girt about with the armour of a good woman's love to do battle with the Philistines and in quest of a knighthood?

'A cheap gibe, you say. Oh well, perhaps. But you did defeat the Philistines and you did get your knighthood and much else besides. However, there was a catch to it all; one which even now contributes to your unhappiness. You began to wonder how strong your genius was if you had to rely so heavily on your wife to enable it to function. Hence that nasty vice between whose jaws you were caught. You needed Alice with a need beyond mere love but at the same time you resented her for it. You demanded her approval but that uncritical adulation of hers was infuriating. Convincing or not, though, you had to have it.

'And now she's gone and I'm bitterly sorry for you, Edward, because I know you and your genius and I know you'll have lost faith. In your heart you're convinced your Muse died with her and that willy-nilly your creative life is over . . . And you're left with what most human beings would dearly, dearly love: not one but several works which will ensure the immortality of your name and which will give pleasure and be discussed long after you and I are dust. But that still isn't enough for the baby Edward, is it? Not content with being Elgar you still want to be Beethoven. Why? I truly can't imagine. I don't understand it. Ah, now you're looking resentful as well as furious. You're going to say that with the fickleness of taste I could never be quite sure you may *not* be Beethoven in two hundred years' time. But you know you won't be.

Brutal truth? Your range is too narrow, your output too small. Your famous heart is maybe too much with you – indeed, I've never known anyone, Edward, who so carried about with them their autobiography. And while you may have changed the musical history of England you haven't touched that of Europe. It's Stravinsky now, and Schönberg and Webern. A sad irony, that. By sheer historical misfortune you led the renaissance of English music from the tail end of a European style.

'You know all this, of course; but not content with an astonishing achievement you're eaten up with resentment that it was not still greater. So now you renounce your own works and music itself. It's all horses and theatres and impresarios in bars. It's flying machines and microscopes and chummy diversions. The crusading knight has at last gone over to the Philistines. The child denied the sweetshop declares his loathing of sweets. Oh Edward . . . My God, it's so unfair of you. And the unfairest thing of all is I suspect I know what you're thinking after this impassioned outburst of mine – some knowing masculine vulgarism about forty years' pent-up unrequited love. Well, that isn't it either. I've had far too interesting and amused a life of my own – a family life at that – to have carried on such a proxy affair for even a tenth of that time. No, I think you can't recognise the nature of the upset you induce in people when you pretend to belittle the whole of music as if you owned it and your achievement as if you hadn't earned it. You think they take offence at your tone or are worried about having provoked a famous man.

'But do you know what I think of as I hear you maintain your name will perish even as you know perfectly well that it won't? I think of my own Eusebius and all those like him who had no time to do anything and are already handfuls of earth. I think of my son who was so pretty and lively and sulky and who too liked long walks to the villages in the jungle round here and days drifting about the river. I think of my boy who frisked in the sun for nineteen short years and whose bodily remains are now lying beneath some hideous mass gravestone carved with sententious quotations about his unnamed name living for ever. That, Edward, is what I think when I hear an old man's self-pity which is merely an overweening egoism in disguise.'

The piano had long ago fallen silent. Insects still clung and battered themselves on the meshes at door- and window-frame but now no sound passed out beyond them except a woman's soft crying. The red and silver beads of their eyes saw a thousand reticulated versions of the room with a thousand identical tiny figures sitting at pianos with hands pressed to faces. On chitinous legs for hours they clung and stared, bouncing slightly; and at their backs was the tumultuous silence of all Brazil.

Later still she watched from her bedroom window as the night grew pale and that invisible current of dawn flowed across the earth which makes sleepless hours retreat into the shadow of their own unreality. And as she looked it took shape, the mountain, its foothills rising from misty jungle and ascending through opalescent regions to where the tip burst and sparkled and flew its freezing banner. It grew in her, unchanged, untouched by rhetoric and argument and imprecation, the whole immovable vaporous pile of it until for the first time she imagined it crumbling, dispassionately viewed the inward collapse, the slipping to ruin of the entire bulk. It shocked her, exhilarated her, shocked her once again.

'Ah Edward, Edward,' she said. 'Damn you.'

Miles Moss arrived punctually aboard the *Hildebrand* and spent most of the morning below, he and Edward dabbling happily with slides and stains. Later both men went ashore together and lunched at the Club before taking leave of each other with regret. The priest returned to convince Captain Maddrell that a memorial service for the vanished doctor would on second thoughts be neither appropriate nor well attended while Edward made his way to the Schiller Institute. It was, he realised with some surprise, his last day in Manaos. Tomorrow morning at seven – or so Steward Pyce claimed – the *Hildebrand* would begin the return journey to Liverpool. He was somewhat unclear as to how he had filled the last five days but the time had gone quite pleasantly and he had met one or two capital fellows – the Rev. Moth (for such he had privately re-named the man) most assuredly being one of them. A knowledgeable chap who had turned out to be no mean micros-copist himself, hardly the typical priest, not at all earnest or dowdy or sidling. Edward thought that Brazil certainly had a way of showing people in an unexpected light; practically no-one he had so far met on this trip had been quite what one might have supposed. He did not extend this line of thought to the point where it would make the prospect of a winter-bound England loom dull and forbidding. His mind was that of a man for whom the mere excitement of the journey home eclipses his knowledge of what arrival will mean.

The sight of the Institute, severe behind its quiet shrubbery, did something to subdue him. It suggested having to be serious, it hinted at confrontation. Lena's mood was not easy to assess, either, as she greeted him in the hall. The air was cool and withdrawn, faintly scented with beeswax polish and what seemed to him burnt jam. Their footsteps on the marble staircase echoed grittily in the afternoon hush. On the half-landing Schiller's bust stood outlined against the creepers at the window whose leaves, on this shadowed side of the house, were still hung with drops of sparkling rainwater from the midday storm.

'It hasn't been long enough,' said Lena in her office. 'Such a ridiculously short time. I don't just mean too short for you to do justice to Manaos or whatever. I mean it's too short for us to have overcome our awkwardness. Forty years are impossible to undo in five days.'

'I don't know that "undo" is a happy choice of phrase. Presumably neither of us would wish to undo the bulk of our lives. One doesn't willingly unravel oneself.'

'No, no,' she said unhappily, 'of course not. I only meant . . .' After a pause she asked, 'What will you do now, Edward?'

'Eh? Why, go home. Oh, I see. In the future? What will I do? I don't know. What will you do? What will anyone do? Grow a bit older, maybe, and then die. Such at least are my plans.'

'You're infuriating, my dear Edward, but since it's exactly the infuriation you've always been able to arouse I find myself fond of it. I meant – and I shan't apologise for presuming things I can't know – I believe I detect in your whole manner and everything you've said since your arrival that you no longer have much faith in your future creativity as a composer. I don't know if I should commiserate with you or whether after a lifetime such a respite comes gratefully?'

But he remained silent, staring at the tips of his pipe-clayed tropical shoes with the faint puzzlement of a child still uncertain whether it's being encouraged or scolded. Finally when the silence had extended itself in all directions he said, 'Whatever you may think, I shan't miss it. It's a hard and anxious business confronting blank paper all one's life. But I still work, Lena; I don't think you realise how much I work. I'm always travelling around England, conducting here, conducting there. I've made a lot of recordings too, you know.'

'I know that, Edward. We have most if not all of them in the Library here. I think . . . I think all I wanted to say was what an exciting phase in your life you've reached and how very glad I am for you. Truly I am.'

'Exciting? Travelling in cold trains to underheated halls to conduct my wretched music for diminishing and ever more elderly audiences? Exciting, reading sniffy reviews of such events – when they're reviewed at all – by hack journalists only too eager to write me off as out of fashion, faintly embarrassing, downright vulgar? I suppose you could say it was excitement of a sort, but then you could say that about an attack of apoplexy.'

'I didn't make myself clear. Dear Edward, that side of things comes to all artists who have the misfortune to live long enough to see themselves become unfashionable. It must be infinitely horrid and depressing, not least because it's fickle and unjust. No, when I said exciting I specifically meant the marvellous future which the gramophone holds out to people like yourself. I should think in your case it's the perfect invention. You like clever machines and it offers you the prospect of a kind of immortality no major composer has ever had. So far as I know you're the first to have conducted his own work for the gramophone, certainly to have conducted so much of it.'

'H'm. Probably because most aren't up to much as conductors of their own music.'

'Of course. But you can do what no other composer has yet done. You can leave a legacy of performances which will show for ever your special talent.'

'And what *is* my special talent?'

'I'd say it was for giving interpretations of your music which are always convincing yet no two of which are ever the same.'

For the first time he smiled. 'Well, bless you for that, Lena. I always used to say I wanted my stuff to go elastically and mystically and I'm afraid I haven't much faith in modern conductors. They haven't the heart for that sort of thing, most of 'em.

Mystically doesn't mean *religiosely*' – he drew the word out with an exaggeration which heaped contempt on sententiousness of all kinds – 'it means an awareness that the music is only half expressed by the actual notes. Of course. And as for elastically, well, it should go with a brisk snap and never rigidly. A thousand fluctuations in tempo but much too delicate to write a full-blown *tempo rubato* into the score. And obviously those fluctuations will depend on one's mood at the time of the performance, they'll change from day to day. That's the mistake they keep making, in my view, these modern conductors. They're so keen to make a name for themselves by producing their own definitive versions of great works – X's Ninth, Y's *Parsifal*, Z's Brahms' One – they simply turn out beautifully-crafted fossils. Whereas I know one must re-live a piece of music each time one plays it and in consequence no two performances *can* ever be identical and still less definitive. Nor should they be. The idea's cretinous.'

'Then that, Edward, must quite simply be your work from now on, to leave as much – no, all of your music – in different versions. That way there will never be any doubt, no matter which way the weathercock of fashion swings. Anyone will be able to hear that your music is still alive, still beating. It'll be an immense task for you and it's highly creative, only maybe a slightly different form of creativity. I can't tell you how I long to hear your records. They will arrive here packed in sawdust and I shall take them out of the crate and blow the shavings off them and put them on the gramophone in there. And then I shall have you to the life with me in the room.'

'Ah, Lena, you're trying to encourage an old man,' he said, not displeased. 'I admit I'd had some such project at the back of my mind simply because I'm so despondent about the future of my music. At least after I've gone there will exist reminders of what it *could* sound like. I can sometimes foresee only too clearly how my stuff will be treated in future. By the time they can bring themselves to play me at all they're going to linger over it, damn them. They'll make it wallow in horrid nostalgia because they won't be able to think how else to play it. They'll wring out every last drop of purple, just see if they don't.'

'Of course I hope you're quite wrong but it's all the more reason for making your records now.'

'Yes. Exactly. Something permanent.'

She heard herself saying 'Well, as permanent as anything ever is' quite sharply, as if impatient with herself for having played yet again into the willing hands of his hubris. 'One no longer has quite the same unshaken faith in the durability of such things – neither masterworks nor the civilisations which gave them birth. You find yourself despondent about the survival of your music whereas sometimes I see only a vision of a more general dust. After all, even Beethoven' (how impetuously the comparison came to her mind!) 'even Beethoven himself wrote in sand and on the same beach as the rest of us, only rather higher up so his marks may remain a while longer than the rest. But one day I believe will come a freak tide and sweep the entire beach clean: Dante, Michelangelo, Shakespeare, Bach, Mozart, Goethe, even Schiller and Edward Elgar. Everybody. Just a smooth sheet of sand blotting in the sun like a mirror going opaque. Time for a fresh batch of scribbles. Or for none.'

'You take a bleak view of the future I must say,' said Edward, clearly disturbed by her unexpected usurpation of his usual role.

'Do I? I don't think so. Civilisations have been coming and going now for a great many thousand years and no doubt they all had their Edward Elgars. Things move on: it's in their nature. Not that they're going anywhere. Just the universal wheels turning, and as they grind so the dust falls out. You and me.' She was speaking now with a subdued passion and not without a trace of triumph as well.

'According to you, hardly worth bothering to make a mark in the sand at all.'

'I think wisdom may consist in being able to say that without the least tone of injured self-esteem. I've never myself quite learned that trick. I suspect the proper aspiration would be to cross the beach without leaving a single footprint.'

It was the solidity of the room and the things in it one noticed, he was thinking, to say nothing of the house itself. Scattered about this building were more than a ton of Bösendorfer piano, tens of tons of books and records. The plaster busts of Beethoven and Bach, the bronze Schiller on its plinth, the buckram volumes of music, the marble clocks, the dense tropical hardwood which sheathed and enclosed as with armour – a veritable mountain of stuff implying a continuity more enduring than any single one of its elements. The whole was a fully-equipped compendium, an outpost of European culture. Remote maybe, and dwarfed by the surrounding continental expanse; but like an amoeba caught in a drying puddle it could survive almost indefinitely in a cystic state, containing within its hardened cell walls the essential nucleus, the fragment of the original seed which would swell and crack and propagate anew when the climate changed and water returned.

'I think Beethoven's bit of beach will survive as long as there are ears.'

'I'm afraid I don't,' she said. 'Ears change. No-one now can read Shakespeare without explanatory notes; one day he will be accessible only to scholars with dictionaries.' A moted shaft of sunlight, thin as a pencil, somehow found its way through the leaves and a shutter chinked by termites to fall onto her lined cheek like a death-ray. 'I don't share your confidence, Edward, I only wish I did. I'm too conscious always of time and of what lies out there.' She lifted a hand wanly towards one shoulder without moving her face. It pointed to an entire compass of directions.

'Savages? The human hinterland? What do they care about Beethoven, you mean?'

'The war changed everything, didn't it?' she said. 'We came quite close to wiping out our own civilisation. Really quite close. Then where would the ears have been? There's something exhausted about us, had you noticed? Nobody who's energetic ever commits suicide. And what *they* have' – again her hand raised itself – 'is energy.'

'Not that I've noticed, they haven't. They're either standing stark naked on the river bank with their mouths open or they're asleep in hammocks. I'm not saying I blame them, only that the casual observer searches in vain for signs of anything other than terminal lethargy.'

'That *is* energy. While we're frantically working to exterminate ourselves they're pleasurably occupied in multiplying. History is very much on their side. And so are numbers, believe me.' A third time her veined hand indicated more than the window over her shoulder. 'I'm not talking just of Brazil, naturally. Mercifully we shall neither of us live to see it but I can envisage a time when we have cancelled ourselves out and they with all their numbers and natural resources will simply come and cart away the entire beach in order to build concrete cities for themselves. Then it'll be their turn to come and search the jungles covering London and Berlin for our lost temples and speculate about our priesthoods and our tyrannous élites. And they won't be – what is it you like to call such people? Yahoos? Of course, Jonathan Swift. No, they won't be yahoos. They'll simply be the next civilisation. And there'll be others treading on *their* heels. It's no cause for despondency, after all. No-one loses more than anyone else. Or gains. If we're despondent we have only ourselves to blame for inventing hopes and pretending we haven't got eyes. London, Berlin, Vienna, Paris, New York . . . They're all Babylon.'

It was profoundly irritating, he later thought on his way back to the wharf, to be lectured on transience at the age of sixty-six by a person not significantly younger and then to be told that any annoyance it might cause is merely due to a lack of the wisdom which *accepts*. Presumably if one had been cut off for the last quarter-century in the middle of primaeval rain forest one's mind would have become a little rusty and peevish, but all the same he did think with a bit of effort on her part . . .

'But of course dearest Edward,' she said before he left, 'when all's said and done I'm dreadfully envious of you. It's foolish, isn't it? Especially after all I've been saying. The fact is, no matter what may happen when we're dead we are at this moment alive and you have left a deep mark on the beach. You've made such beautiful scribbles. You've had a voice, and practically no-one else has one. How lovely to have had a *voice*. I can't be more myself than I am and yet I'm merely lost in the inarticulate crowd. But practically any single bar of your music is utterly you and nobody else in this universe. Ah, damn you, Edward my dear, dear man. Damn you.'

Hours later and she was still weighed with remorse for having been able to spare him her previous night's inward tirade only by replacing it with gratuitous meanness. Now and then a peppery self-justification lightened her mood, telling her that news about the fleetingness of human affairs was fairly stale and enjoyed widespread acknowledgement. But this was soon supplanted by a return of shame and regret that, after all the years, she had been able to find only tones of upset and tokens of injury with which to greet the man she most envied and admired. And loved, of course, whatever that meant. Maybe after all it had to entail not becoming abject, not allowing the other all the spoils. How stupid it was, though, two old people heading for their respective graves unable for so many reasons simply to embrace, to bid each other an uncomplicated farewell.

But such reflections came too late now. Tomorrow he would go and she would never see him again. From her pavilion she might glimpse the *Hildebrand*'s smoke dissipating in the morning sky, for she didn't think she had the courage to go down to the port and wave. And in a couple of months' time when she heard again that melancholy C echo over the town among the vultures and know the ship had returned her hand would tremble slightly as she took the passenger list from Raymundo and scanned it eagerly for the name which would not be there, not ever be there.

She wrote a strange sad note and despite the lateness of the hour took it down to the port herself, handing it in at the gates for immediate delivery to the ship. Steward Pyce brought Edward the envelope with his morning tea at six-thirty but he on seeing it laid it aside unopened for when he felt a little stronger (as he put it to himself) and then, in the general excitement of departure, forgot about it.

For in the hour which preceded the *Hildebrand*'s sailing the *despedidas* were in full swing and the decks and gangways crowded with people who, regardless of their nationality, all seemed imbued with the spirit of Brazilian leavetaking. Young English clerks returning home on furlough, several wasted by past fevers, came on board accompanied by girls whose tropical dewiness was in as much contrast as the brown of their skins. Fans jigged violently, straw and linen hats flapped, for the heat which already bore the *urubus* so effortlessly up above the town bore equally down upon the revelries of farewell. Edward, watching it all from his usual eyrie of Captain Maddrell's private piece of deck, spotted Molly and Fortescue coming up the gangway. Knowing quite well they could only have come to say good-bye to him he groaned at having to leave his undisturbed vantage point and contend with heat and people.

'You surely haven't come all this way just to see an old buffer off?' he greeted them. 'I think that's very noble of you.'

'We couldn't possibly have let you vanish without another word,' said Molly. 'I had to say how grateful I was for your company on the way over. You were a great help and encouragement and I shan't forget it.'

'I was? Well, young lady, I'm very pleased if so. I may equally say you both cheered me up. I'm now somewhat dreading the return voyage, to tell the truth. I feel I haven't the energy to make new friends and it'll be rather a gloomy passage. But never mind, I can think of you in the sunlight of Manaos,' and he waved a hand at the light which streamed at all angles upon the ship.

'I'm off to Iquitos the day after tomorrow,' Molly said. 'I don't know if I shall ever get there; I may see something too interesting on the way. But I'm definitely moving on.'

'Ah. You will paint well, won't you? Don't do it too much from the life.'

'Not too much from the life?' She was laughing.

'You must watch and watch to get the details but you must *work* from the imagination. I commend to you the words of William Morris: "No man can draw armour properly unless he can draw a knight with his feet on the hob, toasting a herring on the point of his sword." There, that's enough advice.' He looked from one to the other. 'Good luck to you both in your intrepid pursuits.'

'It's what she wants,' explained Fortescue unnecessarily. 'She'll be back, won't she?' He glanced sideways with uncertain fondness. 'Everybody upriver returns to Manaos.'

They said their good-byes in a very English fashion amid the general exuberance. The last Edward saw of them was their heads bobbing down the gangway past oncoming porters crowned with luggage. He watched the increasing frenzy for another half hour, heard a bugle sound for all non-travellers to go ashore. Suddenly a brass band of cockaded Brazilians, which had been forming unnoticed among the comings and goings on the quay below, struck up *Land of Hope and Glory*. Using a low bollard as a makeshift dais a conductor wearing a band-master's uniform complete with frogging and white gloves energetically danced at the water's edge. They played with immense verve, rather accurately for the most part and in the key of F. Edward was taken completely by surprise and experienced a rapid conflict of emotions. First he wished they'd stop, or at least change the tune. Then he wondered why it was in F and whether South American brass were differently pitched. Finally he found himself admiring the utterly un-English rendering of the over-familiar tune. Had he been able to make himself invisible he would have stayed to watch. As it was, though, he caught all eyes on the quay below staring up at him, the raised arms and pointing fingers, and realised this was a deliberate tribute. With a gesture defensive, submissive, vaguely acknowledging, he retreated hurriedly into the day cabin behind him. There he heard the piece through to the end, mopping his face with a handkerchief.

But it was not long before the band had switched to something he didn't recognise and he judged it safe to re-emerge. He was surprised to find it had moved a little further away – no, it was the ship itself now perceptibly opening up a widening ditch of water into which the loops of the bow mooring-ropes splashed before being hauled aboard. A cheer went up from the onlookers on the quay echoed by the passengers lining the rail. A forest of hands waved, pale, dark, bare, gloved. A few streamers criss-crossed the gap, sagging at the ends of their trajectories, to be grasped, held taut, snapped by the *Hildebrand*'s retreating tonnage. Tears came to his eyes; the business of departures. The ship slid out into the river.

At the last moment he picked out a figure in the shadow of a godown wearing a light dress and carrying a green parasol. Gravely he raised his hand and waved. Maybe the figure lifted a white glove in response, maybe the parasol tipped slightly in farewell; there were too many people, it was too far to tell. The whole scene danced and blurred through brimming lenses. But he went on waving very slowly, regally, a dapper figure alone at its own stretch of rail. A minute later the whole of the town's frontage was clearly in view, already sliding astern. Across the doors of a massive warehouse, now partially obscured by the boom of an English crane, a sign in blue capitals blazoned out the future. CRONIFER GmbH, it read; ONIFER, FER. Gradually the entire town slipped from sight, the last view Edward had of Manaos being of the glittering dome of the Opera House with above it the specks of vultures turning and turning their ragged vortex.

The *Hildebrand* was almost in sight of the confluence of the Rio Negro with the Amazon when a noise rising swiftly above that of the engines made Edward look up. A small yellow biplane was diving steeply at them from astern. For one extraordinary timeless instant he thought of an attack, but then the machine pulled up a scant ten feet above the masts and its huge shadow swept the length of the ship.

'Forty!' he said aloud, the passing chill replaced by exhilaration. The plane pulled vertically up, fell over on its back and swooped down towards them once more. This time it flattened out astern and wheels skimming the surface of the water overhauled them, waggling its wings in salutation. He caught a glimpse of a figure in the cockpit, face masked by goggles, unhelmeted hair blown straight back, a hand raised. Excitedly he waved back and thought he saw the face turn towards him, maybe imagined a wide grin. Then the machine was past and climbing again. From then on until the ship had reached the twin lighthouses the yellow biplane performed aerobatics in the tropical sky for an audience of eagerly upturned faces. It finally turned away with a farewell wave of its wings and a dark burp of exhaust. He watched it dwindle until like a gnat it was lost among river and cloud and forest.

X

The day after tomorrow it's Pará again & a thousand miles of the Amazon will have slipped by in a dream. The nights are loud with saxophones & revelry in some of which I've taken part. No doubt one day someone – quite likely Maddrell or even Pyce – will remember me as a gay old dog. It has all remained a dream nonetheless. I catch sight of my body in mirrors behind the bar &c doing the most extraordinary things such as standing with its head thrown back & its mouth open, laughing. It seems to have become all moustache and waistcoat. I'm not at all certain who the 'I' is writing this Journal nor whether he inhabits that body. Once upon a time, tho', I'm sure he was a person who thought of dreams as productive. Indeed I cd. even now catch myself writing that dreams are all that matter. How else can anyone live but in the imagination? (A cruise ship is the perfect provoker of such a question – the general silliness has to be seen to be believed. And participated in . . .). Well, the world's undoubtedly now & then diverting but it's awful flat & thin stuff on which to get through threescore years & ten . . . Sardonic visionary! What if the imagination fails or suddenly defects? With what alacrity the world rushes in to fill the gap with blandishments!

Yet in spite of everything the desire if not the ability to create still does remain. Manaos left its painful reminder. A lifetime's work (unfortunately not as voluminous as the phrase implies) now beginning to gather dust on library shelves & in the score-cupboards of orchestras & choral societies & I now know nothing has really been achieved, far less assuaged. Did Schumann feel the same before trying to kill himself in the Rhine? I'm not myself about to follow the late Dr Ashe's brave example, at any rate. Suicide is not in the least unthinkable but there are limits. The Rhine is one thing, the Amazon quite another. The Severn now . . . but an ever-ungrateful thing to do to such a dear old stream. It would be like killing oneself in a friend's house.

I see from a copy of Thoreau in the ship's library that he wished 'to go soon and live away by the pond, where I shall hear only the wind whispering away among the reeds. It will be a success if I shall have left myself behind.' Even as I write it out I'm shaken with desire, my pen is unsteady with it. But always those bold leaps, those brave retreats from the world are made on paper. Or if not, then they're made by people who still have <u>energy</u>. But I'm tired & dispirited beyond revival. It's all work. The imagination's all <u>work</u>. Nothing is heard except through listening. Nothing is seen except through watching. Nothing is understood except through thinking. Nothing worthwhile ever <u>presents</u> itself. What choice did we ever have but to do this work? It demands to be done. And yet shockingly, cheerfully, most people allow everything to skid off the retina & whiz through their ears like wind, leaving nothing behind. It's a kind of death. A corpse couldn't have less say on the paths the worms take through it.

Well, now I too have run out of whatever it takes to deflect worms. My hand in the lamplight holding this pen has grave-marks on it & yet is recognisably my hand. Surely only the other afternoon it trailed idly in the Severn amid summer's hum or was wrapped in kite string & left with white grooves visible hours later? Harder to bear is having come <u>so close</u>, as close as the distance between pen & page the instant before writing. For as nib touches scorepaper a door slams far away & whatever it <u>really</u> was is cut off & we're left with pieces of tune wriggling in the foreground like shed lizard tails. We work from haunted memories of nothing (but O! such nothings!).

I'm old. Nowadays great yearnings have little meaning. A life indentured to the imagination is a mad anachronism. No doubt quite rightly, too. Why bow oneself beneath such a hopeless task, so ghoulishly watch that inner passing? 'It is thy very energy of thought/Which keeps thee from thy God.' That was what the Angel said to Gerontius in a bit of the poem I didn't set. Maybe I should have. Well, having got everything wrong & before it's finally the worms' feeding-time I suppose I should 'use well the interval.' But the energy is lacking. I & my body seem unable to do anything now but be carried along with the rest of the gallimaufry aboard this ship. We drink & play chemin-de-fer & watch the antics of a self-described 'roaring cad' who shrieks a lot (I fear he reminds me rather of some of poor Frank's more dangerous friends). On & on we go, drinking & laughing & gassing & thus we shall arrive the day after tomorrow in Pará.

And on an afternoon sitting on deck beneath stately ephemera of clouds there came a lurch which was not so much an insight as a momentary shift of viewpoint. He was aware of an absurdity: of an old man wrapped in eminence and wearing his carapace of clothes being carried along within an iron boat, and yet inside his head a bluish freedom – very calm and pleasurable and crossed by vapours constantly turning in upon themselves. Among the things beside linen and metal which so easily came between this old man and his real domain: the roaring of crowds, the roaring of guns, the roaring of cads. On the far side of such confusions rose *les barricades mystérieuses* which guarded the land beyond, whatever those cloudy ramparts were which now excluded even himself. (The enigmatic quality of this phrase, the title of a piece in Couperin's 6th *Ordre*, had always delighted him even though he knew it probably referred to something banally topical in eighteenth-century Paris.) These barricades cut him off from a lost world for which he ached, had always ached. Was he not like Professor Challenger's pterodactyl which triumphantly escaped from the Queen's Hall in London and headed south-west out across the Atlantic towards its prehistoric home? (He glimpsed himself in passing, a black and monstrous outline swiftly crossing the moon.)

Intense though it was, this longing was yet quite calm, just as it had been when he was young and as if it could only be met by a lifetime's devotion. Had not Plato described music as a science of love-matters occupied in harmony and rhythm? The love was correct, he thought, but it was evident Plato had not been a composer else he would surely have mentioned the harsh conditions for the existence of that love: a loneliness which not marriage, not even friendship might dissolve.

What had it been, this life, that work? The loneliness? Nothing, because the longing had remained unchanged, being the only thing which did not diminish and die. Nothing at all. No rewards, no knowledge. Only an inner exile. Somewhere in a land far ahead his wife and his sword mouldered side by side, *fortiter et fide*. Somewhere in a city astern an unanticipated ghost was still going solidly about her business. And here in his deck-chair the wilderness he carried about him ached even as it enfolded with its view of an infinite emptiness entrancingly decked out. It echoed with a voice such as might be raised from a tower to greet the breaking of day in an ancient land. And from it there rose – by what bizarre alchemy he could not guess – a great fume of pleasure and compassion. This was how it had always been; nothing much had changed after all. From the kite-flown skies of boyhood to the cloudscapes of Amazonas his whole business remained with this longing, the limitless garden, and with the love which flew up before the least footfall into it like minor moths from long grass at dusk.

Afterwards when he tried to recall his trip Edward was vague about the return journey. He could not imagine how he had spent the time, above all the two days in Pará. Impressions came to him of luncheon and dinner tables, but who had sat around them? He had no idea. He still associated that town with Kate and Dora, the ladies of the outward journey. Merely knowing they lived there had given the place a certain flavour in his mind, something to do with gaiety and candour, though he had never again set eyes on them.

But if he could not remember Pará he did have a clear memory of the last of Brazil. The slow vanishing astern of a continent and people he knew he would never see again had stranded him in his deck-chair with a sense of finality as of a door closing on yet another incident in his life which had caused him disquiet. As Marajó Island with its majestic portals of cloud receded he was left poised above three thousand miles of rolling waters, thinking he had failed without knowing what had been attempted nor what might have made success. A revivified Muse? Too foolish. The hopeless conundrum came again which had balked him ten days earlier at the library window of Lena's institute: that it ought to be possible to slough off the tyrannous cocoon in which one became encased – of yearning for days gone, of distaste for the present and dread of the future. Only thus might an artist enter his domain.

A flaw of the affection, then. A failure of imagining, a despair born of thwartedness – whatever his infidelity he had been judged and still found wanting. And he looked back at the dark stain through which he had travelled as at something seen at more than distance, oneiric, ungraspable as cirrus, scribbled by winds.

He crossed the Atlantic in full retreat before steady westerlies. Somewhere between Pará and Madeira, which they reached on

Christmas Day, and in a gesture of exorcism he put his Journal in a weighted sack together with Lena's last letter, still unopened, and threw it all into the sea. It was only later he discovered that his manuscript sketch-book must have been tucked into the Journal, for he never found it again. By then a different abandonment was sweeping the ship with its seasonal roarings.

'Merry Christmas everyone . . . '

'. . . *comfort and joy* . . . '

'. . . *not* goodwill to all men, that's a mistranslation, you know. It's to all men *of goodwill*. Absolutely not to rotters and bounders . . . '

'Happy Christmas.'

'Down the hatch.'

Bemused in the midst of all this he caught sight of a rosy and clubbable Sir Edward in the bar mirror raising his glass in a toast and simultaneously raised his own. A holiday – of course, that was what it had all been. A well-earned holiday, and a very jolly one too.

The *Hildebrand* finally docked at Liverpool at nine o'clock on the morning of December 31st. The last day of the year was grey, the air held its breath with the sense of oncoming snow.

'Did you have a good trip, sir?' asked Tom Shannon, who had been on the quay since seven.

'Capital, thank you. Rattling good time. Oh-oh,' he clutched suddenly at the young man's arm with a gloved hand, 'steady as she goes. This ground is more mobile than I remember it.'

'It'll firm up, Sir Edward.'

'No doubt. Thank you for meeting me, Tom, it's most kind. Having to get off a boat like this first thing in the morning with all one's belongings – it's like being chucked out of a hotel into the street . . . I say, is that my luggage? Well hang on, I have something for you.'

When he had passed perfunctorily through the Customs shed Edward unstrapped his suitcase and scrabbled among underwear before handing his escort a blackish lump. 'There,' he said proudly, doing up the bag again, 'there's a bit of exotica for you.'

'It's extremely kind of you, sir . . . What exactly is it?'

'An alligator, can't you see? I agree it's crudish. The point is not the model but what it's made of. It's compressed stuff called *guaraná* which makes a dashed fine drink.'

'This is a drink?' Tom turned the lump uncertainly in his hands.

'Many, many drinks. You're supposed to scrape it with a file made of dried fish-tongue to get the powder, so they tell me. Personally I'd be inclined to try a nutmeg grater.'

'Rather a pity to spoil it,' the young man said putting it away in his pocket. 'It would look well on the mantelpiece. Not the sort of thing everybody has in Knowsley.'

'Well, just as you like.'

'Your train leaves in half an hour, sir. You must be anxious to get home.'

'Oh yes, I suppose I am. Can't wait to see the dogs.'

At the station Edward surprised himself by finding his ticket, an impressive document since the voyage was inclusive of the rail journey to London. Safely into the guard's van went the great cabin trunk, its japanned expanses no longer as virgin as six weeks before, being scratched here and there and having acquired the crayoned hieroglyphs which only Customs men and porters understand. Once in his compartment he settled his bags and then himself. From beneath the carriage a cloud of steam was drifting up beyond the window making a ghost of Tom Shannon as he waited patiently on the platform. Suddenly Edward sprang to his feet and threw his weight on the leather window-strap. The pane fell with a bang and warm steam eddied in.

'I say, Tom, ghastly thought's just struck me. Sorry and so on but I seem to have given all my immediate worldly wealth to a very fly customer named Pyce. You wouldn't by any chance have a cab fare about you? It's really too embarrassing. I'll be all right once I get to the club. I'll cash a cheque and send you back the money first thing tomorrow, of course. Oh Tom, bless you. Noble indeed.'

As the train laid its plume of smuts across a bleak and wintry landscape the excitement of arrival ebbed away. Everything was exactly as comfortless as he had known it would be. He was back. Maybe he had never left after all. Maybe six weeks ago, six minutes ago, he had fallen asleep in the club as he so frequently did and there would come a deafening rattle in his ear as of wheels over points and junctions and he would suddenly awake to find the tea-things arriving on a silver tray. A panic at having left something far too late gripped him. It spoke urgently of being drawn back into an elderly world full of the servility which conceals an utter want of interest. And behind this world another, a vast and stolid provincial precinct grey with cathedrals and choral societies.

But it was not a dream. When an hour or two later his cab drew up in St James's he could see the familiar doorman hurrying out across the pavement towards him, a large umbrella poised in readiness. As he wearily marshalled his gloves and stick this man leaned in across the trunk strapped in front to pay the driver. Then his own door opened and cold air blew in together with a few whirling white fragments. Passively, like any invalid or supplicant, he watched a sleeve which seemed to extend for ever reaching slowly down towards him as if stretching from another world, dusted with snowflakes and encrusted with gold braid. He took the white-gloved hand with resignation and was dragged deferentially out.

'Welcome home, Sir Edward! Welcome home!'

EPILOGUE

Edward Elgar lived on another ten years without composing anything of much significance. He did however make recordings of his own music whose value as historic and artistic documents justified his friends' encouragement in the face of his own gloomy predictions.

From time to time in that final decade he would look out his notes and sketches for various projects – principally a piano concerto, an opera and a third symphony. Late in 1932 the BBC, largely at Bernard Shaw's urging, commissioned the symphony for £1000. Throughout the following year there were brief flickers of the creative flame interspersed with such distractions as the heady pleasure of at last becoming an aeronaut. At the end of May he flew to France to conduct the Paris première of his Violin Concerto with Yehudi Menuhin, combining this trip with a visit to the dying Delius at Grez-sur-Loing. Back in England he tried again with the symphony, which was progressing but feebly. The first signs of his own cancer appeared although at the time he was more anguished by a disease increasingly evident in Europe. He had already written to Frank Schuster's sister Adela:

I am in a maze regarding events in Germany – what are they doing? In this morning's paper it is said that the greatest conductor Bruno Walter &, stranger still, Einstein are ostracised: are we all mad? The Jews have always been my best and kindest friends – the pain of these news is unbearable & I do not know what it really means.

He died in February 1934, working on his symphony until the last. On that very day the *Hildebrand*, which had been sold to a man in Monmouthshire for £11,000, was being broken up. The ship had been built in 1911, the year of Elgar's Second Symphony and arguably the high summer of his output. Thus by a strange coincidence its lifespan happened precisely to encompass the declining years of the Amazon cruises as well as of the creative and calendrical life of Sir Edward Elgar.